HERO SPELL

LIBERTY VALLEY LOVE: BOOK 4

JOSIE MALONE

ISBN: 978-1-955784-02-3

Published by Satin Romance
An Imprint of Melange Books, LLC
White Bear Lake, MN 55110
www.satinromance.com

Published in the United States of America.

Cover Design by Lynsee Lauritsen

Hero Spell is dedicated to my sister writers of the Evergreen RWA chapter who have always helped make this book better. I will be forever grateful to them for the title, the critiques of various chapters, and the suggestions to improve the story. As the saying goes, "Friends are the sisters we choose for ourselves."

Thanks again. I couldn't have written this book without you.

PART I

"Magick, monsters and mayhem – just another day in Paradise...."

— AUDRA DAWSON

1

_____

Everett, Washington - February 1st, 2018

AUDRA DAWSON WATCHED AS HER BEST FRIEND CASUALLY sauntered into the Fandango Room at Billy-Bob's Cowboy Bar & Grill. Ginger's curvy body was wrapped in a fringed blouse, green suede skirt, and high-heeled cowboy boots. Pink and red curls framed her face and brushed her shoulders. Her makeup was better suited to a Saturday night out than an afternoon party. But the look worked for her, as the ample tips she made bartending at Billy-Bob's could attest.

"So," Ginger drawled, as she approached, "how are things coming along? You look ripe for murder. You look like someone kicked your dog, then stole your man. Or maybe," she eyed Audra critically and amended, "like you've been talking to one of your sisters."

Audra slowly lowered the roll of green crepe paper and tape dispenser she held, placing them neatly on a nearby table. "Clancy just blew through long enough to tell me the wedding is off."

"After you made special arrangements for the lingerie shower, she and Kate insisted they had to have two weeks before the ceremony?"

"You wouldn't believe all of the begging, conniving, and family blackmail it took to get this place, plus the hefty deposit I had to pay. And that's not even counting the big family Christmas and all the extra stuff the twins 'couldn't live without' at school this quarter. I'm so glad," Audra said with mock solemnity, "that someone who knows their way around duct tape, rope, and a shovel, is here to help me bury the bodies."

"That's me." Ginger did a little victory dance, more suitable for a twenty-something than a woman fighting her fortieth birthday. "I'll break out the champagne so we can get good and soused before we clobber them."

"Don't tempt me. This is a damn nightmare."

"More like the day of your dreams. You've been patient. You respected your sister's boundaries while she played holy hell with everyone's heartstrings. Now you finally have a shot at Ethan." Ginger headed for the bar and the bottles of champagne. "Are you going to call him and offer a sympathetic shoulder?"

"Not until I figure out what to do about this shower." Audra pulled out her cell phone and dialed her sister Kate's number. It went straight to voice mail, so she had to be on the line with someone. "It's me. I need to know what has your tail in a knot. And what the hell am I supposed to tell Mom?"

Thirty minutes later, she hadn't heard back from either sister. She and Ginger were on their second glasses of champagne when the door opened. Her mother came in, followed by her older sister, Marlene.

Darlene Dawson looked around the half-decorated lounge—obviously checking the streamers that weren't hanging from corner to corner, the unfinished party favors that hadn't been arranged in plastic cowboy boots. "What's going on?" She pinned Audra with the cobalt blue gaze that made everyone in the Dawson family 'fess up to a million and one sins. "Why are you slacking? Where are the twins? Shouldn't they be helping you?"

Audra blinked. She'd forgotten all about the two baby drama queens. She had five younger sisters, all of whom saw her as a cross between Public Enemy Number One, General MacArthur, and Dear Abby. "They got tied up with some college thing and said they'd be late."

"Those two have lazy down to an art form," Marlene said. "What can we do to help, Audra?"

"I don't know." Audra shrugged. "Clancy came in and told us the wedding is off. She and Kate have changed their minds. They're not marrying the Killian brothers, not in two weeks, not on horseback on Valentine's Day at the Lazy B, not ever."

"Lions, tigers and bears—oh my." Darlene eased out of a denim jacket and eyed Audra, then Ginger. "Pour us each a glass of champagne, Ginger. Give me your phone, Audra. I left mine at home in my other purse. I need to call and warn the boys' mom before she arrives with her entourage and that gossip gal from the local paper. It'll be okay, honey. Better broken engagements than divorces."

Audra stared at her. At fifty-seven, her mother was more of a realist than a romantic. While she claimed she loved both men who proposed to two of her daughters, Darlene was the first to quote divorce statistics and remind everyone that "happy ever after" belonged in movies and books, not real life. She'd even told Kate and Clancy that marriage was an institution, and they didn't have to be committed yet. Why didn't they live with the guys and forego getting hitched?

"What do we do now?" Audra asked. "How do we handle it when everyone arrives expecting a party?"

"We tell the truth," Darlene said, taking a filled glass from Ginger. "Your sisters have changed their minds and then we'll have a party anyway. I have a horsy sitter doing chores and I'm spending the night at Marlene's. We can't return the cake or get back your deposit, so we may as well enjoy the afternoon."

"The girls will sort this out sooner or later." Marlene accepted her own glass. "There's too much between them and the boys to let these engagements end today. Believe me, sooner or later, we'll see Clancy and Ethan and Kate and Gavin married."

Ginger brought the bottle of champagne over to Audra and whispered. "I hope not. Snag the guy, quick. You take Ethan and I'll jump Gavin. They deserve to have grown women in their beds, not temper-tantrum-throwing twits."

———

April sunlight sparkled off the neatly mown, emerald lawn in front of the two-story log cabin that Ethan spent years restoring on the Killian homestead. Audra parked her Ford 150 near the back door and switched off the engine. She'd debated what to wear for hours before settling on black jeans, low-heeled boots, and a black shirt with a Southwest print. She didn't want to look desperate even if she was or as if she was chasing the man who thought he loved her sister.

Even though I'm after him, Audra thought, and *I'd be soooo good for him. I'd never do anything to hurt him. I wouldn't break his heart into tiny jigsaw puzzle pieces for fun.*

The back door opened, and she beamed at the big man in the opening. Six-foot-six, he wasn't just all muscle, even if he looked like a lumberjack in a plaid flannel shirt, blue jeans, and wool socks. His corked boots waited on the porch. An engineer for Boeing, he had brains too.

Her pulses thudded in excitement as she slid out of the pickup. "Hi there." She walked around to the passenger side and pulled out the picnic basket. "Hope you're hungry. I brought dinner."

She strolled toward him and watched a smile creep across his rugged features and land in silver-gray eyes. Even with the salt and pepper brown hair, he still reminded her of the boy she'd met so many years before.

"Sweetheart, if you're cooking, I'm starving." He took the basket from her. "I smell fried chicken."

"And the rest of your faves too." She'd spent her one day off a week cooking for him and loved every minute of it. "So, how was South Carolina? I can't wait to hear all about the new plane."

Ginger filled a glass with Riesling and put it in front of Audra. "Drink up. You're spending tonight with me and I'm driving so you can get snockered. How could this happen? You've given your heart and soul to Xanadu Arabians for the past three years. How did they have the gall to pass *you* over for farm manager when you've been running the place for the last six months?"

Audra choked down a swallow of wine, trying to drown her tears. She couldn't cry in Billy-Bob's, not when everything would be reported back to family, friends, and other horse professionals in the county.

"What are they thinking?" Ginger wiped down the bar. "Didn't old man Bergstrom say they had the best breed auction ever with you in charge? They actually turned a profit last year."

"I know." Audra chugged down the rest of the white wine. "I was there, remember? He said I could stay on as Jack Abbot's assistant, that Jack would be glad to let me run the breeding program."

"Jack is a lazy, worthless good-for-nothing, and he's now reached his level of incompetence." Ginger picked up the empty glass and replaced it with a full one. "He'd have you doing all the grunt work while he reaped all the bennies."

"I know." Audra stared into the depths of her wine glass. How could she say she'd miss the horses more than the people at Xanadu, especially the filly she'd raised from an orphaned foal? And the Bergstroms wouldn't sell her the horse she loved. She struggled to swallow the lump in her throat and keep up her professional front.

Taking a deep breath, Audra said, "Jack is a good trainer if he gets close supervision, but there's a lot more to running a purebred horse operation than handling the stock. Bergstrom said that if I went to work at my mom's, he'd sue her because of the non-competitive clause in my contract. I don't know what I'm going to do. My family will freak if I move out of Washington State to find a new position."

"I've changed jobs for years, my dear, so let me tell you the proper response when you get screwed by a boss. Tonight, you get drunk. Tomorrow, you move in with me. And then, we call around and find you a stable management job that's out of Xanudu's reach. As for your family, it'd do them a world of good if they had to grow up and stop dumping on you."

———

Lynn glanced around the cafeteria but didn't see her brother anywhere. Where had he disappeared to now? He was supposed to eat lunch with her and the other eighth-graders because he didn't get along well with kids his own age. Granted, he'd made a few friends with some of the sixth-graders, but Jake was just too smart for his own good. Maybe, things would be better at their new school in the fall.

Carrying the tray with her pizza and salad, Lynn headed for the table where her best friend, Cassie already sat. "Have you seen Jake?"

"Yeah. He took his lunch and went outside. He said he had some serious thinking to do."

Lynn sighed and put her food on the table. "Thanks. Be right back." She found her brother sitting alone on a bench in the school courtyard in the June sunshine. "Do you want to tell me what's going on with you?"

He peeled plastic wrap from his peanut butter and jam sandwich. "We have a problem."

"I'll say. You're out here when you're supposed to be with me."

"No, Lynnie. We need to cast a spell and I have to think it up."

"Oh no." She shook her head. "Not again. Mom's fine. She and

Sean are getting married and we're going to Eastern Washington in two weeks. And Audra Dawson is doing great at running the farm."

"Yeah." Jake bit into his sandwich and chewed. "She's a hero and she needs one."

"What?" Lynn stared at the sandy blond, blue-eyed demon posing as her younger brother. "You can't do that. Not to a stranger. You can't conjure up a man for our new manager."

"She needs somebody who makes her laugh. A guy who loves her best of all." Jake looked at his watch. "You better go eat your lunch. I'll tell you when I need you to help me."

"I'm not doing it, Jake. No way. No more 'love' spells. Not again."

———

He'd left Pullman at five this morning and he'd arrived in Everett in time for a late lunch. He pulled into an empty slot in front of the veterinary office, recognizing the new white Ford 150 his father had posted pictures of on the practice's website. Joe Watkins eased out of his Jeep, stretching to his full five-feet-eight-inches, and rolled his shoulders. In faded blue jeans and a Washington State Cougars sweatshirt, he didn't look like the new Dean of the Veterinary Medicine department.

Well, he wasn't the Dean yet, he reminded himself. He'd been offered the position, but he hadn't accepted it. He'd asked for time to think about it. *For now, I've come home to visit Dad, see a few friends and relations, plus be the best man at Sean Killian's wedding, but only if I like the bride. Hell, I may even attend my high school reunion.*

And for the first time in years, he wasn't teaching the summer session that started in mid-June. He'd enjoy the nine-week break, call it a vacation, and think about taking a sabbatical to write the perfect book on equine medicine. Or then again, he'd have enough time off to realize he wanted to go back to school with the kids and take over his department.

He headed inside, scanning the waiting room with its comfortable sofas and chairs, magazines on the tables, and chew toys in a basket in the corner. Some things didn't change, and his old man was one of them. He'd never gone for the new plastic seats. If his patients had to wait, they might as well enjoy their time. And so should their humans.

A heeler-border-collie pup looked up from where it ripped at a stuffed teddy bear and greeted him with a baby yap. The slender brunette, in jeans and a sloppy sweatshirt, flushed. She looked as if she wanted to cringe back in the chair, disappear with the puppy, leash, and all. "Sorry."

"No worries." Joe grinned at her and didn't say a word about recognizing her from the newspaper and TV articles. She'd undoubtedly heard enough about being battered by an intruder to last a lifetime. "Puppy shots?"

"Yeah. It's the last booster and his rabies, too." The woman relaxed a little.

Joe lingered inside the doorway. "Aren't you Nina Armstrong, the gal with the horse rescue place? How's that going?"

She eyed him suspiciously, then inclined her head accepting the questions at face value. "It's fine. Donations are up and horse abuse is down, so everything works."

"Good to know." With the economy the way it was, he didn't believe her for an instant, but wouldn't say so. He nodded at the puppy who kept chewing on the toy. "You have a cute fellow."

"Thanks. Pooka loves Doctor Art. He's the best."

"He's an inspiration." Laughing, Joe crossed to the desk but didn't see Sarah Holmes, the receptionist who'd run the office forever. He walked to the first examining room and opened the door and spotted his dad bandaging a gray kitten's leg. "Hey, is there a doctor in the house?"

2

Friday, July 13th, 1888

BETH CHAMBERS-MORGAN SAT ON TIGGER, SCANNING THE RIDGE in the light of the full moon. Luke growled, then stood next to her horse, stiff and obviously on patrol. The stallion backed up, tense, tossing his head. He pawed the ground, trying to turn back. She glanced at her brother-in-law who sat on a strawberry roan gelding next to her. "You don't have to do this, Kyle. I trust the cops on the other side to capture Smith."

"I want to see your world and know for myself he's back in the hoosegow," Kyle said, a frown creasing his forehead. "If it doesn't work, I'll come home the next time the door is open."

"I don't know that I can open it for you," Beth said. "It may take both me and the *Guardian* on the far end. And I don't know who she is. All I can do is tell you again to see my father, Will Dawson. Tell him that I'm all right and ask him for help."

Kyle nodded. "I'll do it as soon as I arrive."

"Fair enough." Beth leaned over to hug him. "I promise I'll try to bring you home in September 2019. That will give you a little more than a year. You can see to it that Smith gets arrested and stands trial for his crimes. Don't tell anyone other than Will where you come from."

"You've warned me three times already. I'll keep my trap shut so nobody thinks I'm more loco than a bed bug. Anything else?"

Beth hesitated for a moment. "Do you remember my friend, Nina? The one that Smith attacked? The reason I came looking for him?"

"Yes. He left her for dead when he stole that horse she'd nursed back to health, the one belonging to Trace Burdette."

"That's right." Beth lifted her chin. "See if you can find a way to let her know Wonder is back home and I'm happy too."

"I'll do my best," Kyle said.

"Okay then." Beth reined Tigger to the left and concentrated on the hill. The rising moon shone on the trail, and she nodded. "The way is open. Go careful if you wish."

"It's what I want," Kyle repeated. "Take care of Rad and name your first baby after your pa and me." He urged his horse forward, obviously eager for the next adventure.

Beth waited until he was out of sight, and she no longer heard hoofbeats. Then, she gave him another half-hour before she concentrated on the trail and the gateway to the future, making them disappear into the foggy mists. Tigger tugged on the rein, tossing his gray head. She grimaced before she petted the Arabian's neck. She'd sworn Kyle to secrecy when he caught her heaving her guts out at the smell of the camp coffee after she and Rad joined the posse this afternoon.

She didn't look forward to telling the man that she hadn't stopped his brother from chasing a serial killer through the years. She swung Tigger around and headed across country to where the posse had camped for the night. Luke raced ahead, his tail a banner to follow. "Come on guys. Let's go home."

She heard the German shepherd's bark of greeting before she saw Rad on his black Appaloosa mare. Her husband, her 'forever mate,' her partner in everything, even the weird stuff. A smile leaped in her heart. She waved at him.

"He get off safe?" Rad asked as he rode up to her, stopping the mare next to her stallion.

Beth gazed at his dark blue eyes. "You knew?"

"I saw his face when we caught up with them this afternoon. Kyle hasn't been happy here, especially since I gave him those books of yours. Maybe, he'll find what he's hunting in your world."

"This is my world now." She met him halfway when he brought his horse close enough to kiss her. She rested a hand on his cheek. "You're my world."

————

A burst of noise settled into the disc jockey blowing *Reveille* on his trumpet. The buzz of the alarm on her cell phone followed. Next came the Siamese cat on her pillow patting her nose.

Audra groaned. It was definitely five in the morning, time to get up and that sucked.

She rolled off the sofa bed to her feet, stumbled across the room to turn on the coffeemaker. While the java brewed, she opened a can of meat for the cat winding around her ankles. Pyewacket ate better than she did. "Fancy-shmancy," she told him. "If I don't get some money in the mail today, you'd better start liking generic."

The seal point Siamese sniffed disdainfully at the idea and dove into his gourmet feast. She took a pouch from the box of high-priced kibble, opened it, and poured the contents onto a saucer. Then, she walked across the loft into the bathroom and turned on the shower. When she glanced back toward the kitchen, she spotted the cat heading back to bed. He crawled under the blankets to hide and sleep. He had the right idea, she thought, but then again, he didn't have morning chores waiting for him.

Half an hour later, dressed in black jeans and a western blouse, damp dark red waist-length hair braided, contacts in, make-up perfect, a plastic to-go cup of strong coffee in hand, she headed downstairs. Twenty ponies to hay and grain, a cow to milk, calves, chickens, and new baby pigs to feed. She grimaced. Wow, she missed Xanadu and the help who did the early a.m. rounds. But she wasn't bitching, she told herself. She'd feed, water, muck stalls, and get it all done before Silver Lake Pony Ranch opened for business at nine a.m.

Her new boss, Elinor Talbot was more than fair, and the two kids – total charmers. Soon, they'd be off to Eastern Washington to visit relatives for the week of July 4th, and Audra would have Silver Lake Pony Ranch to herself. She could hardly wait. Elinor had already said that it would be okay to sleep in the house rather than the apartment over the mini-stable.

It didn't take long to feed hay to the three pony mares and their foals. Once they had a chance to eat the alfalfa grass, Audra would come back and do the grain. The babies needed to have their buckets held so their greedy mamas didn't pig out on the food. Her cell phone vibrated, and she pulled it out of her pocket. "Good morning."

"It's me," Clancy said. "I have to meet with the Silver Spurs folks to discuss their show. I won't be in this afternoon."

"We're supposed to bathe fifteen ponies today," Audra said. "We've rescheduled three times already in the past two weeks because you had other things to do, and day camp starts next Monday, June 25th. You know that!"

"This is a two-day 4-H horse show and I need the money," Clancy retorted. "We don't all have major bucks like you."

Audra drew a deep breath and counted silently to ten. "I've worked every day since I was sixteen and supported you and the rest of the family. Could you get here by noon? We won't start bathing the ponies before it gets hot outside. I can't do all the prep for a new day camp by myself."

"Well, you better suck it up and get started, Buttercup, because you don't have a choice." Clancy ended the call.

Audra tucked the phone in her pocket. She shouldn't be surprised her younger sister bailed. Even giving one horse a bath with a garden hose was hard work. Fifteen? Forget about it. Clancy obviously had. She made a habit of avoiding anything she considered menial labor and often said that the maid would pick up the slack. Not that anyone in their family had a maid, of course. That was Audra's job.

But at least Clancy called, Audra reminded herself, trying to stay positive. The twins would *no-show* and accuse her of being mean when she asked why they didn't keep a commitment. They'd raised holy hell last February when it grew closer to Clancy and Kate's double wedding, and they had more chores on the ranch.

Then, their soon-to-be, brother-in-law, Gavin told them to stop the party times at the university instead of studying for their classes. When they didn't, he spoke to their mother about the antics. Payback was starting World War Three between Kate and Gavin and she called off the wedding. That sparked an argument between Clancy and Ethan and their engagement ended too.

It was beginning to seem as if the four of them would eventually reconcile, Audra thought. *Meantime, it's just easier to do everything myself. My Cinderella license never expires.*

Finished in the first barn, she headed for the next. She flipped the light switch inside the door. Various ponies appeared at the front of their stalls, heads hanging out and an old strawberry roan, Bonanza nickered at her. More whinnies followed as she climbed the ladder into the loft. She rolled two heavy bales of hay through the hole in the floor, and they dropped down into the middle of the barn.

When she climbed back down, the first bale was already in the wheelbarrow. Eleven-year-old Jake pushed it while his older sister peeled off chunks of the alfalfa grass and dropped the flakes of hay into the mangers.

"What are you doing?" Audra asked. "Don't you have school?"

"Yeah, for two more days which majorly sucks." Lynn picked

up another armload of hay and answered before her brother could. "We have to hurry. Mom hates driving us. If you get the grain, I'll check water tubs. Jake will feed the steers. Mom's milking."

Audra blinked. "Okay. I already did the mare barn."

"I know," Jake told her. "Tomorrow, remember it's my job."

Audra controlled the impulse to salute and followed orders. The grain was in the feed room adjacent to the hayloft, and it didn't take long to load the orange wheelbarrow kept by the door. When she hired on to manage the pony farm, she'd thought stock chores would be her sole responsibility on weekdays. Apparently not!

A half-hour later, they headed for the house, Lynn carrying the eggs she'd collected when she fed her chickens. Elinor hauled a bucket of milk and Jake jogged ahead of them, ready to feed the three dogs who eagerly escorted him toward the porch. Well, make it one dog and two puppies.

"Six forty-five and we're all done," Elinor said cheerfully as they entered the kitchen. "Audra, you're amazing."

"Me? Your kids did most of it." Audra watched the buzz of activity continue.

Dogs fed, hands washed, Jake set the table for breakfast. Lynn stored the eggs in the fridge and brought out the carton already there, along with a white paper package of meat. While Elinor dealt with straining the milk, Lynn laid strips of bacon in a cast iron skillet on the stove burner, then cracked eggs into a bowl. When Audra offered to help, she was put in charge of making orange juice.

Ten minutes later, they sat down to scrambled eggs, bacon, and toast. A conversation about school, summer plans, and training the foals filled the air while they ate. At seven-thirty, the kids raced out the door for their bus. Quiet reigned.

Elinor sighed, stretched, and got up to bring over the coffee pot and refill their cups. "So, are you crazy yet?"

"Not yet," Audra smiled. "Is this the typical morning routine? Do your kids always help with chores?"

"Yes, but don't feel too guilty. They get paid for it." Elinor sipped her coffee. "So, what's on the schedule for today? This is the first summer I've done day camp. I'm really counting on you and Clancy to show me what to do. When will she be here?"

Audra's heart felt as if it tumbled into her boots. "Clancy didn't call you."

"Not today," Elinor said. "I haven't seen her since Saturday. Why?"

"She won't be in." Audra sighed. Damn it, why did she always end up in the middle? "She had a meeting with a show organizer."

"I see." Elinor narrowed dark blue eyes, then ran a hand through curly black hair. "I don't mean to step on your toes, Audra, but I'm going to tell her not to play, *divide and conquer* with us."

"What?" Audra shook her head. "I don't get it."

"Well, if she was one of the kids at the high school, I'd say she's trying to play us against each other," Elinor explained with a patient, teacher's tone. "They do it to me all the time since I'm a substitute now and they think I don't know the regular routine. I may have to put up with kids playing mud pies with my mind at work. I don't have to put up with this crap on my farm."

Audra froze, trying to gauge her feelings. Bewildered, confused – no that didn't cut it. She was stunned. Nobody in her entire thirty-four years had ever called out one of her younger sisters on their responsibilities, much less nailed them when they failed to keep their word. She, Audra, was just expected to cover for them regardless of the personal cost.

"I should have told you earlier. Clancy loves judging horse shows and—"

"Stop right there." Elinor held up her hand. "You are not your sister's keeper. She's a grown woman and she needs to act like one. Now, let's move on. What are we doing today?"

Audra nodded and pulled the to-do list out of her jeans pocket. "Bathing the ponies, clipping bridle-paths, fetlocks, billy whiskers, checking their hooves to see if Sean needs to trim them before next week. Cleaning all the tack. Washing the saddle blankets. Brushing saddle pads. Inventorying grooming equipment. Each pony needs a personal kit—"

"Hold it." Elinor interrupted. "What does Clancy hate the most on your list?"

"Cleaning saddles and checking cinches and breast collars."

"Okay. We'll leave that for her." Elinor made a note. "And if she doesn't show up, we'll replace her, and she can work for your mom instead of doing day camp here. You have another sister we can swap for her, right? And I sure as sugar don't want the twins."

"Brigid would come here in a heartbeat. Won't that make trouble between you and Clancy? She's your friend."

"Yes, but friends don't sabotage their friend's livelihood," Elinor said. "And I wouldn't be a good friend if I let your sister crash my boundaries without saying something."

Wow, more new ideas, Audra thought. *I'm going to learn so much working here.*

While she put the ponies out in various paddocks and mucked stalls, she analyzed Elinor's reaction to Clancy's behavior. The older woman hadn't been angry or lost her temper. Instead, it had been a case of finding an appropriate solution to a problem. And it was an answer that Audra wouldn't have come up with on her own.

She moved onto the next stall. This was her first Monday on the job. When she worked Saturdays, she arrived after chores to take over the farm so Elinor could go with Lynn to her horse shows. And there were trail guides and working students to shovel manure and put down shavings. Today, it was Audra's job. Clean stalls meant newly washed ponies would stay that way for at least a little while.

———

He'd slept in this morning, woke to find his father had left for an early emergency, a sick horse at Xanadu Arabians in Monroe. Art

Watkins didn't return home. Obviously, he'd gone straight to the vet clinic after saving the expensive animal. Joe stopped at the neighborhood Teriyaki place and picked up lunch before heading there himself. If he wanted to see his father on this visit, he'd have to go where the old man lived and it wasn't in their old home.

In the office, he spotted Sarah directing the proverbial traffic flow of patients and their owners. Short silver hair, tall, rail-thin in the blue scrubs that matched her eyes, she smiled when she saw him. "Well, look what the cougar dragged in. Put that food in the breakroom. Grab a jacket out of the laundry and I'll get you set up in Exam Room Two."

He blinked. "I didn't come here to work. I'm just visiting."

"Right. Get over yourself, young Doc. Snohomish Equine lured away your dad's last associate as soon as we whipped her into shape. He's been going twenty-four-seven ever since." Sarah stood, a stack of files in her hand, and gestured to a woman about her age waiting with a cat container. "I'll take it easy on you today. Daisy, bring that feral rescue with you."

A few minutes later, he was in the small examining room, a purring young cat in his hands. "So, what's the plan for this guy?"

Petite with silver hair, Daisy looked slight and dainty in slacks and a flowered top. She met his gaze and smiled. "You don't remember me, do you? I was your English teacher back in the day. I retired and now I help at the feline rescue in Liberty Valley. Your dad donates all the vet care we ever need."

"Sounds like him." Joe stroked the half-grown tabby. "You don't look much like the woman who made football players shake in their cleats, *Baldusi the Baleful*."

"Oh, I still have my moments and I haven't heard that in years." Daisy laughed. "Your dad brags about you whenever I see him. What brought you home this summer?"

"Sean Killian called, and I agreed to stand up for him at his wedding."

"Anything else?" Her smile teetered on dangerous. So did the narrowed gaze. "Or should I say anyone else?"

"It's time." Joe turned his attention on the waiting cat. "Some things are meant to be, and I have a destiny to follow."

"Sounds intriguing. Keep me posted."

———

With the stalls cleaned, Audra put a flake of hay in each manger. She lingered in the foaling barn long enough to feed the mares lunch hay before going upstairs to the L-shaped loft and studio apartment. The walls gleamed under their high-gloss coats of school bus yellow paint. She'd opened the mini blinds on the large windows on the east wall before she headed to the barn for chores this morning. Decals of galloping ponies in the bathroom and kitchenette on the short end of the L provided a whimsical cowboy impression to the area.

A long table and half-dozen chairs took up the center of the room. Against the right-hand wall were three study carrels, a gift from Ethan who'd visited the Boeing surplus store. The computers in the carrels were from Gavin who'd set them up with their own network and then hooked them up to a separate printer. One corner cut off from the rest of the room by file cabinets and two bookcases held a desk and computer that Elinor said Audra could use.

The couch with its double bed was at the far end of the long wall. Next to it was a short dresser that doubled as a nightstand. Some of her clothes hung in the closet near the staircase. She kept most of her jeans in a suitcase. Soon, she'd move into the house and this room would be a workroom for the campers. They could eat lunch here and do their horsy handouts. She hadn't said anything to anyone, but oh how she missed the three-bedroom manager house at Xanadu.

Pyewacket sat on the windowsill nearest the kitchenette, patting at sunbeams that danced across the glass. That gave her the opportunity to make the bed and fold the sofa into place. She poured herself a cup of coffee and fixed a sandwich. Once she ate, she'd organize the supplies she needed to bathe the first pony in the heat of the day.

An hour later, she finished scrubbing Bonanza's faded red coat with a sponge. Using the hose, she rinsed his left side, then his right. She sprayed his mane and tail one last time. He was the soul of patience while she dried him off with giant bath towels. She worked hair conditioner into his mane and tail, then combed the thick blond hair. "You look beautiful," she told him.

He snorted and nudged her in an obvious search for carrots. She laughed and led him over to Elinor who proceeded to trim the old Welsh gelding's fetlocks, billy whiskers, and bridle path. Audra led Lightning to the hitch rail. He eyed the bucket of soapy water, the sponge, and the garden hose. Then, he snorted, reared, and attempted to bolt back to the security of the paddock.

Audra planted her booted feet in the gravel drive and jerked the lead line, wishing she'd put on her gloves. How could she when she needed to wash his gray coat? "Whoa! Stand."

Seven hundred pounds of Arabian-Welsh pony struggled to break free, but luckily, she had a rope training halter on his head. She pulled him back to the closest apple tree and snubbed him to the trunk. While he considered what was coming next, she filled an empty bucket with warm water and picked up a dry sponge. She dunked it in the bucket and returned to Lightning. She wouldn't go all out on him. Instead, she'd just wipe him down. His next bath would be much more intense.

Between clucks and soothing words, she wiped down his neck. He trembled and she kept up the soft chatter telling him how good he was and how pretty he'd be when he was clean. She worked her way over his left side, then down his legs, and around to the right side. She rinsed out his mane and tail, not bothering with the shampoo or conditioner. After that, she replaced the bucket and sponge by the hose. She picked up her battery-operated clippers and headed back to the pony, switching on the motor.

He tolerated the buzzing very well. And stood like a rock while she cut the extra hair on his lower legs around the fetlock joints.

Next came his whiskers. No problems there. She could tell by the way Lightning tensed that he didn't want her anywhere near his ears.

"Okay, buddy. I got it." Audra shut off the clippers and put them well out of the way so they couldn't get stomped by a dancing pony. She glanced at Elinor. "I think this is going to take both of us."

"Be right there." Elinor paused by the porch and picked up a couple of carrots. Leading Bonanza, she came over to stand next to Lightning and feed both geldings treats. "This is how I trim him. It may not be politically correct, but it works for us."

While Audra watched, Elinor parked the bigger strawberry roan next to the gray and sandwiched herself between the two ponies. She eased out her scissors. Lightning and Bonanza squabbled over the pieces of carrots she occasionally offered, nipping, and nudging each other out of the way. Meantime, Elinor cut tufts of hair out of the gray pony's ears and then clipped the extra hair underneath the headstall strap that held the halter in place. More tiny tidbits of carrots served up as rewards meant Lightning wasn't upset when she finished.

"That was amazing." Audra gazed at Elinor as she led the two geldings side by side toward the barn. "Need help getting them inside?"

"Nope. These two old duffers like being together," Elinor said. "Why don't you grab our next victim?"

"You got it." Audra laughed and headed for the paddock where more ponies waited for bath time. Galaxy was the closest to the gate, first up to hog more than his share of treats so she haltered him, wound through the rest of the equine crowd, and led the palomino Shetland over to the hitch rail.

By the time Lynn and Jake arrived home from school, they'd finished four more ponies. It didn't take long for the kids to change and jump in to help. Lynn brought out her Welsh mare. She washed Gypsy's mane and tail, making them a snowy white. Jake led Blaze, a bay gelding out for his turn, and helped scrub the golden-brown coat.

"I show Gypsy all the time," Lynn said. "She just had a bath last week so she's good to go for a while. And I keep her trimmed, so she takes high ribbons in halter class."

"Good to know," Audra said. "We should be able to do two or three more ponies today, but the rest will have to wait till tomorrow. We don't want them to catch cold."

3

AT NINE THAT NIGHT AFTER DINNER AND A HOT SHOWER, AUDRA wanted to crash, but she still had work to do. Oh, it wasn't for her day job managing the farm. It was time to turn on the computer, open the file on her flash drive, and get started, but she could hardly stay awake. However, she had a deadline that couldn't wait. Wrapped in a fleecy purple bathrobe, she brewed a pot of strong coffee and slid a *Lorrie Morgan* CD into the stereo. Audra kept the music down low so it wouldn't disturb the mares and foals who lived downstairs. So far, the neighbors weren't complaining, and she wanted to keep it that way.

She opened the word-processing program and went into her own files. Sipping coffee, she read the chapter she'd finished the night before. A few typos and a couple of weak word choices needed strengthening. Now, she was ready to return to Trilunon, the fictional world where an evil queen was supposed to serve as a regent for her orphaned nieces but stole the throne instead and married the princesses off to their mortal enemies.

According to the allies of the rightful rulers, the queen expected a triple murder, but Audra would end the story much differently. And right now, the oldest of the three girls, a renowned dark sorceress would consummate the hated marriage and use sex magick to bring her new husband into compliance with her whims and deepest desires.

Two hours later with lots of wild, raunchy sex on the screen, she saved the chapter. She needed at least three more pages to complete the scene, but five in the morning came early. The hero would just have to wait till tomorrow night for the heroine to finish the blow job, but he probably wouldn't whine or snivel too much. That was the fun part of fictional men, unbelievable stamina.

Laughing, Audra closed the computer and headed for the sofa bed. She snuggled down with Pyewacket who purred beside her. "There will be cat food in your future. This book will be finished on time."

The next day started as a rerun of the one before. Chores, breakfast, cleaning the barns, opening the farm for pony rides, and six ponies left to bathe. She should have it done by early afternoon and then she could move on to organizing tack for camp. Saddles to clean, blankets to wash, pads to brush down and she needed to create a shopping list for the Co-Op in case one of them had to pick up replacement gear before next Monday.

Halfway through Tonka's bath, a blonde in a brown Ford Escort pulled into the drive. Audra continued soaping the Morgan-Welsh gelding's black coat and waved a greeting. She smiled when she recognized Sandy. "Hi there. What's up?"

"Elinor called and told me that I could have extra hours this week as soon as I finished at school," Sandy said. "So, I'm here. And as the Silver Lake Pony Ranch saying goes, where do I jump in?"

"Really?" Audra caught her breath. "I don't believe it. I was feeling totally overwhelmed. There's so much left to do before the kids come next week."

"Well, Marcie has a late American History class today. She'll be along as soon as she takes her final exam." Sandy picked up the extra halter and lead from the hitch rail. "Who's next on the list?"

"Flicka."

They didn't bathe the mares with new foals. Instead, once the riding ponies were clean, they moved onto the saddles. Audra moved blankets around in what she privately considered her version of *fashion police*, carefully coordinating colors to be sure each horse would look its best. Once she'd assigned the blankets and pads, Marcie labeled them with masking tape so it would be easy to tack up come Monday morning.

Meanwhile, Sandy and Elinor pulled out the new blue buckets from the discount hardware store. They were supposed to be for painting but would make perfect grooming kits. Sandy proceeded to put names on each set of brushes. The campers would have a hoof pick, curry comb, body brush, soft brush, and a mane and tail brush, all of which were assigned to a specific animal.

No way would Bonanza be groomed with Tonka's brushes and vice versa. It might seem a little anal to people who weren't running a day camp, but Audra had learned a long time ago that giving each equine a groom kit saved money in the long run. Then, she didn't have to buy fifteen new sets of brushes each summer to make up for the ones that had been lost the previous year. And most horse people survived on a budget. Very few ran their stables to lose money like the Bergstroms at Xanadu.

———

"I can't believe we're out here, doing this again." Lynn stood in her long, flowered pink nightgown, bare feet in the dew damp June grass. "What are we waiting for?"

"Five more minutes," Jake said. "It's not midnight yet."

Lynn heaved a dramatic sigh. "Why do we always have to do these stupid spells at midnight, Jake? And the summer solstice? What's up with that?"

"Because it's the longest day of the year. It's a time when the Sun King gets celebrated and that makes it perfect to find a real hero," Jake said. "And we need a strong guy for Audra. A wimp won't do. It's when this spell will work. Come on, Lynnie."

She took the three pages of notes he offered, feeling sorry for

Audra. What had the poor woman done to inspire Jake to find her a soulmate? *"On this night and in this hour, I call upon the Ancient Power. Oh, brave Gods and Goddesses bright, bring us your enchanted light."*

"We must help a woman who has no fear," Jake chimed in on the chant. "Help us bring the perfect hero here."

The spell listed all the qualities the right guy for Audra needed. He'd have integrity and do what was right regardless of how hard it might be. He'd show courage day in and day out. He would be like her and do things because they needed to be done, but he'd also alter plans when it was necessary. And he'd have a good sense of humor too.

Personally, Lynn thought the would-be guy sounded like a superhero from a graphic novel. And there was no way he'd show up, but that was how she'd felt when Jake started this with Mom. Miracle of miracles, they now had Sean in their lives. And they'd be going to Disneyland in September, a place she'd always hoped to see.

So, who knew? Maybe it was like what Jake had said last spring when they cast the cowboy spell and brought Sean to them. "Tomorrow's science is today's magick."

For tonight, Lynn finished the spell with a flourish of her hand. *"I now say this spell is done. May it harm none. In no way, will this spell reverse or place upon us a curse. As we will it, in days that number three, so must it be."*

———

Zane O'Malley turned off the TV, picked up his can of beer, and finished it. He opened the last of the six pack and took a swallow. He'd figured the cool summer weather would change, warm up to what was normal for this season. Then he'd begin putting out the trays of antifreeze around the garage and back yard. He hadn't started yet. What was the point?

Very few animals would be desperate enough to drink what he

offered. The wild ones would avoid the liquid because it smelled like humans. And he hadn't seen very many stray dogs or cats in the area who were willing to try the rat-poisoned laced food he'd put out for them, much less the anti-freeze. Well, he'd try to be patient.

Blast City opened tomorrow out at the reservation. Fireworks would begin exploding in the rural part of the county in the next couple of days and animals would run off soon. If he didn't start finding dying critters in the next couple of days, he'd visit the library and go online. There were bound to be people looking for homes for disposable pets that he could add to his graveyard collection.

Mount Baker National Forest? – Friday, July 13th, 1888?

Kyle Morgan turned in the saddle to check his back trail. He hadn't heard anyone or anything since he rode over that strange hill. Yet, he couldn't shake the feeling that someone or something lurked behind him, pursued him. Why? Gary Smith should be hours and miles ahead of him.

He reined S.O.B. back onto the trail winding between the evergreens. The strawberry roan Appaloosa pinned his ears, crowhopped twice, and then stomped down the track. The horse seemed angrier about riding into the dimming light than fearful. A breeze rustled through the pine boughs. Off to Kyle's right, a creek chuckled over rocks. A squirrel chattered.

And the fog rolled past the giant cedars. Vapor cloaked the trees in foggy shrouds. The gray cloud thickened, and Kyle made his decision. He'd stop for the night. He swung out of the saddle and led the gelding forward. Eventually, the trees parted on a clearing. Knee-high grass would provide a meal for the horse. And there was water.

He'd settle for a cold camp tonight. Smoke from a fire would draw Smith to him and Kyle wanted to be ready for the killer, not end up one of his victims. Being left as a carcass for the coyotes to eat didn't figure in his plans. He had places to go and a new adventure to chase. Later, he'd read one of the books his older brother had given him and learn more about the world he intended to enter.

Finding Rad and living with him hadn't turned out the way Kyle planned. So, he'd ride careful, just as he promised Beth. Somehow, someday he'd find a home, a life he was meant to have, even if he didn't know the details yet.

———

Silver Lake Pony Ranch, Wednesday, June 20th , 2018

Her cell phone rang as Audra headed down the stairs to the barn. "Hello."

"Hi Destynee," A sunny female voice greeted her. "It's Kendra. Did I call too early, or can we talk about your edits?"

Audra blinked at the name of her alter-ego, the one she used for her books. "No, this is fine, Kendra. I'm headed out to feed horses. But, let me pull up a stair to sit on and you can tell me what you need."

"Oh, it's just the usual, honey. More sex." Kendra giggled. "Destynee LaFleur has a reputation for writing the hottest erotic romance around and this book needs to be smoking."

Audra frowned as she sat down on the step, sipped her coffee, and recalled the project completed four months ago, a story about a female werewolf. "But she went into heat in the first chapter and jumped the hero in an alley the night they met."

"That was a terrific opening," Kendra agreed. "Too bad the rest of the book doesn't match it. She needs to be a consistent character and if she can't keep her paws off her mate—well we have to see it all the way through the book, and she becomes almost celibate halfway into the story."

Audra sighed and drank more coffee. "Oh hell, I'm sorry, Kendra. I don't know how I lost track of her."

"Oh, stuff happens in real life, and an actual woman could take a break as she gets to know her new guy," Kendra said. "But this is a book, and it has to make sense. And you're easy to work with so I know you'll fix this. I'm making notes of where you need to strengthen her character and libido. I'll get the edits to you by next week."

"That works," Audra said. "The farm will be closed over the holiday so I should be able to get onto them during the week of July Fourth."

"Okay. I know you said you moved, and I forwarded your new address to the accounting department, but they screwed up and sent your check to where you used to live. And it came back, so I sent it to you by overnight mail. You should have it today, along with your contract for the new book."

"You're amazing." Audra hoped that her smile could be heard through the phone since it couldn't be seen. "And I'm working on that one."

"About the witches?" Kendra heaved a huge sigh. "I'm so going to miss my shifters."

Audra laughed. "Not for long. The second witch is a shapeshifter and she turns into a wolf and has wild sex with her wizard who has the same power. Who loves ya, baby?"

"All right, Destynee!" Kendra squealed. "You're the best."

Chores done, breakfast finished, the kids headed off for the last day of school. Audra brought over the coffee pot and refilled her and Elinor's cups. "What's on for today?"

"I have a coffee date with Daisy Baldusi, my next door neighbor at nine," Elinor said. "Do you want to come along?"

Audra considered the idea. There was so much left to do. "I want to, but we still have saddles to clean, and half the blankets need to be washed and—"

"And will the work take any less time if we go next door for an hour and a half?" Elinor asked. "Or will we both feel refreshed after a mental health break?"

"I don't know the right answer," Audra admitted. "I've never left a job when there was work to do."

"Then, it's a good day to start." Elinor glanced at the milk-can-shaped clock on the wall.

"Okay, my turn to put out the horses in their paddocks and pick the stalls. Your turn to collect blankets and load up my truck. I'll drop them by the laundry after we visit with Daisy on my way to get the kids at school. We always go to *Dairy Queen* on Fridays for ice cream. Since today's the last day, I promised we'd go when they finished class."

"Wow, you're a great mom. Will you adopt me?"

"No, but I'll bring you back a sundae." Laughing, Elinor finished her coffee and took the cup to the sink before she headed outside.

Audra drank the rest of hers and followed suit. She wouldn't say anything to her boss, but it sure seemed different here than it had when she was growing up. She didn't remember any fuss being made about the last day of school. Of course, her mother had six girls to raise, a ranch to run, and a husband who was least in sight until Audra's twelfth birthday when he left for good.

Since her mother was pregnant with twins, Audra took over running the ranch and raising her sisters, becoming the other parent. It was a job that needed doing and she'd done it. She'd figured it was only temporary and she'd be off for a life of her own when she graduated from high school, but it hadn't happened.

Instead, she got her first job when she was barely fifteen, old enough to hire on at the nearby fast-food joint and bring home her wages trying to make up for the child support that her father didn't pay. And nothing was different today. She was still trying to fill his shoes twenty-two years after her father exited stage left.

She sorted the saddle blankets into black trash bags. They'd be washed and returned to the pony farm to hang on fences and dry in the early summer heat before being used on Saturday. Her phone rang and she answered. "Hello."

"It's me," Clancy said. "How are things going?"

"Fine," Audra said. "How'd you do with the Silver Spurs folks?"

"Good. We got their show organized and they've recommended me for a couple of others. I'll be able to do day camp, but most of my Saturdays will book up after all."

"If Elinor needs to hire a different weekend instructor, you'll have to tell her," Audra said. "She's already told me that it's not appropriate for me to come between the two of you."

"You're the new farm manager," Clancy said. "This is your job."

"Sorry, but she does the scheduling. I don't." Audra shifted the phone so she could grab another blanket. "So, what else is new?"

"Not much. The twins want to live on-campus next fall and Mom said they'd have to bring it up at Sunday dinner and the family could discuss it."

"I think it's a good idea," Audra said. "Working to pay their bills and going to school would help them learn life skills."

Utter silence greeted her words. Then Clancy said slowly. "They thought you'd pay for it."

"How can I?" Audra asked. "I'm working on percentage here, Clancy. I won't see any big money before September. And by then, the balloon mortgage on the ranch is due. And this may come as a surprise, but the deposits I put down for the caterer, the florist, the reception hall, the music for yours and Kate's weddings—that was all non-refundable. And your dresses weren't cheap. I'm flat busted."

"I should have known you'd throw that in my face. You do whenever we talk."

"No, I don't," Audra said, feeling like a kid again.

"Yes, you do."

Okay, so it took one to know one. Maybe I am being childish, but damn I'm tired of being constantly criticized.

"Throwing it in your face means I present you and Katie with a bill. I haven't done that. And if the twins start paying their own tuition and their way, well I'm good with it too."

She shouldn't have been surprised by the sudden end to the phone call, but she was. Anytime Audra mentioned she didn't have the money they wanted, her sisters didn't have time to talk. They figured she'd be able to come up with the bucks somehow and if she didn't or couldn't, she was being stingy. She supposed if she were a *good* sister, she'd give the check she expected today to the family, but it didn't make much sense, not when the money really wasn't hers yet. It was only an advance payment on her share of the book sales.

Years ago, when she was first starting out, one of her writing mentors had told her to always bank the advance payment so she could return it if she wanted out of her contract. She'd only had to do that once with a different publisher, long before she signed with Kendra's house. Even though she trusted this company, she knew she'd keep at least half of the funds in her savings account and not touch them. It would be part of her *just-in-case* money. But July was coming and that meant her royalty check would definitely be all hers!

"Ready to go?" Elinor popped into the tack room and picked up one of the trash bags. "So, Clancy just called and bailed for the weekend. She has horse shows. Do you have a sister we can hire to replace her, or do you know somebody else? I don't want to promote Penny to instructor again. She still needs to earn my trust after her stunts last spring."

"I can ask Brigid what her show schedule is," Audra said. "She could probably fill in for some of the days. I know she's judging at the county fair in August."

"Okay. F.Y.I., I told Clancy this was strike two after not showing up to wash ponies. And she pulls one more skip-day and I won't need her for camp." Elinor glanced over her shoulder. "You should probably be ready for some whining and whinging."

"Thanks for the heads-up." Audra tied the last bag shut. "We'll have to organize a way to clean the saddles."

"That's easy." Elinor waited outside the tack room to padlock the door. "Sean suggested we have a saddle-cleaning sleepover on Saturday. We invite all our horse-crazy students to spend the night, load up on pizza and junk food, and clean saddles. Sandy and Marcie can run it and they'll love it which means we can sleep in our own beds that night."

"Where will the kids sleep?" Audra followed her to the driveway, and they put the bags inside the pickup cab. "Do you want them in the classroom?"

"Oh, hell no, honey. You wouldn't get a wink of sleep. They can crash out on the living-room floor." Clucking to her dog and the puppies that belonged to Jake and Lynn, Elinor took all three canines up to the kitchen door. Once they were inside, she came back with a plastic carton from the bakery. "Come on, Audra. Let's go have coffee. We've earned it."

———

He spotted two squad cars and an unmarked Crown Victoria sedan parked at his dad's favorite doughnut shop. Did that mean a robbery or other crime had happened? Or was he about to become involved in a long-running joke with cops and pastries? Joe didn't know, but since he was running late after a spay and neuter visit at a local shelter, he figured he should accept the risk and take maple bars to Sarah.

He parked and walked inside to wait his turn while a young woman filled boxes with various freshly baked goodies from the showcase. He recognized his cousin, a big, blond, former football star in high school. At forty, the guy still looked like he could tackle anyone or anything that got in his way. He must have been promoted at the cop shop since he wore plain clothes, a dark brown suit jacket, shirt, striped tie, and slacks.

Joe nodded a greeting. "Hello, John. Are you racing me to the maple bars?"

"Nope, you can have them all." John Watkins turned slightly to eye him. "I thought you were busy at the college."

"Home for the summer." Joe folded his arms. "As soon as I walked in the vet clinic, Sarah put me on the schedule. I spent the morning making sure half-grown kittens practice safe sex and responsible reproduction."

The comment earned chuckles from the other officers waiting for their orders and a faint smile from John. "So, you're on Sarah's set-in-stone, not-to-be-messed-with agenda and you believe maple bars will ensure she cuts you slack?"

"It's worth trying," Joe said.

Another smile, this one a little wider and John shook his head. "It never worked for me with Beth Chambers, and I used to take her the ones with extra frosting. Good luck, Joe. You'll need it. Sarah's been running your dad's world for years."

The amusement faded as the other cops picked up their orders and left. John waited while the clerk filled two cartons with an assortment of doughnuts, but no maple bars. "See you around, Joe. You can buy me a beer and tell me why you've really come. It's been fifteen years. You haven't spent an entire summer here since you earned your doctorate."

"True." Shrugging, Joe stepped up to the counter and the glass case to start choosing more than maple bars. "I've waited long enough. *Getting by* gets old, John."

"We're singing from the same song sheet." Carrying the boxes, John headed for the door. "Wish I'd realized it sooner. Let me know if you need help."

4

AUDRA WALKED BESIDE ELINOR OUT THE DRIVEWAY GATES, UP THE street, and across the lawn to the back porch of the brick house next door and followed the other woman into the kitchen. The room was decorated in country style, complete with red checked curtains at the windows and a matching tablecloth.

Daisy turned from plugging in the coffee pot at the counter. "Good morning."

"We have éclairs," Elinor said, carrying the box over to the table. "Daisy, this is Audra Dawson, my new manager. Audra, this is Daisy Baldusi. She taught me all I know about teaching English to high school kids who don't want to know it."

A petite woman with a cap of short silver hair, Daisy came across the room and held out her hand. "Nice to see you again, Audra. I've heard a lot about you from Jake and Lynn. You're costing them money."

Audra blinked. "Say what? They're great kids. How do I cost them money? Their mom pays me."

"You do at least half their chores." Daisy grinned mischievously. "So, they don't get paid for them. Lynn says they'll make up for it when they move to Sean's after the wedding and Jake worries he'll never get his new fishing pole."

"And I can't win for losing," Elinor sighed as she opened the carton of six chocolate frosted éclairs. "There are two for each of us." She shook her head. "I catch hell from Sean when I treat them like mini-adults. And I get it from them when I hire somebody so they can be kids. I definitely need chocolate."

Daisy laughed and took down three cups from the cupboard. "Sean's always a real sweetie, not like his older brothers."

Allowing the memories of past years to roll through her mind, Audra eyed the older woman. "How do you know me, much less Ethan and Gavin?"

"I was their English teacher and yours when you did summer school at Snohomish High back in the day," Daisy said. "They were several years ahead of you, Audra. Ethan was the football star and Gavin lettered in basketball and track. Another boy might have tried to compete with them, but Sean shone in academics. He was a brilliant writer. He and Joe Watkins were at the top of my class all four years, not that anybody expected Sean to amount to much when he was the class clown."

Audra managed a smile. When her family moved up to the Lazy B in Liberty Valley, her life revolved around taking care of her sisters, the ranch, and her mother. School passed in a blur, but she had a few memories of her favorite English classes and the teachers. Attending a special summer school creative writing course had been a one-time experience.

"I'm a little nervous about meeting Joe," Elinor said. "Sean invited him to be best man at our wedding."

"Oh, you'll get along fine with him," Daisy said. "He's a good boy."

For a jerk. Audra hoped her face didn't reveal that emotion.

She'd known Joe when they were in the Silver Flying A's, her aunt and uncle's 4-H club and he always helped her with which-ever wild horse she rode. She'd learned quickly never to get attached to the year's project animal because as soon as it was trained, her father would sell it and buy her a new unbroken monster at the auction. When he left, the tradition continued. She was constantly training a new mount. And Joe continued to jump in and help. She had a major crush on him, but suspected he saw her as just one of the guys, even if he called her, *his brown-eyed girl*.

When she was a junior in high school, and he was a student at Washington State University, he invited her to the Apple Cup. The football game between his school and their archrival, the University of Washington was a major event every year whether it took place in Seattle or on the east side of the mountains in Pullman. She'd been thrilled until the moment she found out it was just a joke.

She focused on the conversation between Elinor and Daisy who chatted about the wedding less than two weeks away. While the ceremony would be small, a reception at the end of the summer on Labor Day weekend would be much larger. Elinor planned to invite everyone she and Sean knew to the party.

"I've already irritated his father," Elinor said. "I told the Senator the reception wouldn't be a political event for him and his cronies. He can only have twenty-five of his closest friends."

Audra bit into her first éclair, savoring the custard filling and admiring her boss even more. "At Clancy's wedding, it was a circus and a half. I finally told him if he wanted to use the shindig to pay off social obligations to his friends, he better cough up the bucks to pay for them."

"Did that work?" Daisy asked, bringing over the coffee pot to top their cups.

"Yes." Audra pushed her cup forward, smiling her thanks. "I wasn't trying to be a hard-ass, but two weddings are expensive, and it took almost every cent I had in the bank."

Elinor propped her elbows on the table and leaned closer. "*You* paid for the weddings? Why?"

"Because it's all my mom can do to pay the bills on the ranch and make sure we have enough money for the next year's expenses," Audra said. "I cover any extras for the family and my dad gambles away every cent he has."

"Families are so much fun." Daisy returned the coffee pot to the burner. "Now, tell me about the honeymoon, Elinor. Where are you two going?"

"Sean and I are taking the kids to see my father's family in Eastern Washington for the traditional Talbot reunion," Elinor said. "Then all of us are going to Disneyland the first week of September right after the reception. Mark it on your calendar, Audra. You've got the farm."

"Wow. Sounds like fun," Audra said.

"Yeah," Daisy agreed. "How about if we leave the kids to watch the pony farm and you and I go, Audra?"

"Works for me." Audra laughed. "Then again, maybe not. I'm already in trouble with Jake and Lynn for doing their chores. I don't want to know what happens if I mess up their trip."

After their coffee date, Elinor headed to the laundry and to pick up the kids at the middle school. Audra stopped in the barn to collect halters and lead lines, before catching ponies for the afternoon lessons. She'd groom and saddle the ones who still had blankets. Those who weren't tacked up would be ridden bareback.

She'd tell the students they needed to learn balance and if she held them to slower gaits, they wouldn't break what she privately thought of as her *anti-splat* rule. No falling off. And then she didn't have to pick up the pieces or have ponies galloping all over the ring causing more accidents.

She was in the middle of grooming Lightning when Elinor stomped into the barn. "What's up?"

"Millennials," Elinor snarled. "You can't live with them, and you can't just bury them."

"Okay. That's good to know. I live for the information highway."

A smile slowly replaced the scowl and Elinor stopped outside the stall. "The laundry has new owners, and they don't allow people to wash their horse or dog blankets in the machines anymore. That wouldn't irritate me if they'd replaced the washers, but they didn't. It's too late to get the saddle blankets to the gal at the tack store who does special orders—"

"Besides, she charges a small fortune," Audra said. "I'll call Aunt Marlene and see if I can bring them by and use her washing machine. The only problem is I have to stay, or she'll try to do them for us."

"No worries. You do the blankets and I'll teach the lessons," Elinor said. "Your sundae's in the freezer. Have you ever organized a large-scale sleepover? Sean told me it's different than a birthday party for the kids. I can't see how."

"Because we charge for it." Audra continued combing Lightning's gray mane. "The kids bring money and chip in on the food. Want me to make a poster and sign-up sheet before I go?"

"Yes. Give me that comb and I'll take over." Elinor glanced at the door as Jake rushed inside. "Walk please. Don't scare the critters. I need you to help me out. Go get Audra's sundae from the freezer and take it to her in the classroom."

"Why?" Jake asked, screeching to a stop. "I wanted her to help me train Awesome."

"She's making a poster for the saddle-cleaning party and then she's going to Marlene's for me," Elinor said. "Sean's bringing fried chicken tonight, so he'll help with all the babies."

"We could try working the three of them in a class when I get back," Audra said, handing over the mane and tail brush. "If it's okay with you folks, I'll bring Aunt Marlene back with me. It'll make up for me not letting her do the laundry for us."

"That would be a blast," Jake said, a big smile spreading across his face. "I want to take Awesome to shows when he gets older, and he needs to learn to work with other horses."

"Great, so we have a plan." Elinor began brushing Lightning's tail. "Are you two still here?"

"No. We're gone." Jake sauntered beside Audra out of the barn. "Do you really like brownies and ice cream, 'cause that's what we got you."

"Love them. Can't live without them." Audra teased. "Now, I

just have to keep the ice cream from dripping on the computer keyboard."

"Awesome. I'll go get it for you." He grinned up at her. "I'm glad you're here, Audra. It's like what Sean says."

"And what is that?"

"Sean says people can pretend to care, but they can't pretend to be there. And you follow through and do what you say you will. That's rare."

"It's called integrity," Audra said. "And like Aunt Marlene says, a person has to be able to look herself in the mirror every day."

"Got that right."

Audra watched him run toward the house while she headed for the upstairs apartment in the mare's barn. She'd designed so many posters that it wouldn't take her long to create the ones for the sleepover. She'd make enough copies for Elinor to give them to this afternoon's students. And while the computer loaded up, she'd call her aunt and arrange to wash the saddle blankets. She stopped as the mail carrier pulled through the gates and went to meet the driver. A check and a contract! Oh, boy!

———

It took a half-hour to reach her aunt's house in Snohomish. Audra parked by the back door and picked up the first trash bag. She carried it to the porch and returned to her Ford pickup for the next one. By the time, she'd ferried the last two bags to the porch, the first one was already in the laundry room and the industrial washer had started its cycle.

"You were supposed to let me do them," Audra scolded her aunt.

Marlene grinned and her hazel eyes sparkled. "Yeah, but now while they wash, we can go to the bank. You said you had errands to run."

"You just want to swing by that Greek restaurant, the one with seafood gyros," Audra said. "Well, come on. Let's go. But you'll owe me a favor. I promised Jake I'd bring you back to help us with the foals. We're going to have a big class with all three of them."

"Sounds like fun." Marlene picked up her jacket and purse. "Thanks for thinking of me, honey. Sometimes, Wednesday nights get lonely."

"It doesn't have to be Wednesday." Audra gave her aunt a quick hug, thinking of her uncle who'd died from cancer. "I miss him too."

"Yes, but I worry about you." Marlene locked the door, shook back long gray-streaked black hair. "You've never married. I had Roy. Who do you have?"

"Hey, Pyewacket would have a fit if somebody else was in our bed." Audra headed down the steps and back to her truck. "Besides, the guy I want has someone else in mind."

"Then, you need to let him go. If he can't see you, he's not meant for you." Marlene climbed into the passenger seat. "You deserve somebody special."

The statement lingered in Audra's mind while she did her errands, had lunch with her aunt, finished up the blankets, and then they returned to the pony farm. Her heart leaped as she spotted the late model Cadillac parked in front of Elinor's house.

Ethan had come to visit. She slid out of the driver's seat and bent to pet the dogs when they pelted across the yard to greet her. She looked up in time to see Sean Killian walking toward her, a friendly smile on his face.

He greeted her with a quick, sideways brotherly hug. "Elinor says you saved the day. Thanks, Audra."

"Hey, it's my job." She reached in the back of the truck for the first trash bag. "We need to hang these on the hitch rails to dry. Did Jake tell you his plan for horse training?"

"More like baby training." Sean walked around the rig and kissed Marlene's cheek. "I hear you're helping. When Ethan arrived, I figured he could cowboy up too."

"Why is he here?" Marlene asked, pulling out the second bag of blankets. "Is he getting ready to go back east to build airplanes again?"

"I don't know." Sean took the bag away from Marlene. "He said he needed to talk to Audra."

"I wonder why." Audra hoped her tone didn't reveal her excitement. Ethan had come to see *her*. *Hooray for Hollywood!*

There he was, coming down the porch steps. He was so light on his feet. A big guy, he moved like the star athlete he'd been in high school and college even though he'd turned forty-five last spring. She smiled as he approached. "Hi, Ethan. What's up?"

"Not much." He took the last bag from her. "Where do you want these?"

"We'll hang them on the hitch rails and fences to dry," Audra said. "They have to be out of reach of the puppies."

"Okay." He wasn't smiling. In fact, he looked concerned about something. "Why don't you show me where you want them?"

"All right." She led the way to the paddock fence that divided the yard from the big barn. She opened the bag and pulled the first blanket, a red striped one. "So, how are you doing?"

"I'm fine. It's Clancy."

Audra's heart sank. What was it going to take for him to notice a different woman, one that really cared about him? *Me, me, me!* "Why? What's wrong? She sounded excited earlier when we talked. She's had several horse shows come through, so she'll be judging this summer."

Ethan nodded and hung up the next blanket. "She says Elinor's mad at her and she doesn't know why. Do you?"

Audra pulled out the third saddle blanket, a blue striped one this time. She shook it out and laid it across the fence rail. "I'm not real comfortable with this discussion, Ethan. I know Elinor offered Clancy a management job here and she didn't want it. She said it was too much responsibility when she told me about the job. After Xanadu, I either came here or I found a position out of state."

"I got that." Ethan ran a hand through his salt and pepper dark hair. "I don't think your family could handle it if you left."

"I know." Audra didn't add they'd have to support themselves and find somebody else to be either the villain or kick-ass heroine in their dramas. "But to be honest, I think it's time for me to start looking elsewhere. I didn't mean to step on anybody's toes by coming here. I'm only trying to do the job that Elinor hired me to do."

"Well, she really appreciates your help." Ethan hung up the last blanket and folded up the bag. "She told me she didn't know what she'd have done if you hadn't been here this past week."

"Yeah, I know. We've been busy getting ready for camp." Audra measured him coolly, struggling to control her temper and hurt that Clancy had played set-up again, making her the arch-enemy. Ethan had fallen for the scam one more time. Why couldn't he see through her sister's machinations?

"It wasn't easy for us to wash fifteen ponies by ourselves. We were lucky Sandy and Marcie were able to rearrange their sched-ules and help."

"What about Clancy?"

Audra raised a brow. "Oh, come on, Ethan. After all this time, you should know better than to expect your princess to do menial labor. Scrubbing ponies, washing blankets, organizing groom kits, that's for the peasants. And Sean came up with a great idea for cleaning saddles. Granted, I won't have a life Saturday night, but what else is new?"

"She bailed on the prep work?" Ethan asked, a muscle twitching in his jaw.

"Yes, but I picked up the slack." Audra didn't add the rest of what she thought. *I'm under the elephant, just like always.* Instead, she turned and walked away.

She needed time and space to think. So, she headed to her apartment. Tears burned, but she didn't let them fall. She knew better. Crying never solved any problems. And then the person who hurt her won the battle. She took a deep breath and headed for the fridge. She wanted a drink, but she had to go back to work so she opened a soda.

Cola in hand, she crossed to the desk. She turned on the computer and opened the file that held her new book. She hadn't done much with the villain, so it was time to bring him to life and let him kill someone. The shape-shifting witch was doomed to die. Not easily, however. It was time to torture the woman and throw her down a flight of stairs.

Okay, so it wouldn't last. She'd be reincarnated and come back again to find her true love.

An hour later, calm restored, Audra was ready to return to the fray. She saved her work on the portable hard-drive, then shut down the computer. She fed Pyewacket and headed back downstairs.

Hearing voices, she went into the horse area. She found Jake grooming Awesome while Marlene worked on the colt's mother, Chipeta. In the next stall, Lynn and her friend, Cassie were hard at work brushing Star and her baby girl, Comet. Sean and Elinor were busy with the last mare, Taffy, and her dark gray foal, Licorice Whip.

"What happened to Ethan?" Audra asked. "I thought he was going to help with our first foal class."

Sean shrugged and continued brushing Taffy's rose gray hide. "Oh, Clancy whistled, and he went running."

When they finished grooming a short time later, Audra had her students remove the lead lines so the foals would be independent on their way to the big outdoor arena. Still wearing their new halters, the colt and two fillies trotted after their respective mothers to the outdoor corral for their first real class. All the other work with the youngsters had been solo, so this would be an adventure. Awesome tore off running and bucking with Comet in hot pursuit. Licorice decided this was the perfect time for a snack and stayed next to Taffy, contentedly nursing.

"What do we do," Jake asked, "chase them?"

"No, they can run faster than you do, and we don't want to scare them," Audra said. "So, let's practice what we're going to teach them with their dams."

"Like what?" Lynn petted Taffy's almost white neck, waiting for the mare's foal to finish drinking. "We've been brushing them, putting on and taking off their halters, and leading them around the stalls."

"All good baby steps," Audra teased and saw Lynn's smile, quickly hidden. The girl had to be cool, no matter what. It was a teen thing. "Now, we want them to walk behind their moms. We'll start doing everything they'll need to know when they get older so nothing humans do frightens them. If they're going to stay here for the rest of their lives—"

"They are," Jake interrupted, not waiting for his mom to say anything. "Chipeta would freak if we sold Awesome. She already looks for Paragon and he'll be home in September after Clancy gets done with him."

"Okay," Audra agreed. "Then, these babies have to be suitable for beginning riders in four years. And that means we start teaching them their jobs now."

Even though everyone knew how to lead ponies, she reviewed the techniques she wanted them to use. They practiced walking on both the left and right sides of the mares, squaring them up so they were balanced each time they stopped and then turning small circles. Licorice Whip happily followed her mother through the patterns, so of course, Lynn and Cassie thought they were all that and the proverbial bucket of chips.

When Awesome charged back to his mother, Jake clipped on the lead rope. He began to lead the colt forward, a few steps at a time. If the sorrel balked, it was time to stop and practice backing. Soon, Comet was involved in the class too with Elinor and Sean taking turns between the mare and the filly.

Audra knew most trainers would only have worked with the foals for twenty minutes, but she'd never believed in that. The more hours she spent with them, the better they'd be and right now, they just loved the attention. However, she also didn't want to overwhelm their baby brains, so she ended the class by having the foals led back to their stalls behind their mothers an hour later.

"I don't believe it," Elinor said, scratching Comet behind her ears. "They learned so much, so quickly. Audra, you're an amazing instructor. I don't know anyone else who could have trained three foals and a bunch of novice horse people at the same time."

"Are you calling me a novice, woman?" Sean unfastened the halter on Star, then wrapped an arm around Elinor's shoulders. "I'll have you know as an arrogant cowboy I resent that."

"Yeah, well I'm not as smart as you are when it comes to horses," Elinor retorted, "and I'm the first to admit it." She leaned against him and smiled up at him. "Of course, telling you that you're the cowboy with the mostest means your hat won't fit for long."

He grinned and dropped a kiss on her hair. "Well, you're the cutest cowgirl I've seen all day."

Leaving them to coo and cuddle, Audra went to check on her other students. Lynn and Cassie were focused on Licorice and Taffy, grooming them again and feeding treats to the pair. The filly nibbled on crusts of bread while her dam crunched carrots. In the next stall, Marlene held Awesome while Jake brushed out the colt's mane. His mother stood at the manger, eating a night ration of alfalfa pellets and grain.

"Great class, honey," Marlene said. "If you keep training these little ones, they'll be ready for shows this summer."

"I'd rather hold off till fall," Audra said, resting her elbows on the half-door of the stall. "So many diseases are airborne and young horses are especially vulnerable. We don't have anything to gain by exposing them to the outside show world, especially since they're not registered, and Jake says they're not for sale."

The boy glanced over his shoulder and grinned at her. "Got

that right. Thanks, Audra. I'm going to keep practicing with him, so he remembers everything we learned tonight."

"All right. We'll have another class tomorrow evening."

"Only if you take the day off," Elinor said, coming to join them. "Next week is going to be crazy, so I want you to rest up Thursday and Friday."

5

Everett, Washington ~ Wednesday, June 20th , 2018

ZANE O'MALLEY TURNED OFF THE TV, PICKED UP HIS CAN OF beer, and finished it. He opened the last of the six pack and took a swallow. He'd figured the cool summer weather would change, warm up to what was normal for this season. Then he'd begin putting out the trays of old-style antifreeze around the garage and back yard. He hadn't started yet. What was the point when it'd taken so long for him to find the toxic kind he wanted, the one deadly for pets and children?

Very few animals would be desperate enough to drink what he offered. The wild ones would avoid the liquid because it smelled like humans. And he hadn't seen very many stray dogs or cats in the area who were willing to try the rat-poisoned laced food he'd put out for them, much less the anti-freeze. Well, he'd try to be patient.

Blast City opened tomorrow out at the reservation. Fireworks would begin exploding in the rural part of the county in the next couple of days and animals would run off soon. If he didn't start finding dying critters in the next couple of days, he'd visit the library and go online. There were bound to be people looking for homes for disposable pets that he could add to his graveyard collection.

———

Joe pulled in the circular driveway of a huge three-story house and followed the paved loop around, all the way to the large matching barn and indoor arena. He spotted a young woman wearing a sweatshirt, breeches, and boots hurrying toward him. He opened the door of the clinic's pickup and went to meet her. "Got a colic? Doctor Art's tied up in surgery, so he sent me."

"I'm Christy." The shapely brunette held out a hand. "Are you his new associate?"

"Not yet. He's my dad," Joe said. "I'm Joe. I teach veterinary medicine and I'm home on vacation." He walked around to the rear of the truck and opened the canopy. "So, what do we have going on?"

Christy glanced anxiously toward the indoor arena. "My son had a few friends over to celebrate the end of school. They went out to feed carrots to the horses and found my new mare down, rolling in her stall. Oscar came to get me. Jake got her up and started walking her."

"Sounds like everybody did the right things," Joe added a pair of long plastic gloves to the supplies in the bucket. "Okay, let's go look at her. We'll want to make sure she hasn't twisted a gut. When was the last time she ate?"

"At noon when she got her lunch." Christy started walking toward the barn. "She didn't seem nervous or upset. She'd cleaned up her breakfast hay and grain. And she has an automatic waterer in her stall."

"Does she use it?" Joe asked. "Some horses don't."

He watched bewilderment replace the concern on Christy's face as she considered the question. He opened the door for her, and they headed into the arena where four boys watched a fifth lead a dainty bay mare around the ring. Joe gestured to the blond youngster, and he trotted the horse across the ring.

"Hi, I'm Jake." The boy frowned. "Where's Doctor Art?"

"Surgery," Joe said. "He sent me. I'm his son, Doctor Joe Watkins. What's her name?"

"Sable Moonlit Charm." Jake rubbed the mare's white star, then the snip on her nose. "It's kind of redundant, don't you think?"

"She's a purebred Arabian from Bergstrom's Xanadu line," Christy said, managing a weak smile. "And registered horses often have redundant names."

"Why?" Jake asked.

"To show her family lineage." Joe peeled back the mare's upper lip to check for pale gums, a sign of shock. "What's her barn name?"

"Sable Moonlit Charm," Christy said. "What else would I call her?"

Joe released the lip and petted the horse's golden-brown neck. "Sometimes, people use shorter names at home." He reached into his pocket and pulled out his stethoscope. "Okay, I want to listen for gut sounds. Jake, can you hold her while I do it?"

"Sure," Jake said. "I listened already, but I didn't hear anything on either side."

Joe hid an appreciative grin. "Good to know. Let me see if I can confirm your diagnosis."

The mare was a pretty thing, he thought, slipping the ends of the stethoscope into his ears. A healthy, shining bright coat. About sixteen hands, two white socks, one on her right front and the other on her left hind outlined by the traditional black hairs known as points on bay horses. Those and that dashing long star would make her a looker in the show ring, especially with that ebony mane and tail. He worked his way alongside her, murmuring reassurances, and listened to her intestines, first on the left, then on the right. No distinctive rumbling on either side, so the boy was probably right.

"Did you give her anything for the pain?" Joe stepped back. She hadn't tried to lie down, and she wasn't kicking at her sides.

A hint of red crept into Jake's face. "Sorry, Doctor, I forgot. I had Christy get some muscle relaxant from the barn fridge and we gave Charm enough for an eight-hundred-pound horse," He looked at his watch. "Approximately forty-five minutes ago. It was an amount a lot less than she weighs, but Doctor Art always wants us to under-medicate, not over. So far, no poop."

"Well, you did the right thing," Joe said. "Christy, I need a bucket of warm water. Can you get that here or do you have to go to the house?"

"We have a shower stall in the barn," Christy said, gesturing to one of the boys. "Oscar, will you get the doctor his water?"

"Sure, Mom." Another blond boy came forward, this one in fashionably ragged jeans and a gray t-shirt and took the bucket. "Be right back."

"And we're about to get gross," Joe winked at Jake. "I'm going to have to see if she's twisted a gut and clean out her insides. Can you keep holding her?"

Jake nodded and moved to the same side of the horse. "I get to watch, right?"

"As long as she doesn't move or try to kick my head in," Joe said, pulling on the first long plastic glove. "You can clean out a horse with a bread sack and a bit of shortening."

"That's how my mom does it," Jake said.

Christy winced. "No, not really. Your mom doesn't do this herself, does she?"

Jake nodded again. "Sure. I helped her when we doctored Daisy's horse. It was the middle of the night and Doctor Art was at a different emergency, so we had to do it ourselves. We used clothespins to clip up Twazeim's tail. What are you going to use, Doctor Joe?"

Joe chuckled. "Oh, I think I'll use Christy." He smiled at her. "You can help us out, can't you?" She gave a tentative nod and he bunched up the horse's tail and passed it to her. "Okay, stay on the right while I put my hand where no guy really wants to go. Ready?"

Christy nodded again. "Yes. If Elinor can do what you're doing, I can hold Charm's tail."

"Good to know." Joe squirted a bit of lubricant on his glove and worked it through the plastic covering his fingers. Then, he eased up behind the mare. "Steady, girl. It's going to be all right."

————

"You should have seen him," Jake said. "He just stuck his whole arm up inside her butt. It was major awesome, Lynnie."

"It sounds major awful to me." Lynn kept brushing her palomino mare. "Only you could go to a pizza party and end up having fun pulling poop out of a horse, Jake."

"I didn't pull poop out of her butt," Jake said, indignant. "You didn't listen. Doctor Joe did it. And it was like a total horse-pucky mountain. He got clumps of turds out of her."

"Still sounds gross to me." Lynn dropped a kiss on her horse's white mane. "Don't you ever do that to me." She shuddered dramatically. "Gypsy's a lady, thank Gawd."

"She's a horse and horses get colic." Jake climbed up on the stall door. "And guess what?"

"I'd be too scared to guess anything when it comes to you." Lynn switched brushes and began to buff Gypsy's golden hair. "I'll bet Christy totally freaked. She's such a princess."

"No, she was cool." Jake propped his elbows on the door and leaned his chin on folded hands. "She did what I said when I said. And she was happy we saved her new horse." He lowered his voice, looked cautiously over his shoulder. "Where's Audra?"

"Upstairs in the mama's barn," Lynn said. "Mom gave her the day off. Why?"

"Because Doctor Joe's the one," Jake said. "He's for her."

"No way. You told me she needed a hero."

"Any guy who stands behind a big horse and sticks his whole arm up inside her to pull out clumps of poop is a hero," Jake said. "Doctor Joe could have been kicked or stomped and he didn't even blink. He just did what he had to do. And he saved Charm's life. So, he's a hero and he gets Audra."

Lynn tossed her head. "I'd like to see you make that happen. And there's no way I'm helping, so don't even ask, Jacob Owen Talbot."

———

Chores started early since Lynn had a horseshow. Audra fed the mares, then headed for the main barn to parcel out hay to the rest of the ponies. By the time she was ready to grain, she had company. Jake and Lynn appeared with two sacks of feed in the wheelbarrow, and they worked their way through the row of stalls to the line of grain buckets.

"How were your days off?" Jake asked, waiting for her to measure alfalfa pellets. "Did you have fun? What did you do?"

Audra grinned at him, then measured scoops of pellets into each pail. "Slept late, watched TV, and rested up to get ready for day camp next week." She didn't add that she'd started the revisions on her book or that she'd tried to plot out the new one and ran into difficulties. Writing was her private life and the same went for her alter-ego. It didn't stop her from emailing Gavin Killian and inviting him to lunch so she could pick his brain about *The Tempest*, the Shakespeare play she planned to use as a framework for her witch book. "What about you two? What did you do?"

"I hung out with the guys from my class on Thursday," Jake said. "One of Christy's horses had colic, so I helped her deal with that."

"Who is Christy?" Audra asked.

"A student here, but she's a grown-up," Lynn explained, using the hose to spritz the green alfalfa pellets, moving from pail to pail. "She owns lots of horses, but Sean says she needs to learn how to take care of them because she has gaps in her knowledge, so Mom gives her lessons."

"Nobody knows everything," Audra said, "and if they say they do, they're lying." She finished up with the alfalfa and started with the corn, oats, and barley mixture, adding a scoop to each ration. "Life is a learning experience."

"Don't you think the vet should come and check the foals?" Jake asked. "They're almost two months old."

"They look healthy to me," Audra said. "Why do you think they need a doctor?"

Lynn glared at her brother. "He's all impressed with the vet. The guy saved Christy's mare, but we don't need him here. Our horses are fine, Jake. And Doctor Art said we don't have to take the puppies in for their next set of shots till we get back from Eastern Washington."

"Okay, then." Audra frowned thoughtfully at the feed, thinking about supplements. "Well, let's get this done and move on so Lynn will be on time for the show."

"Works for me," Lynn said.

The next two hours raced by. Soon Lynn and her horse were headed off to Snohomish to the stable where the show would take place. Jake and Elinor left in her truck, eager to help and to cheer Lynn and Gypsy into the blue ribbons. Sandy and Marcie, the two college girls who worked as trail guides, arrived together and hurried to the barn to groom and saddle the ponies for the day.

In what seemed like an instant, Sandy reappeared at the kitchen door, concern on her face. "Audra, something's wrong with Lightning."

"What?" Audra put her coffee cup in the sink and went toward the door. "He was fine at breakfast."

"His nose is streaming snot, and his mouth is foaming," Sandy said. "He can't lift his head. Should I call the vet?"

"Sounds like he's choking to me." Audra made sure that Elinor's dog and the kids' puppies were in the house, then shut the door behind her and went with Sandy to the barn. The gray Arabian-Welsh pony stood in the center of the stall. His head drooped to his knees. She picked up a halter and went inside, crooning softly. "It'll be okay, sweetie. I promise."

"What do we have to do?" Sandy asked.

Audra flicked a quick glance at the blonde. "I'm going to start massaging his throat and glands. You need to finish grooming and saddling the rest of the ponies. We don't want the first ride to be late. That will throw us off schedule all day."

Marcie came to a stop outside the stall. "I can't believe you expect us to just go on like nothing's wrong."

"I do expect it," Audra said. "I'm here and I'll fix this. And it will be much easier for Lightning if he sees the usual routine, than if we huddle around him."

The girls reluctantly moved in the direction of the tack room, shooting dirty looks at her. Ignoring them, Audra gently began rubbing Lightning's throatlatch, slowly working her way down toward his chin and then back up toward his neck. Several minutes passed and she kept massaging the pony.

Up to the throatlatch, down to the chin and back up again. Mucus continued to stream from his nostrils and mouth. So, she hadn't cleared the blockage in his throat yet and she kept up the steady rubbing.

The barn door opened, and she saw her sister, Brigid step inside. She was a typical Dawson woman, tall, curvaceous, and ornery down to her *Ropers*. "Over here," Audra called and continued to massage Lightning's chin, jaw, and throat. "How are you?"

"Okay." Brigid came over to the stall, dressed for teacher duty in a crisp western blouse and ironed blue jeans. She'd braided her long strawberry blonde hair and it hung down her back. "What's up?"

"Choke," Audra said. "And I'm on Sandy and Marcie's list

because I won't let them hang out instead of getting ready for the day's business. So, how is the family soap opera?"

"Still a soap opera." Brigid smiled, but it didn't touch her green eyes. "The twins are having fits because you won't pay for them to stay in the dorms."

"I can't afford it," Audra said. "What do they think? When they weren't looking, I won the lottery and I just try to keep them barefoot and at home? Will they ever grow any brains?"

Brigid laughed. "Don't count on that. Bring a bottle of antacids when you come for dinner tomorrow. They'll be hassling you the whole time we eat. Now, where do I jump in? Clancy said there was a lesson book, so I'd know the status of each student."

"It's in the kitchen on Elinor's desk," Audra said. "I haven't brought it out here yet."

"Okay, I'll get it," Brigid said. "And I made doughnuts from an old family recipe. I'll put the box in the kitchen too and we can fight over them during lunch. Maybe the guides will be speaking to you by then."

"Well, I'm not counting on that either. I seem to be the resident witch." Audra rubbed her way down to the pony's chin. "Be sure to put the doughnuts where the dogs can't get them. And bring me a cup of coffee, will you? This is taking longer than I thought."

"Want me to call Art?" Brigid asked, leaning on the stall door.

"Maybe." Audra stopped the massage and stepped back to eye the distressed animal. Was it her imagination or had the steady flow of mucus slowed down? No, she decided and flexed her hands before she started on the throat area once more. "I guess you'd better. I'll keep trying to get the blockage in the throat to break down. See how fast he can get here."

"You got it." Brigid turned toward the barn door and hurried away, the tail of her braid bouncing against her hips.

———

He hadn't planned to go out on calls during his visit home but had to admit he liked it even if he hadn't admitted it to his father or Sarah yet. Being back in barns and around animals was different than standing behind a podium lecturing college students. And he enjoyed getting his hands dirty, more than he'd thought possible. This was what veterinary medicine was really about. He pulled into the gravel drive. The Silver Lake Pony Ranch wasn't anything like the Taj Ma-Barn where he'd been a couple of days ago.

A statuesque redhead came out of the country rambler, heading for him as he parked. "You're not Art."

"No, I'm Joe Watkins. Which of the Dawsons are you?"

The question earned him a long, steady, green-eyed look before she answered. "I'm Brigid. Do I know you?"

"You probably don't remember me," Joe said. "I was before your time. So, who has choke?"

"Lightning. He's in his stall. What can I help carry back there?"

Joe shrugged and opened the back end of the truck. "I've got it."

Another look as she waited. Joe finished by putting a long piece of surgical tubing in his bucket and they headed past the house in the direction of the old two-story barn. She walked silently beside him, still assessing him from under her lashes. He tried to remember if he'd ever known her and decided that she must have been one of the pack of Dawson girls, but she didn't stick in his mind. Of course, how old could she have been when he left home twenty-one years ago to attend his freshman year at Washington State University in Pullman?

"The vet's here," Brigid called as she opened the barn door. "It's not Art."

"Really? Which one of his wanna-be doctors did he send?" A petite woman glared at them from the back corner stall. "And why didn't you step up and drop-kick him through the goal-posts of life? I want Art."

"We don't always get what we want." Joe crossed the open

area to where his patient waited, a light gray mid-size pony, white mucus seeping from his nose and mouth. "I want a million bucks and a good-hearted woman, but here I am with you." He eyed the short, curvy redhead in front of him. "And you are…?"

"My sister, Audra," Brigid introduced them as she approached. "This is Joe Watkins, Art's son."

"No way," Joe said. "What happened to you?"

"I grew up," Audra snapped. "You should try it."

"You didn't grow much." Joe reached for his stethoscope so he could monitor the pony's vital signs. "You always reminded me of that fairy in *Peter Pan*. What was her name? Oh yeah, *Stinkerbelle*."

He heard a choked-off laugh from Brigid, then concentrated on the suffering equine. The phoned-in diagnosis appeared to be correct. An object was lodged in the horse's esophagus. Saliva with bits of grain flowed from the gelding's nostrils and mouth. "How long have you been massaging his throat?"

Audra glanced at her watch. "An hour and a half while I waited for you to show up."

Joe opened the gray's mouth to check the pony's teeth. A visual exam followed by a physical one revealed no sharp points on any of the molars. He should have been able to chew his breakfast, not choke on it. "Have the symptoms lessened or increased?"

"It's been about the same." She turned her attention to the other woman still standing nearby. "Brigid, I'll handle this. Will you make sure that the trail ride is underway? Then, you can start the first morning lesson."

"Okay, you've got it." Brigid walked away.

"Still acting large and in charge." Joe released his hold on the jaw and stepped to the right side, ignoring the gelding's attempt to bite him. "Looks like we'll have to intervene and get rid of the blockage."

"Gee, are you getting smarter in your old age? Do you think that could be why we called for a doctor?" Audra asked. "Maybe, you could use your cell phone and find us a real one."

"Not happening, sweetheart." Joe slid his fingers up the underside of the pony's throat, assessing the glands. "The tissue around the obstruction will continue to swell and pressure necrosis may start to affect the esophageal wall. There's no time to wait for another veterinarian. This guy comes first."

6

DURING THE NEXT HALF HOUR, SHE REMINDED HERSELF JOE Watkins was an arrogant jerk and she'd hated him for years. It was hard to remember when he was so gentle but effective with the sick pony. He asked all the right questions, ruling out other substances that could cause excess salivation like rat poison. Lightning hadn't been injured and didn't have a broken jaw.

That meant running a surgical tube through his nostril and down his throat to move the obstruction toward his stomach. To her surprise, Joe didn't pull out a twitch right away to immobilize the pony. Instead, he opted for a light dose of a local anesthetic to ease Lightning's stress.

"While this takes effect, can you get me some warm water to flush the blockage away?"

Audra took a deep breath and didn't correct him on the proper use of the words, *can* and *may*. She nodded and passed him the lead line. "He has issues with guys so don't let him bite or kick you. Sean's sister will nail you to the wall if you try to sue Elinor."

"Is she the owner of the place?" Joe asked, a faint smile creasing his lips and warming sky-blue eyes. "Not you?"

"I'm the manager," Audra said and waited for a smart comment. When none came, she decided that perhaps he'd matured a bit more than the teen she remembered and went to the house to bring back the water.

Lightning had started to relax when she returned, his eyes half-closed as he drowsed and drooled on Joe's light blue coveralls. She fought the urge to smile at the man. Despite being almost forty, he only had a few speckles of gray in his black hair. He never had been a big guy, still more lean and wiry than the buff heroes she usually wrote about.

"I think he's ready," Joe said. "You've probably held a horse while the vet does this before, but I'll need you to do what I say when I say it. Deal?"

"Of course," Audra agreed. "I'm not stupid. If you screw this up, it'll damage the nasal passages, cause a nosebleed or injure his lungs."

Joe swished the plastic tubing in the water. "I'm so glad you trust me."

"Only to take care of him, not with anything else."

"I'll change your mind." Joe pulled out the long three-eighths-inch tube and squirted surgical lubricant into his hand to smooth over the plastic. Then, he stepped up to the pony and eased the rounded tip of the tube into Lightning's nostril. "Okay, buddy. Here we go."

He was careful. Audra had to give him credit for that. He slid the tube slowly through the right nostril, never forcing the plastic line. She shifted her hold on the pony's head to help him partially flex it so he could swallow. Joe didn't try to push the tubing into the stomach. He stopped when it was at the esophagus.

"Hold the line for me," Joe said. "Don't push on it or pull it out."

She nodded in agreement. "When it comes to him, you're the boss."

Running water through the tube seemed to do the trick. The flow of mucus from the nose and mouth eased as the lump of grain was flushed down toward Lightning's stomach. The pony heaved a huge sigh of relief when Joe removed the plastic line.

Audra rubbed Lightning's face. "You'll be fine now, fella. Promise."

"Only if you watch the hay for cockleburs, plant barbs, sticks, and other foreign debris," Joe said. "Not that he can have any hay for three days. I want to see the grain you're feeding. What choked him?"

Audra glared at Joe. "I don't feed crappy hay in my barns. He gets an alfalfa-grass mix and there's no garbage in it. He also eats alfalfa pellets and good grain. Who the hell do you think you are?"

"The guy who's going to inspect your loft and feed room after I clean up here," Joe said, in even tones. "And the owner will be hearing from me so get over yourself, *Stinkerbelle*. Clear that hay out of his manger and he'll need fresh water in his bucket. You may want to add a bit of apple juice so he takes on extra fluids."

"Anything else?"

"I'll be leaving him electrolytes and pain relievers with instructions for you to follow. No hay until Tuesday while his throat heals. We don't want him to choke again. The next time could be fatal. And when he goes back on hay, I'll want it dampened for him."

"I'm not an idiot. I know that." Audra unbuckled the halter and hung it outside the stall. She removed the pile of hay from the manger and gave it to Lightning's best buddy after a quick inspection proved that it was as fresh and green as she thought it should be.

She was grateful the pony felt better, glad the vet saved him, and she could be nice. It was hard to remember her mantra as she showed Joe through the barn and let him inspect the feed. So many doctors would have been pulling out their pen and pad by this point to write up the bill and she appreciated the fact that he honestly seemed to care about Lightning.

Sure, she did. So, why did she want to kick him in the butt?

They finished up at the house in time to join Brigid and the guides for lunch. Joe petted the puppies when they rushed to greet him.

"If you wash your hands, you can have a doughnut with your coffee," Brigid said. "Otherwise, forget about it. I don't want them to have dog hair instead of sprinkles."

Audra watched as Joe laughed and obeyed orders. When it came to her baked goods, Brigid didn't take any prisoners. "How did the trail ride go?"

"Good," Marcie said. "We made twenty bucks in tips."

"Then, you must have done a great job." Audra went and washed her own hands, pretending not to notice that Sandy still wasn't speaking to her. "The guides keep their tips and so do you, Brigid."

"What about you?" Joe asked. "Does anybody notice that the place wouldn't run smoothly if the manager wasn't around to deal with emergencies?"

Audra passed him a cup of coffee. "I don't expect people to notice what I do. So, it doesn't surprise me when they don't."

He nodded. "What about changing your appearance, so you look like a clone of the other Dawsons? Do they like you better that way too, *Stinkerbelle*?"

Utter silence fell in the kitchen as the three other women stared. Audra wasn't sure if it had to do with the nickname or the questions. She shrugged, headed for the kitchen table and the bakery box. "In case you haven't figured it out yet, nobody likes management, Joe. They figure crap floats to the top. If you hadn't spent so many years hiding in the halls of academia, you could have had a good dose of reality."

"Reality bites." He followed her. "I still think you should have bailed on your family and gone to New York to be that prize-winning writer who lived in a garret."

"I didn't know you wanted to go anywhere, Audra," Brigid said, removing the lid from the box. "I thought you were doing what you liked."

Audra pulled out a powdered-sugar-coated, old-fashioned doughnut. "Oh, he's blowing smoke. I had a few delusions when I was in high school."

"They call them dreams." Joe nabbed a doughnut for himself. "You had those creative writing scholarships when you graduated. Too bad you couldn't use them."

"Yeah, well we don't all run away from our responsibilities."

In an odd way, it felt comfortable to spar with him. She didn't care about him, so she didn't have to be nice to him or watch her mouth or listen to him whine and snivel that she was a total witch except it was spelled with a *B* instead of a *W*.

When he left fifteen minutes later, she walked him out to the truck to get the bill and the meds for the pony. "Don't pad it," she told him, "or I'll charge you for my vet assisting."

"Yeah, well I should get extra for training you to do things my way."

"It was a one-time occurrence. Normally, we don't need a vet here to mess things up."

"I'll change that when I come back to check on my patient."

Audra laughed. "Now, I know you've been teaching too long. Real vets don't make check-up calls, Joe. And we definitely don't pay for them."

"I'll take out my fee in your sister's doughnuts," Joe said. "And I'll be back."

"Just like the *Terminator*," Audra mocked, taking the papers and the bottles from him. "I don't believe you, and I won't hold my breath waiting to see you."

Between supervising trail rides, coordinating lessons, and running the office, Audra made a point of monitoring Lightning's condition. He dozed most of the afternoon, drank some water, and then slept again. When it was time for the sedatives, she mixed them into a small mash of grain and more liquid. He ate it and didn't choke on the feed.

At different times during the day, she found herself remembering Joe Watkins and forced him out of her mind. However, she still wondered what he looked like in regular clothes, not the coveralls. What did his dad say about Joe's ponytail? Granted his black hair wasn't that long, just past his collar, but she couldn't imagine Doctor Art or Sarah Holmes, the receptionist from Hell letting it slide. There must have been some serious teasing around the vet office.

High cheekbones, a strong jaw, rugged features – somebody or some critter had broken Joe's nose in the last seventeen years. The half-smile on his lips reached his eyes and she liked that. She'd also enjoyed not worrying about his feelings, an odd experience. She didn't have to pretend to be something or someone she wasn't with him. And he'd been so good with Lightning.

Instead of letting the gray gelding out in the pasture with the other ponies at the end of the day, she kept him in his stall. Since horses were herd animals, she didn't let his best buddy, Bonanza out either. The two old gents didn't seem too concerned about the special treatment, although Lightning wasn't having hay for supper.

"Marcie and I are running home to get our stuff," Sandy said, coming into the barn. "We'll be back in two hours to take care of the kids and clean the saddles. Elinor just arrived with Lynn and Gypsy."

"Okay, thanks for the good job today," Audra said. "I'll see you later."

The young woman remained quiet for a moment, then said, "I'm sorry I was rude this morning. You were doing your best to take care of Lightning and you didn't need me to hassle you about it."

"No worries." Audra pasted on a professional smile. "What happens on Saturday doesn't get dumped on Elinor when she walks or drives in the farm gates."

Sandy stopped in the doorway of the barn, turned back, and stared. "Audra, I'm apologizing because I was rude to you, not because I'm worried about her. It really bothered me when you told Dr. Joe that you figured we all thought you were *crap* since you're the manager and I don't think so. I was just freaking about Lightning, and you had enough to handle. You didn't need me acting like a brat."

Audra petted Lightning's neck and contemplated the situation. She'd never expected an apology. She was the Dawson in charge of the Silver Lake Pony Ranch and accustomed to catching hell when things went wrong. Nobody in her family ever considered the personal cost she paid for doing all the emotional laundry in their extended clan.

"It was a scary situation and I'm glad you noticed he was in trouble and came to get me," Audra said. "Otherwise, he could have choked to death. We both did what needed to be done."

"Yeah. I hadn't thought of it like that." With a quick wave, Sandy disappeared out the door.

Shaking her head, Audra petted the two ponies again, then headed out of the barn to greet Elinor and her family. With Gypsy in tow, Lynn was on her way to the palomino mare's stall, so Audra lingered to hold the gate for the young teen. "How'd it go?"

"We got two firsts, a second, a fourth, and two eighth places," Lynn reported, pausing to straighten her horse's white forelock. "I messed up my patterns in the medal class and then Gypsy refused to cross the tarp in Trail."

"Sounds like we do more practice at home," Audra said. "Hey, you were in the ribbons all day. That's rather good."

"I didn't place in Hunt-Seat or Medals, and I took last place in Trail class," Lynn said, a frown creasing her face. "That was a waste of my entry fees."

"But you learned something in those classes," Audra pointed out. "And you're not always going to win. It's a life lesson. How you deal with it is up to you."

"What would you do now?" Lynn asked. "Your sisters are judges at most of the 4-H horse shows. What do they recommend?"

"I'd put your horse away and give her a good grooming," Audra said. "Her supper is in the manger. Marcie scrubbed her water tub and refilled it. Then, I'd load Gypsy's grain bucket up with pieces of carrots and chunks of apples. She earned them."

"I will." Clucking to the mare, Lynn led her inside the barn.

Audra shut the gate behind the pair and headed for the house. She hadn't answered the girl's question, but she was fairly sure Lynn wouldn't realize it for a while. By the time she did, maybe taking good psychological and physical care of the flashy little mare after a busy, high-stress day would become a habit. As Uncle Roy always said, "*A good rider looks after the horse first.*"

When she reached the house, she found Elinor at the sink, filling a small bucket with warm water, preparing to milk the cow. "I saw Lynn," Audra said. "Sounds like she had a pretty good day."

"She doesn't think so." Elinor glanced over her shoulder with a quick smile. "She was majorly upset all the way home because of her placings."

"We don't win all the time," Audra said. "Better to learn that at fourteen, than at twenty-four or forty-four."

"Good point." Elinor turned off the faucet. "So, what happened here today? Anything I need to know right away?"

"Yes. Lightning had choke this morning." Audra went through the steps she'd taken prior to calling the vet, the treatment provided, and the prognosis. "He's on pain medication and off hay for three days. When his throat heals, he can have alfalfa pellets again, but Joe recommended smaller ones and more of a liquid mash."

"Joe?" Elinor frowned. "Who is that? I always use Art Watkins, not one of his associates."

"Joe's his son, a professor of veterinary medicine at W.S.U." Audra struggled to ignore the warmth that seeped into her cheeks. At almost thirty-five, she was too old to blush over a guy. "He's home on vacation."

"I wonder if Sean knows," Elinor said. "He wanted Joe to stand up with him at the wedding." She hesitated, then added. "I'm a little nervous about meeting him."

"Why?" Audra crossed the room and picked up the two clean milk buckets. She led the way back to the kitchen door. "He's an arrogant, smug know-it-all, but you're a certificated high-school teacher. You can handle him."

"Wow, all that and you let him work on Lightning?" Elinor followed her out the door.

"I didn't say he wasn't a competent vet," Audra told her. "We were in the Silver Flying A's together and we had some issues."

"I can believe it," Elinor said, laughing.

While the other woman milked the cow, Audra fed the chickens and locked them in the house for the night. She took care of the baby pigs, trying not to feel sorry for them. They would grow up and then next spring would be butchered for meat. Poor little things. It was enough to make a person become a vegetarian.

As she headed back toward the house, she spotted Elinor climbing the steps to the feed room, directly adjacent to the hay loft in the big barn.

Turning, Audra crossed the paddock to join her boss. "What's wrong?"

"I want to look at the alfalfa pellets," Elinor said. "The feed store was out of our regular brand, so I bought a different kind. If these are bigger than normal, that would explain why Lightning choked on them."

"Considering the age of some of the ponies, we're lucky that only one had problems." Audra opened the door, then followed Elinor inside. Thirty bags equaled a month's supply of pellets, a hefty investment for the farm in more than one way. "As their teeth wear down, it becomes more difficult for horses to eat their feed."

"Yes, and if this new feed is the culprit, we'll have to return the pellets and replace them on Monday." Elinor frowned thoughtfully. "I think I'll call around and see if any feed stores are open on Sunday. Then, we could pick up an emergency bag of our regular feed to get us through tomorrow."

"Makes sense to me," Audra said.

They'd just reached the kitchen and sat down at the table with their coffee cups when the dog alarms, as Audra thought of the three heelers, went off. The canines raced off the porch, barking at something in the driveway.

"That should be Sean and Jake," Elinor said, not moving from her seat. "Since we're closed, I don't have to worry about them being puppy chew toys, do I?"

Because it could also be the first of the kids arriving to clean saddles, Audra stood and went to look out the window by the back door. Sure enough, Elinor was right. Sean and Jake came toward the steps, each carrying pizza boxes while the dogs danced around them.

Suddenly, the biggest blue heeler stopped and turned. Then he charged off to confront a dark red Jeep pulling inside the gates. The driver had sense enough to come in slow and watch out for critters which won Audra's momentary approval.

That faded when she recognized the man behind the wheel. Joe Watkins. What was he doing here? Had he really come back to check on Lightning? What did he think she'd been doing all day? Sleeping behind a stump?

She opened the back door and went to take the pizza cartons from Sean. "Looks like your good buddy came to see you and the Mud Monsters ride again. Did you call Aunt Marlene and tell her that he was here?"

"No, General." Sean grinned, handing her the boxes. "I didn't know he'd have time to come around, so why would I?"

"Why do you call her, General?" Jake asked. "I didn't know you'd been in the Army, Audra."

"I haven't been." Audra smiled at the boy. "They just like to hassle me because I give them orders."

"Well, somebody has to, or nothing would get done," Jake headed into the house followed by his puppy. "Mom, the vet's here and he's a friend of Sean's."

"I'm glad he's someone's friend," Audra muttered and took in the rest of the pizzas. She counted the cartons on the table. Five large pies should be enough to keep the kids content while they cleaned tack. She spotted Elinor's cup by her chair, but the other woman was nowhere in sight. What happened to her? For that matter, where had Jake gone?

Audra swung around as the door opened behind her. Joe and Sean entered the room, both in western shirts, jeans, and boots. "This had better be a social call," she said, sipping her coffee. "I didn't call for a vet and we're not paying you."

"I said I'd be back to check that pony, *Stinkerbelle*." Joe chuckled and elbowed Sean in the ribs. "I told you she still adored me, and you didn't believe me."

7

AUDRA'S SCOWL REACHED DARK BLUE EYES AND JOE WONDERED when she'd opted for contacts to alter their golden-brown color. And why had she bothered? He had the same question about her molasses brown hair, now a deep mahogany red. In high school, she hadn't looked like her younger sisters, and it never seemed to affect her. What or should it be who convinced her to make the change in appearance? And why had she gone along with it?

"The pony?" Joe asked again. "How is he?"

"Let's go look at him and then you can hit the road." She put her cup down on the counter and walked past him to the door. "We have more important things to do tonight than entertain you."

He grinned appreciatively, enjoying the snarkiness. "Sean invited me to join you for supper and since I don't have any other plans, I jumped at the idea."

Another narrow-eyed glare and she stomped out the door, muttering cusswords barely under her breath. He laughed again and followed her across the porch. "Thought this was a kid-friendly establishment. Don't you have rules about potty-mouth?"

"They rate right up there with trespassers. I knew we should have locked the front gates." He picked up his medical bag off the porch rail, then went down the stairs and strolled after her in the direction of the barn. He could catch up, but why bother? Tight-fitting blue jeans hugged the curve of her hips, sassy backside, and long legs. She might be petite, but dynamite came in small packages.

Lightning wasn't alone in the barn. A blond boy stood outside the stall, and it took a moment for Joe to recognize the youngster as the one who helped with a colicky mare a few days before. The pony dozed in his stall, ignoring the human company.

"What's going on, Jake?" Audra asked. "Is he all right?"

"I guess so." Jake didn't move. "I just wanted to tell him how sorry I was. I didn't mean to make him sick."

"Really?" Audra picked up a halter and lead from the hook near the door. "How did you do that? I thought he just choked."

"But it's my fault," Jake said again. "I was so determined—" His voice trailed off when she stopped and looked at him. "I mean—"

Joe opened his bag and removed the stethoscope. "Were you the one who fed him the alfalfa pellets?"

"No," Audra said. "That would be me."

"Sounds like it's her fault then." Joe glanced at Jake. "Maybe, you should tell the boss to fire her."

"Not gonna happen." Audra walked into the stall with the nylon halter. She eased the noseband onto Lightning's face. "My boss was the one who accepted a substitute feed with a different size pellet."

"But I was the one who wanted the vet to come," Jake said, staring at them. "That makes it my fault."

"Sorry, kid." Audra buckled the halter. "Wanting Dr. Wonderful to visit your farm doesn't mean you made Lightning sick. It's your mom's fault for bringing home the wrong alfalfa pellets and it's my fault for feeding them to this old duffer. Even if I'd poured boiling water onto the grain, it still could have choked him."

"And if it was grain soup, he probably would have refused to eat it," Joe said. "Ponies and horses can be fussy sometimes.

Besides, I'd have visited anyway. Like he told you, Sean and I are old buddies, or he wouldn't have asked me to stand up for him at his wedding."

Joe watched Audra turn away from the pony to face him. She glared over the stall door at him. "I know Elinor said you were supposed to be in the wedding party, but I hoped she was only joking."

"Afraid not," Joe winked at her. "I wouldn't have missed Sean's wedding for the world. I just don't know how he convinced his folks that this time shouldn't be a circus."

Another of those long steady looks that used to strip him down to the soul when he was a kid and then Audra smiled. Pure danger in her boots. "You really haven't met the bride yet, have you?"

"No, but I'm looking forward to it."

———

Lightning passed the exam with flying colors. His respiration was good. So was his temperature and heart rate. Audra let Joe leave the stall before she removed the halter and left the pony to sleep. She patted Jake's shoulder. "Feeling better now?"

"Yeah. I'm glad he's going to be okay."

"That makes two of us," Audra said. She replaced the halter on its hook, then eyeballed Jake. "How did you know about Lightning? You just got home. Did your mom tell you?"

"No, Lynn told all of us." Jake led the way to the barn door. "Sandy texted her at the show this morning."

Audra caught her breath, shocked at the revelation. "Did your sister tell your mom?"

"Sure. Mom said for her to tell Sandy to quit playing games on her cell phone and get to work if she wanted to stay employed. Mom told us if you needed her, you'd call and if you didn't, then everything was okay." Jake grinned at Joe. "And it was because Audra got you to come and take care of Lightning."

"And she'd already done everything that could be done before

I got here," Joe said. "In many cases, massaging the throat often does the trick."

"But not this time," Jake said.

"No, that's why she called me," Joe said. "Audra knows what to do for him, so Lightning will be fine. Of course, I'll be around to make sure."

"Oh, lucky us," Audra murmured.

He grinned at her, and she reminded herself that he was a major jerk. Hadn't she learned anything about trusting him? Except when it came to animals, she told herself. He was a good veterinarian, but as a human being, he stunk. And he was the same guy who'd made a fool of her so many years before. It was unforgivable and she knew all about those kinds of men. She learned about them before she went to preschool.

Two hours later, she found herself sitting in a booth at *Mexicali Rose*, a restaurant across from the Everett Mall, still wondering how on earth it had happened. What was she doing here with Joe Watkins, Elinor, and Sean? Audra knew she'd intended to stay at the pony farm this evening and manage the saddle-cleaning party.

Instead, she was next to Joe, a giant menu in front of her and trying to decide what she wanted to eat. "I still can't believe this. I've never walked out and left other people to polish tack."

"Then, it's about time." Elinor smiled at her. "I told you since I was paying Sandy and Marcie, they'd run the event. Believe me. They want to get back on my good side after that little stunt on the cell phones this morning."

Before Audra could answer, a young man arrived with glasses of water, a basket of warmed tortilla chips, and a bowl of salsa. He said something in *Spanish* and then translated, "Your waiter will be here in a few minutes."

"And by then, we may have decided what we want to drink," Joe said. "Is it *Sangria* or margaritas tonight?"

"Well since I'm not cleaning saddles or supervising kids tonight, I'll go for the *Sangria*," Audra said. It'd been ages since she'd had the fruit-laden wine punch and she was ready to celebrate. "Anybody else want nachos?"

"Me," Elinor said, cuddling close to Sean. "Let's get a large order to share."

While they waited for the drinks to arrive, Elinor asked questions and got Joe talking about growing up in rural Snohomish County. "When did you and Sean meet?"

"In 4-H," Joe said. "We were both seven when we joined the Silver Flying A's and Marlene spoiled us rotten."

"Much to Ethan's and Gavin's disgust," Sean added, with a reminiscent smile. "My older brothers always told me not to ask her for homemade cookies or they'd thump me when I got home. So, I'd get Joe to ask, and we made out like bandits."

"They used to take them and hightail it for my tree-house," Audra said.

"Your tree-house?" Joe tugged on her braid. "Who helped your Uncle Roy build it?"

"He built it for me so I could get away from my little sisters, the pests." Audra retorted. "And the price of admission was two chocolate chip cookies."

"Which Joe always paid," Sean said. "How many books did you read up there?"

"All of them." Audra relaxed, as she remembered the days in Aunt Marlene's orchard. The tree-house had been a sanctuary, a place where she could dream away a sunny afternoon and not witness the constant arguments between her parents.

"What kind of books?" Elinor asked. "It's the English teacher in me. I'm insatiably curious about the written word."

Audra laughed and leaned back in the booth as the waiter arrived with their drinks. "When I was a kid, I read everything from Carolyn Keene to Walter Farley to Marguerite Henry. What about you, Elinor? What did you read?"

After their leisurely dinner, they returned to the pony farm. While Elinor and Sean checked on the saddle-cleaning party, Audra went with Joe to look in on Lightning. The pony lay in his stall, sound asleep. His nostrils and mouth were still clear of mucus. He was obviously well on the way to his normal good health.

"Let's not wake him," Joe said. "Sleep heals too."

"All right." When they left the barn, Audra switched off the lights. "Thanks for dinner. I never expected you to pick up the tab for me."

"I can be a gentleman sometimes." He caught her elbow.

When he drew her to a stop, she stared up at him. "So, do you think I'm going to kiss you?"

"Well, I had high hopes, but I'll settle for me kissing you."

She shook her head. "No way, Joe. I haven't seen you in years and I'm not going there yet."

He feathered a thumb over her mouth. "I can wait. Just call if you change your mind. Or you can even whistle. I'll come a-running."

"So, not happening." She stepped back, trying to ignore the faint disappointment when he didn't follow. "I'm not interested in you."

"Maybe, you're not saying it yet, but I'll change your mind."

She lifted her chin, determined not to surrender to the old feelings that tried to resurface. She was an adult, damn it! "Want to bet?"

"I never bet on sure things." He turned and headed for his Jeep.

The farm normally opened shortly after noon on Sundays when Elinor and the kids returned from church. However, with a saddle-cleaning party and sleepover, a houseful of teens and tweens meant a change in the regular schedule. Audra took charge of the barns and the chores while Elinor cooked a pancake breakfast. She'd said that she would take Jake and Lynn to the evening services.

After they ate, Marcie and Sandy took all the kids to groom and saddle up. A lesson followed by a trail ride took up the rest of the morning. While she taught horsemanship, Audra's mind strayed to the night before and the bizarre date with Joe. She'd never expected him to turn up in her life again and she wasn't sure how she felt about his arrival.

He was the first man who'd tried to kiss her in years. Generally, she made any moves when she was interested, and it didn't mean they were often reciprocated by guys. No matter how much time she spent with Ethan, he never touched her and sometimes she wondered if he even knew she was female. What was she supposed to do to get his attention? And did she even want it?

She shook her head and focused on the students in the corral. Of course, she wanted Ethan. She'd been in love with him for years. Joe might be fun, and he could still make her laugh, but he wasn't the man for her. If she counted on him, he'd be gone in a cloud of dust. Somehow, someway, she'd find a way to show Ethan that she was the woman for him. He deserved the best and she could give it to him.

After she fed the lunch hay to the ponies and medicated Lightning, she headed for the house to check the reservations for the afternoon. Elinor hung up the phone as Audra entered. "That was Joe. He wanted to know what time would be good for him to come by to see the pony and you. If he's not careful, he'll be giving Doctor Art a bad name since he never does this kind of follow-up care."

"I don't think so. Everybody knows Art's the one who trained Joe and he's just following in his dad's footsteps. Art always stops in at my mom's to check the stock when he's in east Liberty Valley, near the Lazy B." Audra glanced at the coffee pot. "Okay if I have a cup?"

"Help yourself. I'll take one too. So, what's up with you and Joe? Were you two a couple in high school or what?"

"No, not really." Audra took two mugs from the cupboard. "We knew each other in 4-H, and he used to help me with my horse projects. But we both grew up and went our separate ways. He headed off to college and I stayed home to help my mother raise my younger sisters."

Silence fell. She poured coffee into the cups and took one over to Elinor. "What? You're thinking something."

"Wondering something," Elinor admitted. "Didn't you want to go after your own dreams when you were a girl?"

"How could I?" Audra sipped the thick strong brew. "My father was never around, and he sure wasn't paying child support after my folks divorced. Somebody had to step up and pick up the slack or we'd lose the Lazy B. It's been in the family for over a hundred years."

"I didn't know it was that old," Elinor said. "Marlene never said anything about it."

"It wasn't in Roy's or my father's branch of the clan," Audra said. "Most of the Dawsons moved to other spots in the county over the years. My dad couldn't hold a job. When I was ten, the extended family got together, did the Dawson version of an intervention, and arranged for us to live on the Lazy B. After he left, we discovered that he'd mortgaged the land for money to gamble. It's been up to my mom and me to save it for the next generation."

Elinor nodded. "History comes alive. You should talk to the high school students about your family sometime. I could introduce you to a few teachers."

"I don't know that much about the family, but my Grand-Uncle Will does. If they want to hear about the wild old days in the area, I could ask him, but he's not politically correct at the best of times."

"Neither is history," Elinor said. "Teachers should know that and pass it onto their students. Otherwise, things never change for the better."

Audra watched as the other woman crossed to the desk to look at the reservation book. "What's up?"

"My wedding is a week away and I don't have a dress," Elinor said. "Do you want to go shopping with me and Clancy tomorrow night?"

"Sure," Audra said. "I can remind Clancy tonight when I'm up there for dinner."

"I already did," Elinor said. "I had to touch base with her, so she'd know I wasn't holding a grudge about her hiding out while we prepped for day camp without her. She needs to learn the old-time lesson of *'if you want a friend, you have to be one,'* but life will teach her that. And I don't have to. Neither do you."

Audra almost choked on her coffee. "What does that mean?"

"That you're her sister, not one of her parents and you didn't take her to raise." Mischief crept into Elinor's face, and she smiled over her cup. "As Jake would say, I double-dog dare you to tell her that."

If she did, she'd have to pass it on to the rest of the girls, Audra thought, or Clancy would. No point in sharing that. It was sufficient to think about the idea of standing up to her siblings and wondering how it would go over with the Dawson clan.

Between trail rides, lessons, and taking care of Lightning, the afternoon flew by. At four, Audra headed upstairs to shower and change for the mandatory monthly Sunday dinner with her family. She opted for black jeans, a blue checked western blouse, and her dress boots. She brushed out her hair, then braided it again.

In the mirror, she glimpsed dark roots and knew she needed to get into Ginger's schedule so they could color her hair back to Dawson red. That reminded Audra of Joe and his comment about changing her appearance, so she looked like the rest of her family. Was she supposed to think there was something wrong with fitting in?

On her way through the kitchen, she filled the cat food dish and his water bowl so Pyewacket wouldn't miss her. He didn't move from his perch on the windowsill, so she left him to chase afternoon sunbeams and dust motes. "Back later, guy."

No answer, but what had she expected from a cat?

Grabbing her purse, she locked the door behind her and headed down the stairs. She was halfway to her Ford 150 when Jake intercepted her. "Hi. What's up? Is one of the horses sick? In trouble?"

"No, but I gotta talk to you about the wedding," Jake said. "I just found out that *small* means no cake."

"That sounds like a disaster in the making." Audra struggled not to laugh. "Did you talk to your mom about it?"

"She says it's too late to get one now and we'll have one in September at the reception. It isn't good enough for her and Sean. Next Sunday is going to be special." Jake dug into his pocket and pulled out a wad of bills. "I've got thirty-seven dollars here from the carrots I sold. Is it enough for Brigid to bake a cake for them?"

Audra's instinctive response was to refuse to take the money he held out to her and say that she'd arrange it with her sister. But Jake had his pride, and he was a smart kid. He'd hate it if she patronized him like he was a preschool escapee. "I'm sure it's enough to pay for the materials and she'll want to give your mom and Sean a present too. A cake is perfect."

She took the money he handed her and tucked the bills into her jeans pocket. "I'll talk to Brigid tonight and tell you about it when I get home. Okay?"

"That's perfect." He beamed at her, then turned and headed for the house.

She wished she could straighten out her problems as easily as she had his. Heaving a sigh, she strode to her truck and unlocked the driver's door. She'd do dinner with her family, then be free of some of their daily drama for another month.

It took just under an hour to reach the Dawson ranch in the Cascade foothills. She drove across the old single-lane wooden bridge and up the curving gravel drive to the three-story house. She spotted Clancy coming up from the indoor arena and the twins sauntering from the barn. Audra grimaced. All she needed was Kate to return from Montana and the day would be complete.

No, not really. What I genuinely want is peace and quiet and it's not about to happen.

Collecting her purse and keys, Audra locked the truck door. She smiled at Clancy who reached her first, then started toward the back porch. "Hey. How's it going? How was the show yesterday?"

Stalking beside her, lavender eyes narrowed into a glare,

Clancy demanded, "Did you tell Ethan I bailed on the prep work at Elinor's? He ripped into me about it last week."

"You're kidding." Audra stopped dead. She turned and stared up at the taller woman. "I'll have to send him flowers, or better yet, some of Brigid's chocolate chip cookies. I never thought he'd grow another set after you cut them off years ago. How did that happen?"

8

UTTER SILENCE AND BEFORE CLANCY OVERCAME HER SHOCK, THE twins arrived. Like their sister, they were traditional Dawson women, tall, shapely redheads. Audra felt even more of an outsider despite her colored hair and contacts. Would she ever be one of them?

"We're glad you finally made it," Vonnie said. "Why are you so late, Audra? You always get here right after lunch and jump in to help with all the work."

"New barn, new boss, new rules," Audra said easily. "This is the best I can do, so you better get used to it."

"Well, we're still happy you're here." Wendy brushed past her twin to hug Audra. "We want to talk to you before supper. Is this a good time?"

"Works for me," Audra said. "What's up?"

"Have you two finished the lower barn?" Clancy demanded. "I'm not feeding or watering those horses for you. I have my own stock to look after and a whole barn to finish."

"It's done," Vonnie said. At a look from her twin, she added. "I have two more stalls to clean and bed, but I can do that later."

Audra intervened before the three of them started a shouting match. "Then, go do it. Wendy can sit with me on the porch and bring me up to speed, can't she? We could also talk about it at supper when Mom and Brigid are there."

"And Kate," Clancy added. "She'll have something to say."

"She always does, but she's still in Montana breaking horses, isn't she?" Audra asked.

"Dragged in at three this morning," Clancy said with a sweet smile, too sweet. "She quit that job and Mom's been fielding calls all day from the Dawsons over there. She's major pissed. When Kate gets out of bed, expect all hell to break loose."

"Lovely," Audra muttered. Why couldn't these family dinners ever be a peaceful get-together instead of *Drama City*? She eyed the twins again. "Okay, let's get it done, Wendy."

Ensconced on the swing in the corner of the wraparound porch, Audra waited for Wendy to return with her laptop. Obviously, something was up. Otherwise, her baby sister wouldn't have brought her a glass of icy lemonade and a saucer of homemade chocolate chip cookies before heading up to her room. The twins were the youngest in the family and totally spoiled by everyone. They were waited on by other people and that road only ran one way since they didn't do anything for anyone else.

While she nibbled on a rich, buttery cookie, Audra gazed around the yard at the various buildings, the barns, cabins, and bunkhouses that lined the drive. Everything looked so normal, the same way it had for over a hundred years. It was home. She glanced toward the kitchen door as Wendy returned. "So, what's going on?"

"Vonnie and I want to live near the U-Dub next fall, not on campus, but close." Wendy sat down and opened her computer. "I've made up a budget so I can show you the costs. We need you on our side to convince the rest of the family that it's feasible and won't cost as much as living in one of the dorms."

"All right. Show me the facts." Taking the computer, Audra studied the professional-looking spreadsheet, scrolling through the numbers. Her sister had included everything from rent to groceries to gas for the car the twins shared.

"Nice job," Audra said, "but you haven't figured in money for clothes and entertainment. You'll want to take in the occasional movie or go out for a meal occasionally."

"You mean you're not going to freak out at the idea?" Wendy asked.

"Oh no," Audra said, returning the laptop and picking up the glass of lemonade. "I think it's a great concept. Living on your own will teach you two so many life lessons. I don't see how you plan to pay for it. That's not on this screen, but you and Vonnie must have plans for jobs in Seattle. Have you visited the Student Employment Center at the university? Just don't take on too many hours. The main priority is to keep up your grades. You're juniors this September and you both need to think about what comes after graduation."

Wendy's light blue eyes widened. "We thought you'd help us out—"

Audra leaned back in the swing. "Really? How did you come up with that? I just changed jobs and a pony farm can't pay what a big purebred horse breeding operation does."

"But you always have money," Wendy said. "Mom says to ask you every time."

"I've worked since Dad walked out," Audra said. "First, I ran the farm while Mom was pregnant with you and Vonnie and did jobs under the table for the extended Dawson clan. Dad didn't pay child support, so somebody had to get a job and step up to be the other adult in this family. Guess what? There weren't many volunteers. I started frying burgers at Billy-Bob's for Uncle Jim when I was fifteen. He paid me minimum wage plus tips."

"I know that." Wendy tossed her head, red hair flying. "Everybody always talks about what a hero you are. It's a family legend."

Audra ignored the sarcasm. "That's a surprise. Mom appreciates my input, but you don't. Try walking a mile in my *Ropers* as Aunt Marlene says."

"Vonnie and I would hire a lawyer and make Dad pay."

"Good luck with that. He's a compulsive gambler and he

doesn't have it. You're talking a guy who sells his blood to get a poker stake."

Wendy grimaced. "Yuck, you know the grossest things."

Audra sighed. "I'm only twelve years older than you are, so why don't you quit twisting my tits for it?"

Wendy's jaw dropped. "I can't believe you said that."

"Well, contrary to your opinion, I don't have balls so I can't tell you or Vonnie to stop busting them. And I already asked Clancy about cutting off Ethan's, so I think I'm good for today." Audra drained her lemonade and put the glass on the porch rail. "Give me the computer."

Obviously still stunned by the reaction that her request had caused, Wendy handed over the laptop. "Audra, are you okay?"

"Fine. Better than I've been in years." She scrolled down the total column, highlighted it, and multiplied by nine to come up with the real amount the twins would need for living expenses at the university. "This is the nut the two of you need to crack to live in Seattle. I'm glad you're thinking smart and not planning to be on campus. That would cost even more. Resident camp starts tonight, doesn't it? If each of you sleeps in one of the cabins with the girls, Mom could do some rescheduling and get by with two fewer counselors. That would give you a start on saving up."

"I'll have to talk to Vonnie first."

"Well, do it quick. Final check-in for the campers starts in three hours." Audra picked up the last cookie and watched Wendy hightail it toward her room before heading off to find her twin.

The back door opened again, but this time it wasn't one of her sisters. It was her mother in jeans, a western blouse, and boots, red hair curling halfway down her back. Obviously, she'd spent the day working the farm alongside her other daughters. Audra finished the cookie and waited for the fall-out.

Cup of coffee in hand, Darlene strolled across the porch and sat down next to her. "Did the twins spring their big plans on you?"

"Yes," Audra said, "and Wendy wasn't happy when I told her to get a job to pay for it."

Darlene sputtered into her mug. "I thought you'd tell them it was a stupid idea. They don't need to pay rent, utilities, and grocery bills when they can live at home."

"They turned twenty-two in March, Mom. You can't shelter them here forever."

Tears swam in Darlene's cobalt blue eyes. "But they're my babies."

"I know." Audra wrapped an arm around her mother's slender shoulders. "They always will be, but it's time to let them test the waters. They'll either sink or swim. And there's no guaranty that they'll actually live off-campus when they have to earn the money themselves."

"That's true." Darlene sniffled and leaned against Audra. "Neither of them ever worked anywhere else, not like you. They wouldn't even pick berries or pull weeds for Marlene and she's an easy touch."

"Well, they might surprise you," Audra said. "I told them they should do camp counseling this summer. We're short on staff again, aren't we?"

"Always," Darlene agreed. "I wasn't looking forward to camping out in a cabin with ten teenage girls. This way, I won't have to guilt Brigid into it either or ask you to rearrange your schedule."

"If the twins will do it," Audra said. "Again, no guarantees." She paused. "Why did Kate come home early? I thought she'd be in Montana for the rest of the summer."

"She caught a flu bug and it stuck around," Darlene said, sitting back up on the swing. "She can't train horses when she spends half the day puking her guts out. So, she arranged for a replacement and drove home."

"Clancy said the family was upset with her and you had to smooth things over."

Darlene sighed. "I swear that girl loves to stir the pot and make it boil. Your Aunt Lurlene called to make sure that Kate arrived safely and was resting up. We had a genuinely nice chat. She wants me to come to Vegas with her and Marlene in September."

"You should," Audra said. "I don't remember the last time you took off with your sisters, so you ought to take a vacation this fall."

"I will when you do." Darlene finished her coffee. "Now, I'm going to check the cabins and make sure they're ready for the campers."

"I'll drop these off in the kitchen and then I'll help." Standing up, Audra picked up the glass, saucer and took her mother's empty cup. "Any other dramas I need to know about?"

"Only your Grand-Uncle Will," Darlene said, rising to her feet. "He's having a few problems since Beth disappeared in the National Forest and the search for her was called off."

Audra had helped bring back the Jeep and the horse trailer from the trailhead last April. She'd joined the search for her adopted cousin, a county homicide detective, but there was no sign of the woman or her dog or horse. They seemed to have vanished into thin air, along with the suspected serial killer that Beth pursued.

Darlene sighed and shook her head. "Poor old man. He wanted to use one of our cabins for some of his Army buddies and I had to refuse because I need them all for camp. So, he went downriver to the Rocking J. Astra says he's put in a woodstove and bunks for the guys but told her that they wouldn't need springs or mattresses. He's still annoyed with me for telling him when Beth was picking up men every night at Billy-Bob's between combat tours. Will you swing by and check on him?"

"Yes. I suggested that Elinor arrange for him to speak to some history classes at the high school next fall." Audra decided she wouldn't ask her mother exactly what she'd told Will. Darlene wasn't known for her tact. "I'll pop in and talk to him about it tonight. Teaching kids about the past would give him a new interest and might help take his mind off Beth for a while."

By taking the backroads to Everett, she could stop at the Rocking J and see Great-Uncle Will on the Jamison place. Audra sighed. She'd wanted to arrive home early enough to do some writing, but that didn't look like it was going to happen tonight. Instead, she was back to saving the world as the Dawsons knew it.

The Rocking J had once been a dairy farm and converted to a horse operation after the previous owners took part in what Darlene Dawson called, the *Kill the Cows* program in the 1980s. When there was a surplus of milk, the government offered to pay dairy farmers to go out of business. The catch was they had to brand the cows on their faces, then send them to slaughter. The branding was to prevent the farmers from selling the dairy cattle to other milking operations.

Darlene had issues with anything that smacked of animal abuse to the point that she turned off *Humane Society* TV commercials. While she hadn't minded people changing from one rural business to another to make a farm profitable—good luck with that—Audra thought, her mother hadn't hesitated to share her opinion of *cow murder* with anyone who'd listen, and she abhorred the practice of abusing the animals first.

So, when the original owners tried opening their boarding stable, Darlene insisted that the entire Dawson clan blacklist them and the new horse business didn't make it. Most of the Dawsons were involved in showing, breeding, training, and teaching horsemanship all over the Pacific Northwest and Inland Empire regions and family gossip was a mainstay. That meant the Jamisons who were Dawson cousins, were able to buy the Rocking J dirt cheap, but they didn't have great luck with the place.

For some reason, whatever they tried didn't work whether it was horse training, teaching horsemanship, boarding, and riding camps. Astra insisted it was because they couldn't find good help, but Audra had a different opinion, one she didn't share with her shirt-tail cousin. It took a great deal of time and energy to run a riding stable or ranch.

One person couldn't do it alone. Between Astra working full-time at a Seattle law firm to make partner, Meteor running a catering business in Eagleville, and Venus up to her eyeballs with kids and critters, the Rocking J suffered. Of course, Darlene claimed the reason the Jamisons had a tough time was because of the bad karma related to killing innocent animals.

The long driveway swooped around the farm and ended in a cluster of rundown buildings. Audra recognized her uncle's pickup near one barn. She frowned as she spotted the Watkins Veterinary Practice truck, then saw Joe opening the canopy. She parked next to the other rigs, turned off the engine, and climbed out. "What's up? What life or death injury brings out a vet on a Sunday night?"

"A puncture wound." Joe glanced over his shoulder and smiled at her. "I'm glad you're here, *Stinkerbelle*. I could use someone to hold the mare and I don't want your uncle to get hurt."

Audra ignored the teenage nickname. She wouldn't give him the satisfaction of knowing it bothered her. "So, where are the Jamisons? It's their horse, isn't it?"

Joe loaded medical supplies into a metal bucket. "Well, I understand that Estelle is up in her room with a headache. Astra is prepping for a big court case starting tomorrow. Meteor is catering a party somewhere. Venus was juggling a toddler on her hip, trying to hold onto a five-year-old boy with one hand and the horse with her other. Multi-tasking is one thing, but that was ridiculous and dangerous for the three of them."

"I hope you were nice when you told her it wasn't working." Audra told herself it wasn't personal when she checked him out. The brown Carhartt coveralls were practical but didn't do anything for his broad-shouldered, narrow-hipped body. "Did you send her to the house?"

"I had to. I could barely examine the mare without the baby screaming she wanted a pony ride. That was when Venus told me she was basically here by herself."

Audra waited for Joe to step back, then closed the canopy for him. "Because Orion is out with his buddies too, isn't he?"

Joe shook his head. "Do I want to know where Estelle came up with those names for her kids or why? Can you imagine trying to get through public school with them?"

Audra grinned appreciatively. His question was one she'd considered too, especially when Venus opted for more conventional names for her two kids. "According to my mother, her older sister, Earlene ran away from home, changed her name to Estelle, and joined a commune."

Joe laughed. "Well, that explains a lot. Now, let's go save a life."

"Works for me." Audra walked beside him into the barn where her uncle stood with a small, fifteen-hand palomino mare. "What happened?"

"Took a kick to the right shoulder." Will pointed to a bloody U-shaped cut on the horse's golden hide. "Joe says it was pure luck she didn't break a leg, or we'd have to put her down."

Audra stepped up and adjusted the rope training halter on the mare's head. "I'll hold her."

"I'll let you." Will passed over the lead line. "Did Joe call and ask you for help?"

"No, Mom sent me on your trail." Audra smiled at the older man. "You're in so much trouble."

Will removed his hat, ran a hand through thick white hair, and then replaced the *Stetson,* laugh lines deepening around golden-brown eyes. "Your momma needs to develop a sense of humor."

"Anything else?" Audra asked, struggling not to laugh. She stroked the mare's white blaze. "I mean as long as we're making a list of personality improvements."

Will frowned thoughtfully, then rubbed the silver beard stubble on his jaw. "Reckon I could say she oughta help out Venus instead of blaming these folks for what was done here."

Audra waited while Joe filled syringes. "That would do it. Mom will be back to saying you're losing it."

Will shrugged. "Nothing I ain't heard before. Did Brigid send me supper to make the lecture go down smoother?"

This time Audra laughed. "How did you know?" She

unsnapped the ring of keys from her belt and passed them to him. "It's packed in a box on the front seat of my Jeep. Pot roast, mashed potatoes, gravy. Veggies are in a separate covered bowl and there's a couple of biscuits too."

"If there's doughnuts, I get one, Will." Joe put the capped syringes in his pocket. "Those are amazing."

"And you never had them the way my grandma and Great-Grandma Mina made them. Folks used to call them a little taste of heaven."

Audra shook her head as she watched him head off toward the Jeep. "Yeah, and that must have been an adventure. He wants Brigid to fry them in pork lard and it can't come from the grocery. She's supposed to get the pork fat from the butcher in Snohomish and render it down herself."

"Is that all?" Joe pulled out a squirt bottle from the bucket. "Shouldn't she be cooking on a woodstove? Then, she'd have to find out what kind of firewood she needs to get the right flavor. And split it herself to be a real pioneer woman."

The idea was enough to make Audra laugh again. She could just imagine her sister's face if she had to cook something outside of her industrial, stainless steel kitchen. Brigid thought camping was what she did at *Motel 6* when she attended a cooking event. "And she'd have to watch the boiling fat carefully, so she didn't burn down the house."

"So much for authenticity." Joe squeezed the bottle and rubbing alcohol dampened the mare's neck, filling the area with the pungent odor. She stomped her left front hoof in warning, then tried to jump away. "Got her?"

"Yes." Audra jerked on the lead and the knots on the halter bit into skin. The palomino froze long enough for Joe to give her the first sedative. While he prepped the second syringe, she circled the horse around and held her for the next shot, a longer-acting painkiller.

"Now we wait for them to take effect," Joe said, stepping back. "What are you doing after this? Do you want to go for a drink?"

Audra considered the question while she watched the horse. She should stay and talk to her grand-uncle but he seemed fine to her and looking out for other veterans had always been his mission. She glanced at the barn doorway as he returned.

In his early seventies, even in jeans and a flannel shirt, Will still carried himself like the career soldier he'd been. He held the paper sack that contained the doughnuts, and she shook her head ruefully. "Tell me that you ate supper first."

He chuckled. "You sound like my Great-Grandma Mina and Beth. They both always wanted everything in the proper order."

Audra eyed him, hearing what he said and reevaluating her original assessment. She watched the men share the doughnuts and listened to them talk about Beth. Her uncle didn't sound worried but concerned that his adopted daughter find happiness.

He's in total denial.

Could this be the way Will handled pain and loss? Who was she to say he was wrong? She waited for a break in the conversation. "So, who is coming to visit? Someone home from Iraq or Afghanistan?"

"No, but that's a good cover story," Will said. "They're distant kin."

9

A LITTLE OVER AN HOUR LATER, AUDRA SAT ACROSS FROM JOE AT a booth in the local watering hole outside of downtown Everett. Her sisters loved Billy-Bob's Cowboy Bar on Friday and Saturday nights when there was live country western music, but Audra admitted she preferred the place when it was quieter. Four men in well-used western wear bellied up to the antique wooden bar, happily sitting on the saddle barstools. A few others clustered around the pool tables at the far end of the room. Ginger pulled the taps, filling the pint canning jars that served as glasses for beer.

Audra leaned back against the cushions on her side of the booth. She flicked a glance at the framed poster of John Wayne from *Hondo*, his breakthrough movie. The ruggedly handsome cowboy actor didn't have the appeal of the guy sitting opposite her. Joe had left his coveralls in his pickup. He wore a summer-sky blue t-shirt tucked into black jeans.

And the tight t-shirt did amazing things for his broad shoulders. He was majorly tempting, almost enough to make her swear off waiting for Ethan to break her celibacy fast. However, as the quote went, 'almost only counted in hand grenades and horse-shoes.' So, she'd just enjoy the opportunity to have a drink with someone she didn't care about. She could relax and be herself. She didn't have to worry. She'd be rude, opinionated, and kick Joe to the proverbial curb when he tried coming onto her.

A few minutes later, Ginger sashayed over to the booth with a glass of white wine and a bottle of Canadian beer. She put a napkin down in front of Audra, then the wine, and did the same for the *Molson's*. "Hey, girlfriend. What are you doing here with the doc?"

"She helped me with an injured horse," Joe answered. "Figured buying her a drink was the least I could do."

"Well, aren't you a sweetie," Ginger purred. "And when are you going to buy me one?"

He grinned at her. "When Audra says I can."

When she brought the second round of drinks a short time later, Ginger put two menus on the table. "Since you're not leaving, you may as well eat something before the kitchen closes."

"Sounds like a good idea," Joe said. "I'm starved. I was fixing supper when Venus called, and I had to run up there. What about you? Did you have dinner with your family?"

Audra shook her head, remembering the soap opera at the Dawson table. Between the twins' temper tantrum about having to pay their way if they lived off-campus, Kate taking one look at the meal and rushing to the bathroom, Clancy sulking and Darlene chattering about Will—it was all high drama. Barely able to eat, Audra had been grateful to escape with the food for her uncle.

She opened the menu and studied the selections. "I could go for a burger."

"Me too," Joe said. "Are you having the "Elvis"—a peanut butter, banana, and bacon on a quarter-pound hamburger?"

Audra laughed. It was one of her inventions when she worked here years ago. To her and Uncle Jim's amazement, the burger wound up being a popular choice, enough so that he'd never replaced it. "No, I'm a traditionalist. I like the mushroom and Swiss cheese one."

"Sounds good, but I still want the Hawaiian with Canadian bacon," Joe said.

"Better get lots of napkins," Audra said. "The grilled pineapple slice can still be messy."

While they waited for their burgers, they talked about their summer plans. To her surprise, Joe didn't plan to rush back to Pullman and spend the summer semester teaching equine medicine. He intended to stick around what most Washingtonians called 'the wet side of the mountains' until late August.

"What about you?" Joe asked. "What are your plans?"

"The usual." Audra sipped her wine. "Day camp. Training horses. Showing and getting the kids ready for parades and the local fairs. Same old routine. Nothing changes." She stopped. "Oh no. I forgot to talk to Brigid about a cake for the wedding next Sunday. I'll have to call her tomorrow."

"Is that your mission?" Joe grinned. "I'm in charge of tracking down Viv and Harold. Jake says that she runs the Altar Guild at the church and will decorate the place. She's supposed to organize a buffet dinner too. His mom wanted a no-fuss wedding, but Jake had other ideas."

"It's lucky he's such a charmer." Audra propped her elbows on the table. "If he wasn't, he could be in serious trouble with all these machinations."

"He has a good heart," Joe said, blue eyes amused. "He just wants the best for everyone."

"That doesn't mean he knows what it is," Audra pointed out. "He just turned twelve."

But at twelve, she'd overseen her world and she had known enough to fake control, she thought. She didn't share that. She didn't have to since their orders arrived, and she could pretend the mushroom burger demanded her full attention. It wasn't a pretense for long.

The scrambled egg sandwich she'd had for lunch wore off hours ago and she savored every bite of cheese, sautéed mushrooms, and beef. By the time, she swirled her fries in ketchup, she could laugh at herself. "Sorry, I didn't know how hungry I was."

"Me too," Joe said, finishing the last of his pineapple. "I can't remember the last time Dad and I sat down to Sunday dinner without one of us having to jump and run for an emergency."

"Animals don't live by calendars or clocks," Audra said.

Joe chuckled. "Your Uncle Roy told us that every time someone pitched a fit about a sick critter."

"And if you don't want to take care of them, move to town and quit your belly-achin'," Audra added.

"Cause nobody wants to listen to it or you," Joe finished.

They both laughed. Audra looked away from him as a big, burly man came toward them toting two slabs of cheesecake topped with fresh sliced strawberries. "What's this?"

"Dessert. I don't see the two of you that often. You both work too hard." He slid the saucers along with clean forks in front of them. He collected their dinner platters, napkins, and silverware in quick, practiced motions. "Ginger will bring you coffee as soon as it finishes brewing."

"Do you have time to join us, Uncle Jim?" Audra asked.

"Nope. Got a kitchen to clean and grocery orders to finish." He winked at Joe. "Besides, I'll bet the doc here won't tip me if I cut in on his action. Then I won't have any poker money. Of course, if he hurts the best short order cook I've ever had, I'll bust his head."

"I knew that," Joe drawled as the older man walked away. "Some Dawson would be sure to tell him. Your family is all over the county."

"And the state," Audra said. "It's why Sean's dad sucks up to us most of the time and stabs us in the back whenever he gets the chance."

"Politicians are like that," Joe said. "Personally, I stopped voting for him when he screwed Sean out of vet school."

"For me, it was when he put Ethan in charge of the family so the Senator and his wife could move to the other Washington and hobnob with other big-wigs."

Her comment earned a steady look from Joe before he dug into the cheesecake. What had he seen? Did she give herself away? No, she decided. He wouldn't realize that her anger came from seeing

Ethan struggle to raise his younger brothers and sisters while he studied for his engineering degree at the U-Dub.

When Joe walked her out to the Ford 150 a half-hour later, Audra pulled out her keys. "Next time, I'll buy."

"No way. I'm trying to score here."

She choked back her giggles and settled for a smile. "You think I'll sleep with you because you bought me a burger? Get over yourself."

"Hey, it was a Billy-Bob burger. That should get me a romp in the sheets."

"So, not happening." She laughed. "Next, you'll want an all-nighter because there was wine."

"And cheesecake."

She unlocked the truck door and spun around, surprised to find him directly behind her. "I have standards."

"Lower them." He put his hands on her shoulders.

"A kiss?" She shook her head. "I suppose you want tongue."

"I'm a guy. Of course, I do."

"The cheesecake wasn't that good."

"Liar. I'll tell your uncle you said that."

Laughing, she shook her head again, still amused and baffled by Joe's pursuit. Then she tiptoed up and brushed her mouth over his cheek, feeling fresh beard stubble against her lips. "Enough?"

"Never." He turned his head.

Their lips met.

Soft, sweet, and innocent, a bare touch of their lips. Did she want more?

No! She pulled away. It was the first time in years anybody had tried, much less succeeded in kissing her. Pulses thudding, she struggled to take a deep breath. "I need space."

He nodded. "I'll be here. Take as much time as you need."

"The summer doesn't last forever." She met his gaze and kept her voice calm as if he didn't matter. She wouldn't let him matter. "You'll be on the road before it's over."

He shrugged. "Who's to say I'll go alone? I could tuck you in my pocket and take you along."

"And who is to say you really mean it this time, *Walk-Away Joe*?"

Gawd, he played rough. For a moment, she allowed herself to imagine hitting the highway with him. What would it be like to just relax and not watch every word she said? How would it feel not to have to live up to her family's expectations? What if she only had to satisfy herself? And not deal with all the drama that came whenever she wanted something that her mother or sisters didn't? Could she even handle that? Or had she spent too many years giving away her soul?

He leaned down and caught her mouth in a quick kiss. "I don't share, *Stinkerbelle*. Remember that."

———

In her apartment, she reminded herself that morning came early, and day camp was due to start the next day. There was no way to know if Clancy would actually show up and work the instructor shift. Audra winced. She probably should have thought of the farm first and kept her mouth shut instead of making that crack about Ethan having balls. Instead, she'd said what she honestly thought and now she might have to deal with the consequences.

And what was she going to do about Doctor Joseph Watkins? His arrival home surprised her and that didn't make sense. She should have expected Sean to ask him to come to the wedding. The guys had been best friends since high school. But why was Joe pursuing her after all this time? There were plenty of other women who'd be interested in a successful veterinarian. Why did he want her? What did she want to do?

It was fun to go out for dinner, nice to talk to someone who didn't think of her as a cross between *Gunga Din*, *General Patton*, and *Dear Abby*. Audra grabbed her nightgown and headed for the shower. Okay, she would step back and enjoy the moment. Why not? She deserved the break from her superhero duties.

———

"I don't believe this." Lynn pulled the blankets over her head. "Go back to bed, Jake. I'm not helping you."

"We have to do the spell again," Jake said. "It took more than once to get Mom and Sean together, Lynnie. And so far, nothing's happened between Audra and Doctor Joe. You have to help me."

Lynn glared at her brother. He wasn't moving. He stood by her bed and waited. "Okay. But this is it. We're only doing it tonight and then we're done."

———

The day whirled by. An hour of writing, followed by morning chores, then grooming and saddling some of the ponies for camp, teaching a dozen beginners how to handle other ponies on the ground. Lunch and a switch in students for the afternoon session. The campers who had ridden in the morning needed to learn everything their counterparts already had about horses.

When the kids left at four-thirty that afternoon, Audra was ready for a break, but she didn't get one. She supervised trail rides and taught the last lesson of the day so Clancy could go home and change for the shopping expedition. Meanwhile, Elinor exchanged the load of alfalfa pellets. While she was at the feed store, Audra medicated Lightning. He was well on his way to recovery.

Then, it was night chores. Sean arrived to cook supper and spend the evening with Lynn and Jake. Audra wished she could join them for homemade pizza and board games. Instead, she was with Elinor in the other woman's toy pickup, headed for the freeway and a trip to the western-wear store at the local mall.

"Okay." Audra struggled to suppress a yawn. "What's first on the agenda?"

"A triple shot mocha," Elinor said, signaling for a turn into a grocery parking lot. "Otherwise, I'll wear my jeans and a Silver Lake Pony Ranch t-shirt to the wedding."

"Better than the jammies I had in mind," Audra said.

That earned a quick smile as Elinor pulled up to the espresso stand. "I don't know how the Senator would feel about that, not when he's trying to convince Sean to expand the guest list."

"Who cares what he wants?" Audra yawned. "I'm not voting for him anyway."

Elinor laughed. "I thought I was the only one who didn't care for his politics."

"Talk to his daughters sometime," Audra said. "Felicia always works for whoever is running against him."

"Wow and I figured Sean had issues."

"He's not the only one. His older brothers do too." That reminded her of Gavin. She still needed his help with her book, so she sent him a quick text. Sooner or later, he'd get back to her and she'd be able to work out the conflict in the story.

They started at the mall, but none of the dresses appealed to Elinor. She wanted a cowgirl look, something the boutiques didn't carry. So, they went to the local Co-op that had the largest selection of western wear. While there was a wide selection of jeans, boots, shirts, hats, and jackets, they only saw a limited amount of more elaborate clothing.

"On to Monroe," Clancy dictated. "There's a store that carries show ring and rodeo attire. We'll keep looking, but we may have to resort to online shopping."

"Not yet," Audra said. "You're right, Clancy. That store is where we found your wedding dress. Granted, we had to wait for them to order in yours, but it was still lovely."

The comment earned a dirty look, but Clancy was on her best behavior, so she didn't opt for sarcasm. It only took a half-hour to reach the store that took up one side of the parking lot and most of the strip mall. They walked through the swinging doors and headed past the selection of show saddles to the section of women's clothes.

Before long, Elinor found the perfect dress. The ivory wedding gown had a modest sweetheart neckline. Lace-trimmed front and back western yokes gave the dress a cowgirl or country girl look. Pearl buttons from the collar to the waist and single-button cuffs. The princess seams flattered her figure and she looked like a dream.

"All you need is this hat." Clancy held up a white low-brimmed Stetson with a flowered hat band and a short veil. "Add some white boots and you'll knock Sean's eyes out."

"Flowers," Audra said. "What is your bouquet?"

"Ladies, this is a simple wedding."

Clancy's mouth dropped open, and she looked totally devastated. "No bouquet? What will we catch? How will we know who the next bride will be?"

"And you definitely need a garter for Sean to throw at the guys," Audra said.

"You must have been talking to my kids." Elinor heaved a sigh. "Lynn told Sean he had to rent a tux, or it wouldn't be a real wedding and I thought if we had a minister, we were legal."

"Shows what you know," Clancy said. "I agree with Lynn. This is a dress-up occasion. We are going to party big-time. Come on, Audra. We need to find a dress so I can stand up with her and it must be a style that looks good on you too. I'm not looking like a freak."

"I'll help you find one, but I'm okay. I have that big balloon payment to make on the ranch in two months, so there isn't any money for extras."

Her sister heaved a dramatic sigh. "What are you going to wear?"

"The midnight blue dress I bought for your wedding," Audra said in even tones. "It's brand new."

"Well, all right then. I just need to find one in the right size for me." Clancy headed over to the far side of the store. "Come help me."

"I'll bet she looks beautiful in that color," Elinor said. "Doesn't it wash you out?"

"What?" Audra eyed her boss. "I don't get it."

"Midnight blue is too strong a color for you, and it undoubtedly makes you look like a ghost. Red would be a better choice. Have you worn the dress anywhere?"

"No. It's in my closet."

"Does it still have the tags on it?" Elinor smiled sweetly, too sweetly. "Where did you get it? We'll exchange it for a bright ruby red one and you can knock Joe's eyes out."

"With red-heeled cowgirl boots? I can knock my heels together and proclaim, "There's no place like Pullman." Everyone will love that."

"If it's what makes you happy, go for it, Audra. Life's too short to be miserable."

Clancy came back with three dark blue dresses. "What's up? Philosophical discussions when we're shopping? I don't think so. Audra, which of these matches yours?"

"It doesn't matter," Elinor said. "Pick the one you like best. Audra and I are exchanging hers tomorrow for a red dress. She's turning over a new leaf. No more quiet desperation."

Clancy tilted her head, baffled. "Quiet what? Audra always has something to say. She never shuts up."

"Henry David Thoreau," Audra said. "Walden Pond."

"And that means what exactly?" Clancy asked, still looking confused. "I don't remember anything about him."

"He was what you might call one of the first hippies," Elinor explained. "I have the book if you'd like to borrow it. Thoreau said, "most men live lives of quiet desperation." I was extending the gender to include women."

"I always forget you're a teacher," Clancy said, "but how did you know, Audra? You didn't go to college."

"I read a lot." Audra deliberately changed the subject. "And I'll have to think about a red dress. I haven't worn one in years."

"Not since Mom said the one you got for the Junior Dance made you look like a short hooker." Clancy strolled off toward the changing rooms. "She'll freak if you wear red to a wedding."

"That's almost a good enough reason to do it," Audra bit back the urge to cry. No matter how hard she worked, she never managed to please her family. Even after all this time, it cut to the heart. "What size of boots do you want, Elinor?"

"Seven. See what you can find, and I'll help Princess Clancy."

Audra nodded and crossed the room to the shoe, make that the boot section. She was tired, that's all. It amazed her that Clancy even remembered the last time Audra wanted a red dress. She was supposed to go to the fall dance years ago, but her mother had thrown a fit about the clinging, knee-length scarlet gown. Then the three-year-old twins were sick and a horse colicked. It meant staying home to save the colt. Everybody else was too busy with the kids to help in the barn.

However, they weren't busy enough to avoid the family drama when her date dumped her. When she called the veterinarian, Dr. Art had already been out on a different emergency. Home on a break from college, Joe had shown up in jeans and a sweatshirt. He helped walk the black all night long, then took her out for breakfast the next morning. Over pancakes and coffee, he'd invited her to the interstate rival football game, the Apple Cup and she agreed to go until she found out it was all a joke.

The potential date with Joe upset her mother even more than the possibility of a romantic night at a high school ball with a sweaty-handed jock. It was one thing to have a guy ask to take her to the biggest event of their Junior year. It was another to have Joe come back into her life, help with a crisis, and want her to go with him to the biggest football game of the year. It wasn't like she had to go to Pullman for heaven's sake. That particular Apple Cup would have been in Seattle.

For the first time, Audra wondered what her mother had

expected. Did she honestly think that any son of Dr. Art Watkins would leave an animal in distress for a high school night of dinner and dancing? Even at twenty-two, Joe planned to be a veterinarian like his father. It wasn't as if the Watkins didn't know the hazards of such a life. Joe's mother had died in a car accident on the way home after late-night emergency surgery.

Audra picked out two different white cowgirl boots. One was a low-heeled, sparkly affair. The other was pearly white with a high stacked heel. She took them back to Elinor who was oohing and aahing over Clancy in a western-style dark blue dress.

"It's beautiful," Audra said. "I like the yoked front and full skirt."

"The pearl buttons really jazz it up," Elinor said. "You're the one who's wearing it, Clancy. What do you think?"

"Oh, I love it." Clancy turned in front of the three mirrors. "I already have boots."

"And I asked the clerk to find the same style in red." Elinor had her sweet smile again, the one that should be classified as a lethal weapon. "Different colors but the same style for my attendants. I like the design and since I'm the bride, I win."

10

Morning came with the cawing of crows. Kyle woke to sunlight streaming through the trees and lighting the clearing. He heard his horse snort and rolled up on an elbow. A doe with twin fawns watered at the creek. He remained still until they bounded away. Then, he eased out of his blankets. He wanted coffee and decided to take the risk of a small campfire. If he used dry wood, there wouldn't be much smoke.

After breakfast, he'd move on and that would serve as protection too. Sooner or later, he'd catch up with Smith and turn the man into the local marshal or what had Beth called it—oh yes, a sheriff's deputy. There would be more than a year to explore this world, although it really didn't seem that different from the one he left behind. He'd read more of the books and see what else he might encounter.

─────

Zane O'Malley sat on the porch and listened to the whistles, then the boom of fireworks. It was hard to believe that the loud explosions weren't city displays, but those of private citizens. He smiled, drank another beer. He'd found two dead raccoons poisoned by antifreeze this morning. He'd hacked up the bodies for the coyotes, throwing the tainted meat out in the woods. If someone's runaway pet found the remains that worked too.

He grinned, opened another can of *Schlitz*. He was just a holiday person!

———

Camp was over for the day and Audra watched as the last two kids were picked up by their father. She stretched and twisted, relieving the ache in her sore back, then started for the barn. She'd give Lightning the last of his medication and take a few minutes of quiet time until chores started. The guides had the last trail ride out in the woods. Clancy was busy with the afternoon lesson. Her younger sister had been her most charming self for the past two days. Audra didn't know what the girl wanted but decided she'd enjoy the respite.

She heard gravel crunch in the driveway, then a vehicle. She gave up the dream of coffee and solitude. Pasting on what she hoped was a polite smile, she turned to greet the customer. It was the white pickup from Watkins' Veterinary Clinic. She ran through a list of the critters, ponies, horses, cows, pigs, cats, and dogs in her mind. Nope, she hadn't called Joe and she didn't need his professional services. Or any personal services for that matter.

"Don't you have a home?" Audra greeted him. "Or at least an office."

He grinned and strode to her. He tugged gently on her braid. "Love you too, Stinky. Got any coffee?"

She sighed and gave up the idea of going to her mini-apartment. Instead, she led the way toward the back door of Elinor's house. "Come on. Why are you here? What do you need?"

"Your help. Venus just called and that mare of hers has the start of an infection. The puncture wound hasn't been cleaned since we were there on Sunday and the horse keeps spitting out the antibiotics I prescribed."

"What?" Audra took a deep breath, tried to remember to count to ten. It was supposed to be a strategy for dealing with people too stupid to live. It didn't work. Fury raced through her. "I was there when you told her what post-op care the horse needed. What part of *keep this clean* was too hard to understand?"

He held up his hands and backed a step, pretending to be terrified. "Don't beat me, *Stinkerbelle*. Now you know why I came to see you."

"Coffee first." Audra opened the door and led the way inside. At her corner desk, Elinor glanced up from the reservation book. "Joe has an emergency and I need to go sort things out. Are you okay with chores if I'm not here?"

"Oh, I think we can handle it." Elinor made another note, hiding a smile. "I have Clancy, the kids, Marcie and Sandy. We'll be fine."

Audra glimpsed Joe's appreciative grin and handed him a cup of black coffee. "If you want cream and sugar, you know where to find it. Quit smirking at her or Sean will smack you upside the head when I tell him."

"Isn't she a cute little thing when she issues orders?" Joe winked at Elinor. "It always makes me want to pick her up, stuff her in my pocket and take her back to Pullman with me."

"In your dreams." Audra refilled Elinor's cup. "I have a job here and people depending on me."

"I'll give you until the end of August to sort out things, *Stinkerbelle*." Joe leaned against the doorframe. "Then, I'll help you pack."

"It'd serve you right if I believed your malarkey." Audra concentrated on filling her mug and taking the first sip of her own coffee, grateful for the caffeine. Now, she'd be ready to take a run up to the Rocking J and talk to her cousin about life. "I still need to give Lightning his pain relievers before we leave."

When Joe grinned at her again, she struggled to ignore the blush that seeped into her cheeks. What was it about him that tangled up her emotions? Okay, so his blue denim shirt did great things for the broad shoulders. She allowed her gaze to roam over his rugged features. What would happen if she untied his ponytail and ran her fingers through his black hair?

She focused on her coffee. Where had that stray thought come from? She shouldn't be interested in the guy. She had her life, and he had his. They had things to do today, and he hadn't come after her because he was interested in her as a woman. He needed someone to play nurse to his doctor.

She glanced at the back door when she spotted a male silhouette. "You may want to move, Doc. We have company."

Joe looked over his shoulder, then stepped to one side. He opened the door. "Hey, Gavin. How are you?"

"Good." Tall, brown-haired, in faded jeans and a flannel shirt with dust on his boots, Gavin Killian looked like an older version of his brother, Sean. A friendly smile to Elinor and then he shook hands with Joe before glancing across the room. "Hi, Audra. I've been getting your messages. What's up?"

She shrugged. "I was playing a trivia game with Ginger, and I got stuck on the theme of *The Tempest* so I figured I'd call you and then I could find out what it means. I'd be able to kick her butt next time."

Gavin laughed. "You two and your games. You ought to be on *Jeopardy*. I haven't taught *The Tempest* in a while, but I remember the basic storyline. Most of the play revolved around revenge, betrayal, forgiveness, freedom, and control. Right now, I'm working on lesson plans for *Taming of the Shrew*. How about some coffee?"

Elinor swung around in her chair. "What do you plan to do with *Taming*?"

"Teach gender bias to college freshmen," Gavin said. "You're an English teacher. What would you do with it?"

The two of them launched into a discussion about the themes, symbolism, and motifs in the play. Marriage, love, the war between the sexes, and money. Audra wished she could take notes. Instead, she concentrated on listening to Gavin and Elinor go off about how they would teach the play and what they'd expect students to get out of it. That was what was wrong with her book, Audra thought. She hadn't been excited about the first play she'd chosen, but she could certainly tweak the story and use the format of the other one. Her warrior queen heroine would make a fabulous shrew.

Joe sauntered across the room and put his empty coffee cup in the sink. He handed her a tiny voice-activated recorder. He leaned down and kissed her ear. "Trivia, my butt. Tell me later why you need to know this. Back in a few."

She stared after him as he slipped out the back door in the direction of the barn. Why did he have to be so damned smart? Nobody else had ever seen through her guise of playing trivia games with Ginger. Her friend didn't understand why Audra always wanted to investigate weird facts, but that didn't stop the older woman from covering for her. If Joe asked, Ginger would double-talk around the subject, throw in some sexy flirtation and the subject would soon be forgotten.

When Joe returned fifteen minutes later, Clancy strolled beside him. She looked like a cowgirl princess in her fringed purple western blouse, tight jeans, and black boots. She came over and filled a cup with the last of the coffee. "Young Doc says he has to go to the Rockin' J. It's on my way home so I'm going with him, and I'll help."

Audra rinsed the glass pot before refilling it with cool water. "If that's what he wants, I'm fine with it."

Elinor gave her a long look. "I don't think—"

"I'm not fine with it," Joe drawled. "I came for *Stinkerbelle,* and Elly already says I can have her."

"Don't call me, Elly. It sounds like the girl on *Beverly Hillbillies.*" Elinor laughed. "I don't use a rope to hold up my pants. I spent too much money on my belt."

"Okay then." Joe came across, took the carafe from Audra, and passed it to Clancy. He snagged Audra's hand, towed her in the direction of the door. Over his shoulder, he said, "The person who finishes the coffee makes the next pot. If nobody's ever told you that before, Drama Diva, I'm telling you now. Come on, Stinky. Time's a-wasting."

"I don't like being called a diva," Clancy said, temper rising on her face.

"Make the coffee," Gavin advised. "And Joe has a nickname for everyone. You don't want to give him a reason to come up with a worse one for you." He opened the door. "Have fun, you kids. Make him buy you a drink afterward, Audra."

"He bought me dinner last time," Audra said, following Joe out the kitchen door. "I'm not going to settle for just a drink."

"Play your cards right and I'll make you breakfast," Joe told her. "But I'm going to want more than one innocent kiss. I didn't even get any tongue."

"A gentleman never kisses and tells." Audra aimed a punch in his direction. "Be good."

"I'm always good. When I'm bad, I'm better. And I don't have to be a gentleman. I'm on vacation."

Audra knew she ought to be angered by his foolishness or the clumsy pass or the way he staked his claim in the kitchen. If she'd been a decent person, she probably would have been. But she wasn't. No one had ever stood up to her sisters, not for her. They always got what they wanted, and she always cleaned up the messes. Telling Clancy to make coffee, wow! That was one for the record books.

Did he have a cape? Or did he just change his clothes in a phone booth?

She climbed into the passenger side of the truck. "Can I keep your recorder for a few days, or do you need it back?"

He smiled, drew the seat belt over her shoulder. "I didn't bring you flowers, sweetheart, and I owe you for the horsy help. Keep it. I know you'll get good use out of it."

She tugged gently on his ponytail, enjoying the feel of his thick hair. "I won't be nice to you."

"I never asked for that." He fastened the buckle, his hand

resting on her hip for a moment too long. "And nice is over-rated. I get enough of that PC crap at work. Just be you."

"I can do that." She felt the weight of the recorder in her shirt pocket. It meant more than any bouquet. "Just remember you asked for it."

When he straightened, she pulled him close enough for a quick kiss. Soft, sweet, but she traced his mouth with her tongue before she pulled back. "That's enough for here and now."

"I don't think so." He lowered his head and his lips claimed hers.

———

He kissed her the way he'd wanted to for years. He twisted a hand in the long mane of red hair and pulled back her head. It should be molasses brown with streaks of gold and one day, he'd convince her to dye it back to its natural shade. Her eyes were closed so he could pretend they were the color of melted chocolate, his brown-eyed girl. His tongue slid into her mouth and coaxed hers to come and play.

When he finally lifted his head, she gazed up at him. "I didn't expect that."

"Well, I'm full of surprises."

She rested a hand on his cheek. "You can say that again."

He measured her slowly. She was petite, but all curves in a gold and blue t-shirt that proudly proclaimed, 'Silver Lake Pony Ranch,' and light blue jeans that snugly fit her rounded hips. He traced her lips with his thumb. "Where do you think this will go?"

"Wherever we want it to, Joe."

"For now, I guess it better be on the road to the Rocking J."

Another smile before she nipped his thumb. "Then, you better start driving."

"Good idea." He stepped back, closed her door, and walked around the front of the pickup.

PART II

"When magick is required, a wizard does what he needs to do...."

— JAKE TALBOT

11

SEAN OVERSAW DINNER TONIGHT. THAT MEANT FRIED CHICKEN from the Colonel's with all the trimmings. Jake finished putting out real silverware since his mom hated eating with plastic utensils. Lynn poured glasses of milk, setting them around the table.

"There's only four," Sean said. "What about Audra? Isn't she eating with us?"

Elinor pushed back from her desk. "She went to help Joe with an injured horse."

"Really?" Sean grinned. "Tell me more. He was totally stuck on her when we were kids, but it never went anywhere."

"It almost didn't today." Elinor opened the refrigerator and brought over a jar of strawberry jam. "Clancy wanted to go with Joe to the Rocking J and he insisted on taking Audra instead."

"Is that why Clancy was majorly ticked during chores?" Lynn asked. "She kept stomping around the barn."

"Oh, I think the fact Joe told her to make the coffee when she finished the pot had something to do with it too," Elinor said, putting the butter dish on the table, then tearing open the paper sack that held the half-dozen biscuits.

Sean peeled plastic lids off the coleslaw, then the potatoes and gravy. "Why did she have to be told? Who did she think was going to make coffee for all the caffeine fiends around here?"

"Probably Audra," Jake said. "She does all the stuff nobody else wants to do. I wish I could talk to Lynnie the way that Clancy talks to Audra, 'cept my mom won't let me order my sister around. Sean, when you and Mom get married, can you tell her that Lynnie must do what I say? I'm the youngest and I'm special. Clancy says that's the rule."

Sean laughed. "No way, cowboy. I like my ears just where they are. I don't want them scorched off my head." He eyed Elinor. "Now, why didn't I ever notice that Audra picks up a lot of slack for the Dawson girls?"

"Probably because she's been doing it forever," Jake said. "People don't notice when things are always the same."

That earned him a steady look from Sean and a frown from his mom. Before they said anything, the dogs barked from their confinement in the living room. Jake glanced over his shoulder and saw Ethan Killian at the back door. "We've got company."

"Well, at least now I know why he's here." Sean headed for the door.

"Because it's Wednesday and we always have chicken?" Lynn asked, her tone innocent, too innocent.

"No, because Clancy called and sniveled that she was being picked on," Jake said.

His mother's frown deepened. "Will you two please behave? And Jake, I know the pair of you are in cahoots. Otherwise, when you asked Sean to let you bully your sister, she'd thump you the next time she thought neither of us was looking. Now, put on your company manners."

"Yes, ma'am." Jake grinned at his older sister. "You owe me five bucks. I told you she'd catch on even if he didn't."

"It's not fair," Lynn retorted. "You were like so obvious."

"Manners!" Elinor repeated as the door opened and Ethan came into the room.

———

Tall, seventeen-year-old, classically handsome even when he sulked, Orion Jamison folded his arms and leaned against the wall of the arena. "How do you expect us to clean up that horse when you have to tranquilize her to work on the injury, Doc?"

Audra shot the sandy-haired boy a glare. "She's not sedated, you fool. That's why he's holding her and I'm the one doing the work. Now watch and learn."

The palomino mare danced around the two of them despite the training halter and the knots that applied pressure to nerve points on her face. Audra rinsed out the white rag in the hot water, wrung out most of the water, then wadded the cloth. "Okay, hold her still."

Joe fisted his hand on the lead and clamped down. When the mare stopped, stood shaking in one spot, Audra advanced on the horse. She put the soaked rag on the crusted injury. It took time to clean the puncture wound. It would be faster to have Joe treat the mare the way they had on Sunday, sedating her, and then dealing with the emergency, but the same problem could occur. Her owners wouldn't do the follow-up care and he'd have to be out here again, if not to deal with the initial injury, then to put down the palomino.

"It's nursing that saves horsy lives," Audra lectured, "not a one-time visit from the vet. You need to wash off the drainage from the wound, so her leg doesn't infect. Yes, it's gross to see blood and pus on the hair, but if you don't want to nurse horses, stop buying them. And puke off to the side so it doesn't make you or the horse slip. Then use water-based iodine solution to flush the injury. If she won't stand on the halter and you're not man enough to hold her, Orion, twitch her. You can use your hand to twist her upper lip or the mechanical apparatus. This is life and death, Orion, so quit screwing around."

She glimpsed the appreciative grin on Joe's face and scowled at him when she went back to rinse out the cloth in the bucket that

Venus held. "As for you, if your family can't or won't step up, call Grand-Uncle Will. He'll send someone to help. If you Jamisons want to make a go of the place, all of you have to work together instead of hiding out from your responsibilities."

A blush heated the younger woman's face. She was a typical Dawson. Red-haired, blue-eyed, tall, and curvaceous, she looked enough like Clancy to be a sister, not a cousin. "I'm sorry, Audra. I didn't think of that. She wouldn't stand and Fallyn kept running around the arena, demanding a pony ride and that didn't help."

"Your mother can step up and take care of your kids when you're doing this, or you call mine and have her send Brigid here."

"She can't do that. Mom will lose it," Orion said. "Two and a half years ago, all hell broke loose when Brigid came to babysit. She cleaned the entire house from top to bottom, cooked three casseroles, enrolled my nephew, Quaid in day-care, made Astra catch up all the book-keeping, and told Meteor to keep her underpants on when she left for a date with some logger up town."

"It didn't work, did it?" Venus shot back. "I have two kids to look after besides all of you. And I don't care how the rest of you feel about Brigid. I need help or we'll lose this place. Where will we go when that happens? The last commune in this area folded its tents and moved away years ago. You know as well as I do how people feel about those who are different, and we certainly are."

Audra blinked and shared a look with Joe. That was something she hadn't known. She assumed the little ones that Venus raised were her kids, not her sister's. "I'll tell Brigid you may need her, and she'll come. She adores children." The last of the crust on the wound broke away and Audra used the cloth to wipe around the injury. "Okay, now you need to start filling the syringe with iodine. And always use water-based. Try this with alcohol-based and she'll freak."

"You can't blame her," Venus said, as she followed directions and carefully poured the red liquid into the container. "It would hurt big time."

"Blame has nothing to do with it." Audra took the first full plastic syringe. "Never use a needle. You don't need one. You're saving her life. If you act like it's not a big deal, she'll accept this sooner."

She inserted the tip into the U-shaped gash and pushed the plunger. The palomino reared and jumped sideways when the iodine poured into the wound. Joe pulled the mare toward him. Pus erupted from the cut, then slowed to a trickle. "You okay? Do it again. I want it completely flushed until I'm seeing and smelling blood, not infection."

"You hold her still and I'll do it." Audra handed the empty syringe to Venus and took the second one, already full. "Sterilize the tip with iodine before you fill it."

Despite the horsy temper tantrum, she was able to continue cleansing the injury. When she finished, the mare lunged at her. Audra side-stepped and avoided the teeth. "Where is her grain?"

"I can't believe you're going to feed her after she acted like such a snot," Orion said.

"I'm going to teach you how to give her the meds that she needs." Audra turned to Venus. "Did you crush the tablets, mix them with applesauce and then put them in the feed so it was like a mash?"

Venus nodded, red curls flying. "Yes, but she threw the grain everywhere and refused to eat it."

"Okay, then we need a bigger syringe," Audra said. "Did you bring one to the barn, Joe? Or does Orion need to go get one from the vet cabinet here?"

"Look in my tote box." Joe stood next to the mare, scratching her neck. "What are you planning to do, sweetheart? Mix up the sulfa with the applesauce and then paste her with it?"

"That's why I get the big money." Audra went over to the gray carrier he'd left in the corner of the arena. She dumped eight pills into an empty cup, dissolved them with hot water from his thermos, then added in three spoonfuls of applesauce. She stirred the concoction together. She poured it into the big plastic syringe that was almost the size of a turkey baster.

While Joe held the horse, she stepped up to the left side of the mare. She eased the tip into the corner of the palomino's mouth and slowly pushed the plunger. The medication went in, nice and easy. Joe caught hold of the chin and lifted the head so the horse couldn't spit out the antibiotic cocktail but had to swallow it.

Audra glanced at her cousins. "Any questions?"

Venus smiled. "No. Thanks for coming up and helping, Audra. Now, I know we can do it and I won't have to pay Joe to pop in every day to doctor her. I don't want to lose Sunshine."

"You won't if you take care of her," Audra said. "If you need me, just call and I'll come up."

"And then you'll call me so you're not doing this by yourself." Joe passed the lead line to Orion. "She can go in her stall and have supper now."

The boy fed the horse a piece of carrot, flashing his sister a cocky look. "I can't believe the healing spell you cast didn't work."

Venus rested her hands on her hips. "I've told you before that the Goddess needs help. You can't turn everything over to the Lord and Lady and wait for them to save the day."

"Good point." Audra hid the urge to smile. She wouldn't tell her cousins that it sounded like they'd been raised in a coven, not a commune. "Like Chaplain Forgy said at Pearl Harbor when he was rallying the troops, 'Praise the Lord and pass the ammunition.'"

"You must have learned that during another one of those trivia contests you and Ginger have." Joe waited while Orion put away the horse. "Since Audra did the work tonight, Venus, I'm not billing you. She can."

"You charge an arm and a leg," Audra said, lifting her chin. "If I'm the only one who helps, Venus won't have to pay a vet bill."

"Call it another date night," Joe retorted. "I'm coming with you, so you won't get hurt."

Audra sniffed. "Some date. Where's the wine, the candles, the romantic music?"

"If you quit your belly aching, we'll do that now." Joe headed toward his supplies. "Let me pack up first and then we'll go have dinner. If I'm laying out money for a fancy supper, I better get one great good night kiss."

Audra grinned at Venus. "He's so easy. All that for only one kiss. Most guys would want quantity, not quality."

"Yeah, but you better follow Brigid's rules," Venus said, "and keep on your underpants or Orion will rat you out to the whole Dawson clan."

When they arrived at *Mexicali Rose*, they discovered it was a slow night which meant that they didn't need a reservation to eat at the popular restaurant across from the Everett Mall. Arched doorways led to the dining rooms, brightly colored murals of rural Mexico decorated the walls and huge pottery vases held collections of flowers or feathers.

A hostess in a white peasant blouse and red skirt arrived and asked if they wanted dinner, then led them to a booth with high-backed wooden bench-style seats. The center of the table was taken up with an inlaid picture of riders in a rural setting. The girl put the menus down in front of them, paused to light the candle in the holder at the back of the table, then smiled a quick farewell as she hurried back to the front of the restaurant.

The server came a few moments later with glasses of ice water, a bowl of chunky salsa, and a bowl of tortilla chips. "Would you like something else to drink?"

"Do you want to share a pitcher of Sangria?" Joe asked. "Or shall we look at the wine list?"

"Sangria." Audra opened the huge menu. "I love the way they make it here."

With that decided, she was ready to look through the pages of varied entrees and try to decide what she was in the mood to eat. She heard Joe order a small plate of the nachos that the restaurant was famous for. The chips would be smothered in three kinds of cheese, refried beans, shredded beef, and garnished with olives, tomatoes, guacamole, and sour cream.

As they studied their menus, the waiter returned with a pitcher of Sangria. Lemons, oranges, and strawberries floated in the fruit-filled, red wine punch. He filled a glass for each of them and said their nachos would be up soon. Joe asked for a little more time to choose their meals. Audra opted for an enchilada special while he selected a chimichanga dinner. Their appetizer arrived and both of them dove into the nachos.

"So, what do you think?" Audra asked. "Will Sunshine make it now?"

"If they take care of her, she will." Joe twisted free a cheese-covered chip. "I was serious. Call me if they need you. I don't trust Orion to hold her still, so you stay safe."

She nodded, then reached for another chip. "I have too much on my plate this summer to risk getting hurt. What about you? What are your plans for next week and the holiday?"

He shrugged. "Not much. Dad will be boarding dogs and cats for folks going out of town. We're bound to have a few emergencies. What about you? Elinor said her farm is closed because of the fireworks. Are you doing anything special?"

Working on her book, but she didn't say that. Instead, Audra finished chewing. "Oh, with all the critters on the farm, I'll have plenty to do. Sean says he's taking the dogs back to his place so they can stay with their relatives when Elinor and the kids are gone. Since they'll be living with him after the wedding, I'm supposed to move from the studio into the rambler."

"Let me know if you need help. I'm handy at shifting furniture around."

Audra nearly asked why he wanted to be with her, but the waiter came with their entrees, so she decided to wait. Instead, she asked about his teaching. He started talking about his students and a freshman-level biology course he'd taught during the previous semester when one of the other professors was ill.

During dessert, it was his turn to ask questions. She told him about working at different stables, including her experience at Xanadu, and being passed over for manager. He listened and then asked questions nobody else ever had.

"Why did they pick a man without any experience? It doesn't make sense. How could they make a profit?"

Audra slowly cut into her empanada. "I don't know. I thought they'd be thrilled that the sale went so well last year, but Mr. Bergstrom was really surprised when it finally made money."

"Did you ever think that they were in the horse business for a tax loss?" Joe sipped his coffee. "It's like that joke about how to make a small fortune with horses."

"Start with a large one," Audra said, remembering one of Clancy's favorite t-shirts.

"Exactly. If they wanted to make money, they'd have paid you to continue to operate the farm."

She slowly nodded, then sighed. "Yeah, I can see that now. It was still a heartache. I was saving up my money to buy this horse. I didn't get her. I guess it's just as well. I don't have anywhere to keep her."

"Oh, I'm sure Elinor could have found a stall," Joe said.

"I didn't ask." Audra forced a smile and changed the subject before he mentioned keeping the horse at her family's barn. "So, what are you doing next fall? What classes will you teach?"

12

He pulled into the drive at the pony farm shortly after eleven.

Audra glanced at the late-model Cadillac parked near the back door of Elinor's house. That was strange. Why was Ethan here? She waited for the familiar leap of excitement but didn't feel it. Now, what was that about? All she felt was a sense of dread. He'd undoubtedly come because Clancy had called him. And that meant her sister would blow off the shift tomorrow, leaving her and Elinor to deal with day camp and twenty-four beginning riders on their own.

Joe switched off the truck engine. "Whose car is that?"

"Ethan's." Audra heaved a sigh. "Come on. He's going to yell at me for upsetting his princess and then she'll dump her work on me. Since it's all your fault, you might as well be hammered too."

"I don't think so." Laughing, Joe opened his door. "I'll rescue you, *Stinkerbelle*."

She shook her head. "Nobody can."

"Watch and learn."

She felt a smile tremble into life when he took her hand. They walked into the house together. Ethan sat at the kitchen table playing cards with Sean and Elinor. Audra smiled at the three of them. "Hey, how's it going?"

"Good." Elinor leaned back in her chair. "How's the horse?"

"Terrific," Joe said. "Audra taught the Jamisons how to medicate the mare. My girl's so little that they've decided if she can do it, they can."

Ethan glanced up from the cards he held. "Oh, is that why she went with you, not Clancy?"

"Nope," Joe said easily. "I took Audra because she's mine and Clancy's yours. I don't poach, Ethan. I'm not after your woman or Sean's and now we're headed to Audra's. One more thing."

"What's that?" Sean knocked on the table. "Gin. You lose, bro."

"Nobody orders Audra around but me," Joe said. "So, tell Clancy to cut out the drama diva crap. Got it, Ethan?"

Audra stared at the three men, then dug her nails into Joe's hand. He just tightened his hold. Did he actually think they'd believe she'd let him stay over with her?

"Anything else I need to know?" Ethan asked in a low, deep voice.

"Yeah." Elinor stood and went to the fridge. She opened it and brought over beers for everyone, passing one to Sean, then to his older brother. "I don't mean to be unfair, Ethan, but if Clancy doesn't show up in the morning, I'm going to have to replace her as an instructor. This is a real job, and she has to take it seriously instead of dumping all the grunt work on other people even if one of them is her big sister."

Ethan opened his can of beer. "That's a fair expectation. I'll bring her."

"Why?" Audra leaned into Joe's warmth for a moment longer. She straightened, took the beer from Elinor, then asked. "Is something wrong with Clancy's truck? Did she have an accident? Is she all right?"

"She's fine." Amusement seeped into Ethan's dark gray eyes. "However, you can't expect her to accept you having a life without a fit, honey. And if you think Clancy's snarky, Joe, wait till the other girls find out. Audra's spoiled them rotten, and they will rip your guts out for fun."

"Not Brigid." Joe shook his head when Elinor offered him a beer. "I'll share Audra's. She's never finished one in her life."

"Only because I prefer wine," Audra said. "And why aren't you worried about Brigid?"

Joe put an arm around Audra's waist and looked down at her. "She brought doughnuts to the clinic and said I only had to share them with Dad because she'd made a batch of maple bars for Sarah."

"I hate to break it to you, cowboy, but that is Brigid's stock in trade." Audra opened her beer. "If you make me cry, she'll put laxatives in your doughnuts."

"I'll have to be extra careful then." Joe took the can of beer and drank. "And you can't cry, sweetheart. I may if I have to beat Ethan up for calling you, honey."

Ethan chuckled. "I won't do it again."

"Good choice." Joe guided Audra toward the back door. "It's eleven-thirty. I need to turn into a pumpkin, folks, or I'll be late to open the clinic in the morning. I promised Dad he could sleep late for once."

Audra waited while he closed the door behind them. "You've got to be kidding. This is your great idea? What happens when they find out it's all a joke? They'll hate me."

"Who says it's a joke?" He stopped on the porch.

She turned, stalked down the steps toward her apartment, then whirled to face him. "Well, come on. You can't stay here. They'll know it's a farce, that you don't really want me."

He followed her to the barn. "I'll always want you."

"Like I believe that." When she looked over her shoulder, she saw him lingering to dump the remains of the beer on the grass.

"Tell me that you have some coffee up there. I'll have to stay awhile to make this look good."

"Of course, I have coffee. You're not getting any." She headed up the stairs and unlocked her apartment door. "You're pretending to sleep with me, remember? And I'm not staying up all night to talk to you when I have chores in five hours."

———

Joe followed her up the stairs, admiring the sway of her hips. She stopped at the top to unlock a door, then led the way into a studio apartment. A pole lamp with a red shade cast a dim glow until she flicked the light switches and an overhead florescent brightened the large room.

She stopped in the entry to perch on a convenient stool and remove her boots, then her socks. Since that appeared to be a household rule, he unlaced his as well. He lined up his Ariats next to her Ropers. It made sense. She had enough to do outside and didn't need to make work to do inside.

He glanced around, smiling at the decals of palomino, paint, and bay ponies on the wall. It looked more like a classroom than a manager's living quarters. Classic rock music poured from the small stereo in one of the study carrels. She must leave it on, so the place felt friendly when she walked inside. A seal point Siamese uncoiled from a chair by a computer station on the far-right wall and came to greet him.

Joe leaned down to pet the cat. It sniffed disdainfully and walked away before he touched it. "Who is your roomie?"

"Pyewacket. He came with that name, so I didn't change it. It's from—"

"*Bell, Book and Candle*," Joe said. "Kim Novak and Jimmy Stewart. I always thought it was bogus that she lost her powers when she fell in love. My mother used to say love adds to a person, it doesn't diminish him or her."

"You're a romantic, Joe Watkins." Audra popped the top on a can of meat and spooned the food onto a dish. She bent and gave it to the cat winding through her legs. "Who would have thunk it?"

"Oh, come on, Stinky." He enjoyed watching the play of

emotion across her face. "Admit it. Weren't you disappointed by the ending?"

"It was classic Hollywood. The woman gives up everything for the guy and as soon as the light fades and the credits roll, he leaves her for his secretary."

The deadpan delivery did it. He laughed, enjoying it when she did too. She turned and opened the cupboard behind her, pulling out a bottle of Riesling. He nodded. He wasn't really in the mood for coffee. "Want me to open it?"

"Sure. Then, I can wash the glasses which have been gathering dust."

A few minutes later, they took their wine and went to sit on the couch. She leaned back, relaxing against the cushions, sipping the light gold alcohol. "Do you think Ethan actually believes we're a couple?"

"He wants to and that's half the battle." Joe eyed her over his glass. "A better question might be when he's going to realize how much your sister plays him."

A frown creased Audra's forehead. "He never has, and I know he's smart. He's an engineer."

"Doesn't make him observant where people are concerned." Joe drank more of his wine. "I was always concerned he'd realize you were a better deal."

"No way."

"Yes, way. You looked at him the way I looked at you. I figured he'd wake up and marry you sometime in the last sixteen years. Stunned me when he and Clancy got engaged."

"What about when she kept breaking the engagement? Did that shock you too?"

"No. Your sister wants what she wants when she wants it and if she doesn't get it, all hell breaks loose. She is a drama diva."

"And I'm the calm, quiet sort." Audra wrinkled her nose in disgust, then swirled her wine in the glass before she sipped more. "No wonder I keep cleaning up messes."

"Now you're fishing, sweetheart." He chuckled. "A guy with brains wants somebody like you who walks beside him. If I'd been dumb enough to take your sister to the Jamison's, she'd have bailed once she wasn't the center of attention and Sunshine would be the one who suffered. No, thanks! I'm into saving animals, not killing them."

That assessment earned him a smile before she finished her wine and refilled their glasses.

"Are you ready to talk about the past?" Joe asked.

She heaved a sigh, then inclined her head. "I guess we have to clear the air. So, why did you invite me to the *Apple Cup* back in the day when you'd no intention of taking me to the game?"

"A better question would be why did you agree to come with me and then refuse to speak to me on the phone when I called to make arrangements?"

She choked on her wine and then stared at him. "No way. Do you mean I've been carrying a grudge this long and we got played by my family?"

"You guessed it." Joe eyed her over the glass. "Does this mean you're going to be super sweet to me now?"

"Oh, hell no. You're the one person I don't have to pretend with and I'm not changing that. So, if you have a problem with honesty, there's the door."

He laughed and leaned forward to clink his glass against hers. "No problem here, Stinky."

"Good." She took a deep breath. "I'm sorry my family hurt you."

"They may have done a number on me, sweetheart, but they've done a bigger one on you. We're both old enough to deal with their games now."

"Fair enough and now let's change the subject." She smiled at him. "So, what kind of lover are you, Joe? *Wham-bam, thank you, ma'am* or someone who lasts longer than five minutes?"

"I'll let you decide when you know me better." He put down his empty glass on the end table and reached for hers. Then, he drew her against him, so she cuddled next to him. "That's better for me. How was it for you?"

A burst of laughter. "You jerk. Give me the glasses and I'll refill them."

"In a moment." He framed her face with his hands. The high cheekbones, pointed chin, and large blue eyes still reminded him of one of the fairies who flew through children's books and movies. But she wasn't sweet or gentle. No, if she held a wand, she'd kick magick butt and he could go with that.

He cradled her head in his hands, thumbs making circles on her neck. "I'm thinking about kissing you."

"Let me know when you get past the thinking stage," she mocked.

"I will." He bent his head, captured her mouth. He nipped at her lips. When they parted, his tongue swept inside. This time he wasn't playing. She kissed him back, hands tangling in his hair. She pressed close, her body melting into his. He deepened the kiss, encouraging her tongue to duel with his.

While the heated kiss continued, he pulled her across his lap. He felt her trembling even before he cupped her breast through the t-shirt. His lips found the soft skin of her throat. Her pulse thudded against his mouth. Her nipple tightened against his thumb.

She pulled back a little, stared up at him with huge blue eyes. "How far do you plan to take this?"

"That's up to you." He dropped whisper-soft kisses over her brows. "I should be fair and say that if we make love tonight, I'm not walking away. Are you ready for that?"

"I'm not sure." She reached up, untied the leather string that kept his hair in a ponytail. "No guy's ever made a commitment to me, Joe. I think I scare them off."

"Yeah, you're tough all right." He laughed gently, kissed the tip of her nose. "I'm not going anywhere, *Stinkerbelle*."

"Promises. Promises, *Mr. Not Walk Away Joe*." She threaded her fingers into his hair. "Kiss me again."

"Take off your shirt first." He watched her eyes widen, a hint of a blush creeping into her cheeks.

"You too."

"All right." He unsnapped the denim work shirt.

She pushed it open, so it hung off his shoulders, ran her hands up over his chest. "Nice. Can I say I'm glad you don't shave your hair here?"

He shuddered when she leaned in and kissed one of his nipples. "Isn't it your turn?"

"I guess." She hesitated, then hooked her hands under the t-shirt and peeled it off over her head, tossing it to the floor. Her bra was a lacy navy-blue confection with a front closure.

When she reached for the clasp, he caught her wrists. "Not yet. I want to see you."

"I'm right here."

"No, but you will be." He drew her close, released his hold on her wrists. Now, he could explore her breasts through the bra. He felt her nipples press against his hands. He trailed a kiss over her cheekbone to her ear. "I could kiss you all night."

"No, you can't. The night's half over already." She arched against him, and he remembered to breathe. Lord, she excited him. He fumbled with the closure on the bra, peeled the material back so he could see her small breasts, capped with dark pink nipples.

He bent his head, slowly teased the first one with his tongue before he sucked on it. She moaned, twined her hands into his hair, pulling it around the sides of his head. He found her second nipple with his thumb and first finger, gently rubbing. She sighed and whispered his name, holding his mouth on her nipple. It nearly drove him mad. He rolled the nipple against his tongue, and she clutched his hair.

"Please, Joe. Please."

He smiled against her skin. "I am, aren't I?"

He reached for her western belt, unbuckled it. Then, he unfastened the top button on her jeans, followed it by unzipping the pants. He felt her tense against him and stopped. "Is this—"

"The first time?" She nipped his ear. "Yes. I told you. I scare men off. They barely kiss me, and they don't try to seduce me."

"Then, they're idiots." He kissed her forehead. "And I'm definitely not taking you on a couch the first time we make love. We'll go for a lot more romance."

"It folds out into a double bed."

He laughed. "We'll still do better when we have more time, sweetheart."

She slid her arms around his neck. "You could kiss me again."

"Or you could kiss me." He caught his breath when she shook her head.

Instead, she backed away, slid off his lap to stand in front of him. She pushed her jeans down until they puddled on the floor at her feet. She stepped out of them, only wearing a pair of navy-blue silk panties. In a moment, the underwear followed her jeans to the carpet. "Now, what happens if I kiss you? Getting any ideas, Doctor Joe?"

He reached for her bottom and brought her closer. He wanted to bury his lips in the soft brown curls directly in front of him. "I can think of a lot of things I want to do to you, but I'm trying to be a gentleman."

She bent down and brushed her mouth over his. "You can stop trying any time."

"Oh, I'm just getting started." He kissed her belly button, then pulled her down on his lap again. He felt the warmth of her arousal pressing against him. He trailed kisses up to her breasts again, drawing a nipple back into his mouth.

She squirmed nearer and he stroked her thigh. Then, he cupped the soft brown hair between her legs. She twisted against him, moaning. And he hadn't even touched her, not really. He slid a finger inside her, followed it with a second, let his thumb rub the small bud of flesh.

She rose, threading her hands in his hair. And he kissed her, his tongue tangling with hers as he moved his fingers in and out of her. It was only a prelude to what he'd do when he had her in his bed, but for now, it was enough.

She kissed him back. Then, she pulled her mouth free to explore his neck. To sigh, gasp, moan against his throat while he continued the motion with his hand. She arched higher and her nipple was so close. He bent his head, sucked on one and then the other. She cried out and convulsed on his hand.

Afterward, he slipped out of his shirt and helped her into it. "I told you I wanted more romance."

"But I want you." She pressed close, her hips rocking into him. "And you want me. I can feel it."

He snagged her wrists before she unfastened his jeans. He'd never get them on again and right now, he intended to walk out the door. He'd wait to take her completely, wait until he could make the night special for just the two of them. She'd waited this long, waited for him even if she didn't know it. She deserved special.

"I've barely started with you, sweetheart." He lifted her off his lap and managed to stand. God, he wanted her. He felt it everywhere, through every inch of his body. "I'm going to have all of you with all of me. I'm taking my time even if it kills me."

He headed for the door, gathering up his boots on the way. "I'll see you tomorrow."

"Aren't you kissing me goodnight?" The taunting question slid along all his nerves.

He swung around, caught her chin in his fingers. "Not unless I can put my mouth where I just had my hand."

She blushed. "You macho jerk."

"Okay. Then, I'll do it next time."

13

SHE'D SLEPT IN HIS SHIRT, UNABLE TO FORGET WHAT HE'D DONE A few hours before. Okay, so she wrote about sex a lot. It was totally different experiencing it. She never would have expected that she could be naked in front of a guy and not have him finish what they started. Hell, she'd always been too embarrassed to go as far as she had with him. She yawned, stretched, and snuggled back under the blankets, remembering his kiss, his touch, her first orgasm.

Joe was different all right. Now, what was she going to do about it? Maybe, she'd take his clothes off tonight and return the favor—get him all stirred up and then leave him wanting. It could be fun. She closed her eyes for a moment. Then, she'd get up and hit the decks a-running, or was it just the barns?

A sudden pounding on the door jolted her out of sleep. She threw the covers aside and ran for the door. Pyewacket streaked under the bed. She wished she could join the cat, but she didn't. She paused in the entry. "Who is it?"

"Clancy. Are you coming to work or not?"

Audra unlocked and swung the door wide. What would happen if she told her sister to watch her tone? Instead, it was time for the voice of sweet reason. "If I overslept today, it's not a federal offense. I'll be right down."

"It's after eight. The campers will be here in an hour. Who do you think is going to saddle up?"

Audra whirled when her cell phone rang. She hustled over to the kitchen table and picked it up. "Hello."

"Destynee, is that you?" Kendra chirped, all early morning cheer. "The new artist wants to talk to you about cover art for *A Howling Good Night.*"

"Is that the new—" Audra paused and looked over her shoulder. "Don't let out my cat, Clancy, and go start work. I'll be there in twenty minutes."

"I'm a riding instructor, not a groom." Clancy tossed her head, red hair flying. "I don't saddle or brush horses."

"There's a first time for everything and I really need to take this call." Audra nearly said that she'd worked harder for the last twenty-two years than Clancy had in her entire life. "If you haven't heard it before, no honest job is too demeaning, so I'm telling you now, drama diva."

She heard male laughter and saw Ethan looming in the doorway behind her sister. "Wonderful. Could you take her to start work so I can put on my pants?"

"You bet." He held out a large cardboard cup. "She forgot your mocha in my car. We have the prep covered."

"Hang on, Kendra. I live for caffeine." Ignoring her editor's laughter, Audra sauntered toward her almost brother-in-law. He looked like a mountain in his flannel shirt, jeans, and boots. It was fun to tease him, but she didn't feel any electricity pulsing between them. "I so owe you for this, Ethan."

He chuckled, passing her the cup. "Well, do me a favor and don't tell Joe that you look better in his shirt than he does. The little guy will try to beat me up and I'll never get any of Brigid's doughnuts again."

Audra smiled, sucked on the straw, and let the chocolate-flavored coffee swirl down her throat. "Thanks again."

"Why are you thanking him?" Clancy demanded. "I was in the car when we stopped at the espresso stand."

"Because you've never brought me a mocha in the twenty-eight years you've been on this planet, and you haven't turned over a new leaf today." Audra pointed to the door. "You can go now."

Clancy spun around, stomped out the door and Ethan closed it gently behind them, but not before giving Audra a thumbs up and pretending to leer at her bare legs once more. She suppressed a giggle and went to perch on the stool at the kitchen counter.

"Okay, Kendra. I have coffee now. Tell me about the cover for Howling. I sent in the questionnaire about the characters months ago when I returned the contract."

After she finished with her editor, Audra headed for a quick shower. Then, she dressed, put in her contacts, and did a quick make-up session. She brushed out her hair, tied it back in a pony-tail, grimacing at the dark roots. It was time for a session with Ginger and right now, Pyewacket yowled for attention.

Audra followed the starving cat to the kitchen and fed him the remains from his can of kitty meat. She glanced at the clock. Three minutes left. She hurried across the room, yanked up the covers, and slid the bed back into the couch. Her apartment was fit to be seen. She picked up the laundry basket outside the bathroom door. She'd wash Joe's shirt when she did her clothes after camp.

She hustled in the back door of Elinor's house. Her boss turned from the coffee pot with a smile. "Good morning. Want more caffeine or did Ethan's mocha do it for you?"

"Oh, there's never enough coffee in the morning." Audra put down the basket by the washing machine. "Sorry, I overslept."

"No problem," Elinor said. "Sean stayed over so he did chores with us this morning. Besides, you'll have the whole place to your-self next week and be doing everything. You're allowed a late start." She took a covered plate from the top of the stove. "Have some breakfast. I'll go sign in the urchins. I want you to take the afternoon off when the campers go today."

"I have to grade their workbooks and organize the first camp shows we're doing tomorrow." Audra carried her coffee to the table and the place setting that obviously waited for her. "We're closing Saturday afternoon for a week. I'll rest then."

"You'll rest today after canp. Sandy, Marcie, and Clancy will grade the books and prepare for the show." Elinor put the plate in front of Audra and removed the lid, revealing scrambled eggs, bacon, and pancakes. "Tomorrow at the riding demo, you and I are selling lessons, trail rides, birthday parties, more camp, and leasing to the parents. We need year-round students so I can afford to keep this place after the wedding. Now, eat."

Mocha cup in hand, Elinor collected a clipboard and pen from her desk. "Contrary to Clancy's opinion, I am the boss and what I say goes. And everybody saddles up, not just you, my dear."

Audra dug into the eggs after her employer walked out the kitchen door. She heard a low growl from under the table and glanced down to see Elinor's heeler eyeing her. "Forget about it, Ruler. If you get part of my food, I know your owner will come back in and smack me. She's a tough lady."

"Yeah, Mom is." Lynn came in from the living room, her puppy and Jake's little cattle dog tagging behind. "But she'll let you help us pack tonight after supper if you go straight to your apartment or wherever for a few hours of what she calls, 'me time.' And the dogs got bacon grease on their kibble this morning, so they're fine no matter what Ruler says."

"Good to know." Audra picked up her coffee cup, took a swallow. "I'm sorry I missed out on chores this morning. I didn't mean to dump on you."

"No worries." Lynn dropped to her knees and hugged both puppies. "It was fun to do chores with Mom and Sean again, like old times. The only person who freaked was Clancy. And I felt sorry for her."

"Why? She was pretty steamed by the time she got to my room."

"Oh, that's because Sean and Ethan teased her about being a diva. And Mom told her not to dump all the hard work on you because it wasn't fair, that you wouldn't be so tired if you didn't have to do everything." Lynn cuddled the tri-colored bundle of fur for another moment, then picked up the one that looked more like steel wool. "Did anyone ever give Clancy, the *if you want a friend, you have to be one* lecture?"

Audra cut into her bacon while she considered the question. "I don't think so. Around my mom's place, it's more *if you don't want to do a crap job, leave it for someone else*. And usually, that someone else ends up being me."

"Well, that's not the way it is around here." Lynn ducked away from a puppy kiss. "My mom says it isn't enough for Jake and me to be brother and sister. We must be respectful of each other and act like friends, even when he makes me crazy. Then when things are hard, I can always go to him, and he can come to me."

"Those are good rules," Audra said. "You and Jake are lucky to have your mom."

"And Sean." Lynn gave the puppies one more snuggle. "Okay, I'm going to help Clancy now, so she knows that people still like her. She didn't start out being a diva this week."

"No, she didn't." Audra laughed. "I'll be right there too. Thanks for the heads-up, honey. I appreciate it."

While she finished her breakfast and loaded the dishwasher, Audra wondered if anyone had ever mentioned to her mother that her daughters should be friends, not adversaries. *Definitely not!* Darlene Dawson never would have taken any advice from a young teenager like Lynn. Instead, it would have been grounds for a lecture to Elinor about parenting. That would be an interesting conversation to watch, especially if she had the concession to sell peanuts and popcorn, Audra thought.

She took a few minutes to fill three outdoor cups with coffee. Then, she headed for the back door. She made sure the dog and two puppies remained indoors. While the campers would love the opportunity to play with the canine contingent, an excited heeler, horses, and kids could prove a hazardous combination. Lynn and Jake would take their pups out for walks during lunch and out for playtime after camp.

Audra found Clancy in the main barn grooming and saddling up Bonanza. Ethan was in the next stall working on Fancy, a small silver dapple Shetland mare. Audra passed the coffee cup to her sister. "Thanks for getting this done. I appreciate it."

"Regardless of what some people say, I don't believe you're my servant." Clancy took the cup, shooting a purple-eyed glare at her former fiancé. "Or my slave for that matter."

"I know." Audra handed the second cup to Ethan. "It's my fault. I should have stood up more to everyone instead of blaming myself when Dad left on my twelfth birthday and trying to take his place."

Clancy put her cup on the door and reached for Bonanza's blankets. "I never thought of that."

"Why would you?" Audra asked, on her way to Tonka's stall to start grooming the big black Welsh pony. "You were only six."

"I'm an adult now," Clancy said. "I should have realized that you were a child when I was a child. Why didn't I?"

"Because a child learns from the adults in her world." Ethan slid the saddle into place on Fancy's back. "Did anyone in your family ever treat Audra like a kid again after your dad walked out?"

She meant to work on her book about the witches, wizards, and the war claiming their world that afternoon, but the couch was just too inviting. She didn't bother to unfold the bed. Instead, she just flopped down and pulled the afghan over her body. Too many long workdays on the farm and her book and not enough sleep on those five-hour nights crowded her mind.

So, she'd nap first, then write and finally go help Lynn and Jake pack up for the move to Sean's place. When Pyewacket jumped on Audra's back, he found the perfect spot to warm up, the center of her aching shoulder blades. She debated moving him. It seemed like too much trouble. She decided she ought to be responsible. She pulled out her cell phone, set a wake-up call for eight that night although she didn't plan to sleep that long. Just an hour or two.

It seemed like minutes later when a knock on the door woke her. Yawning, she tossed the blanket aside and glanced around for the cat. He perched on the windowsill, batting at the last of the sunbeams. She stood up, stretched, and went to answer the door. "Who is it?"

"Me," Joe said. "I have dinner."

"Really?" She unlocked and opened the door, finding him at the top of the stairs. He looked awesome in a light blue t-shirt that emphasized his shoulders and muscular arms. She told herself to stop drooling over him and think about supper. "What are we eating?"

"Chinese." He held up two large white sacks. "Hope you have tea. Since we're helping Elinor and the kids pack, I didn't bring wine."

"How did you get roped into the packing?" Audra asked. "Lynn invited me."

"Jake. When he called me about the decorations at the church, I got the word about tonight. I checked in with Brigid and she says the cakes will be ready for the reception. She's making one for the groom as well as the fancy white one."

Audra stepped back and allowed Joe inside. He handed her the bags, shut the door, and took the time to remove his boots. She turned before she rewarded his consideration with a kiss and led the way to the tiny kitchen. She wasn't sure why she wanted distance between them after last night. She just didn't know where they were going, or even if she'd like the relationship when she arrived there. She put down the bags on the small kitchen table. "If you unpack the food, I'll make tea. What do we have?"

"Chicken fried rice, spring rolls, lo mein, broccoli with beef, sweet and sour pork, egg flower soup, and almond fried chicken." He lifted out small cartons as he spoke. "It was a long day and I'm starving so I bought out the restaurant. Do you want plates? Silverware or chopsticks?"

"I never learned how to handle chopsticks," Audra admitted.

"They're too high tech for me and after working all day, I lack the patience to try."

"Sounds like me." Joe opened cupboard doors. "I don't know why it's so hard doing the actual animals when I spend hours lecturing about surgery at school."

Audra laughed and put on the tea kettle to heat. "Exactly. I taught campers to groom the mares and foals, then to lead them. There were only six kids. Marcie had the other six cleaning the barn. Then, we switched groups. After lunch, we sent ours to ride while we took Clancy's students. Taffy's baby didn't want to get up for the afternoon session and I couldn't blame her."

"What did you do?" Joe pulled silverware out of a drawer. "Force her?"

"No point to it. She's the youngest and I didn't want to overwhelm her. We used her older half-siblings, Awesome and Comet. They loved the attention and three kids for each mare and foal worked out fine. Licorice Whip was ready to come to class when Marcie and I traded off."

"That makes sense, and it was a good training experience for the kids and the horses." Joe continued setting up the meal on the table. "What does Elinor plan to do with the foals when they're mature? Sell them?"

"How?" Audra reached in the canister and removed three breakfast teabags. "There's barely a market for registered, pure-bred stock. Nobody wants to spend anything on grade, mixed-breed ponies. You couldn't even get ten cents a pound for them if you sent the bunch off to slaughter in Canada. Elinor says she'll keep them, expand the business and use them to teach children to ride."

"Good plan." Joe tore two paper towels off the roll to serve as extra napkins. "What about weaning them? When will she do that?"

"We're going to try an experiment and do it in a version of the natural way." The kettle whistled and Audra removed it from the heat, switching off the burner. "We'll divide the stalls in half when the foals are about eight months old. We'll keep turning them out to pasture with their moms so they can nurse part-time and let the mares finish weaning them."

She carried the teapot and two cups over to the table. She sat down in the chair he pulled out for her. "Let's eat. I'm starving."

"Looks like we're not the only ones." Joe glanced toward the cat who prowled toward the table. "Do you feed him Chinese?"

She nodded, filling the cups with hot tea. "He has a weakness for fried rice and almond fried chicken. Put some of each on his plate and he'll leave us alone."

Joe chuckled and followed directions. Pyewacket switched directions and headed for his own dish.

They took turns with the cartons, serving themselves and then passing the containers back and forth. While they ate, he shared details of his day, stitching up a young horse that spooked at the sound of fireworks and ran into a wire mesh fence. She told him how Clancy and Ethan helped with saddling and then her younger sister stepped up all day. "She organized grading the workbooks with Marcie and Sandy since they'd taught most of the pages."

"What workbooks?" Joe spun noodles around his fork. "That sounds like a new innovation."

"Elinor created them." Audra cut her chicken into smaller pieces. "She put together different pages. One had a diagram of a Western bridle and the campers had to label the parts. She did the same thing for the saddle and then for the horse. There was a fill-in-the-blank worksheet for grooming. They even had a word search. When we had extra time, the kids colored pictures and wrote down what they learned."

"Are they getting grades on their books?"

"No. Ribbons from first through seventh place and it counts toward who wins the trophy for their riding group." That required a bit more of an explanation. She couldn't believe it when he handed her a fortune cookie. Where had the time gone?

They cleaned up together. She washed their few dishes while he stored the leftovers in the fridge. When she turned from the sink, she found him standing behind her. "What's this about, Dr. Joe?"

"Something you forgot to do when I got here." He bent his head and kissed her, just their lips touching.

Soft and sweet, no pressure, no feeling that he was pushing for more than she was ready to give, so she stepped forward and rested her hands on his chest. "Can't you do better?"

"Not when we're supposed to be helping Elinor and the kids." Joe smiled. "What about you?"

Audra heaved a dramatic sigh. "Do I have to do everything?"

She tiptoed up and caught his mouth with hers.

Three kisses later, they headed for the rambler, hand in hand. When they stood on the back porch, she heard Ruler's low bark of greeting followed by puppy yaps.

Sean opened the door. "The cavalry has arrived. Wonderful. Audra, come tell Elinor that she doesn't have to take all the dishes. You'll need some to cook here and my sisters fully stocked my kitchen."

"But I want to get my dishes out of boxes," Audra said, seeing the concern that wrinkled her boss's forehead. "Do you need more paper to wrap them?"

"I'm good. I've been saving the newspaper instead of recycling it." Elinor smiled at her. "Thanks, Audra. Hi, Joe. Jake's been excited about you helping him pack."

"Sounds like a rescue to me." Joe tugged gently on Audra's braid. "I'll leave you gals to discuss dishes. I'm headed off for manly things."

Elinor laughed. "Okay, then remind my little man that he has to take his socks and underwear. He doesn't get to go commando at the new house either."

Joe saluted and headed for the bedrooms. "Mom's house. Mom's rules."

Spotting the full glass coffee pot, Audra snagged a mug from the cupboard. "All right, talk to me. I don't think I've been to Sean's place in ages. When are we sending the furniture?"

"My house is fully furnished," Sean said. "We don't need—"

"Listen up, Sean. After Sunday, it won't be your house anymore." Audra filled her cup, then went to the fridge in search of the Irish cream. "It will be Elinor's, Lynn's, and Jake's home too. Do you want that or not? Speak up. We can still cancel the wedding. Hey, I'm an expert after dealing with the *crash and burn* of Clancy's and Kate's."

He held up his hand. "Hold it, General. I'm not canceling anything. I'm marrying Elinor on Sunday. And if she wants her furniture in my, I mean our place, I'll move it."

"Aah, that's so sweet." When she turned from adding liquor to her coffee, Audra found the two of them kissing. She leaned against the counter and sipped her drink, waiting for a break in the embrace. "Okay, you two. Do I need to get a bucket of water?"

"No." Elinor looked over her shoulder with a big smile, still standing in the circle of Sean's arms. "We have to talk. My grandfather bought me the farm and some of the furniture has been in the Talbot family for ages. I didn't think it bothered me to leave it, but it does. So, now we figure out what goes and what stays."

"And we can do that on our own," Sean said. "Do you want to help Lynn pack? Be warned. She's trying to figure out a way to talk you out of Pyewacket. He was her kitten before he was your cat."

"I know." Audra left the kitchen to them and went to the teen's bedroom. She was sitting on her double bed, her tri-colored pup in her lap. "What's up, Lynn? Thought we were packing."

"We are, but I don't know what to take."

Audra pulled out the chair by the desk and sat down, drinking her coffee. She focused on the dark-haired girl in jeans and a Silver Lake Pony Ranch sweatshirt. "Well, since I have to pack whenever I change jobs, do you want some advice?"

Lynn nodded, then rested her chin on the puppy's head. "Yes, please."

"Start simple. You know you want your clothes and his toys, right?"

"And King's dishes and his leash and harness," Lynn said, still snuggling her puppy. "But I want the bookcases too. And Sean says that whatever isn't in my new room, he'll buy for me."

Audra looked around the room. The bed and chest of drawers didn't match the rest of the antique wooden furniture which was what Lynn wanted to take. "We have to pack the books anyway. That's a no-brainer. And then, you'll need your desk because it matches the bookcases."

"But not that chair. It's really uncomfortable when I sit for a long time to do homework."

"Okay, so we have the start of a plan." Audra finished her coffee. "Got some boxes? Want me to start with the books while you do your clothes?"

Lynn nodded again. "Do you think Sean will be mad about the bookcases and desk?"

"No, honey. He loves you and your brother. He wants you to feel like you're going to a new home, not moving into his house because he married your mom. And a woman needs to make a nest. It'll be fine."

14

LYNN LOOKED AROUND HER NEARLY EMPTY BEDROOM. SURE, HER bed and dresser were still here. So, were some of her clothes—the ones she'd wear through the weekend and on the trip to Eastern Washington next week. She picked up a box of paperbacks and started for the door. She stopped when Jake hurried into the room. "What's wrong? Is the truck full?"

"Not yet." He took the carton from her. "Sean says there's space for three more boxes. And you have to help me."

"With what?" Lynn asked. "I thought you and Dr. Joe pretty well packed everything in your room."

"We did." Jake dropped his voice to a whisper. "We have to do the spell again."

"No way. We just did it Monday night."

"Nothing's happening between Audra and Dr. Joe," Jake said. "I've been watching them, and they don't kiss or hug. They don't do anything together, not like Mom and Sean did. We have to do the spell again."

"Not yet." Lynn folded her arms and glared down at her brother. "We wait and see. There's no point in nagging. I'm sure the *Ancient Power* you call on in your spell doesn't like it any better than Mom does."

Jake considered the point, then nodded. "Okay, but when we get home on July eighth, we'll revisit the idea. Deal?"

Lynn took a deep breath before she nodded. By that time, Jake might have a new whim or maybe Audra would find someone to date at the wedding. "Now, let's get the truck loaded. Otherwise, Sean and Dr. Joe will never get any sleep tonight. They both have a lot to do tomorrow. So, do we. It's the first day-camp horse show."

———

Audra stretched as she climbed the stairs to her studio apartment. Joe had followed Sean out to his place in Snohomish to help unload the pickup. The furniture and boxes would end up in various rooms of the log three-story house. The kids and Elinor would help unpack later as they settled into their new home. And Sean promised to bring over a kitchen table and chairs tomorrow to replace the ones that Elinor insisted on taking with her.

So far, so good when it came to Pyewacket, Audra thought, unlocking the door. Lynn hadn't asked for him and that was great. The Siamese had been a constant companion for the last seven years and Audra didn't want to return him to his original owner. If she asked him, Joe would talk to his father. The two veterinarians or someone at the clinic might have a line on a kitten and that could prove an appropriate housewarming gift for the teenager.

"I'm not giving you back, buddy," Audra told the seal point cat winding through her legs. "We're partners. I'll talk to Elinor about finding a *mini-you* for Lynn and see if it's appropriate."

He yowled his usual distinctive cry and bumped her ankles again. She knew that meant she better come up with a plate of kitty meat. Otherwise, he'd be replacing her with somebody better at operating a can opener.

A half-hour later, showered and in her long comfy cotton nightgown, she was ready to face her fictional world with its trials and tribulations. Pyewacket stretched out on her bed, content to wash one of his front paws. She looked at the screen again, scrolled back to re-read the previous chapter. Okay, now she was ready to start the scene between the warrior witch and the wizard determined to capture and tame her. Oh yeah, let the erotic fireworks begin! If she couldn't seduce Joe tonight and have sex, at least she'd write about it.

———

The day camp show started in the big corral with half of the students riding while the others waited for their turn in an audience of parents, siblings, and friends. Audra watched the first group of beginners follow Lynn and Gypsy through an intricate pattern that ended with the campers facing their parents on the ponies in a perfect photo-op. Marcie turned off the music and the riders saluted the audience. Lots of applause later, the kids split into two lines to play games.

A small dark-haired girl in a blue t-shirt and jeans tugged on Audra's arm. "Come talk to my mom now. I want to lease Flicka and if you don't hurry, Brittany will get her first."

"Honey, Flicka has seven days a week for you and Brittany to share her." The idea of sharing a favorite pony obviously wasn't a popular one with the eight-year-old and Audra went with the child to talk riding programs to the parent.

Three hours later, the Silver Lake Pony Ranch staff sat at a picnic table in the orchard. Lynn and Jake were on either side of Elinor, listening to the discussion. Clancy pushed around the box of homemade doughnuts she'd brought along that morning. "So, how did we do? How many students booked back?"

"I've got four on the waiting list for more camp." Sandy passed applications and deposit checks to Elinor. "What about you, Marce?"

"I have two that are ready to buy ponies for their kids, but I talked them into the pre-owner package, so the girls will be able to take total care of Tonka and Bonanza."

Elinor blinked. "Did you tell them that I'm not in the sales business?"

"Of course not," Marcie said. "Their daughters need to prove they're responsible enough to look after horses and in a year or so, they'll have moved onto a couple of Darlene's more advanced ponies that they can take home."

"Nice one." Clancy and Marcie exchanged high-fives.

"It seems a bit underhanded to me," Elinor said.

"You need to think about it from the horse's point of view." Audra snagged the last maple bar before anyone else could. "If you actually sold them the two ponies, the girls would be bored with them before Halloween. Then, Tonka and Bonanza would be sold off so the kids could have more advanced mounts. In a few months, those horses would be disposed of, traded, or sold for faster ones."

"This way, we short-circuit all the hoopla," Clancy said. "Bonanza and Tonka stay home where they belong. They teach these girls the basics, then two more beginners, and keep doing that job. It's hard to find patient ponies who like novices. The kids move onto more spirited mounts and when they're ready to take horses home, they come up to Mom's place and buy ones they'll keep until they go off to college."

"At which point, Darlene buys the horses back unless they are training more youngsters in the same family," Sandy added. "She always has a buy-back clause in her contracts and since Felicia Killian is her lawyer, nobody tugs on Darlene's cape. If she doesn't get them, Marlene will."

"I like that," Lynn said. "And nobody gets their feelings hurt when they can't have our ponies."

"Exactly." Audra licked maple frosting off her fingers. "You don't tell them the ponies aren't for sale and they don't have to argue with you about it. You're trying to do what's best for the students. No problems. No worries."

Jake nodded. "Some people don't realize that horses have families and want to stay with them too, but others do. One of the parents told me Chipeta had lots of babies, not just Awesome and Paragon. She said Tonka was actually one of Chipeta's colts. Is there a way we can find out for sure?"

"Next week if she has time, Audra could follow up with Tonka's previous owners," Clancy said. "Couldn't you?"

"I'll check it out." It wouldn't take that long to make some calls. If all else failed, she'd turn her aunt loose on the project. Marlene knew almost every horsy professional in the county. Having to play detective would be payback for Audra helping costume the 4-H club horses for the Fourth of July parade in downtown Snohomish.

"Okay, let's move on," Elinor said. "Any other sales that we need to know about. Audra booked in several new lesson students. Our leasing program will start next weekend. What else do we have scheduled?"

"Two birthday parties," Lynn said. "Do I get a bonus for booking those?"

"Yes," Audra said, "but you have to wait until the event is over and we get paid. Deal?"

"Deal!" Lynn beamed. "What about Jake? He did lots of tours showing people the foals and the mares. What kind of bonus does he get?"

"How many guests did you have?" Audra asked the boy.

He pulled out his notebook and counted the penciled notations. "Seventeen."

"Okay. While you're gone, I'm making you a tip jar," Audra said. "Then, you make sure it's outside the foal barn and people will put in money to see the babies. That will be your bonus for the rest of the summer. For today, you get a dollar per person. All right?"

Jake nodded. "And I can use the money to buy Awesome a new halter. He's almost outgrown his first one."

"Works for me." Audra glanced at her watch. "Suggestions to improve camp? What will make your jobs easier?"

When the meeting wound down, she walked beside Elinor to

the house. Everyone else headed for the barns to do chores. While the horses would have loved some outside time in the sunshine, the nearly constant sound of exploding fireworks in the neighborhood made that impossible. Instead, they were on lockdown. They'd spend the next week in the barn.

Audra had already moved the mother cat and kittens into the feed room. She'd keep an eye on them and make sure they stuck around the farm. If it looked like they planned to run off, she'd resettle them in the classroom once she moved to the house. She thought only cities should have firework displays and those ought to be reserved for the actual Fourth of July. It simply frightened too many animals. She didn't want to think about how many ended up dead or injured.

"It looks like your bonus program is a winner," Elinor said. "I didn't know if it would work as an incentive or not, but I'm glad it did."

"Me too." Audra paused on the porch, waiting for Elinor to open the back door. "What do you think about putting out tip jars in the main barn and around the big corral? Then if the kids aren't signed up for more programs, the staff still gets a financial reward."

"Let me think about it," Elinor said. "I'm tempted to agree, but only if you receive a share of the tips. Camp wouldn't be nearly as successful without your expertise."

———

Kyle frowned as he rode into the clearing again. What was going on? No matter how many times he rode out, he always ended up back here. Nothing seemed to change. The huge cedars still towered two hundred feet in the air. The creek still chuckled over the rocks. The squirrels still chattered, and the crows continued to scold. His saddlebags had the same amount of food and grain that he'd brought with him when he left the posse. And no matter how much grass S.O.B. consumed, the clearing remained untouched.

Kyle swung out of the saddle. Well, since he wasn't getting anywhere, he might as well set up camp. Maybe, he'd catch a fish for supper. And tomorrow, he wouldn't try leaving. He'd stick around and work on the story he'd started about a gunfighter who had a secret. Perhaps, he was stuck in this place for a reason. It could be like the elevator he'd ridden in New York City. The door to Beth's world might take a while longer to open.

———

Elinor's bachelorette party was in the *Fandango Room* at Billy-Bob's Cowboy Bar. Since the festivities took place in the restaurant, it meant Lynn could attend too. Jake had happily gone off to a pizza place with Sean, Joe, and the other men. Behind the mini-bar, Ginger filled champagne flutes with sparkling cider for the people who didn't drink and the pint canning jars that served as glasses with beer. Once she finished with that, she started on the wine.

She'd stuffed her plump curves into a tight dark blue western dress with a low neckline, although it covered most of her chest. There was a good ten-inch gap between the hem of the skirt and her high-heeled cowboy boots. Ginger would make major tips tonight when she took over the cowboy bar in the lounge after she finished this private party.

Audra glanced around the room. Sandy and Marcie had helped decorate the place with bright red and white crepe streamers. Matching tablecloths were on the tables. Flowers filled boot-shaped vases. One of Brigid's beautifully decorated sheet cakes sat in the middle of an oblong table in the middle of the room, surrounded by elaborately wrapped presents.

"I never expected this," Elinor told Clancy as the two of them approached Audra at the bar. "I can't believe you were able to plan this and do day camp too."

"The power of multitasking." Audra accepted a glass of her

favorite Riesling from Ginger. "It's a Dawson specialty and Clancy did a wonderful job pulling this together."

"Lots of practice," Clancy said. "The Dawsons have been getting married and celebrating for more than a hundred years in these parts."

Another appreciative smile and then Elinor went to greet Marlene Dawson at the door. Clancy flicked a glance at them, then lowered her voice to a bare whisper. "Have you seen Aunt Regina yet?"

"No. Why?" Audra sipped her wine and waited for an explanation. Their uncle ran the bar and the restaurant, but his wife did the books. She could make a penny scream for mercy. "Did she come up with the table decorations?"

"Yes, the boots were in the back storeroom," Clancy said. "They use them for a lot of parties, so she threw them in at no charge. She's letting you have the banquet room at cost."

Her stomach knotted and Audra struggled not to gape at her younger sister. "Letting me? But you were the one who organized this shindig. What else am I paying for?"

"Well, the alcohol and the food of course. Ginger's and the waitstaff's wages. Aunt Regina said she won't charge you for the cleaning since the crew does the whole restaurant on Saturday night. The florist will send you a bill. Brigid said the cake was her contribution, so she doesn't expect to be reimbursed."

Nails bit into her palm around the stem of the wine glass. Trying to keep her tone even, Audra stared up at her sister. "I didn't agree to pay for this party."

Clancy tilted her head, lavender eyes curious. "You said it was a good idea when I suggested it."

"Yes, it was." Audra hissed the words. "How did you decide that meant I'd cover all the costs?"

"It's what you always do," Clancy waved at her mom as Darlene arrived. "You always pay for everything. It's a family rule."

Tears burning her eyes, Audra turned back to the bar when

Clancy walked away. "Fill it up, Ginger. If I'm buying, I may as well enjoy it."

"That little bitch." Ginger exchanged the empty glass for a full one. "Okay, this is what we're doing. I'm taking a break and talking to Regina while you run the bar. Once she knows this is one of Clancy's tricks, Regina will step up."

"Why should she? It's not her fault." Audra took a swallow of her wine, trying to drown the lump in her throat. "And this economy has been hell on everyone."

"Yes, and when Clancy and Kate bailed on their shower in February, you never demanded back your deposit. You paid for everything, and she and Jim didn't lose any money that night." Ginger waved to her position behind the bar. "Come on, girlfriend. You know how to do this. How many years did you make drinks to support your family?"

Audra nodded and walked around the end of the counter. "If you can pull this off, I'll owe you big-time."

"And when you finally smack that bitch around, I'll provide an alibi."

"I should have expected something dirty." Audra heaved a sigh as she opened a bottle of house red wine, began to fill glasses. "Clancy's been super sweet for the past couple of days, and it so isn't her style."

"Well, pay attention next time. When Regina passes the word around the business community the girls are responsible for any bills that they run up, you'll be off the financial hook." Ginger hurried away after a brief pause to speak to one of the waiters.

Audra smiled politely as adult guests filtered her way to collect beverages. She did what she considered a professional *meet and greet*, never letting anyone see that her sister had once again cut her to the bone. Her smile widened as her aunt approached. "Hi there. How are you? All set for the parade next week?"

"What happened to Ginger?" Marlene asked. "Potty break? It's nice of you to take over."

"She'll be right back," Audra said. "What can I get you to drink?"

"A glass of truth with a shot of bluntness on the side." Marlene propped an elbow on the bar. "You look like your best friend just punched you in the gut and since Ginger wouldn't do it, talk to me."

"I'd rather not do it here." Audra placed an assortment of different beverages on a small tray and waved at one of the waiters to come and carry the drinks around. "We'll discuss it later."

"No, we won't." Marlene waited until they were alone again. "If we do it now, I'll find out what's happening. Tomorrow or next week, you'll have your defenses up."

Audra lifted her chin and met her aunt's gaze. "Would I be a total dirtbag if I announced that after this round, it's a no-host bar and everybody buys their own booze?"

"Not to me," Marlene said immediately, "and not to anyone else who works for a living. Why don't we do it this way? Your momma buys this round. I'll buy the second. Anyone else who wants to can let Ginger know."

"Mom won't," Audra said in a calm voice. "She'll dump it on me because everyone thinks I've won the lotto. It will be all I can do to make the balloon payment on the ranch at the end of the summer. Elinor's doing her best, but she can't pay me what the Bergstroms did."

"Nobody human has that kind of money except a software millionaire." Marlene glanced over her shoulder as Ginger returned, accompanied by a petite, plump woman with long silver hair wearing a Billy-Bob t-shirt, tight jeans, and fashion boots. "Hi, Regina. We're just working out the financial details, so Audra doesn't get screwed. If Darlene doesn't offer up her credit card for this round, you will charge mine for two rounds."

"Okay." Regina put an arm around Audra's waist and hugged her. "Honey, this is your party. Go enjoy. I'll run the bar. Ginger will hostess and circulate with appetizers and booze. The other waitstaff will come in and out when we don't need them in the main dining room and bar. We'll make this a family doings and there won't be a big bill that you have to pay. I'm sorry I trusted Clancy and you got stiffed. Believe me, it won't happen again."

"It isn't your fault." Audra blinked hard, determined not to cry in front of her sympathetic audience. "When she started being nice to me this week, I should have known I was due to be tortured and then executed for public entertainment. How does Clancy put it? Oh yeah. It's a family rule."

Regina and Marlene shared a look, then Regina said. "I married into the Dawsons and believe me, that's not a rule Jim or I endorse."

"Me either," Marlene agreed. "This is a party, not a way to make your life a crapfest, Audra. Now, let's go have some fun."

15

SHE WAS THE FIRST TO ARRIVE AT THE PONY FARM AFTER THE party. She walked through the barns and checked on all the ponies. They had finished their suppers, and most were asleep in their stalls. A few felt safe enough to lie down, but most dozed standing up because of the explosions from the neighborhood fireworks.

She glanced into the grain room on the way to the mare's barn. Piled up in a corner, the mother cat slept with her kittens. Okay, so they were safe and that meant she could go to her own apartment. Audra paused downstairs to check on her own four-legged companions. The mares stood over their babies, Star stomping every time there was another loud bang. That seemed to call for an extra hay-time snack, so Audra passed out more flakes of orchard grass to the equine matrons.

It should help them settle down and stop stressing over the continued thumping. The noises would grow worse with each passing day right up until Wednesday. It really didn't matter that it was illegal to shoot off fireworks preceding the holiday. The police were too busy to enforce the laws and that meant animals, as well as their owners, were the ones who suffered the consequences.

When she reached her apartment, she peeled out of her dress boots leaving them in the entry. She headed for the bathroom. It didn't take long to remove her make-up and take out the contacts that felt like bulldozers parked in her eyes tonight. She undressed, sliding into her long, cotton nightgown. It was warm and comfy on a night when she really wanted a hug. It wasn't fair, she thought on her way to the refrigerator and the bottle of wine. Why did her life always suck?

Granted, she'd seriously crushed on Ethan over the years, but she'd never set out to hurt Clancy. Too bad the road only ran in one direction, and her sister didn't feel the same way. There were no limitations when it came to using her like a punching bag. Audra filled the glass with Riesling and took a hefty swallow.

And Clancy wasn't the only one. It might have surprised Marlene when Darlene didn't pay for a round of drinks, claiming she'd forgotten her credit card at home. It didn't shock Audra. She was the family rescuer, and she never got any praise for it. Still, Elinor loved the party and the linens she collected for her new home at Sean's place in Snohomish. So, tonight hadn't been all bad.

Audra went into the living area, put down her glass on the end table, and unfolded the bed from the couch. Leaning against the pillows, she picked up the remote, turning on the TV, and clicked through the channels. Finally, she found a western where the woman kicked butt, shooting almost everything that moved while she tried to bring home her lover for burial. At least the actress could ride, a major plus. Too many times, Audra found herself critiquing a performer's equitation rather than enjoying a story.

On the next commercial, she made a plate of nachos. They weren't as fancy as the ones at a restaurant, just chips she covered with shredded cheese, then nuked. She added sour cream and a spoonful of salsa. That made it ready to go. She brought the plate and bottle of wine back with her as another character died in a blaze of bullets. Pyewacket came out from under the bed to see if he could cadge a chip and she gave him one smothered in cheese. He took it and headed to the back of the couch to wipe it out.

When the movie ended an hour later, she debated working on

her book. She wasn't quite ready to call it a night. She put the dishes in the sink, the wine bottle by the garbage so it could go to the recycle bin in a few hours. She went over to check the lock on the door, switch off the lights in the entry, and stopped at the sound of boots on the outside staircase.

She opened the door, ready to ask Elinor what was wrong. But it wasn't her boss. It was Joe. Audra leaned against the doorframe. "What's up, Doc?"

"If I say I am, will you send me home?" He grinned down at her, threaded a hand in her hair. "There's my brown-eyed girl."

She stepped forward, resting her hands on his chest. She felt the steady thumping of his heart. "If you stay, it's for real, Doc. You have to take me to bed, and I don't have sleeping in mind."

"That makes two of us."

She stepped back, took his hand, and pulled him inside. When he eased out of her hold, she locked the door and turned to see him removing his boots. She paused and waited. "So, how was your party?"

"Pretty low-key. Pizza and video games." He grinned at her, unsnapped his shirt. "What about yours?"

"It would have been better if I'd known I was paying for the whole thing, but I worked it out with my Aunt Regina and Aunt Marlene." Audra heaved a sigh. "Sometimes, my family puts the fun back in dysfunctional a little too much."

He framed her face with his hands, bent down to kiss her. "Well, let's see if I can't make things better."

"You did that just by coming here." She pushed the shirt off his shoulders, watching him shrug out of it. "Did I say I was glad you showed up?"

"No, but you will before morning."

She rose on tiptoe to brush her mouth over his. She could have drowned in the tenderness of his blue eyes. She slid her fingers over his chest, dropped a kiss on one of his nipples. "I'm not all glamorous in this nightie."

"It works for me." He chuckled. "And it'll be even better when I get you out of it."

"Promises. Promises." She reached for the leather lace that held his ponytail and untied it. A black cloud of hair hung around his rugged features. She feathered a thumb over his lips. "Kiss me."

He lowered his head and their mouths met, clung. Her tongue enticed his into a passionate duel. He swung her up into his arms, carried her to the bed. He followed her down, still kissing her and she pressed close.

Each kiss led to another. Finally, he lifted his lips from hers. He trailed slow kisses over her cheekbones, to her nose, up to her eyelashes, her brows. She sighed when his lips explored her throat. He unbuttoned her nightgown until it revealed her breasts.

She tangled her fingers in his hair, arching against him. He flicked his tongue over her nipple, then drew it into his mouth and sucked. He teased the other nipple with his thumb. She moaned and tried to wriggle closer.

Eventually, he lifted his head. Their gazes met and she smiled at him. "So, when do you take off your jeans?"

"Not for a while yet." He caught the hem of her nightgown and slowly raised it. "I have plans for us, mostly for making you scream."

She gasped when he slid a hand over her ankle, her calf, up to her knee, then her thigh. "I have a few ideas of my own." She caught her breath when he cupped her. His fingers stroked through the curls between her legs. "What are you doing?"

"I told you already." He pushed the nightgown up. His thumb found the small bit of flesh and rocked against it. Then one finger slid inside of her, followed by a second.

She twisted, found his mouth with hers. He kissed her back. The first kiss led to a second, a third before he trailed butterfly kisses along her jaw to her ear, then down her neck. His mouth teased her nipples, sucking on first one and then the other. His hand moved in and out of her for what seemed like forever. She clung to him, kissed his neck, dug her nails into his back as she rose and fell, matching the motion he started. She exploded in what felt like a thousand pieces as she convulsed around those skillful fingers.

When sanity returned, she saw her nightgown on the floor. How had he managed that? How could he take it off her when she didn't know? She reached for his belt, and he caught her wrists. "What? Turnabout is fair play."

"Not tonight, sweetheart. Next time." He released her, smoothed a hand over her leg up to her thighs. "This time I'm going to taste you."

Warmth flooded into her face. "Nobody's ever—"

"Good. I'll enjoy being the first." He lowered his head, blew softly on the folds of skin between her legs. He cupped her bottom. "Now, let's see if you enjoy it too."

His tongue slid across the small piece of flesh he'd tormented with his thumb. She arched against his mouth, becoming part of the intimate kiss. She twined her fingers into his hair. "Please. Oh God, please."

His tongue drove into her, repeating the same motions he'd done with his fingers such a short time ago. She lifted her hips, up and down, back, and forth as he continued, following the pattern he began. She was his, even if she never told him. He alternated, between soft lapping kisses that barely touched and deep ones that drove her crazy. When she came, she felt him laugh against her. She jerked hard on his hair. "You bastard."

"Sounds like a do-over to me." And he started again. This time it was brief, sampling kisses that roamed over the curls. Deeper ones when his tongue sank into her before he drew the nub of flesh into his mouth and sucked.

She came apart, crying his name. When she opened her eyes, he stood beside the bed removing his jeans. They dropped to the floor. He joined her on the bed, knotting a fist in her hair. She let her fingers stray over his broad chest. She kissed the hard buttons of his nipples. "What do you think?"

"I'm wondering how to convince you that I'd rather see you with brown hair than red."

"Keep talking, Doc." She nipped his chin. "Or you could just leave it up to my family. They keep messing with me and I'll give up trying to win their approval."

"Really?" He brushed his mouth over hers. "Then, I'll go for door number two."

"Good choice." She rolled on top of him, kissed him. "Now, what's your plan?"

"You'll find out."

Kisses led to more touches as they caressed each other until she was under him again. Finally, he slid between her legs, resting his weight on his elbows. Slowly, he eased inside her. He shifted, pushed deeper.

She rose against him. "Is that all?"

"Everybody's a critic." He moved, a long deep stroke.

She met his next thrust with her hips, then a third. She caught his mouth with hers, clawing at his back with her nails. He deepened the kiss and she surrendered. Then, she was moving with him, matching the pattern of his thrusts. Some were shallow, tiny movements of his hips. Others were so deep. The pace increased. He moved faster and she twisted, arching beneath him, determined to take him with her this time.

Before she could, she found herself flying among the stars. She threw her head back against the pillows and called his name. He was still hard, buried inside her. He waited, then started to move again. She met his motions and this time they were together. Each thrust took them farther and farther into the universe. All she could do was travel with him on this journey. He lowered his head and his lips claimed hers. His tongue drove into her mouth as they whirled through a sensual dance among the stars. Their hips met and they climaxed together.

She collapsed in his arms, lying next to him. "Oh, my God."

"You can call me, Joe." He pulled her across him, running his hand over her hair. "I'm good with that."

"I think you're just good." She turned her face into his shoulder. "I've never had sex like that." She paused, then flicked her tongue against his ear. "Are you going to think you're all that if I admit I've never had sex at all?"

"You still haven't." He kissed her eyebrows. "I made love to you, sweetheart, and I don't want to just have sex with you. Okay?"

"I can go with that."

"Fair enough. So, why did you wait so long?"

"I don't settle. And I was holding out for a hero."

"Well, I'm glad you found me." He pulled her closer. "Now, what's it going to take for you to come back to Pullman with me at the end of the summer?"

She sighed and cuddled against him, unwilling to start an argument with him about their future. "Let me just enjoy what we have now. Then, we'll see what tomorrow brings."

"I can go with that." His arms tightened around her. "Are you going to let me sleep with you while I'm here or do I have to go back to Dad's?"

"I want you with me for as long as I can have you, but not on Sunday night." She lifted her head for a moment to meet his gaze. "Lynn and Jake are staying with me after the wedding. You can visit on Monday after they leave with Sean and Elinor for Eastern Washington. I won't share a bed with you when the two kids are in the house. Deal?"

"That works for me." He drew her down for a kiss. "I'll help you take your things to the house after the wedding."

"I like it." She smoothed a wave of dark hair off his forehead. "How long do I have to give you to recover before I jump your bones again?"

———

Due to the constant pounding of fireworks, the pony farm was closed for most of the holiday week. That meant after chores she and Joe returned to her apartment for breakfast. While she fried bacon and scrambled eggs, he made toast and set the kitchen table. She'd barely sat down when her cell phone rang. She picked it up, recognizing the caller as her mother. Audra grimaced.

After the fiasco at Elinor's party the night before, Audra really didn't want to talk to her family, but she couldn't think of a way out of it. "Good morning, Mom. What's wrong?"

Utter silence and then her mother said in a cautious tone, "I wanted to be sure you were coming up tomorrow since everyone is attending Elinor and Sean's wedding tonight."

"Sorry, but I have to horsy-sit," Audra said. "It's not like when I was at Bergstrom's and there was staff to look after the stock. I'm it."

"We could come down there," Darlene said. "That would be fun."

"Except I'll be moving into Elinor's house from the apartment all day tomorrow." Audra held the phone with one hand and filled coffee cups with the other. "I can't haul boxes and entertain the Dawson clan too. I'll see the family at the reception today and then I'll come next Sunday when Elinor and the kids are back to run the pony farm."

"We can help you move," Darlene said. "It won't hurt us."

Audra laughed at the strange idea. She couldn't remember a time when her family helped with any of her chores, not when she was the chief rescuer, and they were good at watching her work. She slid a mug over in front of Joe, then put hers by the other setting.

When her mother still didn't speak, Audra said, "I'm sorry. Were you serious? I figured it was a joke."

"If you're determined to be a martyr, I can't stop you." Darlene's tone implied she was always misunderstood when she only wanted to be a loving mother. "I just thought it would be nice if the family was together for the holiday."

"I'm sure all of you will have a lovely time." Audra picked up her fork. "But, since Clancy racked up one hell of a bill last night,

I won't even try to get the time off work to visit. And I know it's a family rule. The Dawsons run amuck, and I clean up the mess as well as paying for it."

"You are on the pity pot today, aren't you?" Darlene sighed. "I do hope you're nicer at the wedding and not out to embarrass us."

"I'll do my best to make you happy," Audra said in her sweetest tone. She ended the call, fury rocketing through her. She took a deep breath, tried to calm down. It was hopeless and she phoned Ginger. "Hey, girlfriend. Do you have time to do my hair today for the wedding?"

16

Everett, Washington – Sunday, July 1st, 3:00 pm

OKAY, SO THIRTY-FOUR WAS TOO OLD TO HAVE A FIT AND FALL IN it, but after last night's setup at the restaurant and her mother's call this morning, wasn't she entitled to express some frustration? All right, call it rage! She was tired of always standing outside the castle doors while everyone else partied in the ballroom. Or as the family rule went, her younger sisters could throw crap everywhere because Audra always had a plastic pitchfork to shovel up the muck. How did she point out her *Cinderella* license expired?

Audra took a deep breath. Her head felt oddly light without the long ponytail she'd worn forever. She'd agreed to have Ginger cut her hair to shoulder-length before dying it back to the natural shade, a golden brown. She pulled into the parking lot at the church. She hadn't brought the contacts that turned her eyes a dark blue and it was too late to go get them, not if she intended to be on time to stand up for Elinor's wedding.

She switched off the motor, pulled out her keys, and picked up her purse from the passenger seat, sliding out of the pickup truck.

She wound through the vehicles already in the lot, Clancy's, Aunt Marlene's, and Elinor's. No way would this bride be late for her wedding, not since she traded in a frog for a real prince like Sean. And she'd asked Audra to be an attendant. This was a first too, one she'd make the most of—in the new life she'd decided to create for herself.

She lifted her chin. She'd had a makeover although Ginger and Elinor made unlikely fairy godmothers. *There's no way I'll tell them I feel like a brown-haired, brown-eyed stranger in this red dress.* The red skirt swirled around her knees and her red dress boots tapped out a rhythm as she headed across the parking lot to a side door. An usher let her inside and she hurried to the ante-room where Elinor would be preparing for the ceremony.

In her ivory western dress, her friend smiled as the door opened. "What a transformation. Audra, you look amazing."

"Thanks." Audra nodded at her aunt, then her sister. "Where can I jump in?"

"Take over buttoning up the back of Elinor's dress for me," Marlene said, moving to the center of the room and the table where the bouquets of flowers waited. "I'd almost forgotten what color your hair really is, Audra. It's gorgeous. What a terrific cut. It definitely brings out the pixie element of your face."

"Mom's going to freak when she sees that dress," Clancy said.

"Then, she can freak at me." Elinor winked at Audra. "I chose it and I'm the bride."

"And that makes her the boss." Lynn finished wiping smudges of dust off the white cowgirl boots. "It's the rule for weddings, isn't it?"

———

The ceremony went off without a hitch and the reception seemed headed the same way. Snowy white tablecloths, vases of flowers on the round tables clustered in the hall off the church had come as a major surprise to Elinor. She'd gaped at the display, then hugged her kids and Sean before she snagged Vivian, the leader of the Altar Guild who organized the event. A long buffet took up the middle of the room with two of Brigid's cakes as the focal point. Okay, the traditional wedding cake caught everyone's attention. Joe didn't know how she'd found a cowgirl bride with a lasso on the toy groom, but it still made him laugh every time he looked at it.

A half-hour later, everyone was at the various tables. The salads, tiny sandwiches, and fruit samples were decimated but the cakes remained untouched. Joe sat with his best friend, the bride, Marlene who was another mother to both of them, and the two kids Sean intended to adopt as soon as possible. He looked happier than Joe had ever seen him. It wasn't the first time Joe had stood up for Sean at a wedding, but this was undoubtedly the last time.

Joe couldn't stop staring at his date sitting next to him. His Audra, even if she hadn't admitted that yet. A red dress clung to her breasts, hugged a narrow waist, and flared out from the hips. And she had her hair back, a honey golden brown. The short cut made her beautiful brown eyes look bigger.

From the other side, Sean elbowed him. "Stop drooling. It's unbecoming in a guy your age."

"What about the way you look at Elinor?" Joe said. "Aren't you too old? We're only three months apart."

"I'm allowed. It's my wedding."

A blush crept into Audra's cheeks. "Behave, both of you. Joe, it's time for you to start the toasts and keep yours tasteful. Set a good example."

Joe grinned and stood. He leaned down to kiss her, quick. "Have I ever said that you can always be the boss of me? It's so sexy."

Sean laughed, a sound abruptly cut off. He stopped to eye Elinor warily. "Did you...?"

"I kicked you," Marlene told him. "Put on your company manners. I raised you to have them."

Elinor giggled. "Yeah, what she said."

"I'm totally henpecked." Sean appeared amused and pleased by the idea. When he shifted to kiss Elinor, it brought applause from the guests.

Joe raised his glass. "I've been best friends with Sean since we raided Marlene's cookie jar and Ethan threatened to drop us both into snowbanks headfirst." Lots of laughter and the older man shook a fist at him. "Since it was July, it would have been a bit difficult, but we were careful not to tick him off at Christmas."

More laughs. Joe went on. "Sean and I have hung out for years. He's a brother to me and I'm thrilled he brought me a sister. Elinor, welcome to our family." While the guests sipped their drinks, he stepped around to kiss her cheek, whispered. "When do I give you my Christmas list for Santa? I hope Sean told you Dad and I come for holidays."

Elinor brushed away a tear. "There's always a place for you at our house."

"Good to know." Joe returned to his seat. "Did my toast meet with your approval, *Stinkerbelle*?"

She nodded, looking at him over the rim of her glass. "It was nice."

"That's weak. I'll let you write my next speech."

"Nice doesn't get enough credit and it always works for me." She smiled up at him.

"I'll remember that."

Two hours later, they'd seen off the bride and groom. Joe followed Audra as she guided the kids toward the door. "So, what's the plan for tonight?"

"Chores as soon as we get back to the farm," Audra said. "Then, it's movie night."

"I'm in charge of the pizza," Lynn said, "and Jake's making banana splits."

"Sounds like fun. What should I bring?" Joe winked at Jake. "Sean and your mom will have fits if I show up at their house tonight. They want to be alone."

"Then, I guess you better come over to our old place tonight,"

Jake said. "Do you want to be in charge of munchies?"

"I'm a junk food expert. I'll see you there."

"Be in time to help muck stalls," Audra said. "Nobody likes a guy who is only around for the good times and blows off the hard work. Get moving, Dr. Joe."

Most people would have accepted the authoritative tone the way she intended, that of someone accustomed to issuing orders, not as a defense mechanism. Joe glanced past Audra and saw her mother and four sisters within earshot, waiting by the main door to the parking lot. "Do you want me to stick around and cover your back, General?"

She straightened, standing even taller, and lifted her chin. "I can handle it."

"Then, I'll just stay to enjoy the fireworks."

That earned him a glare before she stalked toward her family, accompanied by the two munchkins. She nodded a greeting to the other Dawsons. "I think the ceremony went well, don't you?"

"Yes, it was very pleasant," Darlene said, with one of her professional smiles, the one she used to meet parents dropping off campers. "What were you thinking, Audra? That haircut doesn't suit you."

"Actually, I think it's the color that's dingier," Kate said, in what could have been taken for a concerned tone. "It's mousy, isn't it?"

Clancy glanced at her mother, then at Kate and the twins. "And do I tell her now that red dress makes her look like an escapee from *The Best Little Whorehouse in Texas*?"

"Thank you for expressing your opinions." Audra put one hand on each of the children's shoulders and propelled them through the door. "I'll look forward to seeing you when my hair grows out, I dye it red to be a Dawson clone and I wear clothing that has your approval. I'll drop the money for the mortgage at the bank in September. That's all you want from me, isn't it? To pay and pay and pay for the rest of you to have whatever you want when I don't get the same opportunities?"

Without waiting for an answer, she kept walking. Her family stared after her as if the person they knew, the family dogs-body had been replaced by a kick-ass Marine.

Joe grinned at the group of stunned women. "You have to enjoy my *Stinkerbelle*. She does have a way with words." He eyed the two youngest. "You're twenty-two. Get jobs. The gravy train just hit the station."

"Is that why you came back now?" Darlene demanded.

"Well, I had to wait for them to grow up." Joe reached for the door handle. "You wouldn't let Audra have a life before that time. And now, we can get married, and she can have everything she's ever wanted. I'll see to it."

He ignored the clucking behind him and jogged across the lot to catch up. He'd have to propose to Audra before they contacted her. Otherwise, they'd have her back in harness dragging their family wagon around for the next twenty-plus years. He was through waiting.

He spotted Brigid helping Ethan load wedding presents in the trunk of his car and paused to speak to them. "When are you taking those over to Sean's?"

"Tomorrow afternoon when Gavin is puppy-sitting," Ethan said. "We can hang out together, drink a few beers and play poker. Did the girls give you heartburn for dating Audra? I told Clancy to watch her bitchy mouth today."

"Well, that explains why she said Audra looked like a hooker in her new dress." Joe watched a muscle twitch in Ethan's jaw and decided to add fuel to the fire. "It was after the rest of the family gave her crap for a new hairstyle."

"I think she looks beautiful," Brigid said, "and if you knuckle under to Clancy again, Ethan, I'm putting ipecac in your doughnuts."

"Be afraid, Ethan, be very afraid." Joe laughed and hugged Brigid. "Tell Audra that she looks like a dream."

"I will," Brigid said. "I have a giant bottle of laxatives, so you better be scared if you break my big sister's heart."

"I won't. I already told the rest of your family that I'm marrying her and taking her back to Pullman with me in August when classes start."

Brigid frowned and put the last package in the Cadillac. "You may have to wait until September. She won't leave Elinor in the lurch with day camp."

———

The next afternoon, she walked through the empty three-bedroom house, empty that was of people and dogs, but it still had most of the furniture. Elinor's bedroom and the bathroom were to Audra's left, directly off the large, country-style kitchen. To her right, was the living room with a bedroom on each side. So, which room did she want to claim as hers?

She went into Elinor's room and scanned the space. It was the smallest of the three bedrooms, approximately twelve foot by twelve foot. Okay, it wasn't that tiny—it just seemed so when she considered all the furniture crammed into it, a queen-size bed, dresser, nightstand, and old-time wardrobe. This room was right off the kitchen and the coffee pot with a next-door bathroom. That made it the perfect writing office. All she had to do was take apart the bed and move in a desk, chair, bookcases for research materials, and a file cabinet.

Audra wandered back into the kitchen. It was fully furnished, so she didn't have to do much except unpack her dishes into the cupboards. Sean had brought over a contemporary maple table with room for the six chairs that surrounded it. She headed into the living room. The couch faced the entertainment center and TV. She'd unpack her records and CDs. Her collection of paperbacks and favorite hardcovers would fill the shelves in here. On a rainy day, she'd pile up her snacks on the coffee table right in front of the couch, turn on the pole lamp and cuddle under the quilt her great-grandmother had made back in the early 1900s. What fun!

Next, Audra checked out Jake's old room. He'd taken most of

his furniture. Well, that was good. She now had a place to move the bed and dresser from his mom's room. Either his room or Lynn's would make a good guest room when Brigid wanted a bolthole from the family. Audra smiled, remembering the quick hug her sister had given her right before she left the church parking lot.

Brigid had leaned in to whisper that Audra looked like a proverbial million bucks. Then, Brigid added that it was no wonder Joe couldn't take his gaze off her. Audra felt her cell phone vibrate and pulled it out of her jeans. "Hello."

"Hi, honey." Her mother's tone was cautious. "Just wanted to check in and see if Elinor and Sean got off okay with the kids. How are you doing?"

"I'm fine and yes, they did." Audra sauntered into Lynn's old room. "They were swinging by Sean's to drop off the dogs and then they were headed for Eastern Washington for Elinor's family reunion."

"It was a nice ceremony, and I thought the party went really well too," Darlene said. "I'm sorry about the way things ended. I was concerned about you and I'm afraid I sounded too critical."

"I didn't think going back to my natural color or a flattering hairstyle would be such a big deal," Audra said. "Don't you think it's time I stopped being blamed because I look different from the rest of you?"

"That's not the problem. Nobody blames you, honey."

"You all do. That came across loud and clear yesterday."

"I'm sorry you feel that way."

Audra took a deep breath and decided to mention the elephant in the middle of the room. It was time after all these years. She hadn't won any points trying to fit into the family mold, so perhaps it was time she broke it.

"Let's just be straight-up here, Mom. I don't look like you or my sisters. I look like my father, your husband who left you in the lurch as soon as he learned you were pregnant with twins. I've been picking up the slack since I was twelve. And I'm still catching hell because I look like him."

Silence for a long moment. Then, Darlene finally said, "I never thought about it like that. I was just startled by the change, and I didn't handle it well. To see Art's boy hanging all over you was another shock. You never date. I didn't even know you liked men. You and Ginger have been together for so long."

"We're friends, Mom. That's what friends do. They hang out with each other." Audra stared at the phone, disbelieving. "Did you really think I was gay? That I was hiding in a closet?"

"You never have any guys around," Darlene sounded defensive, then defiant. "What was I supposed to think?"

"You could have asked me." Audra drew a deep breath. "Relationships haven't worked out well for me, especially when I have to constantly break dates because of emergencies on the Lazy B, or if you or the girls want something."

"We're your family. Of course, we come first. Are you saying that you've stopped dating because of us? I don't believe it."

"There was one important guy before Joe, but he didn't want me. He was like the rest of you. I kept trying and trying to make him love me. But he didn't."

"Well, you can be really sarcastic, and people don't want to have to deal with that," Darlene pointed out. "You were extremely rude to me and your sisters yesterday."

Audra sat down on the double bed. It was amazingly comfortable, and she decided it was a definite keeper. "And your comments about my hair and dress weren't mean?"

Darlene ignored the question. "And it was even more hurtful when Joe Watkins said the two of you were getting married. He told us he's taking you away with him and your sisters better get jobs because you're done supporting them."

"Really?" Audra struggled not to laugh at Joe's blatant attempt to protect her. "I'm sorry to hear he shared our plans prematurely. I'll speak to him about it."

"You mean it's true?"

Audra deliberately didn't answer the question. "I have to go. Joe's here. Talk to you later. Love ya."

17

SHE CLICKED OFF THE PHONE AND LISTENED AGAIN. YES, THAT WAS a knock on the back door. She went to answer it, tucking her phone back in her pocket. She missed Ruler and the puppy duo who barked at intruders. Joe stood on the back porch, holding two grocery bags. She opened the door and looked up at him. "So, you're marrying me, Dr. Joe?"

He grimaced. "Your mom called, huh?"

"Yeah." Audra took one of the bags and carried it over to the table. He followed her, looking all cowboy in a western shirt and black jeans. She turned and pressed against him, sliding her arms around his neck. "You just have to be a hero, don't you?"

"How am I supposed to answer that?"

She pulled his head closer and rose to kiss him. "Doc, I think you're going to have to take me to bed."

"In the middle of the afternoon? I'm shocked." He swung her up in his arms and carried her toward the door. "Lock it. We don't want company."

Giggling, she did, then pointed to the nearest bedroom. "Right in there."

"What comes next?" He headed across the kitchen. "I've told you before. You're hot when you're bossy."

"Time for you to kiss me." She sighed when he lowered his head. His mouth teased hers in a soft, light exploration. She tangled her fingers in his hair. "Kiss me like you mean it."

He laughed. Then he did before he followed her down on the queen-size bed.

She moaned when he cupped her breasts through her t-shirt, rubbed her nipples with his thumbs. She had on too many clothes. She arched against him. "Hurry up."

He grinned at her. "I don't think so. I want you wild and begging for me. I get to be in charge occasionally."

"I don't think so." She pulled him close for another kiss. His mouth felt so warm against hers. She traced his lips with her tongue, then surrendered when he took over the kiss, yielding to the fierce passion. While he trailed kisses down her neck, she unsnapped his shirt. She pushed it off one muscled arm, then the other. She slid her hands over his chest, teasing his nipples.

He groaned, pulled back a moment. He caught the hem of her t-shirt. "Yours is going next."

"Promises. Promises." She caught her breath when her bra followed the shirt.

He blew softly on her breast, then licked a path toward her nipple. "Wait until I have my mouth on you. I've been thinking about it since I saw you in that red dress yesterday."

She giggled. "And you never even saw the matching bra and panties."

"I will next time."

An hour later, she lay in his arms, pressed against his side. She toyed with the hair that was longer than hers now. "You don't need to protect me from my family, Joe."

He pulled her closer. "I didn't like the way they treated you yesterday, but I'll let you speak up to them. Of course, if they do it in front of me, I am going to call them on it. Deal?"

She smiled and kissed the hollow of his shoulder. "That works."

"Fair enough." He nipped her ear. "Have I told you that I really like your hair? I'm glad it looks the way it did when you were in high school."

"You can tell me again."

"I have a better idea." He shifted against the pillows, drawing her across his lap. "I didn't get to be in charge before, but I will now."

"Want to bet?"

He chuckled, caught her wrists, and held them behind her back so her breasts arched up to him. His other hand caressed her stomach, sliding ever lower.

She tensed, wanting the next touch so badly she felt as if she'd explode. His fingers finally smoothed the curls between her thighs. His thumb sought, found the tiny bud nestled there.

"You want this." He eased one finger inside her. "Don't you?"

"Yes. You already know it."

"But I want to hear you say it."

He started a slow in and out motion destined to drive her to the stars and beyond. She moved with him. He lowered his head, swirled his tongue around her nipple, then sucked it into the warmth of his mouth.

She cried out as a second finger joined the first, deep inside her. The strokes continued. Hips rising and falling, she met the pattern he set, unable to do anything else. His thumb rubbed softly, rocking into her, sending her spiraling ever upward.

She rose higher to meet his mouth when he moved from one nipple to the other. "Please, Joe. Finish it. Please."

"I will." He nuzzled the soft skin of her breasts. "But not till I'm ready. Beg some more, sweetheart."

She bucked against his hand as the movements continued. Couldn't he tell how hot she was, how wet? She heard the hiss of his breath, felt him harden even more under her, and realized he was just as excited as she was.

And then she was flying among the stars, convulsing on his

hand. She collapsed against him, aware that his hand was still on her. His fingers were still inside her. "Not again. I want all of you this time."

"I already told you, sweetheart. It's what I want today." He released his hold on her wrists. He lowered his head and his mouth captured hers.

She twisted her fingers in his hair, kissing him back just as wildly. His fingers moved inside her, and he started the same rhythm again. His tongue repeated the pattern as he kissed her, in and out until she reached the heights again.

She buried her face against his neck. "You're killing me."

"Not yet." His hands slipped over her back. "I want to taste you, really taste you before I take you again."

"I'll die." She clung to him, shifting on his lap. "Just have me. You want me. I know it."

"Yes, but I want my mouth on you more." He tumbled her back on the bed. "And it's my way. The next time you start ordering me around, you'll know what I have in mind when I say, 'Yes, dear.' And you'll love it."

"You bastard!"

She gasped when he chuckled, kissed her belly button, and worked his way down to the curls between her legs.

His lips found her. "Yes, dear." And his tongue drove deep.

———

Due to the morning chores, she wasn't the first adult to arrive at Aunt Marlene's on the morning of July Fourth. Sandy's mother was there, wiping dust off the red vinyl chaps the riders wore. Felicia Killian moved from horse to horse, adjusting white parade bridles and rapping out orders for the boys to remain with their mounts, not disappear into the back pasture to chase frogs in the pond.

Marlene stood next to the circular driveway, a stack of white blankets on the bench beside her, instructing each new arrival to costume their horses before changing to a parade uniform. In a white western blouse, red bandana, white jeans, red chaps, the middle-aged woman looked like a grown-up version of her club members. She was definitely dressed for success.

Audra crossed to her. "Where do I jump in?"

"Collect the everyday bridles from the kids who rode in and lock them in the tack-room, so they don't get stolen while we're gone." Marlene turned to show the neat braid that confined her waist-length gray-streaked black hair. "Remind the kids with long hair that it has to look like mine. And I don't care if it's a girl or a boy. If it touches their shoulders, I'd better see a French braid. We're doing it just like Roy always did."

Tears misted Audra's eyes as she remembered her uncle. The Fourth of July parade had always been his favorite event and he insisted the Silver Flying A's practice for months, so they'd bring home the trophy each year. Even when he was dying of cancer, he refused to let the club skip the yearly event. He'd trained the kids from his wheelchair and taught Marlene to ride his beloved palomino gelding so she could lead the club into town from the farm.

"I'm waiting for the last two trailer loads of horses." Marlene blinked hard, then lifted her chin. "I want the club mounted up and ready to ride by eight-thirty. We need to be lined up in town by nine-fifteen and we're riding by the two nursing homes in town the way Roy liked."

"You got it," Audra told her aunt. "I'll do whatever you want."

"I know." Marlene paused for breath as Darlene arrived, Kate and the twins behind her. All four Dawson women wore red and white checked shirts tucked into their blue jeans. "I'm glad you're here. Has Brigid taken over the potluck?"

Darlene smiled. "As usual, she's counting casseroles in your kitchen and stocking up the fridge for the big club lunch after the parade. What do you want us to do?"

"Audra's handling check-in when Ethan and Clancy get here," Marlene said. "Twins, make sure that every 4-H kid has a white equestrian helmet and they fit properly. Adjust them as needed. Put someone on saddle checks and make sure that all the cinches are tight."

Vonnie and Wendy nodded, then each headed off in separate directions. Marlene glanced at Kate. "You're still washed out. If you're going to puke, don't do it in my rose bushes. Go take a nap in my room. When you get up at noon, count tablecloths and make sure we have enough paper plates, plastic ware, and cups. You may have to run to the store for more."

"I'm okay." Kate lifted her chin. She'd lost weight and the defiance didn't touch her large green eyes. "I can help. I'll saddle Pryde for the trip into town."

"No, you won't," Marlene said, putting an arm around the younger woman. "Audra, I'll be back to see how things are here in a few minutes. Darlene, will you go check on Gavin? He's grooming and tacking Pryde for me. Come on, Cathleen Therese Dawson. I'll take you to my room. Then, I'll be sure you get there."

Audra frowned as her sister and aunt headed for the house. "What's wrong with Kate? Has she seen a doctor?"

"She won't go." Darlene took a deep breath. "If she's not back on her feet by next weekend, I'll insist she visit the clinic. Will you do me a favor? Switch with me and go check on your aunt's horse. I really don't want to be around Gavin."

"No problem." Audra hesitated. "Ethan should be here with Roy's horse hauler in ten minutes. Will that bug you?"

"No. Clancy can take care of herself right now. Kate can't." Darlene smiled. "Thanks, honey. I can always count on you."

Leaving the matching saddle blankets with her mother, Audra headed for the barn beyond the house. As soon as she entered, she headed for the box stall that held her uncle's old Palomino gelding. Pryde was a huge Quarterhorse in his early thirties. He stood quietly while Joe groomed him. A white blaze and four white socks added to his glamour. White hairs mixed in with the sunshine gold of his muzzle. He nickered when he saw Audra and she returned to the tackroom to collect three carrots.

"Hi there." She grinned at Joe while Pryde munched her offerings. "I didn't expect to see you till the picnic."

"Dad took over at the clinic and I knew better than to go home and sack out. I'd sleep through the parade and never hear the end of it from Marlene." Joe crossed to the door. "If he gets carrots, when do I get a kiss?"

She laughed and went into the stall, giving the old horse the last carrot. She brushed her mouth over Joe's. "What did you do with Gavin? I thought he was doing this."

"One of the kids came to get him to punch holes in a stirrup leather," Joe said. "I told him I'd finish up."

Audra sighed and stepped forward to lean against Joe's shoulder. "I guess I better go run interference. The twins are checking equipment and the drama will start as soon as they see him."

"Yeah, he shared their shenanigans with me. I told him that he should have insisted the dean of the English department switch them out of his class at the beginning of the quarter. Teaching them was a conflict of interest because he was engaged to their sister. Then, it wouldn't have escalated to the point where they accused him of sexual harassment. He was lucky it only cost him his fiancée. It could have destroyed his career."

"Why didn't he ask the dean for help?" Audra picked up the dandy brush and began to buff Pryde's golden coat. "It makes total sense."

"Probably because he'd have looked like a wimp if he said he couldn't handle two students." Joe finished combing out the white mane. "They were lucky they messed with him, not a professor who would have sued them for slander."

"What would you have done?"

"It's not an issue for me. Pre-med would be too tough for your sisters. They'd never get through the four years of undergraduate science or math courses. So, they couldn't even walk into my classroom."

"They're spoiled," Audra said, "not stupid."

"And spoiled women don't become doctors, sweetheart." Joe cleaned Pryde's hooves. "If the academics aren't too much for them, completing an internship would be. It takes guts and brains to become a veterinarian."

He had a point, but she certainly wouldn't tell him that. Instead, she went for the pads that protected the horse from the saddle. She slid them into place on the palomino's back. Joe headed for the tackroom, then returned with the silver-decorated saddle that Roy loved. It was a twenty-fifth-year anniversary present from Marlene for her husband and Pryde never wore anything else.

Audra glanced at her watch. "Time to go. Aunt Marlene wants the kids in line-up in an hour and it takes forty minutes to ride into downtown Snohomish."

"But I didn't get my real kiss yet."

"Complaints. Complaints."

She caught her breath when he snagged her wrist. He pulled her against him, and she melted. How could she deny the magick of his touch? He threaded his hand in her hair. She trembled when he cupped the back of her head, feeling her pulses jump. He lowered his head and their lips met. The fierce kiss ended far too soon when Pryde nudged her in search of another carrot.

She barely managed to whisper. "The parade."

"I know. Wait till tonight, *Stinkerbelle*."

Shortly after eleven in the morning, the latest members of the Silver Flying A's upheld the tradition started by their parents. Audra stood on the sidewalk near the reviewing stand and watched the troupe ride toward her, led by Marlene on a prancing Pryde. The spacing between the kids was perfect. Each horse was the prescribed ten feet from its partner and the same distance from the pair in front.

The red and white costumes on the riders and the horses added even more elegance. Despite the balloons, sirens from the fire trucks and police cars in the parade, and the regular explosion of firecrackers, the horses remained calm. It was because of the way that Marlene trained her kids to expect the proverbial unexpected. *No accidents today*, Audra prayed. *No rearing, jumping, or spooking. Don't act normal, behave the way that you've been taught*, she silently told the horses, remembering all the lessons that her aunt and uncle instilled when she was a child.

Joe gripped her hand. "It's okay. Sean and Elinor say Marlene never changes. She still teaches the kids the safest place to stay is on top of their horses no matter what."

"I know." Audra watched her aunt ride to the far end of the intersection and rein Pryde to a standstill. "I'm glad she makes them wear helmets."

"Me too. Now watch the drill."

A blast from Sandy's whistle caused the forty riders to turn their horses into a single line and face the judges on the reviewing stand. Then, Marcie led the club through a series of maneuvers. Single file to doubles to four horses abreast, heading toward Marlene, before the kids split off and rode back down the street. Next came a series of wheels, with the inside horse standing still while the other four revolved around it. The kids finished by lining up in front of the community leaders where Sandy led them through a timed salute.

After a round of applause and cheers, the club members followed their leader down the main street. Audra felt tears burn her eyes. The onlookers might not know how much effort it took for the kids to ride that well in this situation, but she did. She was proud of them. Whether they took the trophy home or not, it didn't matter. They were still a credit to the club that her aunt and uncle started so many years before.

Audra eased closer to Joe when he slipped an arm around her waist. "What's the schedule for the rest of the day?"

"The picnic at Marlene's. Then, I've got to relieve Dad and take evening hours at the clinic. I can come to the farm about midnight if that works for you. I have to stay until the fireworks are over and make sure we don't have any injured critters."

"That sounds fine," Audra said. "I'm going by Ginger's later to collect some of my things. We'll spend tonight unpacking and taking care of the animals at the farm."

18

HORSES WERE TIED AROUND THE YARD, IN THE ORCHARD AND A few dozed in the small corral. Back in his stall, Pryde munched afternoon hay, accepting carrots as his due. Parents, siblings, and club members circulated around the picnic tables, enjoying the varied menu. Audra had helped bring out casseroles, making sure all the guests were fed before she sat down to eat between Joe and Ethan.

"What happened to Gavin?" Audra asked. "I haven't seen him since this morning."

"The twins got in his face," Ethan said. "And he didn't want to cause problems for Marlene. This isn't one of her favorite days."

"I know that," Audra said. "She really misses Uncle Roy more than ever on parade days when the club brings home the trophy. Unfortunately, you can't surgically implant empathy in those two princesses."

"I'm willing to try," Joe drawled. "Got a scalpel?"

Audra laughed and Ethan chuckled.

"Well, I'll load up a plate for Gavin and take it by Sean's," Audra said. "And I'll stick around to make sure it's people food, not puppy snacks."

"You're a good person, Audra." Ethan kissed her cheek. "Thanks for looking after my little brother."

"It's the least I can do." Audra touched his shoulder. "I'm sorry my sisters have caused so much hell and heartache."

"Not your fault," Ethan said. "You were a kid when they were kids and they've chosen not to emulate you."

"Sooner or later, they'll learn that morality isn't weakness," Joe said. "It's a life lesson. Now, quit flirting with my woman before I use this plastic knife to geld you, Ethan."

When she went into the kitchen after Joe left for the veterinary clinic, Audra found Brigid and Kate putting away the leftovers for the drill team. The older kids always rode in the evening parade up in Eagleville. Ethan had already left with the first load of horses and Clancy was nearly ready to go with the next trailer.

"Are you still hungry?" Brigid asked.

"Not me." Audra went in search of a box that would hold two full paper plates so the food wouldn't spill in the cab of her truck. "Gavin. I promised Ethan I'd drop off supper for him."

"Why isn't he here?" Red-haired and green-eyed, Kate looked like a younger shadow of Brigid. "Attendance is mandatory for all the club members, old and new."

"He was here this morning, but the twins went after him, so he left. He didn't want their argument to upset Aunt Marlene." Audra found a shallow box that had once held a dozen cans of fruit and carried it over to the table. "This will come in handy."

Kate put three pieces of crispy fried chicken on a plate. "Gavin needs to slap them down. It doesn't do any good for me to tell them to leave him alone when they attack if I'm not around."

Audra shared a look with Brigid, then went to their younger sister. "Honey, if you're not mad at him, why haven't you kissed and made up?"

"How can I?" A tear streaked down Kate's pale cheek. "I didn't trust him when he swore that he never touched them, that Vonnie lied when she said he was a perv. And Wendy backed her, not the truth, not my Gavin."

Audra put her arms around the younger woman and hugged her. "Honey, that's not all your fault. They're your little sisters. Of course, you believed them. Don't you think Gavin would have trusted Felicia and Tara if they came to him with a story about you?"

"That's what he said, but how can he ever love me again?" More tears fell. "I ruined everything, and I can't fix it."

Blinking back her own tears, Audra reached up to stroke the red hair and held her sister tight. "Yes, you can. You just aren't ready yet. You must cut the cord between you and the twins. You have to choose Gavin first."

"But she's a Dawson." Brigid gaped at them. "How can she turn her back on her own family? She can't. She won't."

"It's not turning her back," Audra said. "It's stepping up and making sure the whole family includes Gavin, making all of us honor her choice of a man, making everyone respect him."

"Oh, is that all?" Sarcasm laced Brigid's words and she glared at Audra. "Are you putting a phone booth in the front yard too? Getting her a cape and colored underwear?"

"She's right." Kate sniffed. "It's too hard."

"Today, it is." Audra hugged her sister one more time, then eased away. "Finish fixing a meal for Gavin. You don't want to turn Brigid loose with her ipecac. Someday, it won't be too hard to stand up."

"Really?" Grabbing a napkin off the table, Kate wiped her nose. "Promise?"

"You bet. I promise." Audra collected plastic silverware. "Once you get Mom totally on your side, she'll back you and that will make everything easier. And it's only her, Clancy, and the twins who need convincing. Brigid and I already want whatever makes you happy."

A long look from Brigid and then her sister nodded agreement. "We're on your side, Kate. If I were you, I'd convince Gavin to elope and take a job at a university a couple of states away. By the time, you guys moved back here, everything would be hunky dory."

"Not a bad idea," Audra said, but she knew her sister wouldn't do that, at least not yet.

When Audra left a few minutes later, Kate looked a little happier. She hadn't decided to reconcile with Gavin yet, but at least the option wasn't as far away as it had once been. Carrying the box, Audra headed for her pickup. She paused when she saw her aunt and mother in the circular drive watching different members leave and went to say goodbye.

"Are you headed home for chores?" Marlene asked.

"Yes. I'm sorry I'll miss the other parade, but I don't have anyone to look after the stock for me." Audra nodded at her mom. "I'll be up on Sunday afternoon."

"Sounds great, honey." Darlene glanced at the plates. "Is Ginger coming for supper?"

Audra shrugged. "Last I heard she was working most of the day. Why? Did you want me to invite her to come along on Sunday?"

"That would be wonderful." Darlene smiled. "Then, she'll know we're open-minded and willing to accept your relationship."

"Mom, I appreciate the fact that you're so liberal." Audra took a deep breath. "Ginger and I have been best friends for years. We're not gay. We sleep with guys, not each other. And now, I'm going."

Darlene heaved a dramatic sigh. "You don't have to hide who you are from us. We're willing to love and accept you just the way you are."

"Good. Then, I'll bring Joe with me," Audra said. "He's the guy sharing my bed right now. The family can practice being nice to him.

"Got you there, little sis." Marlene laughed and looked in the box. "Taking dinner for you two?"

"No. I told Ethan that I'd drop off dinner for Gavin."

"Why would you when he didn't show up to help today?" Darlene asked.

"He did," Audra said. "He just wasn't willing to have World War Three with the twins in front of the whole club, past and present."

"They want to protect their older sister. It's extremely sweet of them."

"What would be sweet is if you kept standing up to them the way you did last spring, and they took responsibility for the rumors they spread about Gavin." Audra lifted her chin to meet her mother's gaze. "The only other option is for Kate and Clancy to choose their guys over the family and move out of state with them. None of us want that, do we?"

Leaving her mother to think about it, Audra strolled toward her truck. Now, all she had to do was try to get Gavin on board. If he talked to Kate when she felt so remorseful, they might reconcile this summer. Then, both would be a lot happier.

The next morning, Audra carried a bag with breakfast sandwiches and a cardboard tray with mochas up the walk to Ginger's apartment. Having decided that they were a couple, Darlene's next step would be to invite Ginger for supper. As the saying went, *denial wasn't just a river in Egypt.*

Clancy Dawson wasn't just the diva of drama. She'd taken lessons from their mother. Darlene didn't give up once she'd planned anything and this scheme interfered with what Audra had intended to do today, making the corrections to her upcoming book. Juggling the drinks, she bumped the doorbell with an elbow and waited. Finally, the door opened a bare inch. "I have coffee. Let me in."

"It better have whipped cream too." Ginger unhooked the security chain, then stepped back. Blonde hair swirled around her shoulders. She wore a long cotton nightgown, her signal she'd spent the night alone. "I worked till three this morning. Where's the blood?"

Audra laughed and handed over the giant mocha. "It's a triple shot, and you obviously need caffeine."

"Yes, I do." Taking the coffee, Ginger headed for the bedroom. "I'll be right back."

Audra set up the food on the glass coffee table in front of the couch, then plopped down on the couch with her own twenty-ounce latte. After two swallows, she reached for her ham, egg, and cheese sandwich. Halfway through it, she heard footsteps.

Ginger returned in a dark blue fleece bathrobe. "So, why do I get a visit at the crack of dawn?" The older woman curled up with her drink. "How was the parade?"

"Good. The kids took the trophy in Snohomish and the drill team got the other one up in Eagleville." Audra kept eating. "My family was there."

"What else is new?" Ginger picked up the other sandwich. "I don't know how your aunt could have organized forty kids and their horses without the Dawson clan."

"Probably not, but Marlene would have tried." Audra finished her breakfast, then said, "My mother has decided I'm gay."

"Really?" Ginger choked on her sandwich. "What does she think you and Joe are doing? Knocking boots for fun?"

"I'm cheating on you with him."

"Well, you slut."

"Exactly." Audra picked up her deep-fried hash-brown. "To show how open-minded she is, she's invited you and me up for dinner on Sunday. It's to foster a reconciliation between us."

"Really?" Ginger asked again. "Brigid's cooking, right? What are we having?"

"That's all you have to say?" Audra eyed her friend. "What's for supper? Aren't you upset?"

"Why would I be?" Ginger interspersed bites of her sandwich with sips from the mocha. "Your family is trying to get at you, and they want to use me to do it. It's a win-win for them. They get rid of Joe when he hears you and I are a couple, a pretty sick one if you're cheating on me and we're still together. He leaves you because he thinks you're playing him. You and I have a falling out over it when you decide I set this up. And you're on your own so you can support your family for the rest of your life."

"And they think I'm the cynical one." Audra finished her hash-brown and wiped her greasy fingers on a napkin. "I learned from a master. So, what are we doing about it?"

"The three of us are going to dinner on Sunday," Ginger said. "Call Brigid and ask her what she wants us to bring. I'll arrange to get the night off work. Tell Joe that he's escorting both of us. With any luck at all, they'll think we're all sleeping together."

"No way am I sharing him with you. He's mine." That was the first time she'd said it. Now, why did it feel so right? Audra bunched up the wrappers from her breakfast and put them in the paper sack. "Do you want to bring a date?"

"No. If your family is putting the fun back in dysfunctional, I don't know a single guy that could handle the pressure. You said that Joe's different. He's known your family for ages, right?"

"Since we were kids."

The doorbell interrupted their conversation and Audra stood. "I'll get it. Are you expecting company?"

"No. I guess I better get dressed." Carrying her cup, Ginger stood and left the living room. "Be right back."

The bell pealed again, and Audra walked down the short hall to the door. She unlocked it but left the security chain in place. "Who is it?"

"Art Watkins."

"What?" Audra opened the door and stared up at the tall, white-haired man. "Why on earth are you here?"

"Shouldn't that be my question?" He grinned at her, his sky-blue eyes the same color as his son's. "Joe told me that you two are dating and your momma is upset. She called me three times last night and she hasn't done that in years, not since the last time she had an injured horse."

"Yes, Joe and I are seeing each other. And yes, my mother's freaking out." Audra hesitated, then opened the door. "You may as well come in. We're trying to figure out a way to convince her that I'm not gay. Ginger and I are best friends."

"Well, your momma sent me to invite her for supper on Sunday so you two can work out your differences."

"She just doesn't listen." Audra heaved a sigh. "The family would do better if they decided to celebrate my birthday a few days early and they asked my best friend to join the rest of us for dinner."

"Not a bad idea." Art grinned at Ginger as she came into the room, wearing black sweatpants and a sloppy t-shirt. "Good morning. I'm the next wave."

She smiled, pushed blonde curls out of her face. "Sorry, Doc. Audra beat you and she brought me coffee."

"I didn't know that was a requirement." He chuckled. "Now, what are we doing about your family, Audra?"

"I'm starting to consider a divorce."

"You never will cut them off." Ginger sat on the couch. "Next plan?"

Art ran a hand through his salt and pepper hair, concern sliding across his tanned features and landing in his eyes. "When was the last time they had a birthday party for you, Audra?"

"When I turned twelve and my dad didn't show up," Audra said in even tones. "I wanted to wait for him to get home from work to open my presents. Mom took me aside and told me that he wouldn't be there. They were divorcing. She needed me to step up and act like an adult, a partner to her."

19

WHILE THEY CLEANED HER BOXES OUT OF GINGER'S STORAGE area, Audra thought about her birthday. She'd be thirty-five in less than a week and sometimes she didn't feel any older than the child who took on an adult role so many years ago. When he left, Art had promised to talk to her mother and let her know that he approved of the relationship with Joe. Of course, then the older veterinarian added that he really didn't feel it was his business to tell his adult son how to run his life either. Ginger warned Art not to pass that on or Darlene would show him the door.

"What do you have in this carton?" Ginger puffed as she put the cardboard box on the tailgate of the Ford 150. "Bricks?"

"No." Audra laughed. "Books. And you can't see what kind until I get them back to the pony farm and unpacked, Ms. Book-a-holic. I've been throwing books in boxes for as long as I can remember. When the box is full, I bring it to your place."

"I am so spending the day with you and helping you get settled into your new digs." Ginger grinned before she turned back toward the basement. "And I dibs a book I haven't read. There must be at least one or two, maybe a half-dozen."

"Undoubtedly." Audra slid the box into place, then went to carry out another carton. She was going to miss the old-time liquor store near the family farm where the owner saved empty boxes for her. They were the perfect size to pack the assortment of keeper paperbacks and hardcovers. Of course, the downside was that she looked like a total lush. Nobody would believe she barely finished a bottle of wine in a month, well unless she spent too much time up at the Dawson ranch with her mother and sisters. They were enough to make her buy a truckload of Riesling and not share a single glass.

She and Ginger emptied the locker and loaded the truck. A short time later, they were at the pony farm and unloading the boxes. They carried the cartons into the kitchen and stacked them neatly in the back corner.

"Where are they going for keeps?" Ginger asked.

"The fiction will end up in the living room. The research ones go in my office." Audra grimaced. "I should have labeled the boxes instead of trusting their contents to my memory. There's no way I know which ones are which."

"Well, that's why you invited me. I'll be in book heaven. Where's your office?"

Audra led the way into the small bedroom. "Here. It's perfect. I just have to move the furniture out to Jake's old room."

"Why didn't you do it when Joe was here to help?"

"Because when Elinor called, she gave me permission to repaint his room sunshine yellow. We did that instead." Audra glanced at the bed, dresser, and wardrobe. "Oh, God. What was I thinking? This is impossible."

"Not yet. Show me the other bedroom. I want to see how the color came out."

"Okay." They left Elinor's old room and headed through the kitchen to the living room, then opened the bedroom door to what was once Jake's room. They stepped into what Audra privately called her *summertime place*—somewhere that she'd always wake up cheerful – even on the gray mornings that Western Washington had in abundance.

"I love it." Ginger opened the mini blinds on the side window so the July sun lit the room. "I'm almost ready to move in too."

"I don't know," Audra teased. "You do and my mom will know we're a couple."

Ginger shrugged. "As long as you realize that if we were truly together, your family would feel just as threatened and do anything to split us up, that's fine."

Audra froze. She hadn't even considered the idea. What kind of idiot did that make her? She'd simply been concerned because her family didn't know her as a person. What if they did and this was all an emotional game to try and control her life? She'd believed the twins playing mudpies with Kate's and Clancy's weddings was some sort of immature stunt, not a symptom of a deeper problem.

She gazed at Ginger who had tipped her head back to study the cream ceiling, then focused on the walls again. Finally, the older woman picked up the drop cloth to look at the brown rug. "What are you thinking?"

"That we should go shopping and buy an emerald, green carpet," Ginger said. "It would give your new room the feel of a garden. We could get a wallpaper border and do a chair-rail variation."

"And the furniture?" Audra asked. "What are we doing about that?"

"We should go have burgers at Billy-Bob's, pick up some strong men and bring them back to move the furniture," Ginger said. "Either that or you could call Joe and put him in charge of finding guys. But he should lay the new carpet first and then move the bed. Got a tape measure? Let's see how big the room is and how much carpet we have to buy."

"Now, I know why you get the big money." Laughing, Audra went in search of her purse. First, she'd call Joe. Then, it was the way Ginger always said. When the going got tough, the tough went shopping.

———

Standing on the far side of the room, Audra studied the space. The queen-sized bed took up the center of the room, facing the windows. She liked the arrangement. The sunlight would wake her in the morning. The nightstands flanked the bed, lamps on them so she could read at night. The dresser and wardrobe were on the inside wall. She glanced at Joe as he and Gavin carried in a long, low bookcase. "Over here."

"Are you sure you want it on the outside wall?" Gavin asked.

"Positive. It will help insulate the room."

"And if we put a chair in the corner along with a pole lamp, you'll have a reading good time," Joe said.

Before she answered, she heard a shriek from the living room. She hurried out the door and found Ginger hunched over a box. "What's wrong?"

"I don't believe this." Ginger held up a trade paperback of a scantily clad blonde draped over a wolf. "Do you know what this is?"

"I'm going out on a limb here and calling it a book." Gavin's gaze narrowed and he advanced on her. "Is that a Destynee LaFleur? Give it up."

"No way." Ginger gasped. "It's not just a book. It's mine. I got it first."

"It has a cover and pages," Joe pointed out, teasing her. "I'd call it a book too. And I'll give you more money for it than Gavin will."

Ginger clutched the paperback to her chest. "Philistines. I'm surrounded by uneducated idiots."

"They're college professors," Audra said. "They aren't idiots. And they totally fixed up the bedroom. It's looking awesome."

"Not as awesome as this." Ginger stroked the cover of the book she held. "You have an entire collection of Destynee LaFleur's romances, even the ones that nobody can find. Do you know how long I've been looking for this book?"

Audra crossed the room. She knelt, closed up the box. It was going to her office where nobody else would look at the author copies. She scooped up the carton. "I have a feeling you're going to tell us."

Ginger cuddled the paperback. "It's her first book with the original cover. It's been out of print forever and you have ten copies just sitting here. How did you manage it?"

What was she supposed to say? How could she lie to her best friend? Nobody knew about the books she wrote at night, especially not Ginger who was a hyper-critical reader. No answer came and she couldn't meet her best friend's gaze.

"Where did you find the books?" Ginger asked again. "She's one of my favorite authors."

"Along with a dozen others," Audra said. "It's why I always give you a gift card from *Barnes and Noble* on holidays so you can shop."

"But these books?" Ginger stared longingly at the box Audra held. "Can I look again? I won't scream. I promise. Where should I hunt for them?"

"If Audra's had them a while, she can't tell you," Joe said. "They're probably from a close-out sale at a bookstore. And if she has ten of that one, I need a copy. It'll make points with my secretary because I always dump a lot on her at the start of the semester. Things are going to get worse since I'm the Dean of the department."

"Dream on, animal guy," Gavin said. "Kate and I read them to each other. If I take her Destynee's first book and a box of chocolates, I'll be happily married in three days."

"What's going on?" Ethan asked as he came into the room. "I heard Ginger holler."

"She found a book by a favorite author." Audra hesitated, then returned the box to its position in front of her friend. "Okay, you can look for other titles, but remember what you said, no yelling. And you can give copies of the first book to Joe and Gavin."

"Who is it?" Ethan asked.

"Destynee LaFleur," Ginger's tone was hushed. "She writes

the hottest romances. They're amazing and her heroes totally howl at the moon. And Audra has all her titles."

"Romances?" Ethan shook his head. "No wonder I never heard of her. What man would read that?"

"Now, he's what I'd call a Philistine," Joe drawled. "My students love her stuff. They got me hooked on them."

Audra struggled to analyze her emotions. She was happy he read her books, wasn't she? Of course, people liked her stories. The quarterly royalties and her advances proved she didn't just write them for herself. However, meeting actual readers felt vastly different.

"Do you know how you can tell the price is too high for a used copy?" Joe asked Ethan.

"How?" Ethan folded his arms, looking bored.

"It's autographed." Ginger and Gavin chorused, laughing at the puzzled look he gave them.

"I don't get it," Ethan said. "All authors sign their books."

"Not Destynee. Her publisher says she's so busy on her next book, she doesn't have time to hit the conventions or bookstores," Ginger said. "She could be anyone."

"Or he could be anyone," Joe said. "Even Ethan. If he were writing them, none of us would ever know. And there are men who write romance. My secretary told me that."

"He does spend a lot of time on the computer," Audra said, grateful for the distraction. Teasing Ethan would take the focus off her collection of Destynee LaFleur novels.

"I am not a romance author," Ethan told them, a muscle twitching in his jaw.

"That could just be his cover story," Gavin said. "We'll have to ask Clancy. I bet she would tell us how romantic he is and what he does in his spare time."

"You're the English professor," Ethan said, glaring at his younger brother. "You'd be a better author than I would."

"That might be true," Ginger kept cuddling her book. "Destynee uses a lot of literary allusions from classical works. She loves Shakespeare and since Gavin teaches it, then he could be my favorite author."

"And I'd be laughing all the way to the bank because romance captures more than fifty percent of the literary marketplace," Gavin said, "but it's not me."

Late that night, Audra woke to lamplight and the sound of a low chuckle. She lifted her head slightly from its place on Joe's chest. "What are you doing?"

"Reading." He stroked her hair. "Go back to sleep."

She yawned. "I don't know if I can. Read to me."

"I'm in the middle of the book. I don't want to go back to the beginning. I want to know what happens next."

"Then, just read from where you are."

"That won't bother you?" He turned a page.

"No. Read to me." She closed her eyes. "You can stop when I fall asleep again."

The next day, Audra stared at the computer screen, half-amused, half-puzzled by Ginger's, Gavin's, and especially Joe's reaction to her first published book originally released more than sixteen years before. It'd been a good story, but she knew she'd improved in her craft since then and was a much better writer. When Joe read to her the night before, it'd taken a while before she enjoyed the interaction between the characters. She kept hearing the mistakes she'd made when she wrote the book. He apparently hadn't noticed any differences between Destynee LaFleur's early work and her later ones.

The only person who'd penetrated her secret identity was probably dead, murdered last April when she followed a serial killer into the Mount Baker National Forest after he attacked her best friend. Okay, Beth would say he was an alleged or suspected killer. Her adopted cousin was still gone. She'd figured out that Audra and Destynee were one and the same, but Beth was a homicide detective who delighted in solving puzzles.

And I screwed up. I should have used a story that was in the news instead of one she gave me. No wonder Beth recognized the details when she read the published book months later. A more than competent cop, she'd confronted Audra with the facts, not giving up until she got a confession. Audra smiled at the memory. She'd intended to dedicate *Howling* to Beth who willingly provided more background for the hero.

Revisions, Audra told herself. It was time to get back to work if she wanted this book to hit the stores on time. She heard someone shooting off fireworks and for a moment wondered how combat veterans dealt with the constant *pop-pop-pop* sound. Beth said more than once it reminded her of weapons firing. If she had time off around the Fourth, she headed into the National Forest with her dog and horse on an extended camping trip.

Maybe that was the way to deal with her absence. Audra ignored the popping of fireworks down the street and decided to pretend that her adopted cousin was off on another of her mini-vacations in the wild country around Mount Baker. Then her disappearance wouldn't hurt as badly.

Back to work. Audra reread the scene in front of her, remembering her editor's advice. The character needed to be consistent. Now, why was the heroine refusing to commit to her newly found mate? Because it was too soon. Having a one-night hook-up was one thing, but when it turned into a permanent relationship by morning, that would be downright scary. Okay, here was a reason for the woman to be defensive and for the hero to pursue her. Audra began typing.

Lunch was a sandwich and coffee at the computer. She continued working on the edits until chore time. She'd heard intermittent fireworks through the afternoon and that meant the ponies would once again be spending the rest of the day inside. By tomorrow, they'd be ready to run before the farm reopened at noon. Audra saved the revisions, stood, and stretched while the computer went through its shut-down procedures.

She headed into the kitchen, closing the office door behind her. Leaving the coffee cup on the counter, she stretched and twisted again. She'd forgotten how much her back stiffened up when she had a long writing stint. She scooped up her pink quilted vest off a chair at the table and slid into it. Humming, she opened the back door and froze.

A big black, brown, and white shaggy dog lay on the porch. Bluish-green vomit pooled around his mouth. A bullet wound creased the skull and blood still trickled onto the deck. She saw a second injury on his back leg. She heard a low whine and the tail moved in a faint effort to wag.

"Alive? You're alive?" She went back into the house. She grabbed her purse, a stack of towels, and a clean blanket from the top of the dryer. Then she returned to the porch. "Hang on, buddy. I'll get you some help."

She eyed the dog. She was close enough to see that he was male. She estimated his weight somewhere between seventy to eighty pounds. How was she supposed to load him in her truck? He weighed nearly as much as she did. She dug out her cell phone and called the veterinary clinic. No answer, but Joe had to be there taking care of the critters staying over through the holiday week. She left a message, then tried his cell. He didn't pick up. Another message.

First things first. She went to her truck, started it, and put down the tailgate. Then, she backed the Ford as close as she could get it to the steps. She spread a blanket in the bed of the pickup. Next step. She went back to the dog and laid a big beach towel partway under him. A plastic tarp would be better, but she didn't have time to search the barns and toolshed to find an appropriate sized one. "I read about this when I was doing research for a book. Now, we'll see if it works."

The dog whimpered when she began pulling on the towel, sliding him toward her rig. She kept talking, hoping to soothe him with her voice. "Joe will look after you. If anyone can make you better, he can. He'll figure out who hurt you too."

She stopped when the dog struggled to rise. He collapsed on the towel again. She stroked the soft fluffy fur on his shoulder. "Just stay put, buddy. Let me do the work. It's okay."

He tried to lick her hand and she smelled an odd, sweet odor on his breath. She didn't know what it was, but she didn't like it. He was a big dog, but he wasn't mean. If he had been, he'd have snapped at her by this point. Instead, he accepted her help.

More pulling and she was able to drag him into the truck. She arranged his body on the blanket. She didn't cover him with the towel. It would just blow out on the road. She climbed out and closed the tailgate. She locked the house, then drove out the front gates and snapped the padlocks on them too. She didn't know what happened to the dog, but she wasn't leaving the farm open while she was gone.

It didn't take long to reach the vet clinic. The sight of both Joe's Jeep and Art's pickup pleased her. She parked as close to the back emergency doors as she could, then honked the horn. The sound brought Joe outside. She climbed out to greet him. "Got a sick dog here."

"Another one?" Wearing blue scrubs, Joe strode toward her. "Dad brought in a little poodle mix that had ingested antifreeze. We did everything we could, but we lost it."

Audra froze, remembering the strange smell. When they did yearly maintenance on the farm rigs, they had to keep the antifreeze away from the animals that lived on the Dawson ranch. "I'll bet that was what did this guy in. And he's been shot too."

"Well, let's see what we can do." Joe patted her shoulder. "And if I have a meltdown around this damned holiday, cut me some slack. I don't think the founding fathers had terrifying helpless critters in mind when they organized a revolution."

"If we had a time machine, we could ask."

He managed a chuckle and then he was over the tailgate, examining his new patient. "He's a Bernese Mountain Dog, not much more than a pup. He isn't full grown. Shocky. Go help Dad bring out a stretcher. We'll have to wheel him inside."

She followed directions, unperturbed by the tone or the order. She loved the fact animals came first with him. She stopped, stunned for a moment. Did she love him? She shook her head. No, she wouldn't think about that now. She'd put off the thought as long as possible. She'd adored Ethan for so long. How did Joe change her life in less than a month?

Once the dog was in the operating room, she left the two veterinarians to work a miracle. She had stalls to muck, ponies to feed, a cow to milk, and a bunch of other critters to look after. She'd check the lost and found ads on the computer once she finished chores. Joe had promised to look for a microchip. He said the dog was valuable and people might be looking for him. If not, Audra offered to take him.

She really didn't need a dog, but this one was special. She couldn't remember another one who had been so affectionate when he was injured. Obviously, his original owners had loved and cared about him. They'd probably turn up and take him home. If not, he deserved another good place to live. She frowned as she pulled in the gates at the farm. Art had told them antifreeze poisoning was a common problem in the area during the summer. Why hadn't she ever heard about it before? And what could she do about it?

———

Zane wandered through the evergreens that framed the O'Malley farm. He'd had a shooting good time that afternoon and left three dying dogs to be eaten by the local coyotes. The fun part was that the varmints wouldn't realize that the carrion would kill them – due to the rat poison and antifreeze they'd ingested.

He spotted the first two, but where was the big one? He'd found it on the internet. The stupid owners had claimed not to realize how big a Bernese grew or how much energy the pup would have. Zane had promised to give the dog a good home. He'd gotten it for free and once he brought it here, he hadn't bothered to feed it. What was the point? He wanted it to eat the tainted food and it wouldn't do that if it wasn't hungry.

Now, where was the carcass? The coyotes had been around, but it would take a few of them to drag off an eighty-pound body.

Then again, maybe not. If they started tearing the dog apart, they could pull away the pieces. Zane smiled. He'd come out earlier in the day tomorrow and look around for the scavengers. There would be a few more bodies to scatter near his animal graveyard.

————

The sun teetered on the horizon when Joe parked in front of the three-bedroom rambler. He climbed the steps to the back porch and tapped on the door.

Footsteps and then Audra glanced through the window before she opened the door. She tilted her head. "So, how's the dog?"

"Surviving." Joe leaned down to kiss her, threading his hands into her golden-brown hair. "Good rescuing. He may make it if his body throws off the poison. We're having trouble with the microchip. We need Sarah to do her computer magick so we can read it. Meantime, Dad called his contacts at the various shelters and the cop shop. Nobody's reported him missing."

Audra frowned up at him, worry in her brown eyes. "That doesn't make sense. He's a nice dog. He didn't even growl at me when I was loading him in the pickup, and I know he was in pain."

"He's also a big guy and he's only a little more than half-grown. When he's back in good health, he'll eat you out of house and home."

"Well, you have to save his life first, Dr. Joe."

"We're doing our best. Dad will stay with him tonight and I'll go back in the morning." Joe leaned against the doorframe and eyed her. In shorts, a t-shirt, and flip-flops, she looked as if she'd barely turned twenty, not as if she'd be thirty-five next week. "Dinner? Do you want to go out for a meal?"

"No. I have spuds in the oven and a salad in the fridge. Do you want to do the guy thing and grill the steaks?"

"Sounds great."

"Good. Then, I'll open the wine. White, okay? I don't want to look at red."

20

SHE WAS FEEDING HAY WHEN THE BARN DOOR OPENED AND JAKE rushed in, followed by Lynn. Audra greeted them with a smile. "So, how was your trip?"

"Awesome." Jake ran across the barn to hug her, then took the next flake of hay to feed. "We have lots of cousins and we went to the movies and swimming and the arcade and everything with them."

While her brother chattered about his adventures, Lynn heaved a dramatic sigh. "You can't imagine how awful it was putting up with ten boys his age. The only time it was peaceful was when Sean and some of the uncles took a bunch of them on a fishing trip and they were gone all night."

"We camped up by the lake," Jake corrected. "And we cooked our fish over a fire. Lynn was almost grounded when she and the other girls got lots of make-up at a store. The lady slathered so much on her that Mom said that she looked like a clown in a circus."

"Sounds awesome," Audra teased, dropping a flake of alfalfa-grass into Bonanza's manger. She winked at Lynn. "I got in nearly as much trouble when I took Kate and Clancy to get their ears pierced when they were your age. Your mom couldn't have been as ornery as Aunt Marlene and my mom together."

"She tries." Lynn grinned. "And her cousin Helen wanted to get me a perm, but Mom exploded."

"You didn't ask first when you got them earrings?" Jake gaped at her, his eyes wide in shock. "Wow, you are a hero."

"I wouldn't call it that," Audra said, refusing to add that Kate had sworn they already had their mother's permission and just needed a ride to the mall. "I was a risk-taker back then."

That earned a laugh from Elinor as she entered the main barn. "So, where can we jump in on chores? How did things go?"

"Everything went fine," Audra said. "The ponies will need a run this morning. Someone shot off fireworks all week, so I kept them in the barn."

"Good idea, but we can call the cops today and report it if we hear O'Malley do it again. He's the worst offender," Elinor said. "Most of my other neighbors have brains and animals so the craziness ends on the Fourth. Yesterday was the county cut-off so it's over until Labor Day."

Lynn carried two flakes of hay across the barn to Flicka and Tonka. "Uncle Gavin said the dogs were fine. While we were gone, he kept them inside and let them play in the arena at Sean's. We didn't hear any fireworks last night."

"There weren't any around Aunt Marlene's either when we were getting the kids off to the parades," Audra said. "That was good. Like Joe says, loud noises and horses don't mix."

"Dr. Joe?" Lynn asked. "The vet?"

"I thought he was only hanging out while we were here because he's mostly Sean's friend," Jake said, with an innocent look.

"He's the only guy I know named Joe and he's on vacation, so he comes around a lot," Audra told the kids. "I think growing up in the club was one of the reasons he always wanted to be a vet."

"And I'm sure he's exceptionally good at it. He saved Lightning. Well, you both did. You nursed him back to health." Elinor gave the two kids a stern look. "Don't even think about it. Now, go get the grain and we'll finish the chores."

The two vanished out the barn door in the direction of the feed room. Audra focused on her boss. In jeans and a western blouse, Elinor was the picture of a cowgirl, not a disciplinarian. "What's going on?" Audra asked. "I must be missing the subtext."

Elinor fed the last of the hay. "Didn't Clancy tell you what they did to get Sean and me together?"

Audra shook her head and waited.

"Jake decided that he wanted a new dad because my ex never had time for him. Between the fantasy books and his favorite movies, there was plenty of input to show Jake that magick was the answer to his prayers. Somehow, he got Lynn to go along with it and the two of them cast what they called, *the cowboy spell*. And then Sean showed up at their 4-H meeting."

"He's the answer to a magic spell?" Audra struggled to control her giggles. "Does he know that?"

"He knows." Elinor pushed the wheelbarrow into the far corner. "And you don't want those two matchmakers casting a spell on you or doing everything they can to fix you up with a guy."

"I might if I could have Harrison Ford, back when he was Han Solo in the early Star Wars movies."

"You don't get to pick," Elinor said, with a reminiscent smile. "They do. And considering how tricky they are, they may already be out at night doing their little magical routines."

———

Sitting in the passenger seat of his jeep, Audra glanced at Joe. "I can't believe we're doing this. Make that, I can't believe you want to go to my mom's for dinner. You know she and my sisters will be out to get you. You and Ginger are crazy."

"It's a united front." Joe pulled into the parking lot at the apartments. "Go roust your friend. Besides your family needs to get used to me. Otherwise, the holidays won't be fun, they'll be an endurance contest."

"What holidays?"

"All of them," Joe said. "It's not like Dad and I have many relatives. He's the black sheep of the Watkins clan since he opted for veterinary medicine, not law enforcement. And I followed in his footsteps, so I figure we'll be doing Thanksgiving, Christmas, Easter, and the rest with your relatives after we're hitched."

"Married?" Audra stared at him, shocked. "That was just a rescue when my mom was in bitch mode last week."

"Oh, I wasn't joking at the wedding or afterward," Joe said, with a quick smile. "I'm not proposing to you yet. You'll probably say no. Better go get Ginger so we're not late."

Audra unbuckled her seat belt and opened the door. She slid out of the four-wheel-drive, trying to analyze her emotions as she headed up the sidewalk. Finally, she decided she was confused but oddly happy. Why? She didn't want to get married, did she? Of course, she also hadn't planned on an affair with anyone. She'd been chasing a dream so long that she didn't know what she'd have done with Ethan after he succumbed to her wiles.

She giggled. She sounded like one of her heroines in a historical romance. She rang the bell and heard footsteps inside. "Come on, girlfriend. Let's rock and roll!"

Brigid was the only one in the house when they arrived at the Dawson spread. She took the bouquet of mixed flowers that Joe offered and gestured to the counter. "You can put the wine there."

Ginger followed directions and put the three bottles of Riesling next to the waiting glasses. "So, where is everybody? Didn't they remember we were coming?"

"Clancy and the twins are handling chores. Kate and Mom are signing in the resident campers and assigning them to counselors." Brigid took a vase from the cupboard and began to arrange the flowers. She glanced at Joe. "Got a sick cat in the pantry."

Audra went to open the door and Joe followed. "What happened?"

"Catfight in the barn."

"Okay, I gotcha covered," Joe said. "Come hold the patient, Ginger. I'll share the doughnuts that Brigid is going to make me."

"I didn't say anything about doughnuts," Brigid retorted. "I'm feeding you supper."

"Doughnuts," Joe insisted. "It's cheaper than a vet bill."

"Make mine with extra frosting," Ginger called over her shoulder.

When the two disappeared into the adjacent room, Audra snitched a piece of carrot off the tray of appetizers, eying the concern on her younger sister's face. "What's up?"

"What are you thinking?" Brigid whispered. "Mom's going to have a fit when she sees the two of them."

"Well, Joe wants to marry me, and Ginger's open to sharing, so we're here." Audra bit into the carrot fresh from the garden, chewed, and swallowed. She eyed the other veggies on the plate, grape tomatoes, celery, broccoli bits, tiny pieces of cauliflower, debating which one to try next. "We figured the family should get used to our little *ménage a trois*."

Brigid sighed, planted her hands on her hips. She struggled to hide a smile. "Okay, don't tell me the truth. But, when the screaming starts, just don't give me any crap. I warned you."

"I'll keep that in mind." Audra glanced at Joe when he came back into the room. "Need any help?"

"Nope. Just some supplies from the truck and then you can come with us to check the cats in the barn. We'll want to see the other guy."

For once drama wasn't served along with Brigid's pot roast when everyone gathered around the large dining table an hour later. There were a few nasty looks from Clancy, but Kate was on her best behavior. The twins had charm down to a fine art as they talked about the apartments they'd seen around the university. Audra deliberately didn't ask if they'd updated their resumes and found jobs yet.

Over coffee and apple pie, Darlene glanced at Audra. "Have

you decided what you want for your thirty-fifth birthday next week?"

"Homemade carrot cake with cream cheese frosting. Walnuts and raisins in the triple-layered cake," Audra said, "and lots of frosting."

"It's the same every year. No originality there," Clancy said. "Guess you don't get to be creative this time, Brigid. You have your orders."

"Oh, I think the family recipes were probably very original back when they were created," Audra said. "Can you imagine trying to make doughnuts on that old wood stove in the kitchen? Or dinners like this one?"

Ginger took the conversational ball and ran with it. Soon she had the family sharing memories of the Dawson family who had settled in the area more than a century before. Audra reached in the pocket of her jeans and turned on the mini-recorder. Since Joe gave it to her, she carried it everywhere.

She glanced at Joe. He winked at her but didn't interrupt the story that Darlene told about one of the early women in Liberty Valley who followed in her mother's footsteps and became a town marshal. Another story followed of a woman who built her own house from the foundation to the roof.

"Grand-Uncle Will told me that we had horse thieves in our lineage," Clancy said, "so not to think the Dawsons were purer than laundry soap."

"He said bank robbers," Kate corrected. "If they'd been horse thieves back in the day, we wouldn't be here. Back then, stealing a horse was tantamount to murdering someone and the perpetrator didn't last long once the law caught up with him."

Before the argument escalated, Darlene interrupted. "Audra, you never did say what you wanted for your birthday. Why not go back to school? I'm sure you don't want to spend the rest of your life managing one stable after another. What's your dream?"

Audra didn't answer right away. How could she say that she'd love it if she could write her books in the daytime instead of waiting until she finished work? Her family didn't have a clue what she did to pay off the mortgage. "I'll have to think about it."

"How would you pay for it?" Vonnie asked, widening her eyes. "You're the one who says, get a job."

"And what would you want to be?" Wendy leaped to support her twin. "Like you always tell us, it costs too much for college not to have goals."

Joe leaned back in his chair, sipping coffee. He winked at Audra. "Marry me and use my discount at Washington State University. Take as many different courses as you want and do the research so you can follow that high school dream of writing the great American novel."

"Really? You wanted to be a writer?" Ginger glanced at Audra, then turned her attention to Joe. "Me too? Don't all guys want sister-wives? I always wanted to be a great American author. I'd love to go to college on somebody else's nickel."

Audra propped her chin on a fist. "Don't you have to write the books to be a great voice in American lit?"

"There's always a catch," Ginger said. "Most writers say it takes months, even years to create a book. That's a lot of work."

"Everything worth doing has always taken effort," Darlene told her. "Of course, some books seem like they're cranked out on an assembly line."

Kate heaved a dramatic sigh. "Mom's about to get on her hobby horse and ride. Gavin brought me a book by one of my favorite authors and she hates that genre. So, like I said, "Don't read it." It's mine and nobody else has to enjoy it, but I do."

Audra winced. She'd known that her mother didn't enjoy romance, but there was nothing worse than having the fact slammed in her face like a punch in the nose. However, the ensuing conversation covered her reaction and hurt. Why didn't her family want to know who and what she was? Other than someone who paid the mortgage?

PART III

"Create your own reality ~ make your dreams true…"

— JOE WATKINS

21

Audra jolted awake and glared at her radio. The disc jockey babbled on about the lovely summer morning. That segued into the classic Donna Fargo hit. Leaving her to sing about being the happiest girl in the whole U.S.A., Audra grabbed her clothes and hustled for the shower. She and Joe had even gone to bed early, well early for her. It was barely eleven at night. How had she managed to oversleep today?

When she went through the kitchen, she found Pyewacket cheerfully ensconced in front of his cat food dish, eating breakfast. No sign of Joe. She went to look out the window and spotted his truck, Clancy's rig, and Elinor's pickup as well as Sandy's car. So, chores were well underway. This must be some sort of conspiracy to surprise her on her birthday. Smiling, Audra continued to the bathroom.

It turned out to be a wonderful start to the best birthday she'd had in a long time. Organized by Clancy, the day campers brought her flowers, chocolate, and a mocha. Brigid arrived with a carrot cake for all of them to share at lunch. It was more than Audra expected. Because of the responsibilities on the farm, family celebrations were usually held the Sunday after the actual day. When

Brigid left, she reminded Audra to show up alone for dinner that weekend.

"No, I'm bringing Joe," Audra said, walking her sister to the waiting truck. "You may as well get used to him being in the picture."

"It's not me. I'm not the one trying to keep my sisters from having lives. Mom's the one who feels threatened. She's on edge because it looks like Gavin and Kate will reconcile soon. The twins have acted out for the past three days, ragging on Kate until I'd run away from home if I were her."

"Life isn't a game of frozen tag, Brighty. We don't freeze in place to make others comfortable. It's an ongoing dance between our choices."

"I know that." Brigid fished a set of keys out of her purse. "Some people are better with change than others. Vonnie freaks when I tell her that she's just like Mom, but it's the truth. Both go crazy when things are unpredictable."

"And people often are." Audra hugged her sister. "Don't worry so much. It'll be fine. I promise."

"Well, have a good rest of your birthday."

"I will." Audra returned to work.

Hours later with chores done and everybody gone, she enjoyed the luxury of an empty house, empty that was except for her and Pyewacket. He sat on the bookcase by the living room window taking a leisurely bath. She debated being responsible and heading for her laptop but decided to have a glass of Reisling instead.

The cat's hiss followed by two books hitting the floor alerted her before she poured the wine. Her watch cat was obviously on patrol. She looked out the picture window and saw Joe's parked Jeep in front of the house. What upset the Siamese? Then, she saw Joe holding a leash and the dog watering the grass in the side yard.

She laughed. "Poor Pye. You're going to have to get used to company. No more being the only child. And if you go live with Lynn, she has a puppy too."

Pyewacket stalked across the room to perch on the back of the couch. Lashing his tail, the cream-colored cat gave her an evil glare. Audra shrugged and went to open the kitchen door. She walked out onto the porch and crossed to the steps. "Hey, guys. What's up?"

The tri-colored dog cocked his head, then bounded toward her, tail wagging in full sweeps. A lump rose in her throat as she headed to meet the pair. "He remembers me?"

"Why wouldn't he?" Joe asked, coming toward her. "Not every day a beautiful woman saves your life. I'd never forget the occasion either."

Audra dropped to her knees in the summer grass and gathered the half-grown pup in a hug. She buried her face in his fur so Joe couldn't see her tears. At ten, her father had told her that no man wanted to be around a *Sobbing Susie,* and it didn't matter if he had sold her horse right before the county fair when it was too late for her to train another one. She'd better stop blubbering or he'd give her a reason to cry.

Breathing in the aroma of puppy and trying to avoid his kisses, Audra struggled to control her emotions. When she was back in charge and trusted her voice not to shake, she said, "I'm so glad you brought him to see me. Where's his owner?"

"You're it." Joe held out the end of the leash. "Take him. Happy birthday."

"What?" Audra stroked the fur. She caught the dog's head in her hands and gazed into the dark brown eyes. "No way. He's too loving. Somebody put a lot of time and energy into him."

"When he was an itty-bitty bundle of joy. Then, he started growing and she couldn't keep him in an apartment, so she gave him to her brother. He gave the dog away to a guy he met on the Internet. They signed away all rights to him when they saw the vet bill. I've reprogrammed his microchip to show you as his owner."

Audra slowly stood and took the leash. The dog leaned against her, and she staggered. "Okay, you big lunk. Here's the first lesson. Sit."

"He doesn't know that word. You're looking at a guy who failed obedience school."

"I know you did, but what about my dog?"

Joe laughed. "There's my sharp-tongued, brown-eyed girl."

Audra sidestepped close enough to hug him. Then, she focused on the dog again, encouraging him to sit at her heel. "Thank you. He's the best present I've had in years. How much is the vet bill?"

"One night of wild loving should cover it."

"I'm not having sex with you to pay a bill." She grinned up at him. "Your dad helped save him, so what is he doing tonight?"

"He's busy chasing your mom. There's something about you Dawson women." Joe leaned down and kissed her. "Grab your purse, lock up and let's go shopping. Your new roommate needs some supplies."

Audra rumpled the dog's black fur again. She studied her new friend. He returned the favor. Back in what was normal health for him, he loomed even taller, more than two feet tall at the shoulder. He had some filling out to do before he reached maturity, but she hoped he'd reached his full height.

He was coal black with a white chest and rust-colored markings above his eyes, the sides of his mouth, the front of his legs with a bit more reddish-brown fur around his white chest. She giggled when she glimpsed a white horseshoe shape around his nose. He definitely belonged with her. All she had to do was train him to guard the farm and its four-legged inhabitants.

She nodded. "A new life deserves a new name, so I don't want to know what the people who threw him away called him."

"What are you calling him?"

"Navarre after my favorite dog book. I'll have to dig it out and read him the story." She petted the dog again. He was a fast learner and still sat by her heel. "What are we doing with him while we're at the store?"

"We can take him with us. Most of the pet stores welcome four-legged customers. He has good car manners." Joe shrugged. "He'll be fine if you want to leave him at home. It only took one correction for him to leave the cats alone at the clinic when I let him out of the pen."

"We'll take him with us. I want to be here when I introduce him to Pyewacket for the first time." She passed the leash to Joe. "I'll be right back. Let me lock up."

"Works for me."

Their trip to the pet store took almost two hours. Audra found all the things her new roomie needed, two beds – one for inside and one for the porch, toys including a stuffed white squeaky goat that Navarre insisted on carrying, his own dishes, a second retractable leash longer than the one Joe brought. She almost had a cartful when he lugged over a huge sack of dog food.

"Treats for training?" Audra asked. "Should we get him one of those big chewie rawhide bones?"

"Not unless you want to pay for me to do surgery to get the pieces out of his stomach."

She blinked. "But you see them all the time on TV."

"Sean has bred dogs for years and you'll notice he never gives them to his." Joe put the bag of food in the cart. His tone changed to that of a doctor in charge of the world. "Most of the time, companies use chemicals to clean off hair and prep the hides for treats."

"What do they use to clean off the chemicals?"

"Usually, a bleach rinse and that's not good for dogs."

She nodded and looked at the young dog lying on the floor, his stuffed animal between huge paws. "Anything else I need to know?"

"When it's clean, the bone is shaped and smoked. As the dog starts chewing it into pieces, the rawhide will slowly regain its original size. Swallowed, a piece may swell inside your dog's stomach. And the rawhide doesn't break down. Once swollen, the piece then has the potential to cause anything from mild to severe gastric upset, to death and it takes an operation to remove it."

"Well, he's not getting any of those for the rest of his life. What can he have?"

"We'll swing by the grocery and get him some frozen peas, almonds, cashews, and Brazil nuts. If you want to give him some chicken strips, then it's best to make your own."

She laughed. "I can just imagine what Elinor will say when I tell her I'm raiding her freezer and cooking up one of her organic chickens for my dog."

"You can always get dog cookies or strips from Sean the next time he makes them. I wonder if he told Elinor that he cooks for his dogs before the wedding."

Audra laughed. It would be fun to see her friend's face when she learned about that. "Oh, wait a minute. I didn't ask her about a dog before you brought me Navarre. I need to call and let her know that he's going to be on the farm."

"Already taken care of," Joe said. "I told her the whole story yesterday and the deal with the previous owners. She's good with you having four-legged protection."

"Really?"

"Really," Joe said. "Of course, Jake thinks you need a super-hero costume now that he knows you transported a comatose dog that weighs as much as a newborn colt to me."

Audra sighed and shook her head. "What am I supposed to do now? He's already been looking at me as if I have a lasso of truth."

"You can wear a *Wonder Woman* costume for me anytime."

"Don't hold your breath waiting for that to happen, Dr. Joe."

An hour later, they'd finished their shopping. Joe took Navarre behind the store for a walk, then all three of them were on the road. Audra frowned at him when he pulled into the parking lot at Billy-Bob's. "What are you thinking?"

"Dinner," Joe said. "Navarre has his stuffed goat to keep him company. I locked up his food. Let's take an hour for a quick burger and then we'll go settle him in at the farm."

Audra glanced over her shoulder at the sleeping dog. "He sleeps a lot. Should he be out of the clinic?"

"Hey, he has his own personal doctor. You're right. It'll take a bit more time for him to finish recovering from those toxins, but I have faith. He'll make it."

She walked beside him toward the restaurant, enjoying the feel of his arm around her waist. "This is the best birthday I've had in years. Thank you."

"Hey, it's not over yet. I have until midnight to make it even more memorable."

When they entered the main doors of Billy-Bob's, Audra saw her aunt at the reception stand, meeting and greeting customers before the hostess took them to their tables. Coming out of the station, Regina hurried to hug Audra. "Happy birthday, honey. I'm glad you came to see us. How's your day going?"

"It's been great, the most incredible birthday I've had in years."

"Well, we're packed so go grab a table in the *Fandango Room*. I'll send Ginger over with a complimentary glass of wine for you and a beer for Joe."

"That sounds wonderful." Audra kissed the older woman's cheek. "Hope you and Uncle Jim can stop by to chat for a couple of minutes."

"We'll try," Regina said. "Now, scoot."

Laughing, Audra obeyed. She wound her way through the dining room to the closed door on the far side. She opened it and stepped inside to a roomful of people. Elinor, Sean, Lynn, and Jake. Aunt Marlene. Grand-Uncle Will. Venus and her matching sisters, the triplets accompanied by their mother and brother. Joe's father and her mother, along with Kate and the twins. Ethan.

The room was decorated with balloons and streamers from corner to corner, like the motif used for Elinor's bachelorette party. Brightly wrapped presents filled a table in the middle of the room surrounding one of Brigid's sheet cakes.

Audra gaped at the crowd, stunned, and surprised. "What is this?"

"Your birthday party." Gavin came forward with a glass of

wine. "Here you go. You'll need it when Ethan makes them sing to you."

Audra glanced over her shoulder at Joe. "You did this."

"Guilty." He grinned down at her. "You deserve it. Now enjoy, *Stinkerbelle*."

"I'll get you for this. I know when your birthday is in November, Dr. Joe."

"Promises. Promises."

Two hours later, while Joe loaded the gifts of books, dog toys, and clothes in his Jeep, Audra found herself alone with her mother and the twins. "This was really nice. Thanks for coming down. I know how busy you are with camp."

"Well, like Joe pointed out, you only turn thirty-five once," Darlene said. "It's one of those major moments in a woman's life."

"If he's still around next July, he'll probably say that about your thirty-sixth birthday." Vonnie pasted on an innocent look. "And the next one right up till you're fat and forty."

Audra counted silently to ten, struggling to maintain her patience. Was she too old to slap her younger sister? Probably. "Well, we need to go so we'll see you on Sunday for dinner."

"It's a family affair," Wendy said in her sweetest tone. "That means just you."

"If I can't bring Joe, don't bother setting a place for me." Audra headed for the door, leaving the three of them to sputter behind her. So, she was being a bitch, but she didn't care! She'd been all things to all people for far too long. She was thirty-five and from now on, she'd do as she damned well pleased.

"What's up?" Joe met her in front of the restaurant. "Did I ruin your night by arranging a party?"

"No, you made my night." She brushed her mouth quickly over his. "Come on. I think you should get a present now."

He laughed, wrapped an arm around her waist. "I refuse to wear gift wrap, Stinky."

"How do you feel about ribbons?"

22

DAY CAMP OVER AND THE KIDS GONE, THE SILVER LAKE PONY Ranch staff clustered around a picnic table in the orchard. Lynn and Jake sat next to Elinor, listening to the weekly after-action report. Clancy passed the box of homemade doughnuts she'd brought in Sandy and Marcie's direction. "So, how did we do? How many students booked back?"

Once again, the week had been a rousing success. Audra listened to the report on new leasers and potential customers. Navarre lay beneath the table, pressed against her legs. He wasn't sure if he liked the other humans, but he adored Lynn and Jake's puppies. The three of them had a glorious romp after chores. Now Navarre slept deep, still in recovery from his bout with the poisons while the other two pups tussled in the grass under Ruler's watchful gaze.

"Well, it sounds like we have a handle on more students this fall," Elinor said. "I need to talk to Audra so would the rest of you start chores?"

Clancy ostentatiously looked at her watch. "I have to take off to be at the Lazy B by six."

Elinor raised a hand and pointed to the barn. "I'll pass out paychecks when the stalls are clean, watered, and fed. Audra will bring in the ponies before dark. Sooner to it, sooner through it, ladies and gentleman."

"Okay." Lynn slid out from her seat and started toward the main barn. "Are you coming, Jake?"

"In a minute." He glanced at Audra. "Lynn and Mom were talking about moving Gypsy to Sean's in August so she can practice more for the fair. What time will Dr. Joe be here? I wanted to ask him about taking Chipeta and Awesome then."

"I don't know how Joe will feel about moving the colt. He'll barely be four months in August," Audra said. "Why not wait till he's a bit older so the trip in the trailer won't be so hard on him? There's no rush and it would give us time to train him to load so he's not frightened."

"Can you really help me with that?"

"Sure," Audra said. "We'll start tomorrow in his lesson."

"Awesome." Jake beamed at her. "Did you find out about Tonka's mom and dad?"

"Not yet." Audra had forgotten that Clancy volunteered her for the task. "I'll talk to Aunt Marlene and make some calls tonight."

"She'll get to it sooner if she doesn't have the chores staring her in the face," Elinor said.

"Oh yeah, I'm gone." Whistling to his puppy, Jake darted off to catch up with his sister, and the other adults.

Audra laughed and glanced at his mother. "What did you want to discuss?"

"Reorganizing the farm," Elinor said. "In the fall, this place won't need both of us. Sean and I have discussed putting in a Snohomish Pony Ranch on his property and we're thinking to start in the fall. He has plenty of stalls and an indoor arena."

"So, when the rainy season begins, you could continue teaching lessons," Audra said. "Are you selling out here?"

"Not in this economy." Elinor leaned down to pet her blue heeler when he came to stand by her end of the table. "My grandfather bought the farm for me and there isn't a mortgage. My thought is to have you stay on and we'll run it year-round, not just be open on weekends from September to June. I could hold off on substitute teaching until things slowed down."

"Sounds like a great idea. If you try getting people to drive from Everett to Snohomish for lessons, you'd lose a certain number of clientele."

"That's right. Ethan stopped over last night and he's checking into the county permits for putting an indoor arena in here. He's going to swing by tonight or tomorrow to look at the area. My thought is you could teach lessons regardless of the weather."

"You'd need more ponies," Audra said. "Would Clancy teach there or here?"

"In Snohomish when I get busy enough to need her." Elinor held up her hand and took on her teacher's tone. "I know how much you two care about each other, and she'll always be your little sister. She needs to step up and you cut her way too much slack. If she's working with me, she does her share."

Audra breathed a mental sigh of relief and hoped her face didn't reveal that she was pleased, not upset by the idea of separation from the drama diva of the family. Of course, if Clancy truly needed her, things would be different. "I think that's a good idea. If we're divvying up the ponies, then Bonanza and Lightning should go to Snohomish. Clancy's really attached to Bonanza, and it cut deep when the twins sold him off for spite."

"Those two are enough to almost make me believe in corporal punishment." Elinor shook her head ruefully, black curls tumbling to her shoulders. "Not quite, but almost. Of course, they learned to be that mean when they were little, so they should have been trained then. It's going to take a major setback for them to learn to act like humans now."

Well, that's another new idea, one I should have thought of before. Why didn't I?

Audra took a deep breath. "You're right. At some point, life will smack the two of them and it's not my job. If I need an instructor, Brigid will be available once the resident camp season ends. The bakery where she worked last year went out of business, so she doesn't have a job waiting in September."

"And you may want her to move in to help you," Elinor said. "Of course, we'll be taking the farm animals up to Sean's this summer once we have paddocks, pens, and stalls for them."

"Well, can you leave some of the chickens? Brigid uses a lot of eggs in her recipes."

"No worries and I'll bring milk when I come down. I'm not leaving for good. Daisy would never let me hear the end of it if I weren't at her place for coffee twice a week." Elinor glanced over her shoulder, then lowered her voice. "Did she tell you that one of her cats disappeared over the Fourth of July?"

"No. I wish I'd known. I'd have helped her look for it."

"Well, she hunted all over the neighborhood and asked everyone. She put up posters at the local stores too. Then, this morning she found its head on her doormat."

"What?" Mind whirling, Audra gaped at the other woman. "That makes no sense. If a wild animal killed the cat, then it could have been eaten, but nothing feral would leave part of it on a porch."

"It was cut off, not chewed," Elinor said. "She's keeping her other cats in the house from now on and I told her I'd warn you to do the same with Pyewacket. There has to be some sicko in the area."

"It's someone who doesn't content him or herself with torturing cats," Audra said. "Navarre would have died if I hadn't gotten him to Joe and Art in time."

Elinor nodded. "I know. I promised Daisy I'd take the momma cat and her kittens home with us tonight. They'll be safe in the barn there until we find out who is doing this."

"Makes sense. I'll help you put them in a cat-tainer for the trip." Audra frowned thoughtfully. "I was going to ask you about finding a Siamese kitten for Lynn. I know Pyewacket was her cat first, but he's mine now and I can't give him up."

"Let me talk to Sean about it and I'll get back to you."

———

Things felt different when Kyle woke this morning. After break-fast, he'd saddled up and ridden out. The trail wound through huge cedars that towered two hundred feet in the air for most of the morning. Then the trees began to change to maples and alders for the first time. He heard the rush of the river over the rocks. Squir-rels still chattered and the crows continued to scold, but he saw hoof-prints from deer and heard a distant roar. What was that? It sounded like a train, but the noise faded, then returned. The door to Beth's world must have finally opened.

———

Stealing one of the old bitch's cats out of her yard had been a thrill. He owed her for making his life hell back in high school and making his folks send him to that stupid doctor for years. He'd waited even after he saw the posters at the drug store and grocery. Then, he returned the head. He couldn't stick around and watch her cry over it. That would have been even better. He'd wait until dark, then go snoop and see where she buried it. He'd dig it up and return it to the porch, so she'd fall over it tomorrow morning. Maybe, she'd think she was going crazy and see the shrink herself.

He grinned at the thought and kept loading his shotgun to go shooting tonight. The wild critters bypassed the treats he left for them, but they couldn't avoid the rounds he fired. With any luck at all, he'd find someone's pet roaming in the woods. Way to spoil their Friday, the 13th! He always shot to wound, not kill so he could enjoy watching them die. What would it be like to shoot a person? He'd tried asking his cousin, the Army hero, how it felt to cut a human throat, but the *goody-two-shoes* hadn't answered, just turned, and walked away.

Well, one day he'd find out for himself, Zane thought and headed for the woods. Time to go hunting!

———

After morning chores, they went back to bed. The farm didn't open until noon on Sundays, so it meant there was time to make love, sleep, and cuddle before they got up for the day. It was Joe's turn to cook breakfast and she enjoyed watching him work. He reminded her of Brigid, cleaning as he went and using the minimum number of dishes. And the food smelled good too! Audra cut into her stack of pancakes and glanced at Navarre when he woofed. "What?"

"Company." Joe brought over the pot and topped their coffee cups. He lingered to look out the kitchen window. "Dog alarm is right. It's Ethan, Sean, Elinor, and the kids. Why is Ethan here?"

"Elinor and Sean are talking about an indoor arena. Ethan probably came to scope it out." Audra put down her fork. "I need to help open the business."

"After you eat." Once he returned the glass carafe to the warmer, Joe strolled to the door, Navarre an eager escort. "Morning, all. Coffee's on. Do you want some?"

"Not yet," Sean called. "We're looking at the ground and deciding where to put an indoor arena."

"So, we'll be back for coffee," Elinor added. "Sandy, Penny, and Marcie will be along soon. Remind Audra she has the rest of the day off, so she'll be raring to go tomorrow morning with the next session of day camp."

"You got it." Joe shut the door. He returned to the table to sit across from Audra and eat. Navarre flopped on the floor beside her chair. "You heard the boss."

Audra nodded, finished chewing. "She certainly worries that I get enough time for myself. It's different than any other barn I managed. Most of the time, I worked six days a week and was on call for the seventh."

"Sounds like Dad's operation." Joe drank coffee. "I told him I'd handle the calls today so he could take your mom out for lunch. Do you and Navarre want to come with me if I get an emergency?"

Audra forked up more pancakes. "Sure, what else is on the schedule while we wait?"

"If you don't mind, I need to start working on my lesson plans for the fall. My laptop's in the Jeep."

"That's fine." It'd give her time to continue the revisions for her book. She needed to finish them and get the edited material back to Kendra by Tuesday. "And then we're supposed to be up at Mom's for dinner by four."

"Sounds good and we have a plan for the day."

———

Joe negotiated the next set of curves on the two-lane mountain road. This was the trade-off for his father's practice since he refused to euthanize dogs or cats at the county animal shelter. Instead, he opted for helping the police with injured or frightened animals at all hours of the day or night, even on weekends. "Keep an eye out for the sheriff's rigs."

"I am, but I haven't seen anything yet," Audra said.

Navarre looked out the back window, tail wagging. He obviously figured a car trip was only for his entertainment.

Evergreens crowded the road and blocked everything except occasional driveways. Joe rarely glimpsed any houses and yet he knew people lived up here. He saw a sign for the Mount Baker Recreational area and slowed. There still wasn't any sign of the police car or the deputy who called him about a crazed horse.

"Up ahead at the pull-out," Audra said suddenly.

Joe saw the distinctive black and white cars at the same time. A new trailer was hitched to a pickup with the same emblem. He signaled and pulled off the highway to park his Jeep next to the nearest sedan. "Leave Navarre here for a while. When we finish, we'll take him for a hike."

"Sounds good." Audra opened the windows to give the dog a cross-breeze.

"I want to see the horse before I give him any drugs. Sometimes, it just takes another handler to load one, although these guys are usually pretty good with stock."

"Or women. They do have female officers."

Joe nodded and went to the back of the Jeep to grab a set of coveralls and his tote of medical supplies. He'd forgotten about her adopted cousin. Stupid, since Will Dawson had filled him in on his missing daughter. She trained with Audra and Nina Armstrong for endurance riding on a champion Arabian stallion.

"You the vet?" A stocky man in a dark green uniform came to meet them. "Where's Art?"

"Joe gave his dad the day off," Audra said. "Where's the horse?"

"Over here, just past the trail head. We have witnesses who saw two guys fighting and the gelding belongs to one of them."

Joe ignored the cop's chatter and headed for the big red Appaloosa standing in a grove of short cedars. The horse pinned his ears and glared from narrowed blue eyes. A young blond man sat on a nearby rock, hands cuffed behind him. He was tall, lean with a ragged scar down his right cheek, wearing worn, dark pants and a flannel shirt. "I'd stop there, Mister. S.O.B. don't cotton much to strangers."

"S.O.B.?" Audra paused to eye the man, then smiled at him. "Does that mean what I think?"

"Yes, ma'am. I didn't name him. My brother did because the horse always had a mean streak. Heard it got worse when he took on a porcupine as a colt."

Joe frowned when an older man in a black police wind-breaker came toward them. He was a scrawny fellow with graying brown hair with a scraggly beard to match and empty mud-brown eyes. "He doesn't need anything from you. I'll ride him out of here."

"What's his name?" Audra asked.

"Who?"

"The horse. What do you call him?"

"Nothing. He's an animal."

"Better than you are." The younger man spoke up. "He doesn't attack women, Smith."

The smart-ass comment earned a look that promised retribution. Joe saw Audra back away, then dig in her pocket for something. She pulled out her cell phone, pressed buttons.

A ringtone erupted from the older cop's pocket. Helen Reddy's signature song filled the parking lot. The anthem of women's liberation brought the rest of the officers toward them. Joe recognized the new arrival, his cousin, a big blond bruiser in a suit jacket and slacks. He was the first one forward, his gaze narrowed on the older man in the black windbreaker. "Where is she?"

"What the hell do you mean?" Smith demanded.

"Detective Beth Chambers. You're wearing her coat. You obviously have her phone."

"And he did have her badge unless he threw it away, but I didn't find it." That statement from the young cowboy earned scant attention.

Joe watched as the coat was peeled off the false officer. He was handcuffed and put in the back of a squad car, a uniformed deputy standing guard close by.

With gloved hands, John Watkins felt in the pockets of the coat. He looked inside a black wallet, then tucked it gently into an evidence bag. He repeated the same action with a cell phone. Finally, he folded the jacket and eased it into a larger plastic bag. He passed off the items to a nearby officer. "Put them in my car. I'll take them to the lab."

Then, he turned back to the first deputy, jerking his head toward the man who really owned the horse. "You got any reason to hold him?"

"Not now. I'll cut him loose."

John nodded and waited while that happened. Then, he said, "I'm John Watkins. Can you tell me where we'll find Detective Chambers?"

Rubbing his wrists, the cowboy stood and stretched. "I'm new to these parts. Smith said he was going to kill me so I couldn't tell anybody what he'd done to the woman whose coat he stole. I took exception to the idea. You'll find his club back there aways."

"All right. If I have more questions, where can I find you?"

"Contact me." Audra handed over a card. "You knew Beth as another detective. She was my cousin. The Dawsons take care of their own and we'll look after—"

"Kyle. Kyle Morgan, ma'am." He smiled, then turned to look around for something. He came up with a worn leather cowboy hat that had fallen into the dirt. "And I'm in your debt."

"I think it will turn out to be the other way," Joe told him. "Beth's family will appreciate knowing what happened to her."

He wondered about the strange look the other man gave him. Then, Kyle went toward the horse, snagged the reins, and neatly avoided the gelding's nip. "How far away is your place, ma'am? Can I make it there by dark?"

"I'll have the Animal Control cops haul the horse there if you can load it," John Watkins said. "It's the least we can do for the man who helped us find one of our own and there's no point in going off the mountain with an empty rig."

"I don't know about that. S.O.B.'s always traveled on his own hooves. He doesn't do fancy."

Joe grinned. "Well, let's see what we can do to change his mind. Where do you plan to take him, Audra? Your mom's?"

"No way." Audra stepped up to scratch the strawberry roan Appaloosa's neck. "We'll go to the Rocking J. They have room for more horses and Mom will be up to her ears in resident campers. She runs a woman-only operation during the summer and there's no room for this guy or Kyle."

Joe nodded and lowered his voice. "How did you know Smith had Beth's coat?"

"I didn't," Audra said. "I suspected it as soon as I heard his name. We spent time together and Beth vented a lot of anger about her last investigation. She thought Gary Smith murdered several women. After he attacked her best friend and stole Nina's horse, Beth followed him into the National Forest."

"Not a very smart thing to do," Joe commented.

"Foolhardy," Kyle agreed, "but brave."

"Beth always had guts and I hoped Smith would have kept her phone as a trophy." Audra blinked hard. "Let's get your horse loaded and then you can tell me what he did to her."

"No, ma'am." Kyle bunched the reins in one hand, slid the other up toward his horse's mouth. "She'd want you to remember her the way she was, not as a woman he bushwhacked and left to die along with her horse and dog."

Joe watched the words make their mark on his cousin's face before John turned and stalked in the direction of his unmarked car. "Be right back and we'll load up."

It only took a few strides to catch the other man. "What's going on, John?"

"I didn't know she was related to the Dawsons. She didn't talk much about family or introduce me to them." John glared at the driver's door and then jerked it open. "She thought I didn't have her six, so she used her vacation time to go after Smith. I should have been there."

"I don't know what to say."

"Nothing to say, 'cuz. Be there for your woman, so she doesn't think you're just a Friday night hook-up."

23

AUDRA SAT IN THE BACK SEAT NEXT TO HER DOG AND STUDIED THE two men in the front. It'd taken the three of them to load the big Appaloosa in the sheriff's trailer, but they'd managed it. If she didn't know better, she'd have sworn the gelding had never been trailered before. That was impossible. Most mature horses were trucked to various places, not ridden across country unless it was some sort of competition.

Kyle's eyes widened when he saw the Jeep. Joe told him three times to buckle up, then finally explained how before the younger man fastened his seat belt. It made her wonder just how long he had lived in the hills and where.

That reminded her of something her grandfather's brother, Grand-Uncle Will had said about expecting company. Had his friends arrived yet? If not, he might have time to spend with Kyle. Besides, this was the first news they'd had of Beth in three months. It wasn't what they wanted to hear. Audra knew she and her grand-uncle had hoped to see her cousin ride in on her gray Arabian, her retired K-9 partner loping behind. It wasn't going to happen. Tears burned her eyes and Audra choked back a sob.

Navarre whined and pressed against her. She stroked his rust-colored fur, then drew out her cell phone to call her uncle and

Venus. They needed to know what she'd arranged. When she finished talking to her grand-uncle, she met Joe's eyes in the rear-view mirror. "What's up?"

"You're more familiar with this area than I am. Did you ever hear of a town called Junction City?"

Her first reaction was negative, but a dim memory stirred of one of her grand-uncle's stories. "I'm not sure. It could be one of the places that died when the trains came through. We'll ask Grand-Uncle Will. Why?"

"It's where I rode out of when Smith broke jail. There aren't any trains up here," Kyle said.

"Not now." Audra wondered how badly the other man had been hurt. She hadn't seen any bumps or bruises on him. That didn't mean he didn't have a concussion. Maybe, they should head for a hospital instead of the Rocking J. "Did your people have Smith locked up?"

There was a long silence. Then, Kyle finally said, "My brother did after Smith tried to steal the little girl that Rad and his new wife took in."

"You didn't tell my cousin, Detective Watkins that." Joe slowed as they neared one of the outlying communities in Liberty Valley. "Why?"

"Figured he'd think I was as loco as Smith if I admitted I was chasing the man down to be sure the law got him so he couldn't hurt anybody else."

"You have a point." Audra didn't say what she thought it was. She'd heard that a few veterans headed into the back woods to avoid society after the Vietnam War. Had others fresh from Iraq and Afghanistan joined them and created their own hidden society? Was that where Smith had hidden these last few months? She was surprised someone hadn't killed him for trying to abduct their child, not just locked him up. More questions, but it didn't look like she could get answers now.

The conversation died when Kyle saw the first houses, businesses, and school that made up part of Eagleville. His head whipped back and forth as if it was on springs. If she didn't know better, she'd have sworn this was his first trip to town. They passed her family's ranch and then reached the Rocking J a short time later.

Joe pulled down the drive and parked next to her uncle's rig. Audra got out, leaving Navarre carefully inside. While Joe went to find Venus, Audra headed over to where her grand-uncle waited. "I may have made a mistake. This guy could be three bricks short of a load."

Will chuckled and patted her shoulder. "Never apologize for doing a kindness, sweetheart. What's your friend's name?"

"He's not a friend yet. I just met him. He says he's Kyle Morgan."

Will stiffened, then broke away to stride forward, a broad grin spreading across his weathered face. "Welcome home, young Morgan."

Kyle eyed him cautiously, standing by the passenger side of the Jeep. "Have we met before, sir?"

"Yes, but you won't recall. It hasn't happened yet."

That made no sense to Audra, but it obviously did to Kyle. After a moment, he shook hands with Will, then the two hugged, a quick manly embrace. Okay, something very strange was going on and she wanted to know what. She joined them. "Start talking. What's up with you two? How do you know each other?"

Will grinned at her, then at Kyle again. "That's my girl. She always wants all the facts."

"Typical Dawson." Kyle nodded. "Soon as I saw her, I knew she'd sort everything out, same as Miss Mina did when she decided her kin were going straight."

"Who is Mina?" Audra demanded.

Will glanced at the sheriff's horse trailer coming down the drive. "It's a long story. We'll catch you up another time. As for you, Kyle—"

"I know. Bethany told me that if I let folks know everything, they'd lock me up in a loony bin."

Relief swept across Will's craggy features. "I hoped she'd make it there, but I didn't know how she'd get word to me." He paused. "She always hated being called Bethany."

"Well, it's only for family. Mostly, folks call her Detective Morgan or Mrs. Morgan."

"Are you saying my cousin married you?" Audra demanded. "Now, I know you have a concussion. I should have taken you to a hospital."

"Not me." Kyle backed half a step, hands up. "I'm not brave enough to take her on. I just brought her a wedding dress. Rad was the one who talked her into wearing it and marrying him. She and that dog are a pair."

Two hours later, Audra leaned back in the restaurant booth, studying the glass of wine in front of her while she considered the puzzle Kyle Morgan presented. It didn't make sense. Why would Beth choose to stay in some hidden community in the hills instead of returning to her family? Granted some of the older Dawsons didn't accept Will's adopted daughter as one of them, but Beth had always laughed at them. Had she lost her mind? Did someone, Kyle's brother, brainwash her?

"Are you upset about dinner at your mom's?" Joe asked, interrupting her thoughts. "I'm sorry we were late and missed the meal."

"Not your fault." Audra picked up her glass. "It wouldn't have mattered if you didn't have an emergency call and we arrived on time. They still would have forgotten we were coming. It was payback for the party you arranged on my actual birthday."

"If you know that, why do you put up with them?" He made a T with his hands. "Never mind. Don't answer that. They're your family and you love them."

"Exactly." Audra sipped her wine, allowing the golden Riesling to slip down her throat. "Of course, I probably shouldn't have told Mom that we were at the Rocking J with one of Grand-Uncle Will's friends, but I didn't want her to hear it from Estelle."

Joe shrugged, nursing his beer. "At least now you know that

Navarre can be trusted with little kids. He was the soul of patience when the baby tried to ride him."

"Yes, and you know that Sunshine is well on the mend. I'd say it was a good time for everyone. I just wish I knew what to make of Kyle Morgan."

"Give him a couple of days to settle in and then we'll visit." Joe gestured to the menu in front of her. "Have you decided on dinner? Shall I order you an *Elvis* burger?"

"No way." After one more sip of wine, she put down the glass and reached for the folder in front of her. "I'll figure it out. I'm thinking comfort food. I wonder if Uncle Jim has any chicken fettuccini in the back."

The idea woke her in the middle of the night. She could research Rad Morgan on the computer, learn all about him and then go find her cousin. There must be a trail into Junction City, or nobody would be able to enter, much less leave. *Once I talk to Beth and know she's doing exactly what she wants, I'll walk away. She made it through three tours in what she called the 'sandbox.' I know she can take care of herself. Obviously, she wasn't happy here. Is she happy there?*

Leaving Joe to sleep, Audra took her robe from the hook on the back of the door. She went through the dark living room. She saw Navarre zonked out on the rug in front of the couch and Pyewacket snoozing on a throw pillow. She left the family contentedly snoozing. She headed into her office and turned on the laptop. While it hummed to life, she returned to the kitchen. She nuked a cup of yesterday's coffee.

She sat down at her desk and clicked on the Internet icon. She'd start with a generic search and go from there. She typed in *Rad Morgan* and sipped coffee as she waited for the computer to do its magic. A short list of article titles appeared, most about an early Washington state lawman. One link led to an obituary printed in an early Everett newspaper in the early 1940s. She clicked on it.

She skimmed the details. This particular Rad Morgan passed away peacefully in his bed at the ripe old age of ninety-seven. A survivor of Andersonville Prison Camp, he'd come west in the aftermath of the Civil War. Based in the town of Junction City, he served as marshal for many years before Washington Territory became a state. He was known for breaking up the Dawson Gang, stopping child prostitution in the area, and solving numerous crimes. Married late in life, he and his wife had five children of their own and fostered several orphans.....

Audra wrinkled her nose and clicked the back button, not bothering to finish the lengthy article. The guy sounded like a saint. He must have some mud attached to his name, but she didn't want to read about that. She wanted to find the guy who had the same name now and convinced her cousin to stay in the backwoods with him. She began a search for Junction City. If she could find out where it was located, it wouldn't take long to make a trip there and find Beth.

Buttoning his jeans, Joe yawned as he strolled into the room. "What are you doing?"

"Trying to find the place where Kyle claims he left my cousin."

"Want some help? I'll get my laptop."

Despite their best efforts, Audra still didn't discover where Junction City was located in the next day and a half. So, once horse camp ended, she asked Elinor for the rest of the afternoon off to make a trip to the downtown library. A local historian, who just happened to be a good friend of her Grand-Uncle Will, worked there and might be able to help solve the mystery. Audra parked and headed upstairs to the archives.

A dark-haired young woman in a tight black lace corset and short black skirt over net leggings and high boots rushed forward to greet her. "Hey, Ms. A. Gran will be so sorry she missed you. She's off with your Uncle Will and his hunky new friend."

"Damn it. I wanted to quiz her about Junction City."

"I can get that for you. The three of them were all over the files and the old photos."

"It shouldn't be all that old, Lindsay."

"Maybe, not to you, but I calls it as I sees it and we're talking about places that existed almost a hundred years ago." She unrolled a map, laying it flat on a large table. "Okay, come take a look. This is Snohomish County in the days before the railroads came and, in those days, everything was shipped by riverboat or went across country by horseback."

Audra crossed to the table and eyed the paper. A name popped out at her. Snohomish City. "Is that where Snohomish originally started?"

"Yes." Lindsay traced a blue line with a highly polished black and red nail. "This is the town landing. The Cedar Shipping boats left from here and went upriver with supplies part of the year until the weather closed the river. The ships stopped in all these little towns and the trips culminated here in Junction City which was owned by this totally wicked gunfighter."

"Wicked?" Audra asked. "How? Why?"

"Trace Burdette was like totally amazing." Lindsay picked up a large binder. "Read all about it in the Junction City newspaper. I'm so doing my next research project on Burdette and the Lazy B. I'll bet I can get that published in a big-time magazine and rub the history dean's nose in it. Old fogey says women were only good for sex and babies back in the day. Every time I turn around, he wants to cut the funding for Women Studies."

Audra blinked. "The Lazy B? It's the name of our ranch. Coincidence?"

"No. I haven't figured out how the Dawsons ended up with the property, but I'm fairly sure it was through marriage. There'd be a big paper trail of land sales if it happened any other way. Can I check out the attic at your mom's house again and look through the family records?"

"Sure. I'll meet you there. You know the Dawsons never throw anything away. Now, where is Junction City today? Does it still exist?"

"Sort of." Lindsay returned to the map. "See where these two rivers come together? Well, Junction City was originally on the north bank where the two branches met. The town was considered one of the bigger settlements in early Washington State, but the railroads bypassed it."

"Why?"

"Money. It was cheaper to build a rail line on raw land than to buy from all the property owners who'd been farming and ranching up there for years. Besides, nobody knew what the rivers would do during flood season and the last thing anyone wanted was for a train to go downstream."

"I guess that makes sense." Audra frowned at the map. It didn't look as though Junction City was more than ten miles from Snohomish, just a few minutes by car. It couldn't be the same place where Beth supposedly lived, not when Kyle Morgan and Gary Smith came out in the mountains, an hour or more from civilization. "Could there be another town with the same name?"

"Oh sure, but I thought you wanted the one that Gran and your uncle's friend were talking about. Let me pull up the index of all the towns in Washington."

"That's not necessary. I just want the ones in this county or possibly Skagit because the boundary between them is so close when you get up in the foothills."

"Okay, then this is it."

Audra shook her head. It still didn't make any sense. Where was the town? Where was her cousin? She began to look through the photos. Most were old, sepia in tone, showing men in logging attire, teams of horses and mules, giant trees. There were a few scantily clad women. "Who took these?"

"I need to do more research," Lindsay said. "Only a couple had the photographer's name, "A. Morgan." I'm not sure who that is, and neither was your uncle's friend. He said nobody had that initial in his family. That's like totally amazing. If someone asked me about my relatives now, I'd miss a cousin or two. But Kyle knew all of what he called his kin. What about you? Can you list all the Dawsons?"

"No way. Somebody always is getting married or having a

baby." Audra paused, then asked. "Did they say anything about the Dawson gang?"

"Interesting." Lindsay headed for her computer. "People are always fascinated by what Gran calls the lesser element, so those records are already scanned. Let's see what comes up. Of course, if anyone asks where you got the info, I don't know anything."

Audra grinned appreciatively. "Coward."

"You got it. I don't want to hear from your momma that the Dawsons walked on water until I opened up this can of truth."

"Well, she won't be hearing from me that the family stories are based on fact. Grand-Uncle Will has been saying for years that we're descended from bank robbers, but nobody really believed him."

"You should record his stories before he gets much older. Then, you'll have an oral history of your family."

"I'll think about it." Audra kept looking through the photographs. They were a slice of pioneer life, she thought. There were pictures of children standing on huge cedar stumps, a class-room with students and a teacher, families of varying sizes. She stopped and stared at one photo of a couple in the front yard with a large dog lying nearby.

Rugged and handsome in a dark suit, the man held a baby in a flowing white dress. Standing next to him with a hand on his broad shoulder was a woman in a light-colored shirtwaist and black skirt. Hair piled high on her head, she looked as if she was listening to him. It wasn't the fact that they had an obvious attachment to one another that made Audra stare at the old photo. She knew the woman. It was Beth!

24

AUDRA HAD TO WAIT UNTIL THE NEXT EVENING TO VISIT THE Rocking J and see Kyle. When she'd called the previous afternoon from the library, he and Uncle Will had been off somewhere and not expected to return until late. So, she'd made a copy of the photo. She knew most people would say it was just a resemblance between the two women and that she wanted it to be her cousin because she didn't want to believe Beth was dead.

Audra didn't show the picture to anyone else. Instead, she looked through the files on her laptop and compared the photos she had of Beth in her Army fatigues, her dress cop uniform, and more casual attire. The facial features were identical to the old picture of the pioneer woman. There must be a reason and Kyle Morgan undoubtedly knew it. Today, Audra wasn't waiting for answers.

"I'm not that much into denial. I could admit it if she were really gone," Audra told Navarre riding shotgun in the passenger seat of the Ford 150. He woofed a soft agreement, tail thumping when they turned in the driveway at the Rocking J.

Her daughter riding on her hip, Venus came out of the house when Audra parked the truck in front of the house. She slid from behind the wheel. Navarre jumped out of the pickup and jogged over to sniff the little girl. A squeal of delight filled the air. Audra smiled. "You may as well put her down. We don't want to break both their hearts."

Venus laughed and followed directions, watching her daughter hug the huge dog. "I owe you big-time. That guy you brought up is out building a fence with Uncle Will and Orion. If Kyle sticks around a while, I'll be able to turn out the herd on pasture and it will save on the hay bill."

"Hay in July?" Audra watched the toddler pulling on Navarre's neck. The dog tried to lick her face amid baby squeals. "Are you serious?"

"The fences on this place have been falling down for years. I didn't want the stock running the roads." Venus waved toward the knee-high grass in the nearby field. "I hate to see the grazing go to waste. What does your mom do?"

"It depends on the schedule. During the summer, we have six cabins of resident campers, and each night one group rides after dinner. Those horses get supper in the barn. The others are out to pasture for twelve hours. We do almost the same thing at the pony farm. We let the ponies graze in the afternoon but come back in for a light meal. Of course, Elinor doesn't have as much land as my mom does."

Venus nodded, then gestured toward the wraparound porch. "Come have a cup of coffee while you wait for Kyle to get back. Then, I won't feel guilty for picking your brain about how to run this place."

"Sounds good." Walking slowly so the two-year-old and Navarre could keep up, Audra followed her hostess toward the house.

An hour and a half later, the farm truck came through the fields, down a rutted gravel road toward the barn. Excusing herself, Audra went to meet the men, Navarre an eager escort.

Orion stumbled toward her, fatigue on the hoof, carrying his sweat-stained t-shirt. Dirt covered his baggy jeans from the knees to his boots. She smiled at him. "What's the matter with you?

Where's Grand-Uncle Will and Kyle? Did you leave them working?"

"No, they're in the barn." He jerked an arm toward the large two-story building. "Those two are going to kill me. I've been digging postholes since lunch and they just told me that if there was a full moon, we'd keep going. What's wrong with them?"

"Nothing." Audra patted his shoulder. "You aren't used to the way that men work on farms. Go to the house and wash up. Venus is putting supper on the table."

"I hope I can stay awake long enough to eat."

Shaking her head, Audra headed into the barn where she found her grand-uncle and Kyle feeding the horses. "How's the fence coming? I wish I'd realized how dilapidated the place was. I'd have organized a work party."

"Not a bad idea." Grand-Uncle Will grinned at her while Kyle hefted another bale of hay into the wheelbarrow. "Won't your momma have a hissy fit?"

"Probably, but we have a big family. They can pitch in and help each other." Once the three of them finished feeding, she led the way out of the barn. Audra drew the copy of the photograph from her pocket and passed it to Kyle. "Where is she?"

"Not sure. She and my brother have a circuit to ride, but he may make her stay home if she's expecting."

Will grinned. "I never had much success making Beth do anything. I wish him luck."

Audra folded her arms and waited until she had their total attention. "Where is she?"

"It's more like *when*, not where." Will met her gaze evenly. "Honey, with those books you write, you should have a better imagination. Did it ever occur to you that this world has mysteries we haven't solved yet?"

"Of course. Scientists are always coming up with new answers." Audra took the picture away from Kyle, passing it to her uncle. "Where is she?"

Kyle frowned and looked at Will. "Should I tell her?"

"She won't stop until you do."

"All right then." Kyle glanced at the photograph again. "That hadn't been taken yet, not when I left. It was 1888."

"Are you serious?" Audra folded her arms and glared at the two men. "I'm not laughing. I want to know where she is and how I find her. Tell me now."

"He told you the truth," Will said. "She traveled back in time."

"And she took her dog and horse with her? That's crap." Audra lifted her chin, spacing her words carefully. "Why do you believe his farfetched story when he told me Gary Smith attacked her?"

"He did, but he didn't succeed in killing her or the critters," Kyle said. "He tried."

"And I didn't go looking for Beth on a whim when she was a child living on the streets in Seattle," Will said. "She'd told me years ago where to find her and how to teach her what she needed to know to survive in Washington Territory."

"And you know this how?"

"She saved my great-grandmother's life when she was a teenager and helped finish her raising. I ran in and out of their houses when I was a boy."

"What about Kyle?" Audra jerked her head toward him. "What does he have to do with any of this? Was he there when you were a kid? Is that why you said you knew him?"

"It's a conundrum," Kyle said. "Is he in my future? Am I in his past? Will things change by me coming here instead of staying there? I don't know the answers any more than you do. I can tell you that Bethany is as safe and happy as my brother can make her."

"But I can't see that for myself."

"Can't you?" Will wrapped an arm around her shoulders. "Beth told me that you do a lot of research on your computer. Why don't you hunt around and see what you learn about the early days of the Dawsons?"

She managed a nod and blinked hard to hold back her tears. Why did she want to think that her cousin was alive and well somewhere else? It did sound like one of her books. Could her grand-uncle be right? Was there a trail through time, a portal that Beth had gone through after Smith? "Did we really start out as a bunch of bank-robbers?"

"The younger Dawsons weren't very good at it and after Smith shot a bunch of the old-timers to doll-rags, Miss Mina changed course," Kyle said.

"Why did he cut loose on them?"

"Because he's a woman-killer and they wouldn't let him have Miss Mina." Kyle shook his head, regret, and pity on his face. "Poor fellas should have gone in fighting like Zeb Prescott and the Lazy B hands did. They were the ones to get her to Bethany."

"And what did my cousin do?"

"She's a true healer. She saved the girl, but by the time I left, Bethany had already told Miss Mina that she's not getting married until she finishes her schooling. Babies need smart mamas."

"Did she already plan to marry someone?"

"Her adopted cousin. Her uncle took him in when his folks were killed by Indians. Folks did things like that back then and the boy took the Dawson name." Will hugged her again. "I'll bet when you hunt down the truth, you can put it in one of your books."

She drew a ragged breath. "Beth told you about them, didn't she? Most people don't know I write, but she figured it out."

"Yes, and she made me promise not to tell your momma or your sisters, not that they ever asked me. Beth said that Darlene wouldn't get over the fact that you support the family and the ranch by writing love stories. Your daddy broke her heart and she never healed from it."

"Either that or she enjoys being the object of everyone's pity," Kyle said, narrowing his eyes. "Some folks just love being the center of attention and getting everybody in town all riled up."

Audra eyed him while she considered the point. Maybe, he was closer to the truth. Her mother certainly didn't act like love's martyr. Could all of this be a manipulative game? She heard metallic ringing from the porch, the old-time signal that a meal was ready and waiting. Eating here meant learning more about Beth and not cooking at home. Talk about a winning deal!

Joe had the late shift at the clinic. He wouldn't be at the farm before ten and he was an adult. He could look after himself until Audra arrived.

———

Another great day of camp, Audra thought as she signed out the last of the children. She put away the clipboard in the classroom and saw Clancy at the long picnic table. She'd started grading the memory books the kids had made this week. "Need any help?"

"Don't you have to run off again?" Clancy asked, with a toss of her red hair. "You've been least in sight all week. Like it's my fault that Joe arranged a party for you, so we didn't do a family thing last Sunday."

Audra laughed and shook her head. She poured herself a cup of coffee and another for her younger sister, then carried the mugs over to the table. "This may come as a surprise, Devon Clancy Dawson, but the world really doesn't revolve around you, Mom, and the rest of the girls. Yes, Joe did make my birthday the best in more than twenty years. If we're still together in November, I'll do the same for him."

"Why wouldn't you be together?" Clancy put down her pen. "He seems really hooked on you."

"He goes back to Pullman at the end of the summer. I've never known a long-distance relationship that worked. This is just a summer fling and I'm enjoying every moment of it."

"It could be more."

"I don't see how." Audra reached for a stack of the books. "Last time I only wanted to go to the Apple Cup with him and a simple football game turned into a major disaster. This is temporary and I'm good with that."

Clancy heaved a sigh. "And I thought I had issues. Wow, you really don't ask for much from life, do you?"

"Why should I when I know better? I learned a long time ago to do everything for myself. I get in trouble when I forget, but when I remember, it always works."

Clancy gave her a long, strange look. "Ethan says we've really done a number on you, and I guess I thought he was trying to pull my chain. He's right, isn't he? You actually believe all we want is for you to be a superhero and solve all our problems."

"And money. The Dawson family wants cold, hard cash." Audra picked up a red pen. "The twins stopped speaking to me this summer since I said I couldn't pay for them to live off-campus. Guess I'd better start buying lottery tickets if I want the family to love me by Christmas. Of course, that only works if I win."

Clancy winced. "Ouch. That's a major owie. We can do better. You'll see on Sunday."

"Like Jake says, I don't *wanna*. Brigid is bringing down the trunks of family papers and I'm putting them in order so they can be donated to the local Historical Society. That's my new Sunday project, not dinner at the Dawsons."

"Do you want some help?"

"If I do, I'll call in Uncle Will and his friends. They know and love history. Uncle Will has stories about them that need to be recorded so everyone knows that the people in those papers are real human beings. They had hopes and dreams that should be remembered."

Audra didn't add that she hoped to find out more about Beth and her new family. The idea sounded crazy enough when she merely thought about it. Talking about it would buy her a ticket to the loony bin. And letting her family think she was upset about their behavior last Sunday provided the perfect excuse to avoid them and do her new research project. She doubted it would end up in a book, but who knew?

That evening she finished up the last of the revisions for her latest shape-shifting book and sent the corrected manuscript off to her editor. Things were so much faster now than when she'd started in this business. Back then, everything had to be sent by *snail mail* and now her manuscripts sailed back and forth electronically. Responsibilities finished, she could return to the world of her witches and wizards. That was so much more fun.

She glanced away from the computer screen when Navarre stood and stretched. He woofed softly. She saved her work and went with the dog to the kitchen door. He was right. Joe had arrived. "Hey there."

He grinned and came up the steps, carrying a grocery bag. "Hey yourself. I was in the mood for banana splits. I stopped and got the makings."

"Sounds fun. What are we celebrating?"

"Your mom called me at the clinic tonight to apologize for the snafu last Sunday. She said they'd make up for it this week and invited us for supper."

25

"Venus rode out to check the new fence line." A smaller, plumper version of one of Audra's red-haired sister, Meteor tore lettuce into pieces, tossing the greens into a wooden bowl. "She said that you're talking about putting together a work party to help install more fences. Your mom will freak. She wants this place to fall into ruins."

"I know." Audra crossed to the cupboard, opening it to find plates. She began to set the long table that took up the center of the room. "Mom may be so pissed she butts out of my life and gives me time to breathe until the mortgage falls due in two months and she wants me to pay it."

"I knew you had an ulterior motive." Meteor laughed. She reached for a ripe tomato and a knife. "You're not the saint that Venus claims and that makes me like you better. Is your mom hassling you about Dr. Joe? Does she think he isn't good enough for you?"

"I don't think it's that altruistic." Audra considered the idea while she hunted silverware. She was sure that her mom's call to Joe came after Clancy told the rest of the Dawsons that Audra felt like some sort of sacrifice and was starting to get mad. If she distanced herself totally from the family, who would pick up the emotional slack? Nobody else wanted to do the job. And who was to say that Joe wanted all her time and energy devoted to him? She didn't know what came next in her life. She wasn't happy with the status quo, but how did she change things to something better?

Another long look from Meteor's light blue eyes and then the younger woman returned to chopping veggies for the salad. After a few minutes, she asked about possible dates for the work party. The two of them discussed the details of arranging materials, getting tools, and putting on a potluck lunch for the next fifteen minutes. Then, Navarre barked from the porch. Audra went to call him away from guard duty so the adults could join them for the meal.

By the time she returned home, she felt better. She'd already started phoning relatives. Grand-Uncle Will would pass the word to the old-timers that he knew, and she'd email the younger contingent. Everyone would converge on the Rocking J the first Sunday in August. It was a case of bringing your own tools as well as something for lunch. Uncle Jim had promised to deliver one of his huge portable grills for burgers, hot dogs, and sausages.

———

Years ago, she'd organized the attic and since none of her sisters particularly cared to play upstairs, they hadn't changed the arrangements. Kate and Clancy preferred the barns, so if old tack remained near the door, they were happy. Brigid moved the cookbooks down to her kitchen and only visited if she wanted to donate furniture to one of her causes. The twins avoided the place entirely – thank goodness neither of them had an interest in vintage clothing or she would constantly be cleaning up behind them.

Audra passed the wardrobes with their assortment of clothing and ended in the section of the long room that held file cabinets of papers. As a teen, she'd spent days, weeks, and even months sorting through the pages of memorabilia. Now, she headed to the farthest corner where the steamer trunks stood. She opened the first one. On top of a sheaf of papers was an old newspaper lauding the efforts of local boys fighting in the Pacific.

World War Two, Audra thought. That would be interesting, but it needed to wait until another time. Today, she wanted to know what happened to her family before the 1940s. She closed the lid and moved to the next trunk. A photo album lay on top of the papers. She opened the book. Mostly, it was family shots. The pictures of children playing caught her attention. They played baseball. Another group rode ponies. One teen girl triumphantly held up a giant salmon, a fishing pole nearby.

Something in the composition of the photos reminded her of the one she'd found of Beth. Not all the pictures had credits, but Audra spotted the distinctive "A. Morgan." The mysterious photographer wanted to show life in all its facets. Who was it? That was something else she could research on the computer. Couldn't some of the work have ended up in newspapers and magazines?

"Audra, are you up here?" Darlene came across the attic. "What's going on?"

"Not much." Audra closed the album, replacing it where she found it. She smiled at her mother. "Last week, Grand-Uncle Will and I discussed family history. I thought if it were all right with you, I'd put some of the older records in order. I want to video his stories before he gets much older, and they're lost to posterity."

"Sounds like a good idea. Is that why you brought your truck?"

"It has more room than Joe's Jeep," Audra said. "If you're okay with it, we'll take these trunks with us today. I have plenty of storage at Elinor's."

"That's fine." Darlene paused, then said, "I had him put that dog in the rig. It's too big and I didn't want it to scare the horses."

Counting silently to ten, Audra put the lid down on the trunk. She pretended that securing the top with the leather straps took all her attention. When she could control her tone, she said, "Navarre hasn't done anything to frighten the ponies at home. Was he chasing the horses here?"

"No, but I didn't want him to start."

"It's your place, but he's usually welcome wherever I go. Either Joe or I watch him, so he doesn't make trouble." Audra struggled to keep her tone civil. "I didn't want to leave him home. I overstepped the boundaries and I'm sorry. I won't bring him here again."

"Thank you, honey. That would be best. I can't have a dog upsetting the customers."

"Of course not." Biting her lip, Audra stalked across the room. She went downstairs and spotted Joe talking to Ethan and Brigid. "I need help here, guys. There are five containers of ephemera in the attic, and I want them in my truck now."

"Ephemera?" Brigid looked interested. "Any cookbooks?"

"No, but if I find any recipes, I'll email, and you can swing by the pony farm to pick up copies."

"You could bring them by next time you come," Brigid said.

Audra nearly said she wouldn't be back but held her patience and her tongue. If she revealed her anger and hurt, they'd never get the family papers. She'd wait. A few minutes later, Navarre barked as they approached the truck. She lowered the tailgate on the pickup and pointed out where she wanted the trunks. She stayed by the vehicle as the men went back into the house for the rest of the containers.

Joe eyed her as he loaded the last one. "What's up, Stinky. You look pissed."

"I am and I'm leaving. Are you coming with us? Or staying here? Ethan probably will give you a ride to your dad's."

A soft whistle and Joe leaned down to kiss her. "Are you kidding? I love it when you stand up to the Dawson coven. Go get 'em, darling. Navarre and I will wait here for you."

She drew a deep breath. "Did he do something wrong? I don't want to be unfair. If he attacked a guest or chased a horse or something small like a cat, then he should be in the truck."

"He was with me and that, along with breathing, was enough of a sin. He didn't even growl at the cat who smacked him." Joe shrugged. "Your mother may have married into the clan, but she has the typical Dawson control issues. We should have called and asked if the invite included your puppy, not assumed the whole family was welcome."

"That's a good way to say it." Audra returned to the kitchen where she found her mother with Brigid. Ethan washed his hands at the sink. "Okay, we're gone. We won't stay for dinner. I overstepped myself when I brought the puppy, and I don't want to leave him in the truck for hours."

"What?" Darlene gaped at her. "Don't tell me you're having a fit because I said the dog is a threat. Joe should get rid of him."

"He may be huge, Mother, but he's only a puppy. My puppy. You may not have been paying attention a couple weeks ago when Joe gave me Navarre for my birthday. I'm keeping him. He's not any more of a threat than any other canine. I'm an adult and I'm entitled to have pets provided that I'm a responsible owner." Audra hugged her sister. "Call and come by when it fits."

"Let me pack up some dinner for you," Brigid said. "You can take it with you and warm it up at home."

Audra shook her head. "No, but thanks. We can make the Rocking J in time for supper."

"Don't tell me she invited you to dinner," Darlene snapped. "What will Estelle say about that behemoth?"

"Nothing. She enjoys watching Navarre play with her grandkids. Joe and I have a standing invite to visit whenever we're close. He can do no wrong since he saved one of their mares." Audra glanced across the room at Ethan. As usual, he looked like a lumberjack in his flannel shirt, jeans, and boots. "Sorry about this contretemps, but you may as well get used to it if you decide to marry Clancy."

He grinned appreciatively, gray eyes amused. "Thanks for the warning, but your little sister tells me I have no choice. I got your email. I'll be at the Rocking J for the party in two weeks."

"Wonderful. That works for me." Audra strolled toward the front door. Behind her, she heard her sister and Ethan explain about the work party. Well, that ought to give Darlene something more to bitch about. As an added bonus, it'd provide an opportunity to enjoy some peace and quiet for a while since her mother would be sulking until after the get-together at the Rocking J.

———

She'd put the horses out to play in the beautiful summer sunshine while they finished the afternoon chores. Navarre looked up from a hoof paring and gave a deep bark. He didn't move from his position in the aisleway but continued to guard Audra and chew on the natural treat. She grinned and kept scooping horsy poop.

"Anybody home?" Marlene called, from the entrance of the mare barn. "Nobody was at the house, so I came here."

"Back here." Audra paused to wave to her aunt. "Haven't seen you for a few days. What's up?"

"Not much." Marlene came to a stop outside the stall. She bent to pet the dog. "I'm on one of my chore-checking missions. I want to know that the 4-H kids in my club actually do their own horse care, that they don't dump it on their parents or staff. Where are Jake and Lynn?"

"Cleaning the big barn. They told me it was my turn for the little one." Audra eyed her aunt, then returned to picking the stall. She kicked through the bedding, looking for any missing turds. "We zoom through the afternoon cleaning because the campers muck throughout the day. Why are you really here?"

Marlene blinked in surprise, then began to laugh. "I told your momma this wouldn't work, that you'd see through me in a heartbeat. She's all upset because you and Joe didn't stay for supper yesterday. You went off to Estelle's."

"And ordered in pizza when we found out that one of Uncle Will's friends had never had it." Audra carried the last forkful over to the muck bucket, then smoothed out the six inches of pine shavings in the stall. "As the saying goes, better a dinner of herbs where love is—"

"Then hatred and a stalled ox within," Marlene finished the quotation. "You may want to cut your momma some slack, honey. She's having a tough time. She's accustomed to having all of her daughters clustered around and this summer she's lost three of them."

"No way." Audra went to the next stall and began picking up the few piles of manure. "The others still live on the ranch. I'm the only one who stays where I work."

"Yes, but she doesn't have your undivided attention anymore or Kate's or Clancy's. Your mom feels threatened even if she won't admit it." Marlene carried over the plastic-wrapped bale of bedding. "Send her flowers and a nice card."

"You're not saying to go up there every night?"

"How can you?" Marlene began to add clean shavings. "You work more than ten hours a day. She just needs to know you care, so reach out. Now, I have to see Clancy and tell her to get home for dinner more than twice a week instead of hanging out at Ethan's until eleven at night."

"Good luck with that." Audra glanced at the barn door when she heard running footsteps. Navarre stood up a moment before Jake rushed inside. "What is it? What's wrong?"

"Blaze is down in the pasture. He's bleeding from the chest. Mom says come quick."

26

Audra wound her way through the rainbow herd of ponies, bays, palominos, chestnuts, paints clustered at the gate. She hurried toward Elinor and Lynn who knelt by the liver chestnut gelding lying in the middle of the field. Marlene lingered to give special instructions to Jake, and he dashed off in the direction of the bigger barn. Audra glanced over her shoulder as the older woman caught up. "What did you tell him?"

"To go finish the feeding so we can get these folks into their stalls. Something has upset them, or they'd be grazing, not leaving one of their own."

"Makes sense." Audra eased the halter off her shoulder when they neared. She stepped up to the pony and slid the noseband onto his face. She frowned at the deep scratch above his eye. "What happened, buddy?"

"While we figure things out, Jake needs your help, Lynn." Marlene put a hand on the teen's shoulder and guided her away. After a low conversation, the girl jogged across the field toward the barn. "Okay, let's see what we have."

Audra took the tissue her aunt offered and wiped at the chocolate brown fur. The three-inch scratch ran diagonally toward the white blaze that gave the Welsh-Quarterhorse his name. He nuzzled her hand affectionately and she wished she'd remembered to bring some carrots. She glanced over at his stablemates. They huddled near the gate, not even Bonanza coming back to inspect the humans for possible treats.

She petted the pony again. "What happened, Elinor?"

"I don't know. I heard fireworks and then the ponies spooked and galloped to the gate, all except Blaze."

"Not fireworks." Marlene glanced up from where she inspected the blood trickling down the right side of the pony's chest. "Gunshots." She probed gently at the wounds. "Probably a .22 caliber. Elinor, go help the kids and keep them in the buildings in case whoever did this is still around. Audra, use your cell and call Joe. Then, get the cops."

"What about Blaze?" Worry and concern remained on Elinor's face. "I've had him since I opened this place. Will he be okay?"

"We'll stay with him," Marlene said, deliberately not answering the question. "You have kids and other critters to look after right now. Get to it. And call Sean. You'll want him and his brothers."

Elinor managed a nod and hugged Blaze before she followed directions. Audra clenched her fists for a moment to calm down. Then, she pulled the cell phone out of her jeans pocket. She took a deep breath, tried to keep her tone steady so she wouldn't upset the pony. "You don't think he'll make it, do you?"

"That's up to Joe and Art. They're the miracle workers, not me. I do know that thirty years ago when a kid shot a guy's pony for sport, we ended up having to finish the job. Roy was furious. He dragged the boy out and made him dig the hole to bury the poor thing." Marlene straightened Blaze's dark mane. "Of course, back then your dog wouldn't have survived that poisoning either. There have been a lot of advances in vet medicine."

Audra nodded and started making calls. When she finished, she said. "Joe's on the way. He said to cold-hose the chest area to minimize the swelling until he gets here. It'll take a few minutes for me to run a hose from the orchard standpipe, but I'll be back as fast as I can."

"And Sean?"

"He was halfway here, but Joe wants a stock trailer to evacuate Blaze to a clinic with a tilt table so he can operate if Blaze needs surgery. Sean's stopping by Christy's to borrow her fancy horse hauler."

"Cops?" Marlene sat by the pony, holding Blaze's head on her lap. "Who did you get?"

"Uncle Will contacted a couple of Beth's friends. He says that shooting a pony here isn't like hunting up in the hills where someone might have mistaken Blaze for a deer. This was deliberate. He'll be along too, but the detectives and deputies may arrive before he does."

"Okay, sounds like you have a handle on it. Go get that hose."

Audra obeyed, wishing she were as calm as she'd sounded. Her hands shook when she unlatched the gate. Deep breaths, she told herself, but it didn't work. Her heart thudded. She felt like it'd leap from her chest. It'd been so difficult to keep her voice steady when she answered her aunt's questions.

But I managed, Audra thought. *I can do this. I won't be hysterical. I won't.*

When she returned with the hose, she was surprised to find Blaze standing. She eyed her aunt. "Why is he up?"

"He won't want to lie in a pool of cold water," Marlene said. "This fella is a people-pleaser. As soon as he knew I wanted him on all four hooves, he was willing to try. Get started. There's already edema. Let's see what we can do about it."

Audra switched the shut-off valve and turned on the water. The hose flexed in her hands. She began to soak the dark brown chest, starting on the left side and working her way to the right. Red streamed to the ground, some on Blaze's right foreleg, coloring the white sock. She wouldn't call it, blood. She wouldn't. Besides, it wasn't. Not really.

Joe arrived first. Medical instruments in a stainless-steel bucket, he strode across the orchard and through the open gate. In brown coveralls, he didn't look like a superhero, but she'd never been so glad to see anyone. He managed a professional smile. It didn't touch his sky-blue eyes. "Okay, let's see what we have here."

"Are you taking x-rays now?" Marlene asked.

"No. I'll wait until we get to the clinic, Fearless Leader. For now, it's a thorough exam. Then, I'll do an ultrasound to check his lungs before we move him. Sarah pulled up the medical records on the computer for me to scan at the clinic. Dad says all of Elinor's stock is up on tetanus. Of course, I'll be sedating this guy and getting him started on antibiotics."

"Will he live?" Tears stabbed her eyes and Audra blinked hard. "Please—"

She stared up at Joe when he put down the bucket. He stepped closer, pinched her chin in calloused fingers. "What?"

"Sweetheart, I'll do everything I can to save him. I need you to be strong and help me."

She nodded, biting her lip again. She glanced away, took a deep breath, and focused on running cold water over the pony's chest. She wouldn't think about how scared she was or how exhausting it was to always be the strong one. "I'm here."

"Good. I knew I could depend on you."

———

Zane enjoyed the show nearly as much as he had shooting at the herd of ponies. His first thought had been to kill the little showy bay, so he'd gone for a headshot. When he only creased the skull, he opted for four chest shots instead. That stirred up the neighborhood. The do-gooders had arrived first, followed by the cops. The police wouldn't do anything. Hell, they bitched a lot about animal cruelty on TV and in the local newspaper, but they never interfered with his fun over the Fourth of July. He'd bet they patted the old lady school teacher's hand and told her to get another cat to replace the one he killed.

"What's going on?"

He glanced over his shoulder at the man who was his mirror image. Their mothers had been identical twins, and few could tell their sons apart. It made for a lot of good times when they were kids, well good for him. He knew Robert hadn't enjoyed paying for all the trouble that he, Zane had caused. Hell, his cousin should thank him. He'd never have ended up in that military boarding school as a teen or had a successful Army career without him. The guy owed Zane and the least he could do was cough up some bucks and continue the free rent on the farm.

"Or should I ask what did you do now?"

"Just watching the neighbors." Zane shrugged. "Looks like they had some excitement today. You sure you want to move into this crazy neighborhood?"

"I am moving in and you're leaving." Folding his arms, Robert loomed in the doorway, pure menace in fatigues and combat boots. "The contractor got the permits to remodel the house this afternoon. Construction starts tomorrow. The landscaper arrives next week."

"I could supervise the work for you."

Robert laughed, a short, sharp sound. "You? I wouldn't trust you to dig a hole for a latrine. Don't mess with the crew from Hawke Construction. They've done their time in the *sandbox* and they know about guys like you. Nobody will ever find your body."

"And what will your mother say about that?" Zane smirked, unafraid. There had been threats before, but nobody ever believed Robert's wild stories especially since they were true. "You know how she feels about family. She's made it plain since my own dear mom bit the dust."

"You're forty-two years old. The charity ends now." Robert smiled, a bare crease of his lips. His dark eyes remained wary and watchful. "And my folks are so busy being grandparents to my kids and helping my wife pack up for a move to Washington State since I was transferred here, they won't even have time to take your calls. I told you three months ago to find another place to live. I meant it."

A solid thumping on the front door interrupted. Robert turned, strode to the front door. Zane followed, long enough to see the distinctive dark-green uniform the cop wore. Oh, let his cousin deal with this dust-up. That would be nearly as entertaining. No one would believe he wasn't the one who'd gone crazy with a rifle this afternoon. Everybody knew what the constant combat tours in Iraq and Afghanistan could do to a guy. And Robert had gone there five or six times.

Returning to the kitchen, Zane grabbed the backpack of food and slid out the back door. He melted into the fringe of evergreens that circled the yard. He'd come back later after his cousin and the sheriff's deputy had left the area. It wasn't like anyone genuinely cared about that silly pony.

———

She'd tried to write but couldn't enter her fictional world tonight. It had always provided the escape she needed from real life. She'd used her books to hide from her father's rejection, her mother's demands, the non-stop orders from the various employers. She could go to the fairytale realm in her mind and stay there when everything hurt too badly. But there wasn't a freedom ticket tonight. She had to deal, and she couldn't go with the family to the veterinary hospital in Snohomish. One look at Jake's worried face revealed he'd fret non-stop about the other animals unless she stayed to protect them.

She cuddled on the couch with Navarre. She'd channel-surfed for a half-hour before choosing to stare at a series of inane sitcoms. The telephone rang. She grabbed for the landline. "Silver Lake Pony Ranch."

"Audra, it's me. Clancy just got home and told me what happened. How are Midnight and Musketeer?"

"What?" Audra stared at the receiver. A tear trickled down her cheek. "I was out there helping with Blaze while the cops hunted for the nutcase. I could have been shot and you don't even ask about me."

"Don't be silly or hysterical. You weren't in any danger." Darlene heaved an audible sigh, distinctive even over the phone line. "The cliché is *Save the drama for your momma*, but that doesn't mean I want to hear it. I'm sending the trailer with Clancy. I want my ponies back. She can choose if she continues to work there. I'm making the decision for them. They were only on loan to Elinor. Thank goodness I didn't sell them to her."

"What are you thinking? This was a one-time occurrence. Beth's cop friends told me they'd include the area on more of their rounds and they'll be around a lot. Grand-Uncle Will says he and his Army buds will hang out too. We'll be doing everything we can to keep the campers and the horses safe."

"Good. I want those ponies here by ten tomorrow morning or I'll file a report they were stolen."

"My God, you're a bitch." Audra gasped and gaped at the phone. Had she actually said what she was really thinking? "I'm sorry, but it's going to be hard enough finding a substitute for Blaze and keeping everyone calm tomorrow. I don't need to send away two more ponies."

"You should have thought of that before you let someone shoot up the place and nearly kill one of the animals that you were responsible for. Now, you know what I expect. My horses in my barn first thing. Do it!"

Hours later, Navarre's low growl woke her. Opening her eyes, she reached over to pet the huge puppy lying next to the couch. Pyewacket slowly stretched to life and Audra followed suit. She must have dozed off after her last trek out to the barns to check on the ponies and other animals. Escorted by the dog and cat, she headed for the kitchen to see what had roused the animals. Joe stood on the back porch, obviously looking through his keys for the right one.

Audra unlocked and opened the door. "How is Blaze?"

"Good to see you too." Joe chuckled and stepped inside. "He's stabilized and under observation. None of the bullets penetrated any organs."

"That's amazing." Audra hugged him. "I'm so glad that you stuck around for the summer."

"Me too." He bent his head.

Their lips met in a kiss that was more tender than passionate. She framed his face in her hands. "Did you eat?"

"No time for it."

"Okay with scrambled eggs and toast?"

"Sounds wonderful."

"Then, I'll get started." While she assembled the materials, making trips to the refrigerator, the cupboard for a bowl, he watched warily. Audra cracked homegrown eggs into a cup first, carefully saving the shells for the hens. "You've seen me cook before. What's up?"

"Your mother called and ripped Elinor a new one while she and the kids were at the clinic. Sean's pissed."

"Why aren't I surprised?" Audra dumped the eggs into the bowl and began to whisk them with a fork. "I should have known I was her second call, not the first. She wants back the two ponies she loaned Elinor. Of course, Mom being Mom, she isn't willing to wait until Friday when this session of camp ends. No, it has to be first thing in the morning so it will disrupt as many lives as possible."

"All Elinor could think of was to use the mares and foals for some of the kids. She said that she couldn't adjust the time, so the kids rode less, not after advertising that everyone got two hours in the saddle."

"I did consider that and then I decided it wouldn't work." Audra took a few minutes to chop ham and cube cheese. "The mom mares won't focus if the babies start playing or investigate the other horses."

"Plus, the campers who get the mares would squabble with the ones who didn't and vice-versa." Joe filled cups of coffee for each of them. "So, what was your brilliant solution, Stinky?"

"I really played the bitch this time. I called Aunt Estelle, brought her up to speed, and asked if they had any ponies I could borrow until Labor Day. They're sending down four. Venus says they'll sell two of them to Elinor, take back the other two for their kids when school starts. Best of all, they'll handle delivering Midnight and Musketeer to my mom."

Joe stared at her with obvious fascination. "Your mom is going to totally freak. You know that she and Estelle are at odds over everything."

"Yes, and this way, Estelle gets to be the hero and my mom comes off like a real bitch, hitting Sean's wife when she was already down. It should be enough of a comeuppance that he'll continue to shoe the stock up there so he can take the high road."

"And enjoy watching her squirm while he plays the nice guy." Joe carried his coffee over to the table and sat down. "How did you know the Jamisons had suitable stock?"

"I didn't, but they've been buying, training, and reselling horses for the past year. It was worth trying." Audra poured the egg mixture into a frying pan, adding the meat and cheese. "And this way we'll have a good turnout to build fences up at Estelle's in a couple of weeks too. The rest of the family will love helping such a nice person. Everybody wins."

"I don't think your mom will see it that way. Doesn't she have issues with her older sister?" Joe chuckled. When the toaster popped, he pulled out the bread and buttered the two slices. "I'll hold off on bringing Dad up to speed. Then, Darlene will have someone sympathetic to her complaints about you. Since she heard the whole thing at the clinic, Marlene was ticked so it won't do your mom any good to call her."

"So, Aunt Marlene stuck around until you finished?" Audra dished up the eggs and brought over the plate. She sat down in the next chair to watch him eat. "I wanted to come with you guys too, but Jake looked scared to death when you mentioned it."

"He felt better once he knew you'd protect Chipeta and Awesome. Did you have any problems?"

"Nobody came by after you guys left. I padlocked the highway gates. I had the cops on speed dial, but I didn't need them. Navarre and I checked on the ponies and the rest of the stock several times. They were into eating and sleeping." Audra glanced at the milk-can-shaped clock on the wall. "We can do a walk-through when you finish eating."

"Works for me."

27

It felt as if they'd only been asleep for a few minutes when Navarre barked. Audra rolled out of bed, grabbing her robe on the way. She followed the dog's wagging tail and went to the back door, frowning as she saw two men standing on the porch. She flicked on the light and recognized Orion with Kyle Morgan behind him.

She unlocked and opened the door. "What are you guys doing here so early? It's not even daylight."

"Dawn's about two hours away," Orion agreed. "Give me your keys so I can get the trailer and the ponies in off the road. The girls need to get started before it's any later."

"Started on what?" Audra demanded. "I take care of the stock here."

"A protection spell."

"What?" Audra gaped at him. "I don't get it."

"You called my mom. You asked for help." Orion sounded as if he was explaining the facts of life to a small child. "She sent you the horses. She also told my sisters to come down and ward the place so evil can't enter here, and you'll be able to live without fear. Keys, please. We must get going before the sun comes up.

The spell will be stronger if the girls do it now, before the break of day."

Shaking her head, Audra followed directions. She handed him the set of keys and watched him jog toward the gates in the moonlight. She eyed Kyle. "I don't believe this. It sounds so much like my new book, but that was just a story I created. I'm going to have to totally change the characters and setting now."

"Why?" He grinned at her. "Do you think anyone will actually believe your cousins are witches? Or that I came here through a gate in *Time*, sent by a woman that everyone knows was murdered?"

"I just make up stories." She stared up at him. "You knew that before Grand-Uncle Will shared it, didn't you?"

"Bethany told me." Kyle pushed back his hat with a thumb. "Folks aren't really sympathetic to a man writing tall tales, not even my brother. She said you'd understand and help me learn how to write my books. You're a storyteller, one who shares her own truth whether people want to believe it or not."

"I guess that's one way to look at it." Audra watched the horse trailer pull into the front yard and park, with a late-model Lexus behind it. "I still can't believe Astra is here. Venus said she had a big court case coming up, so Meteor would bring the ponies in the morning. How did Aunt Estelle manage to get all three of them to show up?"

Kyle shrugged a broad shoulder. "She said that when the head witch calls, all the little ones better ride their broomsticks where she sends them."

"I'm glad my mom doesn't know about this aspect of Aunt Estelle. We'd never hear the end of it." Audra stepped to one side as Navarre went to investigate her cousins. "I'd better get dressed so I can put the ponies in the corral until I arrange their stalls."

"I'll do that," Kyle said. "I'm here for the day. I helped patrol Junction City for my brother, the marshal. I'm not afraid of trouble, even if I don't look for it."

"Well, that sounds good." Audra glanced toward the vehicles

again and decided her dog would be safe enough visiting with her family. She returned to the bedroom. Joe was already dressed. "My cousins are here with the horses and things are about to get weird. Are you okay with that?"

"How strange?"

"They're going to cast a spell to protect the farm and ward off evil."

"That sounds interesting. Will they let us watch?"

"I have no idea."

She'd forgotten how insatiably curious he was about everything. In a way, that was a blessing. He wouldn't decide she was crazy or that her family belonged in some sort of loony bin. Besides, he was right. She'd enjoy seeing the ritual even if she didn't use it in one of her books. Who knew? It might help guard the pony farm from the nutcase who'd shot Blaze. It certainly couldn't hurt.

———

Audra finished signing out the last camper and waved goodbye. "See you tomorrow." As the car left, she followed it to the gates to close them. Then, she turned and walked toward the house to let out the dogs. Escorted by the canine contingent, she headed for the classroom where Elinor and Clancy had started to set up for the staff meeting.

Jake rushed to meet her, then dropped to his knees and hugged his puppy. "What did you do last night? The farm doesn't feel scary like it did when we left with Blaze."

"I didn't do anything." Audra glanced at Lynn. "What?"

"Where did you get the other ponies?" The teen petted the gold and white collie mix who leaned against her leg. "Your mom didn't send them."

"No. She has back her two and my Aunt Estelle bailed us out." Audra gestured toward the classroom. "Let's go have our meeting. Then, I'll only have to go through the story once."

"Will you tell everyone why there's rock salt and pentacles at the entrance gates?" Jake asked. "Did you do the protection rite?"

Audra stopped and stared at the boy. "What are you talking about?"

"He's into magick." Lynn heaved a sigh. "You can't hide it from him so you may as well tell him. He spotted the wind chimes and strings of bells in all the barns too. They were hard to miss."

Heat flooded into Audra's face as she started for the mare's barn again. She hoped he hadn't seen the witch's jars buried at the four corners of the farm or known their significance. It had been embarrassing enough when Astra handed her the four jars and told her to go pee in them. Normally, Venus said they'd have used just one container, but since the farm had such a serious adversary, more drastic means were required.

She stopped outside the door to the stairs and drew a deep breath. "Does your mom believe?"

"You can't tell her," Jake said, "not about the *Craft*. She had a hard enough time handling it when we got Sean in answer to one of my spells."

"Then, we probably shouldn't share that my cousins and aunt are witches. The triplets did what they called a *cleansing and protection* ritual." Audra held up her hand. "I'm not saying to lie to your mom. I'm just saying that unless she asks, let's keep this woo-woo stuff to ourselves. A lot of people don't believe, and the way Orion explained it to me, even when they're good people, they can undo what he and his sisters did."

Jake nodded. "And we don't invite evil here so none of our visitors will deliberately break the spell. Okay, I just wanted to know. Can I meet them?"

"That's so like you." Lynn laughed and shoved her brother's shoulder. "You find out it's all real and you want to meet the people who do serious magick."

"I've always known it's real," Jake retorted. "Can I, Audra? Will you introduce me?"

"I'll ask your mom if you can come with me to the fence-building party we're having at my aunt's next week." Audra climbed the stairs to the classroom. "What about you, Lynn? It's on a Sunday. Do you want to come and help?"

"If Mom can handle this farm without us, it'd be cool," Lynn said. "Thanks for inviting us."

"Where did she invite you?" Clancy finished putting dough-nuts on a plate. "Can I come too?"

"To Aunt Estelle's for the shindig there next week," Audra said. "Are you really going to be there?"

"Ethan says that he is, and I told him that I'd meet him there after we finish up here," Clancy said. "Mom is freaking about the ponies now, so she's stopped having a fit about everyone going to the Rocking J."

"Why on earth would she be freaking?" Elinor asked, filling coffee cups. "She wanted her ponies back. She got them. They arrived before the specified time too."

"Because Aunt Estelle isn't afraid of my mom's tantrums and calls it as she sees it," Clancy said. "She phoned and gave Mom a karma lecture, that everything comes back on the sender and by not stepping up, there's some bad ju-ju sliding Mom's way."

"What did Mom say?" Audra asked.

"Oh, she told Estelle not to threaten her and the conversation went downhill from there."

"It wasn't a threat." Jake headed for the sink to wash his hands. "It was a warning."

"Yeah, what goes around, comes around," Lynn said, following her brother.

"And what do you think, Audra?" Clancy asked.

"That there are more things on heaven and earth than we know about," Audra said. "I'm just grateful that Aunt Estelle and her kids came through for us."

"Mom said Aunt Estelle claimed to be a witch when they were kids and ran off to learn how to use her powers. Do you believe that?"

"All I know is they helped me when nobody else would,"

Audra said, "and I'll call them whatever they want me to call them."

By avoiding the subject of magick, it hadn't taken long to tell everyone about the deal with Estelle and Astra. Buying the two extra ponies made good sense. Elinor wanted to open a new farm over at Sean's and that meant they needed more stock, not less.

"Maybe your cousin could find us about six more head," Elinor said. "Gentle, small ones suitable for kids and tweens. We barely get any teenagers or adults to ride here and when I start the new place, I can't see that changing."

"So, what training does Estelle think the other ponies need?" Clancy picked up a second maple bar. "They rode great in my class. You didn't look like you were having any problems with them, Elinor."

"I wasn't." Elinor agreed. "So, what's the deal?"

"They have a toddler who loves to run and scream all around the barn and a six-year-old boy who doesn't have any knowledge. Venus thinks that after the two oldest ponies do camp, they'll ignore the hijinks and be happy to just do a few rides."

"They should bring down the older kid for camp," Lynn said. "He'd learn to groom, saddle and ride."

Her mother and Clancy shared a look. Then, Elinor said, "We could comp the week since they loaned us the horses."

"What does *comp* mean?" Kyle hadn't contributed much to the conversation before. He listened, coffee cup in hand. "The Jamisons have pride even when they don't have much else."

"It's short for complimentary," Audra said. "Elinor is saying we'd let the boy come for free as a way to say *thank you* for everything they've done. Clancy, you could swing by the Rocking J on the way here and pick up Quaid, couldn't you?"

Clancy shook her head and looked away. "Get somebody else."

Audra froze for an instant as she saw a tear slide down her sister's cheek. "Oh no. What did you do?"

"Why do you always think I did something?"

"Because you always do." Audra was up, around the table, and hugging the taller woman. "Tell me. What happened?"

"I argued with Mom." Clancy turned her face into Audra's blouse. "I didn't intend to, but she was so mean about everything, especially when I told her she made me look like a fool for loaning ponies to Elinor. She always says we should help others because we got help when we started living at the Lazy B and teaching horsemanship."

"And you believed her?" Audra stroked the bright red hair. "Honey, she talks it, but she doesn't walk that talk."

"She always fights with you and Brigid, but she doesn't do that to me. Then, she told me that if I didn't agree with her decisions, to get out of her house. It was her way or the highway. I hate when she does that to you, but I didn't think—"

"I know." While tears soaked her shirt, Audra cuddled Clancy close. "Do you want to stay here with me? There's a guest room in the house or you can have this classroom."

"I went to Ethan's last night. He's going to Wichita for a week so he said I can stay there. He gave me his room and slept on the couch." Clancy cried harder, shoulders shaking. "If I haven't made up with Mom by the time he gets back, he'll help me find an apartment."

"Sounds like a good guy." Kyle drank more coffee. "Aren't you too old to blubber because you had a squabble with your ma?"

"None of us dare to argue with my mother," Audra said, giving him a stern look. "She never learned to fight fair."

"I never understood that," Kyle said. "Can't win if you're caught up on being fair and ain't winning what a battle's about?"

Elinor sighed and rose to go after the coffee pot. "I don't think you're being fair to your mother. She's scared to death. She can't corral you two, so she settles for demanding the horses back in the barn where she can protect them. And she'd be perfectly happy if you'd both go home to the Lazy B where she can keep you safe."

"And words are just words." Kyle shrugged a broad shoulder.

"Ain't like she's Trace Burdette, and she's gonna put you in Boot Hill if you insult her."

Marcie propped her chin on her fist. "Who is Trace Burdette?"

"The gal who started the Lazy B with her grandpa," Kyle said. "Before she killed you, she'd make you dig the hole. Tale was that if she got real annoyed, she'd have her hands bury you alive."

"No way." Marcie rolled her eyes. "Everybody knows the Dawsons are one of the oldest families in Washington state and they've had the Lazy B forever."

"Because we married Trace's heirs." Audra patted her sister's shoulder. "She was a real woman who lived a long time ago."

"Doesn't feel that long ago to me," Kyle said, holding out his cup for a refill. "Her grandpa raised her, and he wanted her safe, so he treated her like a boy. Everyone in Junction City thought she was one. When he died in an ambush, he left her his pearl-handled pistols and she wore 'em for the rest of her life. Well, most of the time. Not always. She killed men with those guns or her knife, and I heard she was deadly with the bullwhip, too."

"I don't know of a Junction City, or a Trace Burdette," Elinor said, "and I used to teach Washington state history."

"Her biography isn't in a lot of books," Audra said. "She owned Junction City, and it was bypassed when the railroads came through. Her town died, and since she was *unusual*, nobody talked about her. Of course, when I was in school, I never learned about the suffrage movement in Washington Territory or that women still fought for the vote even when Washington became a state."

"By 1888, she was married to Zeb Prescott, running the Lazy B, and raising a passel of orphans," Kyle said, drinking more coffee. "Including a gang of Dawson kids after their pa died."

Clancy lifted her head and reached for a tissue to wipe her eyes and nose. "You mean my family?"

"Yup. They were kin to the biggest bunch of wannabe bad men you've ever seen. Bank robbers, swindlers, gamblers, back-shooting scum." Kyle shook his head, disgusted. "And dance-hall merchants, too! Not an honest horse thief or gunman among them. Their women weren't respectable either, not till Miss Mina."

"Stealing a horse then would get you hung." Audra glanced at the wide-eyed kids then looked back at Kyle. "Don't you dare mention what a *soiled dove* was, or a *hurdy-gurdy* girl either."

"I wouldn't, not in decent company."

Sandy and Marcie turned on Elinor, who leaned back in her chair, laughing. "What are they talking about?"

"History. You two are in college. Open a book. Read." Elinor shook her head, still amused. "If all else fails, go next door and talk to Daisy. I'll bet she'd love the company. She's still lonely since one of her cats disappeared over the Fourth of July."

Another look between the older teens, and then they pushed back their chairs. "We're doing chores," Sandy announced. "After the ponies are fed, we can go see Daisy."

"Can we help?" Jake jumped up. "I want to know everything."

"Yes." Elinor pointed to the door. "Go, Lynn. You're old enough to learn a few down and dirty details about history."

"I don't know about that," Kyle said. "She may be marrying age, but some things just ain't decent."

Lynn's eyes widened. "I'm only fourteen. I'm not old enough for that."

"In olden times, you would be," Elinor said. "And Sean would find a nice friend of his like Joe who'd be a good husband to you. Don't worry. You're a pretty girl. We'd give you a nice dowry."

"That's just gross. I'd never marry an old guy like Dr. Joe even if he did save Blaze." Lynn headed for the door. "I'll bet Daisy says you're joking. Fourteen-year-old girls didn't get married, not ever."

"And I'll bet a week's laundry that I'm right," Elinor said.

"You're on!"

Lynn vanished down the stairs calling for the others to wait. Elinor grinned. "I have to do that more often. Jake won't bet with me since he ended up on dish duty."

"You're a good mom." Clancy blew her nose before she looked

at Audra again. "I guess what you're saying is that all the Dawsons aren't perfect, and neither is Mom."

"And I know I'm not." Audra sat back down again. "I'll cut her some slack because Elinor and Aunt Marlene think Mom's having a tough time. I'm glad you stood up to her and came today. It would have been a lot harder to do camp with a new instructor and new horses."

"I wouldn't bail on you." Clancy took a deep breath. "I know I don't like grunt work, and I can be the princess you call me, but I'm not a coward."

"None of the Burdettes or Prescotts ever was, and their blood runs deep," Kyle said. "If you come from Miss Mina's branch of the Dawsons, you have reason to be proud."

"We do and we are," Audra said. "I don't recommend you fish Trace's pistols out of the gun locker in the attic, Clancy, and start wearing them even if Mom does piss you off."

Clancy giggled. "Are they really still there?"

"I don't know, but I wouldn't be surprised. Dawsons aren't known for throwing anything away."

Clancy touched Audra's hand. "Thank you for being so nice to me. I've been a real witch to you, but I—"

Remembering the night before, Audra gripped her sister's fingers. "I'd never call you a witch, honey. I know yesterday was scary, but I'm glad you're here with me."

"And Brigid is, too. She sent the doughnuts with me last night."

"They're almost as good as Ma Sims' ever were." Kyle snagged the last plain one from the box. "You may have to move back home just so we can get more."

That prompted a real laugh from Clancy. "Typical guy. No, I won't. Brigid will bring a carton down when she comes to visit."

"Okay, now that everything is settled, let's plan the rest of the week." Elinor reached for a pad of paper and a pen. "Kyle, I appreciate your being here, but don't you have work to do for Estelle?"

"I am. She wants me here until the chickens come home to

roost and the fellow who shot the pony is in the hoosegow." Kyle looked around the classroom. "I've bunked in worse places. I can sleep on that sofa."

"It folds down into a bed," Audra said. "I'll show you how to do that later."

"And you'll teach me what Bethany said you would while I'm here. Sounds like a fair deal to me."

"Bethany?" Clancy gaped at Audra. "You mean he's a friend of our cousin?"

"Yes. You could call it her last request for me, and I'll honor it."

"I wouldn't call it a last one." Kyle bit into the doughnut and chewed. After he swallowed, he added, "You go through those papers of your Uncle Will's, and you'll find a dozen more."

Audra winced and nodded. "You're probably right. I'd forgotten she always wrote out a long list before she headed back to Iraq and Afghanistan."

"Sounds like you'll be even busier." Elinor tapped her pen on the table. "Let me know how I can help."

While she cleaned up after supper, Joe went to help Kyle settle into the classroom. Audra thought about everything that had happened in the last two days. She remembered what Meteor had said on her way out the gate. Her cousins had sent the evil back to the evil-doer, times three. He should be facing the consequences of his actions soon.

Audra shook her head as she scraped dishes. She just hadn't expected her aunt to speak to her mom. Normally, Estelle and Darlene avoided one another. And Clancy opting for what she considered morality rather than expediency—who'd have thunk it?

As if the recollections of the day conjured up the reaction, Audra felt her cell phone vibrate. She pulled it out of her jeans, looked at the screen, and then answered. "Hi, Mom. How are you?"

28

AUDRA LEANED BACK IN THE PASSENGER SEAT OF THE JEEP AND flicked a sideways glance at Joe. He was focused on driving and that gave her time to think about the phone call from her mother. She wanted help to reconcile with Clancy but wasn't willing to admit there might be errors on both sides. Instead, everything was all Clancy's fault and that was going to go over like a lead balloon.

According to her younger sister, the biggest problem she had was convincing Ethan that they could live together without the benefit of the clergy. And he wasn't willing to settle for anything less than marriage. Meanwhile, Mom's latest tantrum was a do-it-yourself deal and Clancy wasn't willing to meet their parent halfway.

"Can I help?" Joe asked, slowing for a red light. "You haven't said a word since I told you I had an emergency and asked if you wanted to come along."

"Family stuff," Audra admitted. "My mom wants me to run interference between her and Clancy. It's hard to do since I'm ticked about the horse changes and grateful that my sister is riding for the proverbial brand which happens to be the Silver Lake Pony Ranch, not the Lazy B. And it doesn't mean I think my sister is perfect because I know she's not."

"Why not just say that?"

"Because then I end up being the bad guy. Mom will be mad at me for not supporting her a hundred percent and Clancy will feel the same way."

Joe shrugged. "Reminds me of what Roy used to say."

"What's that?"

"A person who rides the fence ends up with a sore crotch."

Audra laughed. "Thanks a lot."

They wound through one last neighborhood of what she considered cookie-cutter dwellings. Then, he pulled into the circular drive-in front of a fancy three-story house and followed the paved road around to a barn and adjacent indoor arena. He parked his rig. "Well, are you ready to see how the other half lives?"

"You bet." Audra opened her door. She nodded at the young brunette in breeches, boots, and a cream sweater who hustled toward her. It was hard to believe that the other woman had gone to high school with Clancy. "Hi, Christy. What's going on?"

"I don't know. Jack was here to work with the horse I bought up at Xanadu. He was riding her when she stopped going forward. She wouldn't move even when he spurred her and used a crop. It looked to me like she'd lamed up on both hind legs, but he said she was just being stubborn."

"I'd rather hear Joe's opinion." Audra followed the younger woman in the direction of the barn. "I don't remember you buying a horse at the sale last spring."

"I didn't because I had to wait until I had more room in the barn and Nathan got over being annoyed at me. He thought I had too many, so I sold three. Then, I bought Sable Moonlit Charm in June for three-day eventing."

Audra felt the name slam into her heart. She'd bottle-fed the orphaned filly from the day her mother died, a week after Charm was born. The Bergstroms had claimed that they were going to keep her since the dam had been one of their best. Now, they'd sold the young mare to this twit who couldn't tie the laces on her Ropers without help. "I didn't know she was for sale."

"She was totally tearing down her stall and they were freaking out, so I got a great deal on her."

"Really?" Audra glanced across the indoor arena and saw the mare lying down on the far side of the ring. "How long has she been like this?"

"She went down under Jack and refused to get up. I listened and she had those gut sounds that Dr. Joe told me about, so I knew it wasn't colic. I told Jack that and he gave me a ration of crap about being a Sunday rider, so I kicked him out. I put a blanket on her because she looked cold and called you."

"You did the right thing, Christy. I'm going to want to run a few tests, but it looks like she's tying up." Joe rested a hand on Audra's shoulder. "I forgot to bring any carrots. Would you find some, Christy?"

"Sure. I'll be right back." She hurried off in the direction of the stalls.

"She did the right thing?" Audra hissed, her voice a bare whisper. "That stupid bitch."

"Could be worse. They could have started treating Charm for colic and tried to make her walk. That would make the condition worse and increase the chance of muscle damage."

Audra glared at him, then hurried to her baby. The young mare pricked up her ears and nickered, then nuzzled her. Catching the halter, Audra held the horse's head and hugged her back. "Oh, I'm so sorry."

"It's not your fault," Joe said. "You weren't here."

"I wasn't there either to stop them from selling her."

"You couldn't protect her. You didn't own her, and you couldn't have stopped the Bergstroms from selling the horse to Christy. At least, she's been learning a few things from Elinor. I'd be willing to bet there was a time when she wouldn't have stood up to a trainer."

"I guess you have a point." Audra stroked the mare's blazed

face. Charm heaved a huge sigh and closed big, brown eyes. "So, what are you going to do for her?"

"I'll start with a physical exam, run some tests, and then put her on painkillers and anti-inflammatories. I'm also going to have to keep an eye on you so that Jack doesn't end up hung by his toenails or his testicles."

"That all sounds good," Audra said, ignoring the comment about what she might do to the trainer. She decided to pass the word to the other Dawsons in the horse business about how incompetent Jack Abbott was. It might cost the man a few bucks and it would provide her with a great deal of satisfaction. She smoothed the black forelock. "What about hot-packing her hindquarters?"

Joe nodded. "Heat will help ease the sore muscles. Let's see if this Taj-Ma-Barn has any thermal blankets."

———

Kyle put aside his pen and left the pad of paper on the table. His fictionalized story about Trace Burdette was coming along, but he needed to walk around the farm before dark. Elinor thought of her twenty acres as being a big piece of land and that amused him. He ought to ask Will how to find the old Bar M. It'd be interesting to see what had become of Rad and Bethany's spread. The large dog lying by the door rose and stretched.

"Come on then." Kyle followed the dog down the stairs into the small barn. Two of the mares still finished up their hay. The oldest one stood guard over her sleeping foal, half dozing.

Kyle smiled and headed out to the main barn. The rest of the ponies were fine, even the four that had come down from the Rocking J. Next, he checked on the pigs, the calves, and the cow. He heard the soft clucking of the hens as they roosted in the chicken house. Nothing to fret about, he thought.

The big dog stood in front of him, growling. Kyle glanced toward the gate and saw someone, a man standing at the locked gates. Did Miss Audra expect company? She hadn't said anything about it. Well, no reason to be unsociable.

Kyle headed that way, the young dog pacing beside him. "Evening. Help you with something?"

"I'm not sure." The stranger held out his hand. "Rob O'Malley. I own the farm down the street. Saw the cops here last night. Looked like you had some excitement."

"Could say that." Kyle eyed the fellow. He wore a strangely mottled blue suit, pants tucked into low-heeled boots, and an odd sort of hat that covered short black hair. Slowly, Kyle reached out to shake the man's hand. Calloused and he gripped hard, so he might dress funny, but apparently this Rob worked for a living. "One of the ponies was shot."

Rob narrowed dark brown eyes. "My cousin may know something about that. He's been least in sight all day, according to the fellows I have working on my house."

"I'll pass the word. What's his name?"

"Zane O'Malley. I'd tell the cops, but I'm headed back to Georgia."

"What's he look like?"

"Me," Rob said, with a faint smile. "Our mothers were identical twins. Same height, but he's about twenty pounds heavier. His hair's longer than mine too. He doesn't have a speaking acquaintance with the truth and his streak of mean runs deep."

"Fair enough." Kyle stepped back. "We'll keep an eye out for him."

"I told him to move on, but I don't know if he will before I return with my family." Rob grimaced. "He will when I get back."

———

The last week had flown by between finishing one session of day camp and teaching a second one. Then there were the daily visits to Charm and Blaze. Like everyone else on the pony farm, Audra had been watching out for Zane O'Malley, but she hadn't seen the man anywhere. However, there was an entire construction crew remodeling the house down the street. She'd barely made time to work on her new manuscript and do a final set of edits on the book scheduled for a September release.

Audra looked at her grocery list. She had more shopping to do. She pushed the heavy cart through the wholesale grocery. It was time to find the bottled water and a selection of cookies and crackers for tomorrow's fence-building party. She'd pick up three large bags of carrots too, two for the pony farm and one for Charm.

Audra lifted her chin and blinked hard. She wouldn't think about what Joe said last night. If Charm didn't regain full use of her muscles, she'd never make it as a dressage or jumping prospect. The work would be too hard for her. There had to be a special hell for people like Jack Abbott. How could he do something so heinous, overwork a young horse to the point she collapsed underneath him?

Because nobody stood up to him, Audra thought, nobody but her and the Animal Control officers wouldn't hassle Bergstrom's trainer. Jack was the proverbial legend in his own mind and figured rules didn't apply to him. He should have been monitoring Charm's physical condition while he trained her, not tried pushing a willing horse so hard. Well, if she kept thinking about it, she'd be in tears before she finished here. Carrots, she told herself firmly, and she'd look for the organic Golden Delicious apples the filly loved too.

Once she finished up here, she'd run the groceries to the Rocking J. She'd swing by the vet clinic in Snohomish to see how Blaze felt. He was scheduled to go to Sean's barn on Monday and complete his recovery. He'd be ready to do gentle pony rides by Christmas and return to full-time work next summer. It was a good thing he belonged to Elinor. Her ponies did a lot more walking than trotting or galloping. Joe had reason to be proud of himself, even if he didn't brag about his skill.

———

Audra parked in the shade of a towering maple tree. Lynn and Jake were the first to slide out of the pickup, accompanied by Navarre. They trooped toward the house. Two-year-old Fallyn hustled down the porch steps and ran toward them, Venus right behind. Navarre woofed, and loped to meet them, tail wagging. The toddler greeted him with shrieks of delight while he tried to lick her face.

"He's such a good dog." Venus petted him, then collected her daughter before she climbed on Navarre. "If you ever need to find him a home, think of us."

"I will, but don't hold your breath." Audra laughed. "I didn't know how much I wanted a dog until I got him. Now, I can't imagine my life without him. He's such a wonderful companion and a real comedian."

"It is pretty funny when Pye chases him around the house," Lynn said.

"I'll bet." Venus grinned at both kids. "Welcome to the Rocking J. I'm glad you came."

"Really?" Jake asked. "Did Audra tell you about us?"

"She did, but she didn't need to." Venus smoothed Fallyn's strawberry-blond curls. "I saw your work in the garden."

"I didn't think you noticed that Elinor grows most of her own veggies." Audra tilted her head to one side. "The kids do a lot of the weeding, but I think it's because they like to pull carrots for their ponies."

"Oh, I wasn't talking about that," Venus said, juggling the little girl on her hip. "It was the love-bringing spell. How many times did you cast it?"

"The what?" Audra glanced at Lynn and Jake. The girl blushed and the boy looked away. "Okay, you two. Start talking. What have you been up to?"

Absolute silence reigned for a moment before Venus said gently, "Witches take pride in their work. You should share what you did."

"You deserve a hero because you are one, Audra," Jake said. "We cast a spell so the right guy would come to you. It worked when we did it for Mom and Sean so we knew it would work for you and Dr. Joe."

"Really?" Audra didn't know if she believed in their spell or not. They apparently did. It could be pure coincidence Joe returned at this time and they'd resolved their differences. Or perhaps, Fate had taken a hand as well.

"This is my life," Audra told the two wannabe witches. "From now on, I control it. Deal?"

Lynn nodded and elbowed her brother when he started to protest. "Deal. Thanks, Audra. Do us a favor and don't tell Mom. She's not real excited about Jake's magick."

"I'll tell her if she asks me, but she probably won't." Audra smiled at the duo. "Now, let's go meet some folks."

29

JOE HAD PLANS TO MEET AUDRA AT HER COUSINS' PLACE TODAY, but as his father often said, "Sick animals don't have a time clock or a calendar." And when a cow needed help calving, it meant Joe's schedule went by the wayside and he headed off to work. Still, mom and baby were doing fine. He was headed back to the clinic to shower and change, but he could swing into Christy's place and check on Charm. She'd responded to the drugs he supplied and to Audra's fussing. The young mare had returned to life in her roomy box stall. She ate well and was able to stand for several hours yesterday.

He pulled in and parked behind the fancy horse trailer Christy had loaned Sean to use to transport Blaze. What was going on? Was a new horse moving in? Why? It looked like it might be a few months before Charm was back to normal. Still, the filly was young and strong so she should come through this bout of azoturia simply fine. Collecting his tote from the back of the truck, he headed into the barn aisle. He spotted Christy giving a carrot to the bright bay mare. "How is she today?"

"She's been up most of the morning. I think she'll haul to Mount Vernon fine."

"Not a good idea." Joe stepped up to stroke the side of the

mare's face and she nuzzled him. "Charm isn't ready to be hauled that far. It'd be too stressful. Why do you want to take her on a road trip?"

"The Bergstroms are willing to provide a replacement horse so I don't sue them because of their incompetent trainer. I need the stall for the gelding they're giving me. So, I'll run her up to Mount Vernon. She can finish recuperating there until the owner of the feedlot takes the next load to Canada."

Fury rocketed through him and his jaw tightened. He struggled to keep his tone civil, not say what he thought of owners who disposed of animals so carelessly. "You're sending her to slaughter? I haven't finished with her yet."

"I'll write you a check," Christy said. "I appreciate everything you and Audra did for her, but she's going to cost more money than she's worth. And there's no guarantee that she'll come back ready for three-day eventing. This way, I won't have to throw more good money after bad."

"Give me the horse and you won't owe me a cent," Joe said.

"Are you serious?"

"Yes. Do we have a deal?" When she slowly nodded, he put down his plastic carrier of medications. "All right. I'll call Sean and have him bring over his trailer. We'll take her right now and then you'll have the stall. Let's do the paperwork."

———

Audra glanced around the yard. In their spare time, Orion and Kyle had managed to build several picnic tables over the last few weeks. Three of the tables were lined up to provide a buffet crowded with casseroles, salads, chips, and breads. Cakes, pies, other homemade goodies, and gallons of ice cream in the freezer waited in the house, ready to come out for dessert. Uncle Jim had chicken, hotdogs, and hamburgers sizzling on his giant grill. Aunt Regina stocked more bottles of soda, milk, and water in an ice chest.

"I think we're ready for that herd of locusts building the

fences." Estelle came toward Audra holding a small metal rod. "You put this together, so you get the honor of ringing the triangle."

"Seriously?" Audra eyed the woman. Short and plump with long graying red hair, she bore more of a resemblance to Aunt Marlene than her other sisters. "I've never done that before."

"Come on," Estelle said. "I'll show you how." As they walked toward the back porch, she added. "Kyle was so happy when he got here this morning. He showed me his story and told me all about what you're teaching him."

"Have you read his book?" Audra asked. "I've seen a half-dozen pages, but that's it."

"Well, since he writes by hand, he only has a few chapters ready to share." Estelle frowned, blue eyes narrowing thoughtfully. "I don't know if you should teach him to run a computer or not, even if it would help him write faster. He hasn't said if he's staying for good, or if he's just visiting. And I can't *see* him here, five years in the future."

"See him? I don't understand."

"You should. I didn't just leave home because I wanted to escape. I needed to go so I could learn how to control my powers. My daughters and son came by theirs honestly."

The more that she heard about her cousins and aunt, the more Audra knew she had to revise her book so that it didn't bear any resemblance to her extended family. She couldn't expose actual witches to the public. She watched Estelle run the metal rod around the large triangle hanging down from the porch roof. A loud clanging ensued. When it was her turn, Audra repeated the action, successfully creating more noise.

"You could get the same effect by using a cell phone," Darlene said disapprovingly behind them. "Calling the different parties back to the house that way wouldn't create as much racket."

"Or be as much fun," Estelle said, cheerfully. She hung the short rod by the triangle. "I'm glad you're here, Darlene. Your daughters have been so helpful. You must be really proud of them."

"Of course." It was an automatic response, one lacking any sincerity and all three of them knew it.

Estelle patted Audra's shoulder. "Help me out here and go show people where to wash up. It's not a task I'd normally ask *you* to do, but I want to talk to your mother."

"Why not me?" Audra tilted her head. "I don't mind."

"Because where I come from, teachers and bards are of a higher status. I didn't need Kyle to tell me that you hold up a proverbial mirror to show people the way they should act."

Amused and touched by the assessment, Audra laughed. "Well, I think teaching cleanliness falls into my bailiwick."

She headed over to Lynn who supervised the younger kids playing with Navarre. "Come on. Let's help these munchkins clean up for lunch. Are you having fun?"

"Yes." Lynn beamed at her, scooping up Fallyn. "I wish we had babies like these at home. They're so cute."

"What about Jake?"

"Oh, he's in heaven. He went off talking to Orion about magick and dragons. And Orion listened, then told Jake he had a lot to learn."

An hour later, it was time for her to join her family for the meal. Audra glanced at her watch, wondering what happened to Joe. He ought to be here by now. Well, his first emergency had undoubtedly stretched into a second. She picked up a plate and began to fill it with different types of salad. She paused by the grill and chose a piece of chicken. Grabbing a bottle of water, she strolled over to where her mother sat with the twins, Kate, and Brigid at a small table.

"How's it going?" Audra put down her plate. "Are you having fun?"

Kate gave her a long look. "Things have just started to get exciting, Destynee."

"What did you call me?" Audra felt heat rush into her face, then slide away. Her knees shook. "Who told you? How do—"

"Kyle," Brigid's tone was calm. "Pull up a seat. He doesn't understand that you've kept your alter ego a secret. How many books have you written?"

"Thirty-five." Audra sank into the chair that Wendy vacated and pushed forward. "I've sold twenty-eight."

"What happened to the others?" Kate asked. "Can I read them?"

"No. I'm working on my next story. The rest are put away."

"Why?" Darlene glared at her. "Are you ashamed of them? You should be."

Audra stiffened, anger mingling with hurt. "I couldn't sell them. They weren't ready to show anyone, and I haven't had time to rewrite or revise them."

"Why not?" Kate asked.

"Are you kidding?" Wendy brought over another plastic chair. "It takes me forever to write a paper for class. I can't even imagine how long it'd take to write a book that has hundreds of pages. You throw in the fact that Audra works full-time—"

"Yeah," Vonnie chimed in. "How do you manage it?"

Audra carefully didn't look at her mother. Her sisters were always a surprise, but Darlene wasn't going to accept the romance novels without a fight. "I write at night or early in the morning before I start work. It's what most writers do until they can afford to give up their day jobs."

"Twenty-eight books and you can't afford to write full-time?" Darlene shook her head. "That should tell you something. It's pure silliness. You should quit and put your attention where it belongs."

"I couldn't agree more," Brigid said, winning a smile of approval from their mother.

"What?" Audra gaped at her sister, feeling the betrayal slam into her heart.

"You should give Elinor two weeks' notice. Mom doesn't really need me in the kitchen at the Lazy B. She has plenty of other help, so I'll move to the pony farm and take over managing it in the middle of August rather than after Labor Day. You should be writing full-time. I researched Destynee LaFleur on my phone as soon as I heard what Kyle said. Imagine what she could be doing if she came out of the writing closet. Her last ten books have made all the extended bestseller lists. If she promoted and toured, her sales would skyrocket, and she'd be at the top of those lists."

"She needs a website," Vonnie added. "I can design a great one. I do ours for the ranch and it wouldn't be that hard."

"A blog and social media," Wendy mused. "Destynee ought to be a major presence on the writing scene. She could give away copies of her new book at interviews and speak at writing events. More sales."

"Excuse me." Audra waved her fork. "I'm sitting right here. And how would I write with all this stuff happening? I don't have time to do all that. My publisher handles the promotion for me."

"Yes, but they can't do everything we can to make your *nom-de-plume* a household name. We're your sisters. We know all about you and we'll see to it you're famous," Kate said. "You need a literary agent. You don't have one, do you?"

"No, but I have a great publisher and a fabulous editor." Audra glanced quickly at her mother. Darlene's frown grew heavier. "Mom, I know this came as a surprise. Don't you remember how much writing I did in high school? The scholarships I had to go to college?"

"That was when you were a child." Darlene pushed back from the table. "We need you. We depend on you and all this time you've been sneaking around. I've never been so disappointed in you."

"Get over yourself," Kate snapped, with a toss of her head. "You make it sound like she's been out whoring on Aurora Avenue in Seattle. She had a dream. You and Dad did your best to kill it and she did her best to make it work within the parameters the two of you set. Don't the pair of you ever get tired of running your daughters' lives? Or should I say, ruining?"

Utter silence while all of them stared at Kate. Then, Darlene stood up. "I hope you have somewhere to go in mind when you start flapping your gums, Cathleen Therese Dawson."

"Oh yes, I do, because we all know it's your way or the highway, Mother dearest." Kate lifted her chin. "I'll finish saying everything I think and then I'll swing through the ranch and pick up my belongings."

"Don't, Kate." Audra put a hand on her sister's arm. "You don't have to defend me. I can take care of myself."

"Does it ever occur to you that I'm standing up for me?" Kate asked. "I have dreams too, you know. Maybe, if you get to have yours and remain part of the family, I'll get to have mine. Like the saying goes, when you have kids, you're supposed to give them roots and then wings. You're not supposed to trim those wings to keep them from flying."

Despite her mother's furious departure early in the afternoon after the final dust-up between her and Kate, it'd been a good day. Nobody else seemed to have noticed Darlene's tantrum, or at least no one mentioned it. Did that mean her rages weren't as important as her daughters thought? Or had she pitched so many fits over the years that her extended family ignored them? Most of the Dawson clan had eaten, socialized for a while, and then returned to the fence-building projects.

Joe texted Audra that he was busy and would catch up with her at the pony farm that evening. Before she rounded up the kids and her dog to head back to Everett, Audra loaded up a platter of food for him. She'd just finished adding potato salad to the plate when Venus entered the kitchen, followed by her sisters. "What's up?"

"We've been talking to Kyle and Mom." Astra hitched a hip onto a stool at the breakfast bar. Her sisters wore jeans, t-shirts, and running shoes, but she'd opted for slacks, a western-cut blouse with pearl snaps, and dress boots. "You write books and Mom says you're talking about changing the one in progress because it's about three witches."

"I wrote it before I knew it bore such a close resemblance to your family." Audra covered the bowl with plastic wrap, then put the container into the refrigerator. "I thought I was just making up the whole thing and there wasn't a relationship to anyone, beyond the fact that your mom raised four kids on her own and that all of you run this ranch together, except for Meteor and Astra having day jobs. I need to revise it."

"Why?" Meteor grabbed a carrot stick from the tray before Audra closed the door. "Nobody will ever believe that we do magick when we're together. I think it's okay to show up in a book when only we know the truth."

"Me too." Venus leaned against the wall to watch. "So, which witch am I?"

Audra heaved a sigh and gave up the battle. Normally, she only discussed the newest project with her editor, but since it concerned them, her cousins needed to know. "The youngest. You're the warrior queen who kicks butt all over the pages. Meteor is a shapeshifter."

"And me?" Astra asked. "Who am I?"

"The oldest witch sister who keeps everybody in line and tries to protect her entire family from the evil wizard, the villain in the book, and his minions, a pack of rogue werewolves."

"Fabulous. I can so go with it especially if I get to have wild, raunchy sex with a bunch of hot guys."

"You're a criminal defense lawyer trying to make partner at your firm. Lately, you're either in court or prepping for it instead of partying with Beth Chambers," Meteor pointed out. "It's not like the two of you are still hanging out at Billy-Bob's and squabbling over who gets which guy. You don't even have time for a dinner date."

"This is fiction and that's my fantasy." Astra pointed a finger at Audra. "Lots of sex in a variety of ways and places. If I'm living like a proverbial nun for the next few months, I want vicarious affairs."

Audra felt warmth bubbling up inside her at the support. She glanced at Venus. "And what do you want?"

"A broadsword and I'm clouting my hero with it for taking so long to get here to rescue me." Venus eyed her older sisters. "And skanky Astra doesn't have my guy in the sack no matter how much she tries. He tells her to back off."

"And I'm not limited in shape-shifting," Meteor said. "I can be whatever animal I want to be, an eagle, a horse, a wolf, a panther. Total freedom of shape. Astra can chase my guy as much as she wants, but he has to turn her down. Oh and he has to be a shapeshifter like me so we can mate no matter what."

"That goes along with some of what I already had," Audra said. "Well, except for the part about all the sex you gals want, but I am Destynee LaFleur, and I do write hot stories. Anything else?"

"We get signed copies," Venus said. "Personalized ones for our libraries. And normal names in the book so nobody outside our family knows we're the inspiration. You don't mention us in the acknowledgments either."

"If you're good with that, so are we," Astra said.

"I'm good," Audra said. "It's more than I expected."

"We'll be immortalized." Meteor opened the refrigerator, snagged another carrot stick, and crunched into it. "Okay, now that we've settled the future, I need to go clean up the guest room for Kate. She's staying with us for a while until your mom chills out. For someone who hates rejection, Aunt Darlene sure goes out of her way to find it."

"Better to do the rejecting, than to be rejected," Astra said. "I'll help you before I drive back to Seattle."

PART IV

"Magick is destiny and Destynee is magick!"

— AUDRA DAWSON

30

AUDRA HAD A LOT TO THINK ABOUT ON THE WAY HOME. JAKE dozed in the back seat of the super-cab, using Navarre as a pillow. Lynn was busy texting her friends and catching up on the important teen news of the day. Amused, Audra had messages of her own to return, but they'd wait until she arrived home. When had the pony farm become her sanctuary?

Before she became the manager of the Silver Lake Pony Ranch, she always looked forward to her trips to the Lazy B, regardless of where she worked. This summer things had changed. She rarely made it for Sunday supper, much less the two or three weeknights she used to visit. And to be honest, she didn't care. She enjoyed the lack of stress and drama in her life.

Why? Was it just the time, the nights she spent with Joe? What happened? Her mother and sisters were the same, so what was different? Once Audra thought if her family discovered her secret identity, her life would be over, but now she wasn't upset. Had she changed that much? She had some details to iron out and she would. Having the twins decide to promote her career – that seemed totally different! They probably had some hidden agenda, but she wasn't concerned since she could handle it.

She pulled into the drive, recognizing Sean's truck next to

Joe's. What was Ethan's rig doing here? She'd seen him up at the fence party, but they didn't have time to talk. Why was he here? There was Ginger's car and Clancy's pickup. Was something wrong with one of the animals? Why did she have so much company on a Sunday night?

Lynn looked over her shoulder to the rear of the super-cab. "Wake up, guys. We're back."

"I'm awake." Jake yawned and stretched. Navarre opened an eye and thumped his tail against the back seat. "Wow, everybody's here. I wonder what's up."

"Well, let's go find out." Audra parked next to Kate's Jeep and switched off the engine. "Come on, folks."

Joe met them on the porch. Audra greeted him with a quick kiss and handed over the plate. "How was your day, dear?"

He laughed. "Good. All my patients survived. And my girl-friend cooked me supper."

"No, she didn't," Lynn said, with brutal honesty. "She raided the leftovers and put together a meal for you."

"Same difference," Joe said, still grinning. "I get to eat." He leaned over and whispered. "Your mom's on a rampage and making all sorts of calls."

"Thanks for the warning." Audra followed the kids into the kitchen. She stopped, froze when she saw the cake in the middle of the table and the balloon decorated chair. "What is this?"

"We discovered we have a celebrity in our midst." Gavin glanced over his shoulder and grinned at her, then continued pouring sparkling cider into glasses. "If it isn't reason to celebrate, then I don't know what is."

"I don't get it," Lynn said. "Who is the celebrity?"

"Audra. She writes books and they've been published." Jake glanced past his older sister to his mother and step-dad. "Can I have one? I want to read it."

"Not until you're older," Sean said before Elinor could answer. "They aren't for kids. They're grown-up books with lots of kissing."

"Well, then I don't want to read one, not with sappy stuff in it." Jake eyed Audra. "Can't you write books for me and my friends without all that?"

"I don't know," Audra said. "I've never thought about it."

"But you're going to think about it now." Lynn heaved a dramatic sigh. "As long as it has magick and dragons and wizards, he'll be happy. He's weird."

"No, I'm not. I just like fantasy books."

"Who doesn't?" Gavin switched over to pouring champagne into the waiting flutes. "All those battles between good and evil in strange worlds constantly entertain people. If it didn't, I wouldn't have a job teaching Shakespeare."

"That's an interesting way to look at it." Ethan leaned against the counter. "Is that what you tell your students or the dean of your department?"

"The dean knows. It makes for some interesting discussions at curriculum meetings."

Jake ignored the interruption and turned back to Audra. "What about teen books without all the kissing?"

"I'm still thinking," Audra said. "You have to give me more than five minutes, Jake. You know it takes time for a book to come together."

"How long does it take you to write one? It takes me ages to think up things."

"Usually, a year from idea to a published work on store shelves." Audra eyed her sisters warily when they came into the kitchen, accompanied by Ginger. "Do I want to know what you were doing?"

"I was choosing a book for Clancy," Kate said. "She wants to read one, but she needs to begin with the first in your latest trilogy. Can she borrow it?"

"She can have it," Audra said, recognizing the cover on the novel that Clancy held. It was a book that had come out last year. "Did you want me to sign it?"

"Yes!"

The next two hours passed in a whirl. They had cake. She signed books and listened to conversations, answering questions about her writing process. At least nobody asked her where she got her ideas or tried to convince her that she should give up her writing. Joe didn't even bring up her mother's calls again.

That was left for Elinor. While Sean and the kids headed outside, she slid an arm around Audra's waist. "Your mom may give you an earful when the two of you talk next time. She called and tried to convince me to fire you."

"What? Why?" Audra gaped at her boss. "Where would I go?"

"She told me that I shouldn't have a writer like Destynee LaFleur teaching children. I reminded her that I am an English teacher. I know how hard it is to write one book, much less as many as you have. She hasn't given up so watch your back."

"I will." Audra hugged her boss. "Thanks for the warning."

"No worries. See you bright and early tomorrow for camp." Elinor was out the door.

Kate and Gavin were the next to leave. He leaned down to kiss Audra's cheek. "Next time, you need to pick my brain for a book, just tell me that you're in crunch time for a deadline. I'll check in earlier. I know how editors are."

"I will," Audra said, touched by the offer. "Thanks again for today, Katie. If you want to sleep in the guest room down here, you can."

"Not now. I'm happy at Aunt Estelle's," Kate said. "And Mom will get over her snit a lot faster if I'm there than here. Besides, I was serious when I told her that she should stop trying to stomp on dreams."

"She only wants to protect her kids," Ginger said, "and she hasn't realized that you're all grown up. It must be tough to be her and let all of you go when she's held you so close for so long."

"Well, now that she's fighting with Kate, she's forgiven me." Clancy tossed her head, bright red hair flying. "Ethan can move back into his place and be happy I'm gone."

"I didn't say that." He started forward, a heavy frown on his face, echoed in his eyes.

"Sounded like it to me." Clancy kissed Audra's cheek. "See you tomorrow. Kick butt, sis." With another flip of her braid, she was out the back door, Ethan right behind her.

"Well, that makes things much more peaceful." Ginger began clearing the table. "No offense, sweetie, but when your family is helpful and nice, they take up a lot of energy. Nearly as much as when they're not." She paused on her way to the kitchen sink. "I understand why you didn't tell them what you really did to pay the mortgage for them, but why didn't you tell me?"

"I was afraid," Audra admitted. "You're such a good reader and you review books all the time online. I didn't want you to cut me slack because we're friends. Then, it all snowballed on me."

"Okay, that actually makes sense," Ginger said. "When it comes to books, I'd never give you a break. If your story sucks, I'll say so. But no more secrets."

"All right." Audra laughed and hugged her best friend. "Should I tell you now that Joe and I are sleeping together?"

"I already knew that." Ginger sniffed. "You're slipping, Doc, if all the two of you do is sleep."

"Oh, we do more." Joe eased the last of the cake onto a platter. "Since Audra is out of the writing closet, I can't wait to help Destynee with her research."

Audra felt heat slide into her cheeks. "I suppose you're going to say that you knew all along."

"Ever since you used a kerosene-based fly-wipe in one of your stories," Joe said. "One of my students brought in the book and asked if that would actually work. I remembered helping your uncle mix up the concoction when we were kids in the Silver Flying A's, his and Marlene's 4-H club. I told my student it was an old home remedy. So, then I had to read everything you or should I say Destynee wrote."

———

The smell of freshly brewed coffee woke her. She opened her eyes and saw Joe sitting on the edge of the bed, wearing only his jeans. She scrunched up against the pillows and reached for the cup he offered. "Morning. Do you have a call?"

He smiled and shook his head. "No. I need to talk to you before you go to the barn. Sean and I spent yesterday afternoon shuffling stock to his place. Elinor said it wouldn't impact day camp, but you still may have to change the schedule a bit."

Audra yawned and sipped the strong brew, eyeing him over the rim of the cup. "Okay, tell me. What did you two boys do when I wasn't here to watch you?"

Joe laughed appreciatively and leaned down to kiss the top of her head. "First things first. I swung by Christy's to check Charm yesterday."

"Really? Me too. I stopped before we went to the Rocking J. She's looking good. I'll go there after camp today."

"No, you won't because she's not there. Christy intended to send her to slaughter to keep the vet bill from going any higher, so I took her. She's out in Chipeta's stall. That meant we hauled her and Awesome over to Sean's. To avoid a family war, Elinor sent Gypsy too and her personal horse. She said you didn't use any of them in camp, so it wouldn't make a problem."

A lump rose in Audra's throat. She struggled to hold back the tears. "You bought Charm for me?"

"I couldn't let her die." He paused. "That was my first thought. You came next."

"Oh, you idiot." She put the cup on the nightstand and hugged him. "You're supposed to say you bought her so I wouldn't have my heart broken by losing her."

"I didn't actually buy her. I took her in exchange for the vet bill."

"You're such a noble fool." She tugged on his ponytail. "Kiss me, you super hero, you."

"Wow, do I get a reward for saving the horse?"

"Definitely. You deserve it since your daddy is going to yell at you this morning for not understanding that in the real world you don't get to save each and every critter." She pulled him closer, and their lips met. When they came up for air, she asked, "Have you told Art yet?"

"No, I will this morning." Joe smiled, rueful humor in his eyes. "He's going to try to send me back to my ivory tower."

"Well, before you go, I'm jumping your bones." She framed his face with her hands, feeling like she could drown in the warmth of his sky-blue eyes. "You're amazing."

That evening while Charm munched supper hay, Audra groomed the young mare. Navarre lay outside the stall in the barn aisle. His low growl alerted her to company. When she glanced at him, she saw his tail wagging. Then, she spotted her sister in the same jeans and Silver Lake Pony Ranch t-shirt she'd worn to teach day-camp all day. "Hi, Clancy. Are you headed home?"

"I guess." Clancy leaned down to pet Navarre. "It's not that I particularly want to be there when Mom's doing the drama diva routine about Kate. It's just I can't stay with Ethan when he doesn't want me."

"Ouch." Audra heard the pain that her sister's face didn't reveal and thought she saw tears shimmering in the lavender eyes. "How do you know?"

"He never pushes to take me to bed or anywhere else for that matter. I'm the one who makes the moves, and he always steps back."

"He proposed. He wants to marry you."

"Actually, he didn't." Clancy came into the stall, careful to lock the door behind her. "I did. He bought the ring. When I lose it and yell at him, he tells me we'll do whatever I want. It's never what *he* wants."

"But he loves you."

"How do you know? I don't." Clancy picked up a brush and began to work it through Charm's snarled black mane. "I thought there was hope for us when he told me not to be a princess this summer, but then he backed down. I could take a job over at Aunt

Lurlene's in Montana this fall. He wouldn't care. He wouldn't even miss me."

"He loves you," Audra repeated. "He doesn't look at other women. It upsets him if you date anyone else. He warned off Jack last spring. Ethan is almost forty-five, Clancy, and he's old-fashioned. He didn't need Uncle Roy to teach him morality. Ethan's always had it. He does what he says and says what he's going to do. It's probably a reaction to the Senator opting for expediency."

"Well, maybe." Clancy moved to the horse's hip and picked up her tail. "I suggested we elope, and he turned me down."

"Then, obviously he's not worried about standing up to you," Audra said. "Does he want to wait until the Senator is back in the state?"

"No, Ethan isn't big on his parents being around. He wants my family there. With Mom on the outs with you and Kate, he says we have to wait until things settle down." Clancy focused on the tangled knots. "I told him Mom would make up with you as soon as the balloon date for the mortgage gets close."

"Probably too much reality for him." Audra wondered why the truth didn't slice into her heart this time. Was it just the note of acceptance she heard in her sister's voice? Did she feel the same way? Their mother answered to her own set of values, but then again, who didn't? "Why isn't she angry with the twins wanting to promote my writing career?"

"Oh, Vonnie told her that it was so you'd make more money, and then you'll have enough to take care of the mortgage even if you don't have a big-time job because the Lazy B comes first." Clancy heaved a sigh. "You'd think Mom would see through them, but she never does. They do what they think is best and work around her. I heard them talking about the apartment off-campus this year and you helping them pay off their car."

Once again, Audra contemplated why it didn't bother her to hear an assessment of her youngest sisters' motivation. What had happened this summer? What changed things? She didn't mind helping her family, but she didn't feel like she had to change her clothes in the proverbial phone booth or run around in her underwear with a flaming sword.

"They're born survivors, so I guess we should give them credit for it."

"You can," Clancy said. "I can't. If they hadn't played mudpies in my life, Ethan and I would be married."

"I'll tell you the same thing I told Kate at the Fourth of July parade. It's time to step up, Clancy Dawson, and make sure the whole family includes Ethan, making all of us honor your choice of a man, making everyone respect him."

Clancy drew a ragged breath. "Okay, I'll do it when you do it."

31

Joe walked down the hall to his father's office. Art Watkins sat behind a large wooden desk, in the middle of a phone conversation. Since he was obviously doing more listening than talking, it undoubtedly was personal, not a patient's human parent.

Art covered the end of the receiver. "Are you getting ready to take off?"

Joe nodded. "I'm picking up supper and going to the farm. I told Audra I'd be there early enough for her to ride Charm for the first time."

"Okay, I'll see you tomorrow." Art kept part of his attention on the phone conversation. "Her momma is worried that you'll marry the girl and Darlene says a woman who writes porn is not a suitable wife for a college professor."

For a moment, anger raged, but Joe tamped it down. "I'll give her opinion the respect it deserves. I'd think more of it if she actually read anything Audra wrote."

"Well, don't confuse your prospective momma-in-law with facts. This is the first time she's called me in years to talk about something personal, not just an injured or sick animal."

Momentary anger was replaced with amusement and Joe

laughed. "Night, Dad. You can tell her that you're sure I've always known my destiny, or should I say, Destynee?"

It didn't take long to swing by the deli. He selected sandwich makings and an assortment of salads. Now, it wouldn't matter how long Audra trained the young horse. Their supper could wait. When he arrived at the pony farm, he spotted the pair out in the small corral used for ground school. Charm wore a saddle and bridle over a halter while Audra worked her on a longe line. He wasn't the only spectator. Clancy leaned on the fence to watch the mare walk a circle.

"How's she doing?" Joe asked, crossing the yard. He petted the dog when Navarre frisked up with one of his toys, a thick flying disc. "She looks good."

"She's coming back," Clancy said. "We probably groomed her for an hour while Audra and I talked. We just tacked her up and brought her out."

"Has she trotted or cantered her?"

Clancy looked at him as if he'd just crawled out from under a rock. "Don't be silly. Of course not. Charm needs time to regain her muscle tone, not to overdo."

"A short, gentle jog won't hurt the filly." Another scathing look and he almost winced. "I am a real doctor and I specialize in equine medicine."

"You're not a trainer. Jack Abbott had better not call himself one where I can hear him."

Joe grinned but was careful not to chuckle where Clancy might hear it. She climbed through the fence and went to talk to her sister. In a moment, Audra unhooked the line and turned Charm loose. The filly walked a few steps away, then picked up a trot. Next came a few crow-hops and finally a serious bucking spree before she dashed away in a gallop from one end of the ring to the other. She definitely hadn't heard Clancy's talk about overdoing it.

Watching out for the horse, Audra came over to the fence, followed by her sister. "Hey, handsome. How was your day?"

"Good. I'm glad you're letting her stretch out before you ride her."

"I'd rather have her do all the jumps and leaps before I get on." Audra glanced over her shoulder. She sighed, then shook her head. "Honestly, Clancy. I thought she would just walk a little more. Letting her choose the activity level was one of your better ideas."

Clancy shrugged and climbed back through the fence to stand next to Joe. "Well, the doctor actually suggested it. He thought she ought to trot before you rode her. I figured she might try rolling with the saddle on, but I didn't expect the acrobatics."

"Me either." Audra tilted her head to one side, then the other before she gave Joe a steady, brown-eyed stare. "How did you know she was ready for that?"

"I didn't. It was an educated guess." He stepped closer to the rail. He leaned over to catch Audra's chin and kiss her quickly, then eased back. "I've already lowered the pain relievers to the minimum so she can feel it if she hurts."

"Good point."

The filly trotted over and stood near Audra as if to join in the conversation. Charm flicked an ear, then nosed her new owner's shoulder. Without making eye contact with the horse, Audra reached over to scratch the brown neck. "Do you want to do some real work now, or are you just mooching carrots?"

"If she answers, we're making a million bucks," Joe said.

"No, we're not. I'm keeping her." Audra picked up the set of nylon reins hanging on the post. She clipped them onto the halter that the filly wore. "Okay, who's helping the first time?"

"Doc," Clancy said immediately. "He has more upper body strength. He can hold her long enough for you to get off if Charm goes ballistic."

"Makes sense to me." He supposed if he were more macho, he'd have been the one to make the decision, but this way all of them were in agreement. That meant the training session would be positive since no one's ego was on the line. He picked up the short lead line as soon as he was in the round pen. He hooked it on the halter.

He waited while Audra checked the fit of the saddle, tightened the cinch, and messed with the stirrups again. Through it all, Charm stood like a statue, occasionally chewing on the snaffle bit. "Do you want a leg-up this time?"

"No, I'll just do a regular mount. Once she's used to it, I'll teach her to let me get on from anything." Holding the reins, Audra rested her left hand on Charm's neck. Nothing happened, no reaction from the horse. A foot in the stirrup and a smooth jump up, then she swung her right leg over the mare's hips and settled into the saddle.

Charm twitched her ears and turned her head slightly. Audra leaned forward and gave her a small piece of carrot. "Good girl. We'll try walking as soon as she finishes her treat."

"We'll keep this session short, only a few times around the corral."

"You're the boss."

"Right." Joe chuckled. "And if I were dumb enough to believe that, you'd rip me a new one. I know you, *Stinkerbelle*."

An hour later, Charm was back in her stall finishing up the last of the supper hay, now mixed with a pound of long, skinny organic carrots. Clancy had headed to the Lazy B and that meant Audra could enjoy the evening with Joe. She led the way into the kitchen, followed by him and Navarre. She closed the door behind them, sat down at the table to remove her boots. "Do I have time for a shower before we eat?"

"It's a cold supper so you can take all the time you want." He put down the grocery bag on the table long enough to unlace his own boots and then line them up with hers beside the back door. While she checked for phone messages on the farm landline, he unpacked the bag, putting away containers of salad, a mini-watermelon, and the two sandwich wraps. "I had these in the refrigerator in the back of the truck to keep them cool. And a shower – I could go for that."

She hurried for the bathroom. "Me first."

"Me with you."

She laughed, eyeing the small room and the tub. "Think we can fit?"

"I'm willing to try." He closed the door.

She watched him pull his t-shirt out of his jeans. She backed up and sat on the toilet. "Are you going to strip for me? Make it good if you want a big tip."

"You're a tough audience." He eased the shirt up to reveal a flat stomach, no washboard abs, just the muscled build of a man who worked all day. "And I know you're just using me for research."

"It's a hard job, but you can handle it." She looked at his wide chest and felt her breath catch for a moment. He was so gorgeous. Had she ever told him that? She didn't remember. She saw his broad shoulders next and finally his arms. The t-shirt ended up on the floor next to the laundry hamper.

She wanted to touch him, to run her hands over his skin, to kiss him, to taste him. Instead, she waited while he unbuttoned his jeans and along with his boxers, they followed his shirt. Naked, he came toward her. "What about your ponytail?"

"I had to leave something for you to do."

"Okay, I'll see what I can do." Giggling, she stood. She tiptoed up to kiss him, sliding her fingers into his dark hair. He lowered his head and their mouths met for a long moment. One kiss led to a second, a third.

She sighed when he lifted his lips from hers and started unsnapping the pearl buttons on her blouse. "I could get used to this."

"And we've barely started." He pushed the shirt off her shoulders, brushed kisses over the top of her breasts, and then unhooked the front closure of her bra. "Wait until you see what comes next."

She smiled up at him, untied the leather lace that held back his hair. "I'll give directions."

"Sounds like fun. I can't wait."

An hour later, they had made it to the bedroom. She lay in his arms, pressing her mouth against his shoulder. He trailed kisses up the side of her neck to her ear. The whisper of his breath made her shiver. He continued to explore the line of her throat and jaw. Then his lips found hers and their tongues met, clashed in a new passionate duel. Several kisses later, he lifted his head.

She ran her hands over his arms when he drew one of her nipples into his mouth and sucked gently. She moaned and arched up to meet his lips. She tangled her hands in his hair to hold his head in place, sighing when he captured the other nipple, rolling it between his thumb and first finger.

It seemed like a lifetime later when he smiled down at her.

"What?" She tipped her head to one side so he could kiss her ear. "Do you have more ideas, or should I come up with some?"

"Wait until after I have you with my mouth before you start issuing orders."

———

While he dished up the salads and sliced watermelon, she tidied the bathroom. She emptied her pockets before dropping her jeans into the hamper, taking a few minutes to check messages on her cell phone. There were three from her mother, the last two marked urgent. Audra grimaced. She knew better than to call at this hour. The resident camp at the Lazy B would be shut down except for the night staff and Darlene wasn't one of those. Returning the call would have to wait until morning.

"An emergency?" Joe asked from the doorway.

"Not one I can deal with at this time," Audra said. "Mom wants to talk to me."

"You're on your own with that, sweetheart." He turned and walked away.

"What does that mean?" She followed him.

"Just what I said. She called my father and whined and

whinged about you writing porn, so I should know better than to marry you."

"What?" Audra gaped at his muscled back. "But she's my mother. How could she lie like that? It doesn't make sense."

"It does to her." He filled two wine glasses with Reisling. "Are you going to allow her to get away with it or stand up to her?"

"Why does it have to be me?"

"Why do you think?"

The questions simmered in her mind while they ate. She knew her mother didn't approve of romance novels but trying to make trouble seemed a bit extreme. They had cleaned up the kitchen before Audra said, "I don't get it, Joe. Why does it matter if I write books?"

"It shouldn't matter what you do as long as you're happy and you aren't hurting anyone, but you stepped out of her control when you didn't give up your passion. Remember when you wanted to go to college? She said she needed you to help look after your sisters, to help with the ranch. You called your father and asked him to step up so you could accept the scholarships you'd been offered. It was his job to help raise his daughters. What did he tell you?"

"That he was busy, and I should do what my mother needed." Tears burned and she bit her lip, trying not to let them fall. "He didn't even come to my graduation."

"I know, baby, I know." Joe crossed the room, came to her. "I was there."

"You always are." She turned into his arms, buried her face against his chest, and let the tears come. "I don't know what to do."

"What if you start taking care of yourself first?" He stroked her hair. "Isn't it about time?"

She nearly told him the truth. She didn't know how. She'd spent so many years taking care of other people. Now, her own mother was using it against her.

"I never let the writing interfere with anything they need."

"Isn't it about time that it did, that you have a life?"

"What are you saying?" Audra stepped back, wiped at her eyes. "I do have a life."

"Only as much as your mother allows." He folded his arms, stared down at her, concern on his face. "What are you waiting for? Unless you demand some autonomy, she'll keep using you up. Or do you enjoy being the family martyr?"

"I've never enjoyed it." Audra froze when the truth escaped. "But someone has to look after everything. I remember when I was a kid that I'd get home from school and the chores wouldn't be done. The horses would be hungry, or the cows left in a flooding field next to the river."

"Times have changed. Have you considered that? Are you still the only one who can do livestock chores at the Lazy B? Do you need them depending on you? They can get along without you now, can't they? Do you plan on being their slave forever?"

"That's not fair."

"Well, maybe I'm not willing to wait any longer for you to grow up. Your dad dumped his responsibilities on you twenty-three years ago. It's time to walk away and let your family live on their own instead of constantly rescuing them. You've done more than anyone else would."

"I don't—" She paused and changed it. "I won't give up my family for you."

"Not for me. For yourself. Think about it. Call me when you're ready to talk about a future, your future."

She sat down at the table. Navarre came over and stood next to her while Joe walked out the kitchen door. She nearly told him that it was what he did the best, walking away when she needed him most. She wouldn't give him the satisfaction of knowing he hurt her more than her family ever had.

Instead, she locked the door behind him and went to her computer. She had a book to write, a deadline to meet. And in her fantasy world, she let the witches run wild. They cast a banishing spell that sent their new soul-mated wizards flying through time portals. Her heroines didn't need men and neither did she.

———

"Mom wants you to call her." Clancy stood in the barn aisle while Audra put flakes of alfalfa grass hay in the next two mangers. "She says she's left you a ton of messages."

"Sorry, tell her I've been too busy to talk to her. I've been fielding the hell she unleashed on me when she started telling the whole Dawson clan that I write porn. I've had emails, texts, and phone calls from people I haven't seen since the last family reunion five years ago. I'll get to her when I get to her."

"She did that? What are they saying?"

"Half want money because they know all writers are rich. A quarter wants to tell me I'm going to burn in hell because I'm a sinner. The same men who call me a whore want to know if I need help researching. I tell them, no, that they can't live up to my fantasies." Audra pushed the wheelbarrow further down the aisle, picked up more hay to feed the next set of stalls. "The rest are like Aunt Estelle. They offer support and tell me how much they admire me."

"You need a secretary." Clancy carried hay to the stalls on the other side of the barn. "If you spend your life talking to all our relatives, you'll never have time to write a book again."

"I didn't think of that." Audra nearly asked if it could be her mother's strategy. It wouldn't work. Joe hadn't been around the past two nights, so she'd spent them writing and torturing the heroes of her story. "Where would I get a secretary? I don't have anything to pay someone. I need all my money for the mortgage next month."

"You better talk to Mom soon. She wants to go back to the bank and increase the loan again to expand the arena and add a couple more cabins. You'll be supporting the farm until you die of old age. You need to tell her to cut the crap."

"Wonderful." Audra knew the sarcasm didn't pass by her sister. "She wants to stop me from writing and then make it impossible for me to quit. How does she think I'll be able to pay a bigger installment?"

"The Bergstroms called looking for you. She says if you play your cards right, they'll make you the manager of Xanadu, and then you'll have more money than we'll be able to spend."

"I haven't heard from them and I wouldn't go back if they begged. Loyalty is a two-way street. They showed what they thought of me when they hired Jack Abbott to run their barn."

"Maybe, you ought to require as much from your family as you do your employer." Clancy pushed the empty wheelbarrow to the feed room. "If you won't let your boss walk on you, then you shouldn't let us."

"I thought you were the family princess."

"I am but let someone else be *Cinderella* for a while. You've served your time."

32

HEAVING A SIGH, LYNN CLIMBED THE STAIRS TO THE APARTMENT IN the second story of the mare's barn. Why did she always have to be the one to track down her brother? And more importantly what was he doing? He better not have made a mess. She and Sandy had cleaned up here, so the lunchroom was ready if any parents visited it after tomorrow's horse show.

I don't like do-overs, Lynn thought. If Jake made it necessary, she'd tell Mom that he should do the cleaning next time.

She opened the door and saw him staring at a computer screen. "I should have known. What are you doing? Writing a story? Come on. You can do that at home."

"It's not a story." Jake didn't flick her so much as a glance. "We have a problem."

"What? This has been the best summer ever. Well, not Blaze being shot, but everything else has worked out the way you wanted. What's wrong?"

This time Jake did look at her. "What kind of lawyer are you going to be when you don't see what's right in front of you?"

"A good one. Most of them are real focused."

"Not Harold. He always sees the big picture."

Lynn dragged over a chair and sat down by her brother, considering the point he'd made about her mother's attorney. "I bet he learned to do that when he was in the Army and people were shooting at him. What are you doing?"

"Fixing it so we can stay over here tomorrow night."

"Why?" Dread tiptoed through her. "Oh no, Jake. We're not doing the spell again. It's already worked for Audra and Dr. Joe."

"They had some kind of fight. He hasn't been around all week. We have to get them back together. That means we need to spend the night here. I talked to Orion and he says the spell will work better if we repeat it where we cast it in the first place."

"So, what are you doing?" Lynn asked again. "Mom and Audra will never let us do it again."

"I know so I have to keep them busy. Mom's easy. She'll love having a date night with Sean. The tough one was Audra."

Lynn eyed her brother, fascinated in a horrible way. "And you found something for Audra to do?"

He nodded. "I'm making an appointment for her to talk to these people tomorrow night. They're in charge of this super big writers' conference in Seattle on Labor Day weekend and one of their keynote speakers was just in a bad accident."

"How do you know this stuff? I bet they didn't announce it to the public."

"I follow social media. They had this writer coming from back east and she's in the hospital. She'll be okay, but she won't be ready to come out here in three weeks. Most big-name authors are booked a year or more in advance. So, I emailed the organizers and said I was Audra's business manager, and she might be available to fill in since it's an emergency."

"What did they say to that? Get lost, kid!"

"They don't know I'm a kid. They can't see me on this computer. I'm typing emails, not using the camera."

"Well, you'd better hurry up. Mom's ready to go and pretty soon she'll be up here. You'll be grounded past forever if she finds out that you're playing mudpies with Audra's life."

"So, will you."

"What? How do you figure?"

"You're my big sister and you didn't stop me."

Lynn glared at her pest of a brother. "All right. What's taking you so long? Tell them to meet her for drinks and dinner at Billy-Bob's tomorrow after the camp show. She wants a hotel room, meals, and to sign her books at the sale."

"How did you know they had a book fair?"

"Because it only makes sense. If you get a bunch of writers together, they'll have their books available and there are bound to be people who want to buy them."

Audra heaved a sigh as she pulled into the busy parking lot and found a spot for her truck. Why had she allowed Jake to talk her into this dinner with other writers? *Because I didn't have anything else to do except sit home and avoid Mom's calls and try not to call Joe.* She couldn't use the farm as an excuse not when Jake arranged to babysit the critters with Lynn and Sandy's help. And Elinor had been so happy about having alone time with Sean. *Only a monster would try to disrupt that and I'm not one.*

Audra walked into the restaurant wondering how late she had to stay. What was polite in this circumstance? Could she plead some sort of emergency and escape early? She spotted her aunt at the hostess stand and wound her way past the other people waiting for tables.

In a western blouse and a long skirt, Regina looked ready for one of the busiest nights of the week at the cowboy bar and restaurant. She smiled and came towards Audra, hands outstretched. "So, how are you tonight? I couldn't believe it when your mom called and shared your news. You've always been amazing."

"Well, that's one word for it." Audra hugged the older woman. "I'm supposed to meet some folks here."

"They're back by the bar. I'll take you." Regina slipped an arm around Audra's waist. "They were going to order a bottle of champagne, but Ginger told them that you preferred sparkling cider. She'd bring your favorite Riesling when you arrived."

"She's a good friend. I'm glad she's looking out for me." Audra paused. "What do you think? Should I be interested in joining other writers? My mom—"

"Feels threatened by anything that doesn't center on her." Regina kept smiling at her other customers, even though her tone was low and serious. "This is your business, honey. It's like the Chamber of Commerce for your uncle and me. Of course, you need to find your own circle of professional associates who share your interests."

"Mom doesn't think what I do is actually work."

"Then, she should try building a story world after working all day, not just once, but day after day, month after month, year after year." Regina's hold tightened. "You have a gift, honey. Don't let anyone take your stories away from you. They don't have the right. Okay, lecture over. Now, you enjoy the rewards of your hard work."

"I will." Audra hesitated when they approached a corner table where four people waited, three women and one man. Then, she took a deep breath and lifted her chin. She could do this. Her eyes widened as she recognized Elinor's neighbor. "I don't believe this. Daisy? You write romance?"

"Me and thousands of other writers." Daisy pushed back her chair and stood. "But you're the success story here. I haven't sold anything yet."

"You will," Audra said. "You're the woman who taught me how to create a story and never sneered at my werewolves."

"After years of reading high school essays, yours were a treat." Daisy shook her silvered head. "I can't believe I didn't recognize your books when they came out. I think I missed your first ones and just started on the later series. Now, let me introduce you to the conference chair, the publicity and workshop folks."

"I'm glad you missed the early books," Audra said. "You were tougher on me than my first editor. I dreaded your *red* pen marks."

The group laughed and Audra relaxed. It looked like it'd be a pleasant evening after all. No drama here, but maybe she'd make new friends. Wasn't it about time?

Four hours later, she leaned back in the booth and waited for Ginger to finish her shift. The other writers had already gone, leaving Audra with a stack of materials to ponder. She flipped through the program. Starting Friday, there were class sessions before the welcome dinner. Then, there was an editor and agent panel. To her amazement, she noticed that Kendra would be one of the guest speakers.

"So, tell me all about it." Carrying a cup of coffee, Ginger slid into the seat across from her. "Is Destynee LaFleur making an appearance at long last?"

"Yes. I'm the Saturday lunch keynote speaker at the Western Washington Writers Conference. I must write a speech that will inspire everybody from newbies to best-selling authors. Any ideas?"

"Not yet but let me think about it." Ginger sipped her Irish Cream laced beverage. "How did you get roped into this? I couldn't believe it when they showed up and told me who they were waiting for! They wanted to know if you really were a local person and I said you were a lifetime resident of the wet side of the mountains. You need to update your bio on your books. Maybe, you should add a picture."

"That's worth thinking about. They wanted to know if my business manager was accepting new clients. I didn't tell them he was facing the rigors of seventh grade in the fall, so he'd be busy."

"No way." Ginger laughed. "Is that how you ended up here? Little Jake was up to mischief? What a brilliant kid!"

"It's one word for him. Daisy asked me about my agent, and I told her that I didn't have one. If I get stuck on a legal question, I pop in and talk to Harold."

"He's sharp, all right." Ginger hesitated, then said, "If I'm out of line, tell me. Do you have the rights back to your first books?

So many of them are out of print and I'm not the only collector who'd love to have copies."

"Yes, a reversion of the rights was one of the clauses Harold told me to insist on when I started in this business. Why? What are you thinking?"

"That you should talk to your current editor about those books and see if your publisher would be interested in releasing them again. You also need to call and give her a heads-up that you plan to speak at the conference. She might be able to help the book fair chair get copies of your current books for the sale."

"You sound totally familiar with this conference," Audra said. "Will you be attending?"

"You bet," Ginger said. "A lot of authors pass on their newest releases so I'll review them. I wouldn't miss the opportunity to hobnob with real writers. Jim and Regina know better than to schedule me for Labor Day weekend."

"They're providing a suite for me at the hotel," Audra said. "Do you want to share it with me?"

"Won't the doc be there?" Ginger asked.

"No. We had a fight about my family." Audra drew a trembling breath. "I haven't seen him in almost a week."

"Okay." Ginger signaled the waitress. "I'm buying you a glass of wine and you're telling me all about it."

"One glass of Riesling may not be enough."

"All right. Then, I'll order a bottle. Spill your guts, girlfriend. What happened? Why are you and the doc at loggerheads?"

———

She was in the middle of describing a sword fight between the warrior queen and soldier prince when the phone rang. Reluctantly leaving the fictional world, Audra picked up the receiver of the landline. "Silver Lake Pony Ranch. Can I help you?"

"Audra, it's Herman Bergstrom. Your mother gave me this number. I'd like to talk to you about returning to Xanadu."

"Really?" Audra eyed the laptop screen regretfully. This conversation was obviously going to take a while. She saved the story so she wouldn't lose her text and then concentrated on the phone. "Why would I come back to Xanadu? You made it clear what you thought of my efforts when you hired a different manager."

"That may have been premature. Jack is good at a lot of things, but he seems out of his depth with all the responsibilities. I'm spending more time here than I ever did when you were in charge."

"What did you expect, Mr. Bergstrom? Jack wasn't trained to run the place and you knew that when you hired him."

"I thought you'd be here to help him."

Audra nearly asked who had given the Bergstroms that impression and stopped. She had when she put Xanadu Arabians ahead of everything in her life. "I'm sorry, but I'm happy in my new position and I'm not looking to move anywhere else."

"You haven't heard what I'm prepared to offer."

"It won't do any good. I like this place. I work fewer days and I can breathe."

"Everything is open to negotiation. Let's meet and we can talk about what Xanadu has to offer you. Your mother thought you'd be willing to return if you had a freer hand to run the place and I'm open to making changes."

"So am I," Audra said, gently. Too gently, but he didn't catch the edge in her tone. "When and where?"

33

AUDRA HAD TAKEN A GLASS OF ICED TEA AND HER LAPTOP TO THE picnic table in the orchard so she could write in the evening sunshine. Navarre flopped nearby, exhausted from chasing his favorite tennis ball. Now, she could concentrate on the next battle between the witches and the wizards in her latest creative endeavor. She glanced up as a pickup pulled into the drive, recognizing her uncle's rig. Sighing, she saved the chapter and shut down the computer. She'd return to her story world after the visit. She waved at him and Kyle. "Down here."

The two men strode toward her, both dressed in jeans, western shirts, and boots. Kyle wore a loose leather fringed jacket that covered the holster on his right hip. Navarre bounded to meet them, tail wagging. Kyle accepted the soggy ball and then hurled it in the direction of the pasture. Barking in excitement, the Bernese Mountain dog raced to find his toy. Audra laughed as she watched him. "Hi, guys. What's going on?"

"Not much." Will hugged her. "We're organizing a memorial for Beth. I wanted to touch base with you and see if you'd help me clean out her condo. The lease ends on the first of September."

"Of course, I'll jump in." Audra glanced at Kyle. "No way, she's coming back here, is there?"

"I don't think so. She seems happy with the life she's chosen."

"I'm glad for her sake, but I miss her," Audra said.

"So do I." Will paused. He removed his cowboy hat, ran a hand through his silver hair, and replaced the Stetson. "I also need to talk to you about your momma. She's going to run into a wall if she tries to remortgage the Lazy B."

"What are you talking about?"

"It was one thing when she used the money to send her daughters to college," Will said, "but if she goes through with borrowing money to make major improvements the Lazy B doesn't need, the ranch doesn't stay in her hands. It gets passed onto another set of Dawsons, the same way it was given to her twenty-five years ago."

"My dad was the one who mortgaged the farm," Audra said. "I remember Mom worrying about it after he left the last time."

"Yes, and the two of you paid off most of that by the time Brigid was headed for culinary school. Darlene and I agreed that her education was important enough to increase the loan amount," Will said. "We kept on the *pay as you go* plan for the other girls since we didn't want them dealing with gigantic student debts."

"Then, what's the problem with improvements?" Kyle asked. "I don't think Trace Burdette would want her spread falling into shambles."

"No, but the ranch needs to pay for more cabins and expanding the indoor arena," Will said. "The old-timers didn't want to worry about their descendants over-extending themselves and losing the place to strangers. We have plenty of relatives who are willing to raise hell and put props under it to take the Lazy B away from your family. I don't want to enforce the trust. Your momma has taken better care of the homestead than anyone else ever did in years."

"Okay, I'll add that to my list of things to talk to her about." Audra sighed and shook her head. "I guess my vacation from the family has ended."

"Looks that way."

A sharp popping sound broke the stillness of the August

evening. Kyle cocked his head and listened. "Rifle. Who hunts in the middle of summer? It doesn't make sense."

The ponies were safely in their stalls, and Audra listened as more shots rang out, followed by a dog's bark cut suddenly short, followed by an agonized howl. She recognized where the sound came from now, the O'Malley place down the road.

Navarre whined and pressed close to her side. She froze. "I think Zane O'Malley has returned to his cousin's place. I didn't see the construction crew today. He's probably the one shooting."

"I'd bet he doesn't use a paper target." Will frowned then glanced across the road. "Let's go check it out before we call the cops. There are a lot of kids and animals around. I wouldn't want someone to get hurt."

"Wasn't shooting one pony enough?" Kyle asked.

"Apparently not," Will said.

"Let me put away my things and Navarre. I'll go with you." It only took her a few minutes to lock away her computer and the dog. Worried as he apparently was, he still wanted to go with her, but she didn't want him in the way of a stray bullet. She jogged down to meet her uncle who had already turned around his truck. She climbed in beside him, leaving room for Kyle to join them after he closed the main gates.

What was wrong with her? Why was she going with them to confront a man holding a rifle? Was she totally crazy? Audra shook her head. She felt the comforting weight of the cell phone in her pocket. Okay, if things got dicey, she'd call in the cavalry. "Now, I really miss Beth more than ever."

"She was good at her job." Will pulled out on the road, turned left, and drove the short distance to the O'Malley driveway. "Let's see if there's any reason to contact the police."

He parked in front of the two-story farmhouse. They climbed out of the pickup, Kyle taking the lead. She shivered when she heard another shot, then a high-pitched bleating. "Is it a goat?"

"A deer." Kyle strode around the corner of the house ahead of them, pulling a pistol. "Drop the rifle or I'll drop you."

Audra hurried to catch up with her uncle. "What's going on?"

Will shook his head and followed the younger man.

Sighing, she chased after them. She froze when she reached the backyard, fenced off from the paddock near the barn. She saw a dog lying in a puddle of blood directly in front of the building. She dug in her pocket for her cell and dialed the vet clinic. Joe. First, she'd arrange for him to get here and save the animals, then she'd call the sheriff's department.

Kyle had a man pinned face-down in the dirt. Meanwhile, Will waved at her from a corner behind the barn. Audra hurried toward her uncle. A doe lay nearby, her brown sides rising and falling. Blood trickled from her mouth and nostrils. But Will's focus was on the white-spotted half-grown fawn tangled in the farm and field mesh fence, still calling for its mother.

"Wire cutters." Audra whirled and raced back to the truck. She unfastened the tailgate, jumped up, and scrambled toward the long toolbox in the back end of the rig. It only took moments to locate the fencing tools and a package of unused mechanic's rags still in their store wrappings. She hadn't known that deer could make any sounds, much less the noises coming from the fawn, but she would use the toweling to try and bandage his mother.

She ran back to meet her uncle. When she flicked a glance at Kyle, she saw him cutting a piece of rawhide string from the fringes on his coat sleeve. What did he have in mind? Well, she'd ask later. Right now, her uncle needed help. "What are we doing?"

"Getting the fawn out of the fence," Will said. "Did you call for backup?"

She nodded. "Joe and the cops are on the way."

———

Joe hadn't expected Sarah Holmes, the receptionist to be the one that told him Audra had an emergency. He'd thought she'd contact him or come by when she was ready to admit that she was ready to stand up to her family. He should have known there hadn't been enough time for her to decide to step up. He spotted Will's pickup first, parked in front of the house that was in the middle of some sort of renovation. The message had said there were gunshot animals. He opened his door, walked around to the back of the truck. He gathered the materials he needed first before he started toward the rear of the house.

He saw Kyle hauling a dark-haired stranger to his feet, hands tied behind his back. Joe glanced past them and saw Will holding a fawn. Obviously attempting to apply pressure to an injury and stop the bleeding, Audra knelt by a doe.

Joe started toward the injured animal. He glanced at Kyle, then the other man. "What happened?"

"He was shooting at everything that moved." Contempt filled Kyle's voice as he glared at the man he held by the arm. "We ain't had time to find all the maimed and dying critters yet, Doc."

"You're trespassing." The fellow attempted to wipe his dirt-stained cheek on a shoulder. "I'm Zane O'Malley and I live here. Nobody invited you on my property."

"Take him around the front and wait for the cops," Joe said. "I'll get started here."

Hours later, he sat in the kitchen at the pony farm drinking whisky-laced coffee. He shook his head trying to dismiss the memory of the carnage. The doe hadn't made it. No surprise there, he thought. The surprise had been finding an injured fawn hiding in the weeds. He'd stabilized that one and sent it off with its twin to a wildlife sanctuary. There had been five dead dogs, four more dying, and six more shot. Cats, raccoons, rabbits, some lethally wounded, all shot in a mad frenzy. How could one person wreak so much havoc?

Navarre whined and came to rest his large head on Joe's lap. He stroked the black and bronze fur. "Why do I think you know more than you're telling about that hellhole?"

Audra carried over the coffee pot and the bottle of cinnamon whisky. She'd showered, changed to a flannel nightgown. She topped both their cups. She dragged over a chair, sat down so their knees met. "You did the best you could."

"It wasn't much."

"It was plenty." She leaned closer and kissed him. "It was more than some people would do without worrying about how they'd be paid. With you, the animals always come first. It's why I love you."

"You picked a hell of a time to tell me."

"I know." She kissed him again, a gentle touch of her lips on his. "Drink up, Doc. Let's go to bed."

He shifted in the chair. "It's always been you."

"I know." She managed a weak smile that almost touched her golden-brown eyes. "It took me a while to realize it, but I'm not a romantic like you."

"I know."

———

A knock on the door interrupted the chatter around the kitchen. Audra put her roast beef sandwich down and went to welcome Daisy. "Hi, what's going on?"

"We got the new posters made up for the conference, so I brought you a few." Daisy smiled at Elinor and Clancy. "I thought all of you could jump in and help create some buzz about our newest speaker."

"Well, let's see," Elinor said. "Does it have Audra's name now?"

"Destynee LaFleur's," Daisy obediently held up the poster proclaiming that Labor Day weekend would be a "Writing Great Time in the Pacific Northwest." There were small thumbnail photos of all three keynote speakers, followed by the time, place, and major activities at the event. "What do you think?"

"Mom is going to have a foot-stomping, snot-slinging hissy fit." Clancy sipped her coffee. "She told us at breakfast that the Lazy B will host its usual end of the summer barbeque on Labor

Day weekend and attendance is mandatory. There will be trail rides, pony rides, and lessons. She expects Audra to help run the ranch so the rest of us can sell the fall and winter riding programs."

"But you promised to be at our conference." Daisy looked stunned, then bewildered. "What am I going to do?"

"Make sure my reservation at the hotel includes Joe's name," Audra said. "I don't want the desk clerk to make him sleep in the lobby."

"Don't you have to work?" Daisy asked.

"I expect to work at the conference," Audra said. "I haven't been to a writer's weekend in years, but I remember them as being busy from start to finish, especially for the organizers and speakers."

"Why haven't you gone to conferences?" Clancy asked. "You're a writer. I know I learn a lot from other horse show judges when we meet up and I'm sure it's the same in your profession."

"Because the family and the ranch always take precedence," Audra said. "I've never put myself first, but I think it's time I started."

Clancy heaved a dramatic sigh and shook her head. "Well, you'd better call Aunt Marlene and get her on your side. Mom is going to have a major meltdown when she discovers that you've given up your purple martyr's robes."

"Anything else?" Audra wondered if she saw amusement in her sister's gaze. "Or are you done now?"

"Daisy should see if there's a mini-fridge in your room or if you need to request one," Clancy said. She reached for her sandwich, turning to the older woman. "What other promotion will your organizers be doing? Radio? TV? Social media?"

"Before we start that, I needed to know if you've contacted your editor," Daisy said. "You don't want to surprise her, Audra."

"I have a call into her," Audra said. "She'll probably return it in the morning. It's when we usually talk."

———

Joe was working late at the clinic that evening. He hadn't found a Siamese kitten for Lynn yet, but he was on the mission. Pouring a cup of coffee, Audra decided it was time to deal with the boxes and trunks of family history she'd stored in Lynn's old room. Perhaps, there would be a list from Beth or at least a note that would prove her adopted cousin was safe and sound in her new home.

Audra eyed the heavy antique steamer trunk in the back corner of the bedroom. It was all wood with a dome top, trimmed out in leather and brass hardware. When she opened it, she discovered a series of Victorian lithographs covering different compartments. The first one held neatly folded linen handkerchiefs. Gloves, scarves, shawls filled other sections.

When she lifted out the top tray, she found blouses, skirts, and a dark blue dress in the bottom half of the trunk. Had Beth ever worn these clothes? Audra smoothed the material of the dress and felt something hard underneath. She slowly pushed the cloth aside and found a leather-bound diary.

Audra hesitated, then slowly opened the book. Her cousin's handwriting jumped out at her. The first entry was dated, August 30th, 1888.

Dear Audra,

By the time you read this, I'll be dead—LOL—just had to say that! Okay, Kyle ought to be there by now. If not, he'll show up soon and yes, I expect you to help him. He's my bro-in-law and a bit of a wimp around here. He should be Mister Macho there. That's first on my list. Next, tell Nina I'm happy and so is her Wonder horse. Don't let her blame herself for me leaving. If I hadn't, I wouldn't be where I belong. I wish you could meet Rad. He rocks my world—

34

Her cell phone rang while she smelled coffee. It was morning even if she wasn't ready for it. Audra yawned, opened her eyes, and reached for the annoying contraption on the nightstand. "Morning."

"Good morning, Destynee," Kendra chirped. "I saw a tweet that there's a surprise coming to the conference in Seattle in two weeks and your name came up."

"Yes." Audra shifted her pillows and sat up. She took the cup of coffee that Joe held out to her, smiling at him. "I've decided you're right."

"I am?" Kendra sounded amazed. "About what? I get more hunky shapeshifters?"

"About me coming out of my writing sanctuary and making a few appearances." Audra's smile widened as she watched Joe leave the bedroom, providing the privacy he thought she must need for the conversation with her editor. "I need to grow up. You've respected my whims too long."

"I'd never be that harsh with you." Kendra sounded thrilled and excited. "Are you really going to be in Seattle? We can discuss a new publicity campaign and a book tour."

"That sounds wonderful." Audra sipped her coffee. "Next question. I have the rights to my first ten books which are out of print. Would you be interested in looking at them?"

"Looking? Are you joking? We'd love to re-release them. Do you finally have an agent?"

"No, I'm happy with my lawyer. I'll arrange for him to handle the negotiations."

"Fine. I'll talk with him and we'll get the ball rolling."

A few more details needed to be ironed out before Audra ended the call. She finished her coffee, then followed her nose and the smell of frying bacon to the kitchen. "Thanks for giving me the space I needed to talk to her."

"You'll do the same for me." He cracked eggs into the cast-iron skillet. "We both have demanding careers. You've never said if you'll be comfortable living on the dry side of the mountains. Do you want me to consider an offer from another university? There are plenty of vet schools."

"Pullman works for me. I can write anywhere that I can find space for my computer." She went to him, put her arms around his lean waist. She stood behind him, rested her head against his shoulder. "I learned not to wait for my muse over the years, but to put words on paper every day. What about Navarre and Charm? Do you have space for them? Or is there a good boarding stable for her?"

"There are, but we won't need one. I have a small farm, forty acres outside of town, and a wonderful ranch-hand who runs the place when I'm gone or busy at the university. He'll enjoy having a horse to look after, but he'll be telling me to get one of my own so we can ride together."

"It sounds wonderful." She sighed happily. "You're giving me the *happy ever after* I never thought I'd have."

"Same goes." He turned off the stove. "Come here, you."

She laughed when he swung around and pulled her against him. "I love you. I may not say it often, but I really do."

"As long as you're with me, that's all I care about." He tipped up her chin. "My brown-eyed wonder."

Their lips met in a long kiss. When it ended, she said, "I still have things to work out."

"We have time. Just let me know how to help."

"Believe me, I will."

———

The rest of the day flew by in a whirl of chores, day camp, phone calls, and more stock care. With her daily responsibilities under control, Audra headed for Billy-Bob's to have a sit-down dinner with the Bergstroms. Once this was over, she planned to drive up to the Lazy B. She'd told Clancy to pass the word to their sisters that they might want to make themselves scarce if they didn't want to hear the showdown, or deal with the aftermath.

It took less than two hours to work out the details with Herman Bergstrom and everything went just as she intended. She'd advise Jack Abbott or whichever manager they hired, but she wouldn't live onsite at Xanadu since she was moving out of the area. She wasn't going to do any of the daily scheduling, feeding, or training. She'd simply be an online consultant and for that, her attorney would see that she was paid appropriately. Less labor-intensive and more money. Oh yes, she could so deal with that.

When she knocked on the front door and walked into the house at the Lazy B, she was amazed to see all five of her sisters as well as her mother sitting around the table in the kitchen. "What's this?" Audra asked. "I told Clancy I was coming to clear the air."

"And we decided we should be here," Brigid said. "You've done a lot for this family in all your guises. It's time for us to grow up and stop letting you protect us."

"Okay," Audra said, glancing around the table at the rest of her sisters. She was amazed by their support, but proud of the five younger women. She wasn't the only one who'd matured over the summer. "Thanks. I'm not touchy-feely, but I do love all of you."

Kate smiled from her place at the far end. "It may not be a pretty conversation tonight, but we can handle it. Before we get started, I owe you an apology."

"For what?" Audra asked. "I don't remember you doing anything particularly heinous."

"I did my share in breaking up you and Joe when you were teenagers," Kate said. "I wasn't the only one, but I never told you when he called or passed on his messages."

"Sisters do things to each other," Darlene said. "It's called sibling rivalry for a reason."

Kate eyed her mother. "I did it so Audra wouldn't leave or try to have a life. I started to realize when the twins did it to me last February, that what goes around, comes around."

Shock crept into Vonnie's eyes. "You've never said that before."

"What?" Kate asked. "That I can be as a big a bitch as the two of you? Where do you think you learned to be spiteful? From me and I'm telling you now it can ruin your life. Grow up, sweetheart, or the lessons come hard."

"What she said," Clancy agreed. "What you two did was horrible, but we had it coming. Payback sucks."

"I never would have done anything like that to either of you," Audra told the two of them. "Who is to say? Joe's the romantic one, not me. I'm in love with him now, but back then I didn't know how I felt about him. All I wanted was to go to New York and write books."

"And here comes the drama that we all stopped you." Darlene heaved a huge sigh. "You're thirty-five. Isn't it time you got off the pity pot?"

"Yes, it is." Audra met her mother's dark blue gaze evenly. "I've given you the last twenty-three years since Dad left on my twelfth birthday. The rest of my life belongs to me. I'll make the balloon payment on the ranch's mortgage this year. After that, you're on your own."

"How are you going to pay it?" Darlene asked. "Are you returning to Xanadu? Will they give you an advance on your wages?"

"I accepted a position as a consultant for the Bergstroms. I arranged to sell my backlist of books to my publisher." Audra glanced around the table at her family. "I'm giving you two weeks' notice. If you want anything from me, speak up now because I'm moving to Pullman to live with Joe."

"What about the website we're doing for you?" Wendy asked. "How will we contact you?"

"By phone or email." Audra eyed the twins. "You two need to get your ducks in a row because I'm only helping with your education for two more years. By then, you'll have been at the university for six years and that's more than enough time unless you're going to graduate school. If you are, pay for it yourself."

Brigid suppressed a smile. "Okay, so I'll plan to move in at the pony farm the week before Labor Day Weekend so you can leave with him. You go, girl."

"I am." Audra ostentatiously looked at her watch. "And now I'm on the road. You have my cell number. Call if you want to get together." She reached in her purse, pulled out the printed copy of publishing statistics that Daisy had given her at their meeting, passing it to Darlene. "Here you go, Mom. Next time you want to tell someone that I write porn, don't. Share this instead. Gavin could have told you that romance captures more than half the market share and makes billions of dollars each year. I have nothing to apologize for and I've finished trying to please you."

She was halfway to the front door when her mother caught up with her. "Audra, don't go. I need you."

"Really?" Audra whirled around, her tone fierce. "What about me, Mom? What about what I needed when Dad walked away? Why didn't you have to act like an adult? It was your marriage that failed, not mine. You abdicated your responsibilities and dumped them on me."

This time when her mother gasped and reeled back a step, Audra didn't pause to cut the older woman any slack. Enough was enough. "I was only twelve years old, and you taught my sisters to hate me because I failed them as a parent. Well, guess what? It wasn't my job! I was a child when they were children, and you took my childhood away from me. Then, you had the unmitigated gall to pitch a fit about the way I supported the family and paid the bills. How dare you? I write romance and I'm damned good at it. Try reading one of my books before you put me down the next time."

No answer. Audra spun and stalked out the front door. Rage carried her to the pickup. A lump bubbled up in her throat as she drove toward the highway. Tears burned her eyes. She didn't let them fall. She had nothing to cry about. It might have taken her too long to stand up for herself, but she wasn't backing off. Not now, not ever.

She spotted the Watkins Veterinary Practice truck in front of the house when she pulled into the pony farm. She parked next to it and went back to close and lock the gates. Then, she headed for the kitchen door. Navarre frisked up to meet her, carrying his stuffed teddy bear. She knelt and hugged the giant puppy. "Hey, bubba. What do you think about moving to Pullman?"

"Considering how furry he is, he'll love the snow." Joe stood, leaving a stack of papers on the table, and came to meet her. "Your mom's been calling for the past hour. She said you were really upset when you left, and she wants to talk to you."

"It's not reciprocal." Audra put her purse on a chair. She laced her arms around his neck. "Take me to bed, or I'll take you."

"Promises. Promises." He lifted her into his arms. "Lock the door and hit the lights. I'll take you first. My turn to make you feel better like you did the other night when I was hurting."

"Sounds like a winner." She sighed and buried her lips in the hollow of his throat. "Are you going to make an honest woman out of me, Dr. Joe?"

"You always have been one." He kissed the top of her head.

"Thought we'd make a run to Coeur d'Alene and elope sometime in September. Or do you want a big fancy wedding?"

"I just want you."

"You'll always have me."

"Good. I'm ready for always."

EPILOGUE

Audra glanced at her grand-uncle. He'd arrived with several poster-sized photographs of Beth. "Where did you get those?"

"She was always a good friend to you creative gals," Will Dawson said. "I had the pictures that Nina Webster took enlarged. Now, we just need a few easels to display them. Where's that husband of yours? I'll put him in charge of that."

Audra laughed, glancing at the engagement and wedding rings on her left hand. "He'll be along. He went off on an emergency call with Dr. Art. You know how the two of them are. Animals first and people next."

"Why am I not surprised?"

The door opened and Audra turned to see her mother, followed by her sisters. Brigid was the first to hug Audra, then the twins. Darlene took a step forward and Audra met her mother halfway. "It's good to see you."

"I've missed you." Darlene kissed Audra's cheek. "I hope we can talk while you're here. I want to know all about your book tour. Where are you going and when?"

"I'll share the details later," Audra said. "For now, we need to get this affair organized before everyone arrives. Uncle Will, is Nina coming?"

"I invited her. We'll see." Will held a giant poster-sized picture of Beth in jeans and a western shirt, holding the reins of a light gray Arabian while her dog stood sentinel nearby. "I hope she gets here soon. I promised Kyle I'd introduce them."

Audra stopped and stared. Suddenly, she remembered the historical photographs at the library with the initials, A. Morgan. She'd wondered who the late 19th-century photographer had been and now she suspected that she'd just been given a clue. "Well, if you get busy, Joe and I will be happy to handle that."

"I'll keep the two of you in mind."

"Fair enough." Audra went to greet Joe at the door. He looked dashing and handsome in his dark suit. She tiptoed up to kiss him. "I'm glad you're here."

"Always." He brushed his lips over hers again. "I'm always here for you."

"I love always." She took his hand. "And I love you."

THE END

———

Turn the page for a preview of the fifth book in the *Liberty Valley* series, *A Trail Through Time*!

———

Keep up with Josie Malone and subscribe to her newsletter!
https://sendfox.com/josiemaloneauthor

———

Don't miss out on your next favorite book!

Join the Satin Romance mailing list
www.satinromance.com/mail.html

A TRAIL THROUGH TIME

LIBERTY VALLEY LOVE: BOOK 5

"Where no matter what, soulmates find each other."

PART ONE

"This too shall pass."

— NINA ARMSTRONG, HORSE-RESCUER AND
PHOTOGRAPHER

———

Eagleville, Washington – Thursday, September 27ᵗʰ, 2018

CIVILIAN AND POLICE CARS FILLED THE PARKING LOT AROUND THE funeral home, although the memorial service wouldn't start for almost two hours. Nina Armstrong parked her twenty-year-old Ford Ranger in the space reserved for her and switched off the engine. She dreaded facing everyone, but what choice did she have?

My best friend died trying to bring the man who raped and battered me to justice. Quit whining and whinging and go for it. She would do the same for me.

Nina clambered out of the truck and limped toward the brick

building. At least, she was off the crutches. She hadn't been able to make herself wear anything but black jeans, a subdued top under her black western-style jacket. Regardless of the occasion, she doubted she'd ever wear a dress again.

Last month, she'd had hysterics when her brother-in-law tugged gently on her braid at a horse show, causing onlookers to stare at her and her mother and stepfather to suggest she continue to avoid crowds if she couldn't control her emotional meltdowns. The following afternoon, she'd visited Ginger Taylor and demanded the former hairdresser shave her head. Ginger refused, saying a cap-style cut was enough, and promised to deliver the chocolate brown excess from a waist-length braid to the local *Locks of Love* wig-making drive.

It was time to quit stalling. Sooner or later, someone would see her in the parking lot and try to escort her inside. Taking a deep breath, she headed into the lobby and looked around. A photograph of Beth Chambers in her formal cop blues stood on an easel near a door. Nina winced, remembering the day she'd taken the picture. Afterward, the two of them had gone to lunch at Beth's favorite restaurant, Billy-Bob's where they enjoyed giant slabs of cheese-cake with their coffee, not bothering to feel guilty because they'd split one of the huge, specialty burgers and a mountain of hand-cut, crispy French fries.

In the room, several easels held large pictures of Beth. Many showed her in different Army uniforms. In one corner was a candid shot of her in jeans and a Western shirt, holding her horse's reins while Luke, her retired K-9 partner stood by the pair. The light gray Arabian nuzzled her arm and Nina recalled her friend always had horse cookies in a coat pocket reserved especially for Tigger.

Blinking back the tears, Nina went past the cluster of police officers to the front of the room. Beth's foster father Will Dawson stood there with one of his many relatives, a petite brunette that Nina recognized as Audra Dawson, Beth's favorite cousin.

Despite wearing a formal, black suit, he looked like a silver-haired, singing cowboy with one of his favorite Stetsons. Will smiled and reached out to hug Nina when she joined him. "Thanks for coming. I'm glad you made it."

Nina slipped out of the sideways embrace, hoping she didn't offend the older man, but she couldn't bear to be touched, even five months after the attack. "Beth would hate all this fuss."

"Yup, she sure would. She always threw a fit about the *falderal* when we got together every time before she deployed." Will smiled, all the way up to warm brown eyes. "But this way her friends can say goodbye and wish her well."

"And the family can, too," Audra said, turning with a friendly nod. "I'm Audra Dawson-Watkins now. Don't worry about missing my wedding. Joe and I eloped, and the relatives don't know what to make of that."

Nina nodded, glancing around, and seeing several more members of the Dawson clan. "I saw Joe at the vet clinic when I took in my puppy for his shots last time. He was nice. He even gave Pooka the teddy bear that he'd chewed up."

"That's my husband," Audra agreed happily. "Animals first and people barely second. He'll be back as soon as he straightens out the chaplain. Joe will find a tactful way to explain that nobody will be happy if he opts for one of those surface speeches that are so popular and make it obvious, he really didn't know Beth even if she was sent to him for counseling for her PTSD."

The conversation eased some of Nina's nervousness, but she still had to ask, "Have you heard anything more from the District Attorney? Does he have anything new to say about Gary Smith?"

"Oh, the fellow still claims Beth is alive and well in 1888," Will said. "Detective Watkins assures us that Smith's trying for an insanity plea, but he won't get it. He had her coat and everything she kept in the pockets for trophies, plus there was more evidence when they found his saddlebags and that dead horse in the National Forest."

"There's no way Beth would give up her things," Nina said.

"She got her man. Smith will spend the rest of his life behind bars once he goes to trial."

Will drew an antique gold watch out of his pocket, rubbing the case with a calloused thumb. "You're right. She did get her man. And all the Dawsons can live with that. Time for you to stop blaming yourself for what she did, sweetness."

"But it's my fault she tracked him into the National Forest and got herself killed," Nina said. "I'd never want her hurt."

"Same goes for you," Audra said. "She'd hate it if she thought you blamed yourself. She always took care of everyone even before she became a cop. It was her job and she stepped up. Again, no blame attaches to you."

Not for the first time, Nina wished she believed that. The topic changed to her horse rescue operation and she repeated the party line she'd come up with over the summer. "It's fine. Donations are up and horse abuse is down so everything works. I've been adopting out some of my rescues, but that takes work too."

Audra nodded. "You bet it does. Trying to sell luxury items in a down economy is never easy and it may not be politically correct, but horses are tough to support even when people aren't worrying about mortgages and taxes. And looking for homes when the animals are psychologically damaged can't be easy at the best of times."

Nina felt some of her tension ease. She'd prepared to be criticized and judged, not hear this much understanding on so many levels. She glanced across the room and saw Joe Watkins coming toward them. He never had been a big guy, barely six foot. He was still lean and wiry, accompanied by a younger man in a dark suit, carrying a black cowboy hat. Was that the minister? It couldn't be, not with that hat.

Audra turned her smile on them. "Nina, you remember my husband, don't you? And this is a friend of ours and Beth's, Kyle Morgan."

Nina tensed for a moment, concerned he might try to shake her hand. Instead, he stood still, and then slowly smiled until it touched dark brown eyes. While she didn't smile back at him, she relaxed again. He wasn't a giant of a man, shorter than both Joe and Will, but three inches taller than she was at five feet, four. Faint amusement trickled through her, no wonder he needed the hat to make himself bigger. Sun-streaked blond hair reached his broad shoulders and she realized it was longer than hers. She noticed the faded line of a jagged scar that sliced his right cheek and wondered what happened. Was it a war injury? Had he and Beth served together in Afghanistan?

"Where did you meet Beth?" Nina asked. "I don't remember her mentioning you."

"In the woods on one of her hunting trips."

Nina met his gaze, wary now. "Beth didn't hunt."

"He means a camping trip," Audra said. "You're her best friend. You know she used to head for the hills whenever she could around the holidays because she hated fireworks after all those Army tours to the Middle East. They triggered her PTSD."

"Then, why didn't he say that?"

Kyle shrugged. "Wasn't sure what you folks called it. And she was downright unsociable when I stumbled into her camp looking for my brother. Her dog attacked me. Knocked me down and held me in the dirt."

"Not really?" A rare laughter bubbled up inside Nina. "What did your brother do?"

"Laughed. He never was the sensitive sort. Probably why he and Bethany get along so well."

"You mean got along." Tears stung and she blinked hard. Now, she had another reason to hate herself. She'd deprived her best friend of a man who undoubtedly would have been her soulmate and given her the *happy ever after* she dreamed of and rarely mentioned. Nina glanced around the room. "Is he here?"

"No. Rad isn't much for ceremony."

Another thing he and Beth had in common, Nina thought, glancing at the others in their small group. She saw a faint smile crease Will's face and realized he enjoyed hearing the reminiscences. It still came as a surprise that he wasn't blaming her. She knew she ought to move around the room and talk to the other guests, including the police officers who continued to arrive, but she couldn't make herself do it. The same went for the rest of the Dawsons. Sooner or later, someone would point out that if Beth hadn't gone after the man who attacked Nina, there wouldn't be a need for this memorial.

As if her thought conjured him up, a big blond man in a dress police uniform came toward them. Nina shuddered, recognizing Detective John Watkins. He'd investigated her case immediately after the attack and while he never said anything offensive, she'd always been grateful the nurses in the hospital didn't leave her alone with him. Nina hated his censorious looks as if it was her fault, she discovered an intruder on the Armstrong property and tried to stop him from stealing one of her rescue horses.

"I wanted to express my condolences again," John Watkins said. "Detective Chambers was a good person. She'll be missed."

"Thank you," Audra said, in a polite tone, too polite. "That means a lot."

Will nodded agreement and Joe stepped forward. "Let me show you where we'd like the officers to sit. Perhaps, you could arrange that for the Dawsons."

"Sure. I'd be happy to do that. I just wanted to say - - -."

"Now isn't the time for anything else." Joe escorted his cousin away.

Audra glared after the detective as the two headed into the chapel. "If he'd stepped up when she was alive instead of throwing up hurdles during the initial investigation and sabotaging everything Beth did, you wouldn't have been hurt, Nina. When he acts like he was her best friend, instead of her *bête noire*, it just pisses me off. I'm so glad that Joe and Art don't do holidays with his family because I'd be majorly tempted to let Brigid put ipecac in the gravy, she'd send with us."

"Want me to take him outside and kick his tail, Mrs. Audra?"

"No, Kyle. But thank you for offering. Instead, would you

please keep him from harassing Nina? He's one of those men who thinks when a woman is attacked that she asked for it and I don't want to embarrass everyone by screaming at him for being such a backward ape."

"I suppose I should opt for being PC and say I don't need a protector," Nina said, her tone even, "but I appreciate the support."

"It's what Beth would want and that's why we're all here," Audra said. "Besides, I'll just write him into one of my books and let a renegade werewolf kill him gruesomely. That will make me feel much better since we can't poison him."

Kyle chuckled. "Do you do that a lot, ma'am? Kill off folks in your books?"

"All the time, but I always change the names and the morons usually don't recognize themselves, much less try to sue me." Audra glanced toward the door, frowning at the newcomers, a young woman followed by a man with a TV camera. "I don't believe this. We told the funeral home, no reporters. Come on, Uncle Will. Let's go kick them out of here. This is a memorial, not a circus. Kyle, take Nina into the chapel. I don't want them seeing either of you."

"Yes, ma'am." Kyle inclined his head toward the elaborately carved wooden doors. "After you, Miss Nina."

She started toward the inner chamber, glancing at him, grateful he was her height and didn't tower over her. "I think I know why she wants me out of sight, but why is she sending you?"

"Because Smith tried attacking me and stealing my horse up in the hills when the one, he'd taken broke a leg and he had to shoot it. If nobody else told you about it, that's because it wasn't the one, he absconded with from your barn. Emancipation is safe and sound with Trace Burdette. Don't reckon she'll ever let him out of her sight again."

"Emancipation? Do you mean, Wonder? That's what I called him since it was a wonder, he was alive when he came to my place."

"Well, since my brother gave him to Trace after his ma died

and she raised him from the time he was three months old, guess we should use the name she gave him. She was real perturbed when Smith stole him and brought him here. Like I said, she has him back and he's safe and sound in her barn. Granted, she'd like Smith hung for horse-stealing, but that's not likely to happen."

"Not when they're building a case against him for murdering Beth," Nina said. "I still can't believe he got bail."

"He hasn't been convicted yet," Kyle said. "Have you seen him anywhere?"

"No. My uncle's lawyer got a restraining order so he can't come near me." Nina shuddered. "What about you? Has he approached you? Threatened or attacked you again?"

"Not yet. Some folks saw us fighting up on the mountain back in July and called the police. If it hadn't been for that, they never would have arrested him. Those reporters are interested in sensation, not real stories. They don't understand he'll watch their stories too."

"I've been avoiding them as much as I can." Nina drew a deep breath, hoping a change of subject would keep thoughts of her attacker out of her mind as they walked into the chapel. "What kind of horse do you have?"

"S.O.B. is a strawberry roan, Appy gelding."

"Does his name stand for son-of- -?"

"Yes, ma'am. My brother named him because he's nasty and has a bad attitude. Sooner kick you than eat. Spends most of his time with his ears flat back, threatening to bite folks. Rad says he was a stinker when he was a colt even before he had a run-in with a porcupine and lost."

"How did you end up with him?"

"He threw and stomped one too many of Rad's hands and my brother was going to shoot him. Didn't seem fair to me since the fellow still had blood on his spurs and S.O.B. was a mess. Blood all over him and cracked ribs. Told Rad I'd take the horse and he could fire the man when he healed up or I would."

Nina slid into one of the seats closest to the side door. "What did the vet say about your horse? Did Joe or his dad look after him?"

"Didn't need them." Kyle sat down next to her. "No, I doctored him. Got kicked a couple of times, but once Señora Ortiz started giving me old biscuits for him, we made friends. He likes those better than anything."

"Who is Señora Ortiz?"

"She runs Rad's house for him. She and her husband are good folks."

"And she makes biscuits for your horse." Nina smiled. "Where's their place?"

"Oh, it's a fair distance up in the hills. I've been working for the Jamisons at the Rocking J, but their place is getting revved up. Pretty soon, S.O.B. and I will have worked ourselves out of a job and have to move on."

"What kind of work are you doing?" Nina eased back in the chair and listened while he talked about building fences, repairing barns, and looking after all sorts of livestock. His deep voice rumbled softly and reminded her of an old-time cowboy in a classic movie. For the first time in a long time, she felt safe.

She didn't say that. She usually didn't say much anymore. Then, whatever she did say couldn't be held against her. She let his low conversation provide a barrier between her and the other guests as the room slowly filled during the next hour. She recognized Sean Killian, the local horse-shoer with his new wife.

Right after she'd gotten out of the hospital, he'd brought her Pooka, promising a puppy could make almost anyone feel better. He'd suggested the a rough-coated collie mix who loved to snuggle and protected her from the monster in her nightmares would be an awesome service dog someday. Sean had been so understanding when she hadn't attended his wedding, cheerfully accepting a gift basket the next time, he came to trim the horses.

More of the Dawsons filtered into the chapel including Clancy and Kate escorted by their former fiancés, Sean's older brothers. It looked like the broken engagements weren't working either, but

Nina didn't share that. The Jamison family slipped into the row beside them, seventeen-year-old, sandy-haired, Orion taking the seat next to Kyle, nodding at Nina, but not speaking.

She heaved another breath, then glanced over her shoulder when she heard footsteps. Behind her, Marlene Dawson, the leader of one of the largest horse 4-H clubs in the county for almost forty years, took a seat. Her sister, Darlene who didn't look old enough to have six adult daughters sat next to her along with Joe's father, Dr. Art Watkins.

Slowly, Nina realized they had her surrounded and protected. Tears burned, but she managed to nod at them. "Thank you."

"Beth would want us to look after you," Marlene said, "and this is the first chance we've had in a while."

"What she said." Darlene leaned forward. "I haven't seen your family yet. Where are they?"

"They're not coming. They said Beth was my customer, not theirs."

"No point in being stupid if you don't display it." Marlene heaved a sigh and shook her head. "I'll try to run interference for them, so they don't piss off the entire Dawson bunch and all their kith and kin."

"Why bother?" Darlene demanded, narrowing her blue eyes. "You and Earlene never cut me slack when I screw up."

"You're a Dawson too, even if it's by marriage. We hold you to a higher standard and you know Earlene changed her name to Estelle. Stop being such a turd."

"I'm not and I don't see why you always take her side."

Nina felt a smile edge her lips as the two older women squabbled like teenagers. She flicked a sideways glance at Kyle and saw amusement filter into his face, making lines crinkle around his eyes. She wanted to thank him for providing a distraction but wasn't sure how.

Telling a stranger how frightened she was by the people who had known her for years made her sound like the nutcase her family claimed she'd become, not a thirty-two-year-old woman who'd successfully operated a horse rescue for almost a third of her life. She glanced toward the dais where the choir lined up and a young man began to play the small grand piano. She choked back a nervous giggle when she recognized the tune as Helen Reddy's signature song, the anthem of women's liberation, one of Beth's favorites.

Following the song, the chaplain greeted the crowd and thanked them for coming to celebrate a life taken too soon. He spoke about the woman he'd known, the one who served her country as a medic in the U.S. Army, and then came home to continue her service as a law enforcement officer. Afterward, it was the turn of Beth's police captain and several detectives.

Kyle stirred beside Nina and leaned over to whisper, "They're making her sound like a saint. She'd be telling them to spit in the wind and call it a shower."

"Hush." Nina bumped him with her elbow. "They're creating their own reality. If they admit how much they hated her or the fact that the captain didn't stop the guys from harassing her or they never backed her up, they'll look like even bigger jerks than they are. Nobody believes their crap anyway."

"Want me to take them out and slap them around, Miss Nina?"

"No, that's over-kill." She nudged him again. "Watch this. I think Clancy Dawson is about to kick tails and take names."

Without waiting for the last officer to finish speaking, Beth's cousin strolled up to the dais, a red-headed Amazon in a dark blue, western-style dress and fancy cowgirl boots. She took the microphone from an unwilling John Watkins, although she didn't need it. As a horse-show judge during the spring and summer seasons, she was accustomed to commanding an audience in a much larger arena. "Wow, I never knew our Beth walked on water when everyone around her made it rain. Comes as news to me and I'll bet it does to you too."

That brought a round of laughter and Clancy favored the crowd with her sunshine smile. "I'm not going to give you a bunch of hogwash about the Bethany Rose Chambers these cops knew who always protected the weak regardless of what it cost her. I'm going to tell you about the little girl my uncle adopted and the first time he brought her to a family picnic and the way she loaded up her pockets with food because she never knew if or when she'd have another meal which was why my mother and sister always sent her home with leftovers. And when I get done, I want the rest of you to get up here and share your stories about our Beth too. The real person, not the one who had to be perfect at the Eagleville precinct because all of us know a woman has to be twice as good at her job to earn half as much recognition."

Nina glanced over her shoulder at Darlene. "I didn't know she went hungry as a kid. She never told me."

Darlene shrugged, blinking dark blue eyes to hold back tears. "I hope someone shares the way Beth kicked butt and threw coffee cups when she lost her temper. Otherwise, she'll sound like even more of a saint when my daughters get done."

THANK YOU FOR READING

Did you enjoy this book?

We invite you to leave a review at your favorite book site, such as Goodreads, Amazon, Barnes & Noble, etc.

DID YOU KNOW THAT LEAVING A REVIEW...

- Helps other readers find books they may enjoy.
- Gives you a chance to let your voice be heard.
- Gives authors recognition for their hard work.
- Doesn't have to be long. A sentence or two about why you liked the book will do.

ABOUT THE AUTHOR

Josie Malone lives and works at her family's riding stable in Washington State. She's taught children to ride and know about horses for so long that she often discovers she's taught three generations of their families. Her life experiences span adventures from dealing cards in a casino, attending graduate school to get her Masters in Teaching degree, being a substitute teacher, and serving in the Army Reserve - all leading to her second career as a published author. Visit her at her website, www.josiemalone.com to learn about her books.

Subscribe to Josie's Newsletter:
https://sendfox.com/josiemaloneauthor

Contact Josie at:
josiemaloneauthor@outlook.com

www.josiemalone.com

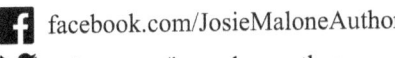

facebook.com/JosieMaloneAuthor

twitter.com/josmaloneauthor

instagram.com/josiemaloneauthor

amazon.com/Josie-Malone/e/B006HC9VMI

ALSO BY JOSIE MALONE

Baker City Hearts and Haunts

My Sweet Haunt

More Than A Spirit

Family Skeletons

Ghost of the Past (coming soon!)

———

Liberty Valley Love

A Man's World

Cowboy Spell

The Marshal's Lady

Hero Spell

A Trail Through Time (coming soon!)